10.00

A CENTURY OF
GAY EROTICA

A CENTURY OF
GAY EROTICA

Credits continue on page 470.

A CENTURY OF GAY EROTICA

JACK SAUL'S RECOLLECTIONS

Anonymous

T hough my weekly couplings with Jack were nearly always exquisite, there would be plenty to tide me over, both between visits as well as long after I would see the last of him in the form of his roughly if salaciously written memoirs. It did not cease to astonish me how much experience this young man possessed, and there was much in his tale that both shocked me and pressed against my admittedly insulated credibility. With many corrections made toward grammar, but few amendments to the facts as originally presented, what follows is a transcript of the tale which cost me twenty pounds, several sumptuous dinners, and perhaps a pint of wonderful spend! —

Dear Sir, —
    I need scarcely tell you that little cocks, and everything relating to them, had a peculiar interest to me from the very earliest

time to which it is possible for my memory to carry me back.

And yet, I was hardly aware of my predilection or at least did not sense its true nature until I was late in my teens. I vividly remember the first time I acted on the acute feelings that I had not yet learned to name.

There was a family party, which was held every year, and attended by as many friends neighbors and townspeople as could fit in our modest farmhouse. A fine young man named Jerry, who was remarkably thin and possessed of delicate features and a shy nature, was seated opposite to me. He particularly attracted my attention, it being the first time I had ever seen him. I was so absorbed in contemplating the pout of his lips, the length of the lashes on his eyes, and the lengthy taper of his fingers, that I could not take my eyes off him, so that he quite blushed.

My avid gaze did not go unnoticed by our fellow dinner guests, including my father who delivered on to my shin an extremely sharp kick. Still, I could barely tear my eyes away, for in my mind he looked like nothing so much as a woman in ill-fitting men's clothes.

And yet in the days that passed, I could barely get dear Jerry out of my mind. I would keep thinking about his large and shining eyes, and how brown and shy they were, and how hurt they looked when I so callously stared at him.

At night while abed, long after I should have been dreaming, I would create fantasies in my head wherein I would take poor Jerry and bind him and tease and taunt him. I would set about proving my daft theory of Jerry's sexuality by removing his clothes piece by piece, and checking for bubbies, and by inspecting the roundish shape of his bum.

Night after night I would run this most pleasing little picture show through my mind as I tangled myself in the bedclothes and rocked back and forth, thrilling to a strange and new excitement building in my young loins.

Then there was one such eve perhaps a year or two later,

where I was to discover the startling climax to my secret pleasure:

Laying upon my belly there in my bed, an overstuffed pillow set in the crook of my pajama swathed thighs, I thought again as usual about Jerry. He had visited recently, and I recalled being quite surprised by his rate of growth. He had towered now nearly six foot, and was still quite skinny, save for where his arse and bosom had queerly softened and and grown somewhat plump. The look of him was had very nearly struck me as comical, though I knew better than to point out the obvious by then; but at the same time, secretly, I found his body aesthetically pleasing. I could not help but gaze at him at every hidden opportunity, but this time no one took any notice of my hungering looks.

But there that night on my belly, I was not thinking of Jerry's friendship, but of his girlish body and what I might do with it, had I my way about him. Why, I thought, I would bind him with twine, so that he might not have a swing at me as I taunted him; and then, with preternatural power I would bring him to his knees, that I might tower over him and rub his pouting, girlish lips with the tingling palms of my hands. Then I would tease him and humiliate him about what a sissy boy he was, and how he looked like a big, lanky schoolgirl with his strange little bust and his chubby arse. I would taunt him until he fairly blubbered and cowered before me, and tears flowed from those great, tea saucer brown eyes and stream down over his soft cheeks. This, I mused, would put a crack in my hard heart, and I would final relent and comfort poor bound Jerry with gentle caresses, and, perhaps even kisses.

Thus did I spend for the first time in my young life! At first I thought I was having an accident in my bed, and that I was pissing my sheets having forgotten to urinate before retiring. But such was not the case. When I thought of kissing Jerry, it fairly made my somehow over-inflated pego suddenly explode, causing me a world of pleasure which bordered upon dementia in addition to the horrific possibility that I had peed in my bed at such an advanced age. The electric orgasm shot gobs of pure, virgin spend into my blankets, to be mashed and spread about by my trembling belly. It was positively wonderful; I would be veritably addicted for life.

Once or twice per annum, when our families gathered on holiday or for a visit, I would make certain to bed near Jerry, the better to inspect the ongoing process of his physical development. Rarely was I disappointed. Why, I can recall one time when Jerry had come for a visit; he was positively miserable, as his mum and dad had set him to work in the fields in the hopes that a harder labor would toughen his demeanor, and perhaps firm up his quite by-then lady-like appendages. They were correct, of course, and my cousin for the first time had grown somewhat larger with firmer teats, a thicker neck and a solid musculature.

Late at night, while lying side by side in bed, I told him that I greatly admired his new physique; that he should be happy of it, and looking forward to baiting girls with such a body. And yet while he thanked me and appreciated my honest and uncruel sentiments, he confessed that he positively loathed the work in the fields, and that the other farmers teased him and recited nasty jokes in his presence, and at times have even mocked having him for a woman sometimes while in seclusion.

As dear Jerry related these things to me there in the darkness, I found my hand sliding down into my pyjamas, nearly of its own accord, to quietly begin frigging my blown up pego. Perhaps it was in the pitch of his voice, somewhat higher and more lilting than a man his age should possess. And perhaps it was in the tales of his being teased and taken by the other farmhands which riled my private lusts. Whatever it was, as cousin Jerry sang his woes, I shot several dizzying loads of spend, quite beyond his notice, into the bedclothes near him.

Time next, but a few months later, I saw that his pleas had been finally heeded, and he had been taken out of his own family's fields. He had rapidly restored his body to its softer and more womanly contours, though I kept my teasing to a minimum, lest I risked his abandoning our nighttime reveries. That eve, as I pushed our bed chatter toward elements which inspired and inflamed my young and inexperienced loins, I found myself inching closer to him under the covers.

"—Oh, no, dear Jerry," I said, mustering all the rare honesty I possessed and thrusting it into the tone of my voice. "I do believe that some of that firmness you developed on your sojourn to the fields has still remained with you, about the regions of your bosom, just here."

"Hmm," said Jerry. "I should truly think not, Jack. Go ahead and have a feel if you like. Not a bit of muscle left, I'm afraid. Soft as a baby's bottom."

To my youthful mind, this would be the culmination of many a waking dream that ended in great wet spots on the sheets or somewhat encrusted pyjamas in the morning. I reached forth and felt the warm, soft fleshiness of his chest, running my fingers over each side, and squeezing up the fleshy excess in my palm.

"I will bet you are right indeed, cuz. Have you given thought to a regimen of calisthenics or some other form of exercise?" My pego was positively alive and dancing about my waist. I truly wanted to rub it against him, push it and shove it against him 'till it exploded; but I was too shy and it was beyond my experience to manipulate such a tableau.

My curious and trembling fingers did manage to creep down his chest and over his belly, as he spoke in response, down to the drawstring of his pyjamas, even as I managed to begin a furious if undisturbing frig of my own self on the sly.

Jerry stiffened abruptly as I pulled at the string and unmade it, then allowed my wandering and mischievous fingers to reach within to have a grope at the mystery between his thighs. To my sheer delight it came awake immediately in my fingers, and I began to frig him with mindless abandon.

He moaned and trembled under my raw and unskilled efforts; and

I nearly burst with laughter at how much terribly smaller he, who was older than I by some years, was when compared to my own endowment. Still I frigged him, and with a squeal he spent a streaming load upon himself, brief moments after I had initiated the evening's attack. To my great disappointment, he turned over and quickly set to snoring, and I had to gratify myself quite on my own.

Rarely did I see Jerry thereafter, as his family moved further away, and when they did come for a visit, he used his elder position to hold up later than I, and spend the evening clucking with the women, whilst I lay in bed on my own and fell to sleep. Then I would not see him for a number of years, as my life would take several interesting turns, and his would settle into one of typical boredom.

About three years afterwards, when Jerry was a married man, happening to be left alone with him for a short time one day, I recalled that initial incident of my unabashed curiosity to his memory. In fact I believe he never forgot it, as he used to regard me with a most peculiar kind of look from time to time.

How he blushed at first: but putting my arms 'round his waist, I asked him to kiss and forgive me, if it was such a long time ago.

"You know, Jack, I will. You were such a tit then," he replied, as he permitted me to take the kiss.

"But, Jerry, I love you so, and am as curious as ever. Can you forgive that?"

His eyes looked anywhere but in my face, as he blushed and seemed deeply moved. Knowing I was quite onto something, I redoubled my osculatory attentions, using what skills I had picked up over my many escapades 'till then. Cooing and chatting, taking to the brandy held in the cupboard for special occasions, fairly soon enough I had raised quite a storm of desire in both our heaving bosoms.

He was married to a rather old and ugly woman, whose money had caught the silly butterfly, who thought that wealth alone could secure happiness.

You may guess the result. A friendly sofa was at hand. We sank down upon it, and, in spite of his pretended resistance, I not only investigated the shaft of love but got it into me. He was one of those smooth and quietly lustful men one occasionally meets with, and when he had once tasted the fine root I introduced into his arse (which was already quite ripe to receive my spendings before Mr. Pego could even present his head), he could scarcely ever be satisfied!

In fact, we ran awful risks. When I was stopping in the house he would leave his wife asleep and come to my room, and when he had fairly fucked me to a standstill, would suck my prick, slap my arse, bugger me with his finger, and do everything he could think of to get even a tenth or eleventh go out of me. Never did we discuss those nights in my bed chamber, nor even did we attempt to fathom how we had fallen so quickly to carrying on in our present circumstances. We simply had a lark for some months, then, and it would be myself who gradually moved on to other adventures.

LORD HARRY

Anonymous

My stay in France soon came to an end, and I cannot recall to mind anything else worthy of note.

A few days before leaving we went down to the family's country seat, south of Auvergne. Here I met Gaston's grandfather on the maternal side, the old Prince de Foix. He was verging on eighty and had seen many vicissitudes in his time, but was still erect of bearing, and was a picturesque figure with his long white moustache and thick mane of white hair.

He was an ardent Royalist and Catholic, and in his declining years devoted himself entirely to these interests, taking no part in social life; but he was very gracious in his manner towards me and nourished an affection for Gaston, hoping he would prove a worthier successor to his dignities than the Prince, of whose abilities and tastes he had rather a poor opinion, judging from one or two remarks of a slightly sarcastic nature which I heard him utter.

I must also mention that the Prince gave an entertainment before I left Paris, and among the guests were some members of Society X as well as Cecil. They smiled at me in a friendly way when I was introduced, but let fall no hint that made reference to our previous encounter.

My visit came to an end at last, and I took farewell of my newly found friends with genuine regret. Cecil travelled with us to London but there I left for Woodbury to spend the last two days of my vacation at home. The reaction from the liveliness of the past weeks was great, but I had not happily to suffer it long, and the morning of my departure for school soon broke.

I had a letter from Rutherford requesting me to look out for him at Bristol, where I had to change trains. As my train drew up, I saw him on the platform and I jumped out and ran towards him. His face lighted up with great pleasure as he greeted me, but he stopped my flow of words and suggested that we should secure our seats before starting to talk. We quickly dispatched a porter to look after our belongings, and after choosing a compartment, settled ourselves down to talk. I had such a lot to tell my friend that it occupied a considerable portion of our journey, and he complimented me on the good use I had made of the last part of my holidays.

All was excitement at the school, and every one was eager to relate the adventures he had gone through during vacation.

When we gained the dormitory we showed interest in surveying one another's appearance after our long separation. The intervening weeks since we had parted added a modicum of development to our bodies; and indeed, we took great pleasure in holding ourselves up for inspection. Bob's growth was most dramatic, and we could not help but run our hands over each dazzling element of his most recent burst of maturity. His neck had thickened, bringing about him a more manly air, and his waist had widened somewhat and was now stacked more densely with solid muscle under an even broader and thicker chest. Even

Bob's member seemed to me a good deal larger than before, and I was sorely tempted to take it just there and then, even before the others had a chance to show off their own.

Duke Jimmy had retained his boyish charm and mischievous demeanor, but he was taller still now, lean and lanky, with the touch of a new air of poise about him. He stripped with little hesitation at all and was proud to display an uncanny sausage of a cock, grown perhaps a full inch in the short months which had kept us apart.

"We have all of us grown and put on some pounds," grinned the Duke, "but it seems I have done most of my growing down the inseam of my trousers, haven't I?"

"That you have indeed, Jimmy," laughed Bob, who then turned and jabbed the nude and reclining de Beaupre playfully about the soft of his belly. "You seem to be in good health, Blackie, and quite well-fed at that. No doubt it's all that pampering dealt you by that Parisian royalty you've been running 'round with."

"Shut up, Rutherford!" giggled Blackie, as he pushed away Bob's prodding fingers. "Besides, Master Powerscourt and I have bent our tastes more toward golden-skinned Adonises than bon-bons. Isn't that right, Charlie?"

De Beaupre winked at me, revealing a tiny and teasing facet of our adventures together to the others, a tantalizing hint of the stories yet to come. The mere thought of that night with Society X, when combined with my gazing at Blackie with fresh eyes, renewed my heat and enthusiasm for the night's coming activities. Though his body was still etched in muscle, Bob in a way was correct. There was a fresh, voluptuous fleshiness about Blackie as his breast and arms and thighs were now filling out to their final masculine form. The salacious curve of his waist now bore the first signs of his insatiable appetite for fine foods and wines, and his formerly flat belly came perilously close to appearing plump over the thick tube of his cock and his large, down-covered balls. All the same, he was truly altogether mouth-watering to me.

"Come here Charlie," said Bob presently, "I'm dying to feel

your hand on me again. It seems like ages since we were last together like that."

I had no objection, and advanced to where he was lying on the bed with pride in my own form. My work with Joe back home had yielded a firm and well-defined youthful image to my body, which had softened little during my time with de Beaupre.

"You look *fabulous*, Charlie," said Bob, as if in response to my very thoughts. "I am growing hard simply gazing at you."

Taking his cock in my fist, I drew down the skin and moistened it with my tongue, lingering over the operation. It came with a pleasing freshness to me, not having seen or touched Rutherford's member for so long. At length, I started to rub it sharply.

I watched as keenly as ever the sight of the swelling purple head, as it was covered and uncovered by the movement of my hands, and it fascinated me just as much as it had done on the very first occasion when I had devoted myself to a similar task with Rutherford. He was enjoying it too, and gazed at me with a smile as I went on with the work.

"You haven't forgotten how to do it since you were away," he said, "but I dare say you have been practicing with Blackie very often—haven't you?"

I laughed and replied: "Well, of course! We had to keep ourselves up to the mark, you know."

Washing Bob's cock with my tongue, I then took him far into my mouth and then back into the tightness of my throat, just as Cecil had taught me to do. Bob gasped and buckled beneath my lascivious movements, and fairly soon he released a rush of spend which poured swiftly down my gullet.

"Now it is *your* turn," he said, and I took the place which he vacated, gladly suffering him to allay my voluptuous sufferings and desires.

Blackie and the Duke were similarly engaged across the chamber, and watching de Beaupre's broadened and tanned body entwined with the smooth, white torso of the lean Jimmy Marmot proved exhilarating. I was brought to a marvelous and delicious spend. Indeed, not a one of us did get into our beds until all had received a taste of blissful joy.

I do not intend to say much about the events of this term, and can only state that it was no less pleasant to me than the one preceding it. There were not many changes among the pupils. Two new juniors had come in, but with these we had no concern. Davenport had left, and there were few regrets expressed at this; Lacy still remained, and we kept our friendliness with him.

Before the close of the term, Jimmy wrote to Lord Harry Marmot, and received in reply an invitation for the whole four of us to spend the Christmas vacation with him at his place in Sodding Chipwich, Hebworth Castle. I obtained the desired permission from my father, and it was arranged that as soon as the term was over, I should proceed to Lord Harry's.

At the last moment, however, both Bob and the Duke were asked by their people to spend Christmas Day at home, while Jimmy's mother also wished de Beaupre to come home to her. I found myself rather awkwardly placed. I did not want to go there alone, and did not want to go home. Rutherford said I could come with him and sent a telegram to Lord Harry explaining the situation. He wired back asking if I could not come by myself, as he should like some one of us to go to him, he being quite alone.

"Why don't you go, Charlie?" said Bob. "That would settle everything nicely. You won't have to wait long for us and I know my cousin will make you feel at home. It seems a shame that he should be kept all by himself waiting for us."

Thus urged, I agreed to the proposal and acquainted Lord Harry with my decision. He sent a further telegram asking me to acquaint him with what train I should come by, which I did. At the commencement of the holidays, I started off alone on the long journey to the North, having impressed upon my friends that they must join us as soon as possible.

It was late and quite dark when I reached the little station where I was to alight, and I did not feel in very good spirits after the prolonged and chilly journey. A tall man, muffled up in a thick overcoat and with a tweed cap pulled down over his eyes, stood on the platform; and as I got out, he came towards me: "Master Powerscourt, I presume?"

I replied in the affirmative and he held out his hand, saying: "How do you do? I am very pleased to meet you. I seem to know you quite well, after all that my cousin Bob and that young scamp Jimmy have told me about you. But come along now."

I was greatly warmed by his friendly person and even more warmed by his very striking appearance.

As the carriage stopped a door was flung wide open, letting a flood of light upon the scene. We stepped out and made our way to the door, the tall towers and buttresses of the castle looming hugely before us in the uncertain dimness of the night.

As we entered, a gigantic black man carefully closed the door, and we went up a steep stone staircase. This led to a spacious vestibule with groined roof and a pavement of stone flags, all in good repair, but quite bare of furniture.

However when we had gone through a pair of double doors, the scene changed and I found myself in a high-ceilinged corridor, thickly carpeted, lighted by foliated casements of painted glass, with antique benches and armories, horns and skins and stands of armor and weapons here and there.

"Welcome to Hebworth," exclaimed Lord Harry, flinging off his cap and coat. Now that he had removed these and was standing in the light, I was able to take stock of him better.

He was under thirty, I fancied, and the absence of a moustache gave him a still more youthful appearance. He had a look of kindly sympathy in his long-lashed hazel eyes, that showed a nature foreign to the cruel callousness of the habitual roué.

"You must be tired and hungry after your long journey, Charlie," he said presently. "Go have a wash, and in the meantime I will have something got ready for you to eat. Peter will show you the way."

The butler conducted me to a dressing room where I freed myself from the stains of travel, and when I had done so, I returned to the salon. Lord Harry awaited my appearance and at once took me to a room nearby. A table near the hearth was laid with an appetizing meal.

When I had finished, the table was cleared by Peter, assisted by another black man, equally gigantic. Lord Harry saw me observing them, and when they had gone out, he said:

"They are two very good fellows indeed, and devoted to me. I hired them in South Africa a year ago, and they have been with me ever since, I call them Peter and Paul, as their African names are too cumbersome for ordinary use."

A little while passed in silence and then he beckoned me to him.

"You are very friendly with my two relatives, are you not, Charlie? Both of whom have mentioned you in the warmest way in their letters so I know the intimacy must be exceedingly close one. They have doubtless spoken to you of me; and have, I am sure, told you that I am extremely fond of promising young men and like to see them enjoy the utmost freedom possible.

"Now, would it be too much to ask you to reveal yourself to me in a state of beauty unadorned!"

I took the hint, when he announced that the room was warm enough to undress, and slowly unfastened my garments while he sat with watchful eyes. I did not especially like the idea, as after all he was an entire stranger to me, but I was impelled by the subtle influence he exercised upon me to carry out his wish.

He made me go on till I stood in utter nakedness before him. When he'd made a good survey of my body, he rose, apologized for having troubled me, and thanked me in the most gracious terms. Drawing up a large, broad couch near the fireplace, he directed me to lie on this at full length, and bending down gave me a warm wine-like kiss, full on the lips.

He then went to a cabinet in a cupboard, from which he took out a book and, giving it to me, bade me read it out loud to him. The request, combined with my condition, created a feeling of reserve in my mind, but I could not well decline to do as I was asked, and after taking the book, I opened it as the beginning and began to read while Lord Harry took his place on a low stool at the foot of the couch.

The volume proved to be an erotic romance of the most lurid description, and after I got through the first few paragraphs, the whole situation so affected me that my face burned anew, and a shiver almost of compunction ran through me.

My companion put out his hand and gently began to toy with my cock, so that I stopped reading, closed the book, glanced with open eyes of dismay at him.

"Do please go on," he said with a winning smile, and a whole world of sweetness and persuasiveness in his dark eyes.

I felt thoroughly subdued and continued with the reading of the book, while he went on with the utmost nonchalance in the fingering of my asshole, as he also toyed with my prick.

I was conscious of another sensation, and a momentary glimpse show me that he was bending over me, and had taken my cock in his mouth. Had it been Rutherford or any other of my friends, I should have experienced nothing but pleasure; but my host's friendship was of such short duration that my horrified wonder at his procedure was indescribable, and a shudder passed through my frame; but he was either unconscious of this, or took no notice of it, for he went on with his self-imposed task with much zest, drawing the skin back to its fullest extent, and sucking and rolling his tongue 'round the knob with voluptuous relish, varying this by taking the whole member between his lips, or licking my balls and thighs.

My cock had up to the present been in its limpest state but by degrees the shock wore off, the lubricity of the book began to interest me; a feeling of curiosity to know more of its contents grew on me, infecting my body with the indefinable sensibilities of passion, while the blood grew warmer in my veins.

This revivification communicated itself into my cock, and it began to stiffen, at which sign he coaxed it with his hands with the utmost persistence, till it enlarged and erected itself with more than usual firmness. As soon as this confirmation had been attained, my companion began again caressing it with his lips and tongue with greater avidity than ever, kissing and sucking and licking the distended knob with the utmost fervency, while with his hands he tickled and titillated my balls and thighs, and pressing open my legs, pushed one finger into my bottom hole. I was in a fever of mingled discomfort and excitement. My voice grew husky.

The finger penetrated so far up my hole and worked about so much in the interior regions as to hurt me, while an occasional pressure of Lord Harry's teeth on the head of my cock, and the force with which he every now and then pressed back the prepuce caused me some little pain, which ultimately yielded to pleasure.

This scene continued for some time, till my awakening lust conquered all other emotions. At length a sudden glow of irresistible delight surged through me, giving promise of something yet more pleasurable to follow. My cock throbbed and grew stiff, sensible of which, my host applied himself to sucking it with still greater insistence, while his hands worked on my balls and in my asshole with feverish quickness.

The fires of voluptuousness flamed still fiercer in my veins, and my body writhed under the influences of this current of licentiousness. My voice faltered, it seemed as if I could hear no more, and the resistance within was forced aside.

I felt a series of throbs and thrills of inconceivable, yet almost agonizing pleasure shoot through me, while my cock leaped with uncontrollable vehemence, and discharged liquid gushes from its end into the mouth of Lord Harry, who sucked it with all his might, causing me an excruciating though exquisite rapture, so that it was beyond endurance; I could see no more to read, my head fell back nervelessly, I gasped and groaned and my fingers clutched the book convulsively, almost tearing it. He looked up with insinuating glances, and requested me to go on reading.

Feeling compelled to obey, I picked up the book again and forced myself to ignore the deep agitation which shook my frame. I began in as calm a tone as I could manage, while my cock ached and smarted and tingled under his tongue and lips, the flesh 'round the root palpitated my balls hung down poignantly sensitive, and my intestines twisted in an interior travail. But I read on, half in a dream.

It was not until I had finished another two chapters that Lord Harry desisted from his attentions; but at last he got up, took away the book and brought a warm dressing gown, which he told me to put on.

When I had done so, my host said it was time to retire, and took me to a very large bedroom, with a huge fire blazing merrily in the fireplace and sent a pleasant warmth throughout the apartment. I looked for my night attire but he said I would not need it, and made me get into the large and luxurious bed quite nude. I was not likely to be cold, as above the embroidered silk counterpane there was a thick down quilt, and a coverlet of soft, warm fur over that.

It was evident that my host intended to sleep with me, for he began to disrobe and when he had divested himself of everything, he too, got into bed.

Turning back the bedclothes so that I was fully exposed, he started to osculate me all over, kissing repeatedly and with the utmost fervency my breast, thighs, shoulders, neck, cheeks, arms and legs, sucking my toes, tickling my back, groin and belly with his tongue, licking my feet, hands and face, imprinting labial caresses all over me. He found out all the most sensitive parts— in under the arms, the nostrils, the ears, the soles of my feet, the palms of my hands, the throat and the inner part of the thighs—and lavished unbounded philanderings on the smooth rotundity of my buttocks, kissing and mumbling them all over, licking with ardor. Finally pressing the cheeks apart so as to obtain better scope, he stretched open the bottom hole with his fingers and inserted therein the tip of his tongue, making me squirm with the peculiar sensation thus created.

When at last he had satisfied himself with all this, he put me flat on the bed and knelt over me in the opposite way, so that his thighs came above my face. Directing me to follow his example he began to suck my cock again. I hesitated to do likewise.

I took hold of his erect member and applied my lips to it. It seemed impossible that I should get it into my mouth, it was so large, but after the first moment's repulsion, I quickly warmed to the work, and sucked and tickled it with my tongue as well as I knew how.

Lord Harry was doing his best to rouse my cock, which had lapsed into inertness, into new vigor. Rubbing it with his hand, sucking the top and working one finger in and out of my bottom hole; while I in return caressed his balls and posteriors with my hands.

He was raised to a considerable pitch of excitement, and his cream was not long in approaching. When it came, he pressed his thighs and belly closer to my face, so as to prevent me from moving my head away, and in another minute my mouth was filled with a tremendous charge of hot, thick cream, which shot down over my tongue and palate and throat, almost choking me, and of course being in the position I was, I had to swallow it. But this only added to my own pleasure.

My member was beginning to rise to the occasion but in a somewhat half hearted way, so when the last drop from his weapon had gone into my mouth, he changed his position and kneeling down by the side of me, worked my cock up and down with his hand in a rapid manner, at the same time tickling my balls and bottom with his disengaged hand.

The process proved rather protracted, but Lord Harry's energy was tireless and at last he attained his goal. My member was sore and inflamed from its first effusion, and pained and smarted particularly when now and then he gave it a little suck, while the continual pulling down of the skin as far as it would go, hurt me a trifle, but again my discomfort soon began to give way to pleasure.

Presently the same glow of voluptuousness as before spread over me, the thrills of vital electricity were once more shooting through my frame. I heaved and writhed and clenched my hands together, my breath came in short gasps; and he bent down and commenced to suck my cock with all his force. My whole body was drowned in a flood of sensuality, my head fell back with upturned eyes, and I sank into a swoon brought on by the intolerable pleasure of my physical sensations, prefacing this lapse of consciousness by a smothered groan and cry.

When I came to, I found that Lord Harry had risen, and was regarding me with interest, but on seeing that my senses had returned, he lay down beside me and with all a lover's ardor, clasped me to him. He kissed me and forced my mouth open with his tongue, making it stay there till our saliva mixed.

He held me thus for some time and then he caused me to turn 'round, when laying close to me, he put his cock between my legs and commenced to go to work gently in a backward and forward movement, while with one hand he took hold of my member and worked it softly up and down, an action which caused me some unpleasantness, as it ached and was sore after its recent experiences, but I said nothing, being curious to ascertain how my host will continue.

This went on for a period and then Lord Harry's movements became rather more brisk, until at last he emitted a copious flow, which bathed my thighs with warm fluid, while he rubbed it with his hand over my balls, cock and belly.

After this I was permitted to compose myself for slumber, which

I was not sorry for. Lord Harry did not seem greatly inclined for conversation, and after a few sentences had passed between us, he recommended me to try to go to sleep.

Lord Harry did not try to prevent me, but until the time that I lost myself in oblivion, I felt my companion's hands caressing me unceasingly all over, but more particularly between the thighs, while ever and anon he imprinted kisses on my back and shoulders and the nape of my neck.

TELENY
Anonymous

There are two kinds of lascivious feelings, both equally strong and overpowering; the one is the fervent, carnal lust of the senses, enkindled in the genital organs and mounting to the brain, making human beings

Swim in mirth, and fancy that they feel
Divinity within them breeding wings
Wherewith to scorn the earth.

The other is the cold libidinousness of fancy, the keen and gall-like irradiation of the brain which parches the healthy blood as with new wine intoxicated.

The first, the strong concupiscence of lusty youth, natural to the flesh, is satisfied as soon as men take largely their fill of love and love's disport, and the heavily-laden anther has sturdily shaken forth the seed that clogged it; and then they feel as our first parents did, when dewy sleep "Oppressed them, wearied with their amorous play."

The body then so delightfully light seems to rest on "earth's freshest, softest lap," and the slothful yet half-awakened mind broods over its slumbering shell.

The second, kindled in the head,

bred of unkindly fumes, is the lechery of senility—a morbid craving, like the hunger of surfeited gluttony. The senses, like Messalina, *lassata sed non satiata*, ever tingling, keep hankering after the impossible. The spermatic ejaculations, far from calming the body, only irritate it, for the exciting influence of a salacious fancy continues after the anther has yielded all its seed. If acrid blood comes instead of the balmy, cream-like fluid, it brings with it nothing but a painful irritation. If, unlike as in satyriasis, an erection does not take place, and the phallus remains limp and lifeless, still the nervous system is no less convulsed by impotent desire and lechery—a mirage of the over-heated brain, no less shattering before it is effete.

These two feelings combined together are something akin to what I underwent as, holding Teleny clasped against my throbbing, heaving breast, I felt within me the contagion of his eager longing, and of his overpowering sadness.

I had taken off my friend's shirt collar and cravat to see and to feel his beautiful bare neck; then little by little I stripped him of all his clothing, till at the last he remained naked in my embrace.

What a model of voluptuous comeliness he was, with his strong and muscular shoulders, his broad and swelling chest, his skin of a pearly whiteness, as soft and as fresh as the petals of a waterlily, his limbs rounded like those of Leotard, with whom every woman was in love. His thighs, his legs and feet, in their exquisite grace, were perfect models.

The more I looked upon him, the more enamoured I was of him. But the sight was not enough. I had to heighten the visual delight by the sense of touch, I had to feel the tough and yet elastic muscles of the arm in the palm of my hand, to fondle his massive and sinewy breast, to paddle his back. From there my hands descended down to the round lobes of his rump, and I clasped him against me by his buttocks. Thereupon, tearing off my clothes, I pressed all his body on mine, and rubbed against him, wriggling like a worm. Lying over him as I was, my tongue was in his mouth; searching for his, that receded, and was darted out when mine retired, for they seemed to play a wanton, bickering game of hide-and-seek together—a game which made all the body quiver with delight.

Then our fingers twisted the crisp and curly hair that grew all around the middle parts, or handled the testicles, so softly and so gently that they were hardly sentient of the touch, and still they shivered in a way that almost made the fluid in them flow out before its time.

The most skilled of prostitutes could never give such thrilling sensations as those which I felt with my lover; for the tart is, after all, only acquainted with the pleasures she herself has felt, while her keener emotions, not being those of her sex, are unknown to her and cannot be imagined by her.

Likewise, no man is ever able to madden a woman with such overpowering lust as another tribade can, for she alone knows how to tickle her on the right spot just in the nick of time. The quintessence of bliss can, therefore, only be enjoyed by beings of the same gender.

Our two bodies were now in as close a contact as the glove is to the hand it sheathes. Our feet were tickling each other wantonly, our knees were pressed together, and the skin of our thighs seemed to cleave and to form one flesh.

Though I was loath to rise, still, feeling his stiff and swollen phallus throbbing against my body, I was just going to tear myself off from him, and take his fluttering implement of pleasure in my mouth and drain it, when he—feeling that mine was not only turgid, but moist and brimful to overflowing—clasped me with his arms and kept me down.

Opening his thighs, he thereupon took my legs between his own, and entwined them in such a way that his heels pressed against the side of my calves. For a moment I was gripped as in a vise, and I could hardly move.

Then, loosening his arms, he uplifted himself and placed a pillow under his buttocks, which were thus well apart—his legs being all the time widely open.

Having done this, he took hold of my rod and pressed it against his gaping anus. The tip of the frisky phallus soon found its entrance in the hospitable hole that endeavored to give it admission. I pressed a little; the whole of the glans was engulfed. The sphincter soon gripped it in such a way that it could not come out without an effort. I thrust it slowly to prolong as much as possible the ineffable sensation that ran through every limb, to calm the quivering nerves, and to allay the heat of the blood. Another push and half the phallus was in his body. I pulled it out half an inch, though it seemed to me a yard by the prolonged pleasure I felt. I pressed forward again, and the whole of it, down to its very root, was all swallowed up. Thus wedged, I vainly endeavored to drive it higher up—an impossible feat, and, clasped as I was, I felt it wriggling in its sheath, giving myself and him an unutterable and delightful titillation.

So keen was the bliss that overcame me, that I asked myself if some ethereal, life-giving fluid were not being poured on my head, and trickling down slowly over my quivering flesh?

Surely the rain-awakened flowers must be conscious of such a sensation during a shower, after they have been parched by the scorching rays of an festival sun.

Teleny again put his arm round me and held me tight. I gazed at myself within his eyes; he saw himself in mine. During this voluptuous lambent feeling, we patted each other's bodies softly, our lips cleaved together and my tongue again in his mouth. We remained in this copulation almost without stirring, for I felt that the slightest movement would provoke a copious ejaculation, and this feeling was too exquisite to be allowed to pass away so quickly. Still, we could not help writhing, and we almost swooned away with delight. We were both shivering with lust, from the roots of our hair to the tips of our toes; all the flesh of our bodies kept bickering luxuriously, just as placid waters of the mere do at noontide, when kissed by the sweet-scented, wanton breeze that has just deflowered the virgin rose.

Such intensity of delight could not, however, last very long; a few, almost unwilling, contractions of the sphincter banded the phallus, and then the first brunt was over; I thrust in with might and main and wallowed in him; my breath came thickly; I panted, I sighed, I groaned. The burning fluid was spouted out slowly and at long intervals.

As I rubbed myself against him, he underwent all the sensations I was feeling; for I was hardly drained of the last drop before I was likewise bathed with his own seething sperm. We did not kiss each other any further; our languid, half-open, lifeless lips only aspired each other's breath. Our sightless eyes saw each other no more, for we fell into that divine prostration which follows shattering ecstasy.

Oblivion, however, did not follow, but we remained in a be-numbed state of torpor, speechless, forgetting everything except the love we bore each other, unconscious of anything save the plea-sure of feeling each other's bodies, which, however, seemed to have lost their own individuality, mingled and confounded as they were together. We had but one heart and one head, for our pulses beat in such unison, and the same vague thoughts flitted through both our brains.

Why did not Jehovah strike us dead that moment? Had we not provoked Him enough? How was it that the jealous God was not envious of our bliss? Why did He not hurl one of his aveng-ing thunderbolts at us, and annihilate us?

Even if death had pitched us headlong into hell in the moment of our sinful lust—well, what then? Hell, of course, is no excelsior—no place of false aspirations after an unreachable ideal of fallacious hopes and bitter disappointments. Never pretending to be what we are not, we shall find there true contentedness of mind, and our bodies will be able to develop those faculties with which nature has endowed them. Not being either hypocrites or dissemblers, the dread of being seen such as we really are can never torment us.

If we are grossly bad, we shall at least be truthfully so. There will be amongst us that honesty which here on earth exists only amongst cardsharps; and moreover, we shall have that genial companionship of fellow-beings after our own heart.

Is hell, then, such a place to be dreaded? Thus, even admitting of an afterlife in the bottomless pit—which I do not—hell would only be the paradise of those whom nature has created fit for it. Do animals repine for not having been created men? No, I think not. Why should we, then, make ourselves unhappy for not having been born angels?

At that moment it seemed as if René and I were floating somewhere between heaven and earth, not thinking that everything that has a beginning has likewise an end.

The senses were blunted, so that the downy couch upon which we were resting was like a bed of clouds. A deathlike silence was reigning around us. The very noise and hum of the great city seemed to have stopped—or, at least, we did not hear it. Could the earth have stopped in its rotation, and the hand of Time have arrested itself in its dismal march?

I remember languidly wishing that my life could pass away in that placid, dull and dreamy state, so like a mesmeric trance, when the benumbed body is thrown into a death-like torpor, and the mind, "Like an ember among fallen ashes, is just wakeful enough to feel the consciousness of ease and of peaceful rest."

All at once we were roused from our pleasant somnolence by the jarring sound of an electric bell.

Teleny jumped up, hastened to wrap himself in a dressing

gown and to attend to the summons. A few moments afterward he came back with a telegram in his hand.

"What is it?" I asked.

"A message from—," he replied, looking at me wistfully, and with a certain trepidation in his voice.

"And you have to go?"

"I suppose I must," said he, with a mournful sadness in his eyes.

"Is it so distasteful to you?"

"Distasteful is not the word; it is unbearable. This is the first parting, and—"

"Yes, but only for a day or two."

"A day or two," added he, gloomily, "is the space that divides life from death:

It is the little rift within the lute,
That by-and-by will make the music mute,
And ever widening slowly silence all."

"Teleny, you have had for some days a weight on your mind— something that I cannot fathom. Will you not tell your friend what it is?"

He opened his eyes widely, as if he were looking into the depths of limitless space, while a painful expression was seen upon his lips; and then he added slowly:

"My fate. Have you forgotten the prophetic vision you had that evening of the charity concert?"

"What! Adrian mourning over dead Antinöus?"

"Yes."

"A fancy bred in my over-heated brain by the conflicting qualities of your Hungarian music, so stirringly sensuous, and at the same time so gorgeously mournful."

He shook his head sadly.

"No, it was something more than idle fancy."

"A change has been taking place in you, Teleny. Perhaps it is the religious or spiritual element of your nature that is predominating just now over the sensual, but you are not what you were."

"I feel that I have been too happy, but that our happiness is built on sand—a bond like ours—"

"Not blessed by the Church, repugnant to the nice feelings of most men."

"Well—yes, in such a love there is always

A little pitted speck in garnered fruit
That, rotting inward, slowly smothers all.

Why did we meet—or, rather, why was not one of us born a woman? Had you only been some poor girl—"

"Come, leave aside your morbid fancies and tell me candidly if you would have loved me more than you do."

He looked at me sadly, but could not bring himself to utter an untruth. Still, after a while he added, sighing:

"There is a love that is to last,
When the hot days of youth are past."

"Tell me, Camille, is such love ours?"

"Why not? Can you not always be as fond of me as I am of you, or do I only care for you on account of the sensual pleasures you afford me? You know that my heart yearns for you when the senses are satiated and the desire is blunted."

"Still, had it not been for me, you might have loved some woman whom you could have married—"

"And have found out, but too late, that I was born with other cravings. No, sooner or later I should have followed my destiny."

"Now it might be quite different; satiated with my love, you might, perhaps, marry and forget me."

"Never. But come, have you been confessing yourself? Are you going to turn Calvinist? Or, like the Dame aux Camellias or

Antinöus, do you think it necessary to sacrifice yourself on the altar of love for my sake?"

"Please, don't joke."

"No, I'll tell you what we'll do. Let us leave France. Let us go to Spain, to Southern Italy— nay, let us leave Europe, and go to the East, where I must surely have lived during some former life, and which I have a hankering to see, just as if the land 'Where the flowers ever blossom, the beans ever shine, had been the home of my youth; there, unknown to everyone, forgotten by the world.'"

"Yes, but can I leave this town?" he said.

I knew that of late Teleny had been dunned a good deal, and that his life had often been rendered unpleasant by usurers.

I cared but little what people might think of me—but he had forbidden me to call all his creditors together and settle all his debts. I was about to offer it again, and relieve him from the weight that was oppressing him, when Fate—blind, inexorable, crushing Fate—sealed my mouth.

There was again a loud ring at the door. Had that bell been rung a few seconds later, how different his life and mine would have been! But it was Kismet, as the Turks say.

It was the carriage that had come to take him to the station. While he was getting ready, I helped him pack up his dress suit and some other little things he might require. I took up, by chance, a small matchbox containing French letters, and smiling, said:

"Here, I'll put them in your trunk; they might be useful."

He shuddered, and grew deathly pale.

"Who knows?" said I. "There might come a beautiful lady patroness—"

"Please, don't joke," he retorted, almost angrily.

"Oh! now I can afford to do so, but once—do you know that I was even jealous of my mother?"

Teleny at that moment dropped the mirror he was holding, which, as it fell, was shivered to pieces.

For a moment we both looked aghast. Was it not a dreadful omen?

Just then the clock on the mantelpiece struck the hour. Teleny shrugged his shoulders. "Oh dear," he said, his voice careless, "seven years' bad luck, I suppose. But come now, there's no time to lose."

He snatched up his portmanteau, and we hurried downstairs.

I accompanied him to the terminus, and before leaving him when he alighted from the carriage, my arms were clasped around him, and our lips met in a last and lingering kiss. They clung fondly to one another, not with the fever of lust, but with a love all fraught with tenderness, and with a sorrow that gripped the muscles of the heart.

His kiss was like the last emanation of a withering flower, or like the sweet scent shed at evening tide by one of those delicate white cactus blossoms that open their petals at dawn, follow the sun in its diurnal march, then droop and fade away with the planet's last rays.

At parting from him I felt as if I had been bereft of my soul itself. My love was like a Nessus shirt, the severing of which was as painful as having my flesh torn from me piecemeal. It was as if the joy of my life had been snatched away from me.

I watched him as he hurried away with his springy step and feline grace. When he had reached the portal he turned round. He was deathly pale, and in his despair he looked like a man about to commit suicide. He waved a last farewell, and quickly disappeared.

The sun had set for me. Night had come over the world. I felt

like a soul belated;
In hell and heaven unmated;

and, shuddering, I asked myself, what morn would come out of all this darkness?

The agony visible on his face struck a deep terror within me; then I thought how foolish we both were in giving each other such unnecessary pain, and I rushed out of the carriage after him.

All at once a heavy country lout ran up against me, and clasped me in the arms.

"Oh—! I did not catch the name," he said. "What an unexpected pleasure! How long have you been here?"

"Let me go—let me go! You are mistaken!" I screamed out, but he held me fast.

As I wrestled with the man, I heard the signal bell ring. With a strong jerk I pushed him away, and ran into the station. I reached the platform a few seconds too late: the train was in motion and Teleny had disappeared.

Nothing was then left for me to do but to post a letter to this friend of mine, begging him to forgive me for having done what he had often forbidden me to do; that is, to have given an order to my attorney to collect all his outstanding accounts, and pay all those debts that had so long been weighing upon him. For I was determined to do that very thing, with his knowledge or without it, that we might fly together from the city.

I jumped back into the cab, and was whirled away to my office through the crowded thoroughfares of the town.

What a jarring bustle there was everywhere! How sordid and meaningless this world appeared!

A garishly-dressed, smirking female was casting lewd glances at a lad, and tempting him to follow her, while, from the look on his face, he was contemplating the loss of his immortal soul and counting it less than the coin in his purse.

A one-eyed satyr was ogling a proper miss—and she to all appearances the very soul of modesty. I thought I knew him. Yes, it was that loathsome school fellow of mine, Bion, only he looked even more of a pimp than ever.

A fat, sleek-headed man was carrying a cantaloupe melon, and his mouth seemed to be watering at the prospect of the pleasure he would have in eating it after the soup, with his wife and children. "For ecstasy a melon," the British colonel had said. What this what he meant? I asked myself if ever woman or man could have kissed that slobbering mouth without feeling sick.

I had during these last three days quite neglected my office, and my manager was ill. I therefore felt it my duty to set to work and do what had to be done. Notwithstanding the sorrow gnawing in my heart, I began answering letters and telegrams, or giving the necessary directions as to how they were to be answered. I worked feverishly, rather like a machine than a man. For a few hours I was quite absorbed in complicated commercial transactions, and although I worked and reckoned clearly, still my friend's face, with his mournful eyes and his voluptuous mouth, with its bitter smile, was ever before me, while an aftertaste of his kiss lingered on my lips. I wrote the letters and drafts that would gather up Teleny's debts and pay them secretly. Would his debtors despise me? I cared not.

The hour for shutting up the office came, and yet not half of my task was done. I saw, as in a dream, the rueful faces of my clerks kept back from their dinners or from their pleasures. They had all somewhere to go to. I was alone—even my mother was away. I therefore bade them go, saying I should remain with the head bookkeeper. They did not wait to be told twice; in a twinkling the offices were empty.

As for the accountant, he was a commercial fossil, a kind of living calculating machine; grown so old in the office that all his limbs creaked like rusty hinges every time he moved, so that he hardly ever did move. Nobody had ever seen him anywhere else but on his high stool; he was always at his place before any of the junior clerks came in, and he was still there when they went off. Life for him had only one aim—that of making endless additions.

Feeling rather sick, I sent the office boy for a bottle of dry sherry and a box of vanilla-wafers. When the lad returned, I told him he could go.

I poured out a glass of wine for the bookkeeper, and handed him the box of biscuits. The old man took up the glass with his parchment-coloured hand, and held it up to the light as if he were calculating its chemical properties or its specific weight. Then he sipped it slowly with evident gusto.

As for the wafer he looked at it carefully, just as if it had been a draft he was going to register.

Then we both set to work again, and at about ten, all the letters and dispatches having been answered, I heaved a deep sigh of relief.

"If my manager comes tomorrow, as he said he would, he'll be satisfied with me."

I smiled as this thought flitted through my brain. What was I working for? Lucre, to please my clerk, or for the work itself? I am sure I hardly knew. I think I laboured for the feverish excitement the work gave me, just as men play at chess to keep their brains active with thoughts other than those that oppress them; or, perhaps, because I was born with the same propensities for work as have the swarming bees or nesting ants.

Not wanting to keep the poor bookkeeper on his stool any longer, I admitted the fact to him that it was time to shut up the office. He got up slowly, took off his spectacles like an automaton, wiped them leisurely, put them in their case, quietly took out another pair—for he had glasses for every occasion—put them on his nose, then looked at me.

"You have gone through a vast amount of work. If your grandfather and your father could have seen you, they surely would have been pleased with you."

I again poured out two glasses of wine, one of which I handed to him. He quaffed the wine, pleased, not with the wine itself, but for my kindness in offering it to him. Then I shook hands with him, and we parted.

Where was I to go now—home?

I wished my mother had come back. I had got a letter from her that very afternoon; in its she said that, instead of returning in a day or two, as she had intended doing, she might, perhaps, go off to Italy for a short time. She was suffering from a slight attack of bronchitis, and she dreaded the fogs and dampness of our town.

Poor mother! I now thought that, since my intimacy with Teleny, there had been a slight estrangement between us; not that I loved her less, but because Teleny engrossed all my mental and bodily faculties. Still, just now that he was away, I almost felt guilty of my neglect of her, and I decided to write a long and affectionate letter to her as soon as I got home.

Meanwhile I walked on haphazardly. After wandering about for an hour, I found myself unexpectedly before Teleny's house. I had traced my steps thither, without knowing where I went. I looked up at Teleny's windows with longing eyes. How I loved that house. I could have kissed the very stones on which he had stepped.

The night was dark but clear; the street—a very quiet one—was not of the best lighted, and for some reason or other the nearest gas-lamp had gone out.

As I kept staring up at the windows, it seemed as if I saw a faint light glimmering through the crevices of the shut-up blinds. "Of course," I thought, "it is only my imagination."

I strained my eyes. "No, surely, I am not mistaken," I said, audibly to myself, "surely there is a light."

Had Teleny come back?

Perhaps he had been seized with the same state of dejection which had come over me when we parted. The anguish visible on my ghastly face must have paralyzed him, and he could not play in such a state, so he had come back. Perhaps, also, the concert had been postponed.

Perhaps it was thieves?

But if Teleny—?

No, the very idea was absurd. How could I suspect the man I

loved of infidelity? I shrank from such a supposition as from something heinous—from a kind of moral pollution. No, it must be anything else but that. The key of the door in my hand, I entered the house.

JUPITER & GANYMEDE
Anonymous

The next day was a half-holiday, and in the afternoon Bob, de Beaupre, the Duke and I set out for a ramble, following the course of a little river which flowed through the woods and meadows in the neighborhood of the school.

As we made our way slowly along, the Duke cried, "Blackie has gone one better than most of us, he has had some adventures with Cecil!"

"Oh, do tell us!" exclaimed Bob and I, eagerly turning to de Beaupre. "Who is Cecil?"

He laughed: "Jimmy is always piling on the agony about me. I believe his brain has turned after listening to one or two of my yarns."

After a little more pressure, however, he gave in and said he would tell us of his first experience with Cecil. What follows is his account.

†††

It was in Paris, about six months ago. There was a great friend of my father named Cecil de Regnier, who used to visit us very frequently. Although he wasn't very old he had been married but his wife had died nearly two years before, only a few months after the wedding. He lived in a big apartment by himself in the Avenue Moche. He was always awfully jolly to me, used to bring me no end of sweets and that kind of thing, and gave me lots of presents. Once or twice he took me to the theater and you bet I liked him very much. One thing I noticed however, and that was how he used to like to squeeze my hand and kiss me when we were alone.

Well, one day he called just as my father was going to a garden fete at the Austrian Embassy, and he asked if I was going too. When my father told him I was not, he said; "Poor boy! He will be awfully lonesome. Let me take him home this afternoon and he can stay to dinner. I will send him back in the carriage after-wards."

My father saw no objections, so Cecil carried me off in triumph and I was soon seated beside him in his victoria, being rattled along as fast as the horses could take us to the Avenue Moche. When we got there, he took me upstairs to his study—a really smashing one, with stained glass windows and lots of guns and all that sort of thing. Cecil gave me some picture books to look at while he took off his hat and cloak, and then rang for his manservant to bring up some fruit and wine.

He made me drink two or three glasses, then called me to come and sit beside him on the big sofa that took up nearly all of one side of the room. "You are a nice boy, Gaston," he said, putting his arms round me and kissing my cheek. I kissed him back, and he seemed so pleased at this that he would not let me go, but kept on hugging me.

When at last he released his hold, he still left one arm remaining round my neck and pressed close against me. He had put on a sort of loose smoking jacket after coming in, and I could see his muscular chest, which fairly glistened in the dappled sunlight.

Then he began to pat my cheeks and stroke my hair and so on, telling me how fond he was of me.

I don't remember what I said and, what with the wine, I tell you I was feeling altogether rather funny. I had never been alone like this with another man before, and though I am not exactly of a bashful nature, I can assure you that I felt as shy as a kid.

At the same time I felt very hot too, and my cock was sticking up as stiff as possible in my trousers. I was afraid he would see it, and that I would be in a dreadful state in case he did, but I dared not put my hand down to shift it so that it could not be noticed as he was looking at me all the time and would be bound to see what I was doing.

"Good gracious!" he said, looking at the big lump where it lifted my breeches up. "Whatever have you got in your pocket?" And before I could say or do anything to stop him, he was feeling for the cause. I went hot all over and felt the blood rushing to my temples, only wishing that the floor would open and let me through.

"You silly boy, let me see what it is!" said Cecil, and I scarcely realized what he was doing before I felt his hands round my waist loosening my breeches. From the haste he showed, I think he was afraid that I was going to stop him and make a run for the door, anxious only to escape. At the same moment, in response to his call, the door to his study opened and his manservant, Maurice, appeared.

"This boy wants to be put to bed!" said Cecil.

Maurice came across the room with a grin all over his face, and the two of them seized me by the arms and dragged me into the next room. I was dazed with the wine I had drunk and by no means pleased; but I was, of course, helpless—as one is, of course, the first time one is drunk—and in a very short time had they removed every stitch of clothing from me and laid me on the bed, naked as I was born.

"Keep him there for a minute, Maurice," said Cecil, and the

servant held me with his strong arms, while his master rapidly threw off all his clothes till he was stark naked. I shall never forget my utter confusion as I saw a man undress for the first time. At the sight my cock, which had grown limp, rose again; on seeing which the servant began to pull it about very freely.

Cecil came over to me and stooped to kiss me. I tried to turn away, but he held my cheeks in his hands, preventing me, and kissed and tongued me until I thought he would suck my breath right out of my body. I had to laugh out loud as I tried to thrust him off.

Then he got on the bed, and my curiosity soon got the better of all my other feelings. He gave the servant a look telling him to leave and took me in his strong arms, but I insisted on kneeling up and having a good look at his body. He was an awfully handsome man with dark hair and deep blue eyes that were almost black, and very white, smooth skin.

I had often admired my own physique in the looking glass at home, but never had I had the opportunity to study the naked body of another man. He was a breathtakingly handsome man, in exquisite form as he was at the peak of his manhood. My eyes lustily devoured his smooth chest and the sculpted muscles of his arms and legs. But, of course, what I was in truth most anxious to see was his cock.

Cecil reclined on the pillows of that enormous mahogany bed and let me have free rein in my exploration of his body, smiling appreciatively at my natural curiosity. In my youthful enthusiasm I fell to my task rather ardently.

"That's it my boy," said Cecil huskily, as I ran my eager hands over his strong chest. I let my fingertips rest nervously on each of his brown nipples, which seemed to excite him greatly, as he moaned with a low growl. I breathlessly let my curiosity drive my exploratory zeal, and soon found that Cecil had a great cockstand. His member was rather large and perfectly formed, below which hung two tight balls, all amidst a curly thatch of brown hair.

My own cock tingled and twitched with excitement at seeing his prick rise and lie across his flat belly. His hips were narrow and his pelvic bones jutted at an acute angle which defined the slope of his stomach flesh into the V-shape of his groin. As his cock was jumping to life under my lascivious gaze, Cecil said, "Touch me."

My reverie was broken. I was almost alarmed, and suddenly shy. As often as I had touched myself in the solitary pleasures, never had I touched another man. But my natural instincts prevailed, and with the help of Cecil's guiding hand I overcame my doubts and reached down to take his cock in my shaking hands. I gingerly pulled back the skin, and began to tickle and stroke the throbbing head of his prick.

"Oh, yes," sighed Cecil. "That's it," he said, as he slightly lifted his head from the pillows.

"Why, Gaston!" he exclaimed, upon seeing me kneeling over him. "You've got quite a cock on you. I didn't imagine!" He smiled deviously at me and my erect member, which was beginning to ache with anticipatory excitement.

I continued to stroke his cock, and Cecil leaned back against the pillows to enjoy my caresses. He smiled and his lids closed over his eyes half way, while his cock danced in my hands. After a few moments he whispered, "Give me your hand," and I complied immediately with his order. The wine we had consumed earlier had completely gone to my head and I was reeling. The following events seemed to have a grace that is usually only found in dreams.

I gave Cecil my hand and he brought it to his lips, and promptly began to kiss and lick and suck my fingers and the palm of my hand. I felt a thrilling excitement, acknowledging that every part of my body was potentially sensually excitable. I watched with rapt attention as Cecil lubricated the palm of my hand.

"There!" he said. "It feels so much better if your hand has some saliva or come, or possibly pomade. It allows you to slide your hand with more ease up and down on my cock." And then he guided my hand back to his coursing member.

My manipulations of his prick were greatly enhanced with the lubrication, and I made note of this new trick for future trysts. Cecil was moaning and his hips were making small circular movements under my touch, and soon he was reaching for my own raging cock. I was anxious for some relief and so thrust out my belly to meet his experienced hand. My balls were aching so much, I thought that perhaps I was going to burst.

With an assured, well-practised motion, Cecil guided my pelvis towards his chest.

"What?" I cried in surprise.

"Come, come, dear Gaston," sighed Cecil. "Let me suck that very pretty cock of yours, and in turn you can taste mine."

I had never heard of such a thing, but with the wine coursing through my veins and his deft fingers coaxing me closer, I knew I could not resist such temptation, and quite readily complied with his order.

I knelt over him, placing my knees on either side of his broad shoulders, which left my legs spread wide, my cock dangling directly over his mouth. In turn, I found my lips magnetically seeking his member. Cecil immediately took my prick in his mouth, licking the top and then took the whole of it down his throat, which made me gasp with pleasure. I felt this wonderful excitement and I shuddered deliciously. I followed his lascivious example, taking his cock between my lips. Tasting his salty essence thrilled me, sending hot waves of desire over my entire being, and soon I was hungrily devouring his entire cock, taking his full length down my throat as he did the same with mine. He began tickling my balls and slyly teasing my asshole. I felt as though I was going to simply expire from so much pleasure. My hips moved mechanically over his mouth, for I could not help but have that response, so intense was the feeling that Cecil was awakening in me. Simultaneously, I caressed his balls lightly and

I even dared to insert my finger slightly into his asshole. Cecil's cock leapt at my insertion, and I felt myself on the verge of coming. He shoved his finger into my anus, and I pressed my bottom down to further receive his touch. I was on fire and moaning involuntarily. I was writhing like a snake over his clever mouth and fingers. Suddenly I felt his back arch and his muscles tense, and Cecil released a great load of spunk, which spurted down my throat, some of it dribbling down my chin. I swallowed his cream, which enhanced my pleasure as I relished the taste of his come. A moment later I was shivering with orgasmic bliss as I shot my sperm into Cecil's mouth and he hungrily lapped up my spunk. Even after my climax, he continued to lightly suck my cock and squeeze my balls. I followed suit, all the while clutching his hipbones as though his body were a lifeboat and I myself cast into an endless sea of pleasure.

I believe I must have drifted into sleep momentarily, my head resting amidst the soft and dewy hairs surrounding Cecil's cock. I awoke to Cecil's exclamations. "What a strapping lad you are!" he cried gleefully.

I laughed shyly and as we continued to lie there in a warm torpor, Maurice, Cecil's manservant, entered the bed chamber. He carried before him towels that were warm and steaming and lightly scented with lemon. He began to lean carefully over the bed and attempted to sponge us. I leapt up and tried to cover myself, but Cecil laughed and said, "Oh my dear boy! Maurice is fine. Come now, lie back and allow him to rub you down."

Upon hearing this, I relaxed and allowed the man to lightly massage me with the heated towels. I noted as Maurice put his face closer to mine that he was not bad-looking at all. In fact, Cecil's manservant was really quite handsome, with fair curling hair and bright green eyes. He was as broad-shouldered as his master, and narrow in the hips, but he seemed to be closer in age to me.

"Poor Maurice!" exclaimed Cecil. "You've been left out of the fun."

"Not at all, Monsieur," replied Maurice, smiling. "It afforded me much pleasure to watch you and Monsieur le Comte."

As he said this his green eyes sparkled, and I felt my blood rising again. I reached out impetuously and grabbed Maurice's cock, that was still semi-erect in the folds of his trousers. He continued to wash my chest and simply said quietly, "Oh, Monsieur le Comte!"

Without waiting to receive approval from Cecil, I hungrily unbuttoned Maurice's breeches and sat halfway up to take a better look at his cock. He was sporting a great member, and I gasped with shock and surprise to find that he did not have a foreskin! I had never seen the like and my curiosity and passion rose in equal measures.

"Maurice! What has happened to your cock?" I exclaimed, examining the new specimen of a male's anatomy with great interest.

"I have been circumcised, Monsieur le Comte."

"Why, Cecil! Have a look at this. Is it not beautiful? Look at the way the knob is perfectly exposed!" I practically shouted.

"Yes," laughed Cecil over my shoulder. "I have had the pleasure of seeing Maurice's beautiful cock on a great many occasions." And at that Maurice smiled mischievously.

I began to stroke his smooth cock and it leapt to greater length, showing that Maurice had quite a huge member that stood out from sandy-colored hair. Below that, a neat sack that held his balls called out for my attentions. I could read how excited Maurice was, not from the impeccable features on his face, but by the way in which his great cock leapt to life under my caresses. Before I knew it I felt my own cock rise to the occasion, and I was rising to my knees to get better leverage on my grip around Maurice's cock.

Suddenly Cecil exploded into a hearty laugh. "Why Maurice!" he shouted. "It looks as though we've found ourselves quite a randy new friend!"

"Yes, sir!" responded Maurice huskily, as I continued to tug on his enormous cock.

Cecil rose up behind me on the bed and began toying lightly with my balls and tickling my bottom, which only served to further excite my already rather heated condition. I impulsively drew Maurice's cock to my lips, and I heard him sigh and felt him push his hips out to greet my oral caress.

From behind me Cecil suddenly inserted his finger into my asshole, which was still to me a novel sensation, and I shuddered at this electrifying new pleasure. I bent forward slightly, as if to urge Cecil to continue with his finger-fucking, feeling desirous of telling him with my posture what great pleasure he was affording me.

As I continued to suck on the manservant's great cock, I delighted in the sensation of his shaft, which lacked the inhibitive foreskin, leaving my hands free to tease his balls and even tickle the rim of his anus. Quite suddenly I felt Cecil remove his finger, and then I felt the tip of his cock insinuating itself into my as-yet virginal asshole. Simultaneously, he reached around and took hold of my cock, that was standing straight out in agonizing pleasure. My member continued to leap and twitch as I experienced each new pleasure. I continued to suck and lick Maurice's cock, allowing my tongue to travel down to his balls and give him a playful lick now and then, only to return to putting my lips all the way round the purple head of his throbbing prick. I could hear low moans from above, and I knew that I was pleasing the manservant greatly.

Meanwhile, Cecil had set to lubricating my asshole with what I discovered later was pomade, seemingly manufactured for this express purpose. Before I knew it, Cecil thrust his cock into my ass. I cried out, as the sensation was so overwhelming. It was breathtaking and a little painful, but that soon gave way to the most hot kind of pleasurable sensations I had yet known. As Cecil thrust his cock deep within my anatomy, I felt as though I might split in twain. I was excited by the pressure and I set to my task of sucking Maurice's cock more assiduously. I even allowed my fingertip to enter his asshole. All the while Cecil never ceased to stroke my cock as he pumped more and more furiously, driving his sword in to the hilt.

Soon I heard Maurice cry out, and I felt his hot liquor flow into my mouth and down my throat. I drank his spunk thirstily, and as he came he stroked my head, which was locked between his thighs. Cecil was making low rasping sounds, and I was so exceedingly warmed and excited by his furious pumping and stroking that I too began to moan with great pleasure. The sounds of our pleasure songs mingled as we began to climb towards our climax together. As I felt his hot sperm enter my hole I felt as though I were filled with molten gold, and I soon was crying out in orgasmic bliss.

I fell over to one side, quite passing out from so much pleasure. When I finally came to, I found Maurice standing over us, smiling, his magnificent cock having been returned to its hiding place in his trousers.

Soon he was arranging the table with an array of liquors and fruits as Cecil and I lay in a languorous heap of shining flesh, gleaming with the perspiration of our sexual efforts. After Maurice silently took his leave, Cecil and I reclined on his enormous mahogany bed, propped up amongst the tapestry-covered pillows as we sipped a fine vintage and stared at the fire that Maurice had started in the grate. At last it was time for me to go, and somewhat reluctantly we dressed. We dined together, during which time Cecil was very charming and witty, but made no further mention in the slightest of the scenes in which we had just taken part.

When the carriage came to take me home, Cecil bade me a tender farewell and made me promise to visit again soon. He had no trouble eliciting my most solemn vow that I would be very pleased to be welcomed back into his exceptional company again.

De Beaupre's clear and vivid narration had moved us greatly as we listened to it, and my cock was so unruly that I had to keep my hand in my pocket and hold it in an endeavor to calm its excitement. I could tell from Bob's and Jimmy's movements that they were similarly troubled. We stopped for a moment as we came to a stile, and the Duke and de Beaupre climbed to the top rail and sat astride it.

Taking advantage of the pause, I took out my cock, which was causing me a good deal of discomfort by reason of its rubbing against my shirt and breeches.

"I could do with a rub right now. I'm so stiff I can hardly walk!" I said. They all looked at my cock standing straight up like a stick and smiled, but de Beaupre said; "Not now, Charlie, keep cool and wait until tonight. It is ever so much more fun then."

"Oh, I say, I can't really!" I replied. "If nobody else will help me, I shall have to do it myself!" and I began to put the threat into execution.

Blackie jumped quickly off the stile, crying; "Don't let him! Make him wait until tonight!" My hands were seized and held while Bob put my cock back inside and buttoned up my trousers, and they all stood ready to pounce upon me in case I should make a further attempt upon myself.

"You will thank us tonight, really, Charlie!" exclaimed Bob apologetically, and I had to make the best of the situation.

After a time we turned our faces homewards and I do not remember anything else worth recording until we retired to our room that night.

"What are the orders for the evening?" asked Bob, after we had undressed.

"I vote that we make Blackie our Master of Ceremonies, and do whatever he tells us," cried Jimmy.

Bob and I agreed, and de Beaupre gracefully signified his acceptance of the honor.

"I promised to give Bob a turn tonight," he said. "So you and Charlie can amuse yourselves together," he added, turning to Jimmy.

"Very well," replied the Duke, "we are quite ready to obey, aren't we, Charlie? How shall we begin?"

"Try a suck," responded Blackie. "You lie one way and Charlie the other. That's what they call in France *soixante-neuf*—sixty-nine, you know, like the position Cecil taught me."

"We'll have a fuck, Blackie, eh?" said Bob.

"I'm ready to try anything you suggest."

Before we started, Jimmy and I stood by to watch the operations of the others. Blackie lay flat on his back on the bed and told Bob to lie on top of him, putting his cock between his (Blackie's) legs. Then Bob began to pump his narrow hips, while Blackie's cock, squeezed between their two warm bellies, was submitted to a gentle and regular friction by Rutherford's movements.

Their orgasm was not long in being brought about. Within a few moments Bob delivered some extra energetic pushes, and cried out as he sank down on Blackie in a state of happy quiescence while his love juice spurted forth between de Beaupre's thighs. Blackie's cock throbbed between their two bodies and gave out a great spurt of come, wetting their bellies which were almost glued together by the warm, sticky stuff.

I found this display quite thrilling, and by the time that their performance was ended my rampant member ached for release. Jimmy was in a similar state of excitement, and fairly dragged me to another bed so that we might share in the rapturous release which we had just witnessed.

Remembering Blackie's command, I reclined on the bed, spreading my legs to provide a better access to my throbbing cock. Jimmy positioned himself in a kneeling position with his knees by my ears. Facing down my body, and providing me with a most inspiring view of his balls and of his projecting cock.

He leaned forward to take my member, first in his hand and then in his mouth. This motion on his part resulted in his cock approaching my face in the most natural fashion imaginable, and I quickly opened my lips so that I might begin to suck his noble organ.

The feel of Jimmy's stiff, warm cock in my mouth excited me tremendously, and I used my tongue and lips on it in impatient eagerness, while at the same time I pulled and twisted his balls about and stroked and pinched his tight bottom, tickling his little pink asshole with one finger so as to do all I could to add to his pleasure.

Bob and Blackie were now spectators in their turn, and watched us with the greatest interest. Presently Blackie entered the fray and began to tickle Jimmy's spine with his fingers. Bob followed his example as far as he was able, by stroking my thighs and by tickling the little opening of my anus. This went on for some little time, until I felt a tingling sensation creeping over me and knew that my climax was not far off.

I judged, too, by the way that Jimmy quivered every now and then, that he was in a similar predicament. He sank lower, thrusting his cock further into my mouth. I heard him gasp, his hot breath pouring thickly over my thighs. Then he almost fell on top of my face, his teeth closed tightly on my member, his own organ palpitated and I felt something wet and warm trickling down my throat.

Next minute the transport seized me. I gave a great heave upwards and then all my muscles relaxed their tension, and I was conscious of nothing but the glorious, thrilling happiness that was setting my entire frame on fire, as my cock jumped about wildly in the act of emptying its essence into Jimmy's mouth.

The wonderful bliss prostrated us both, and we did not move to change our positions until the first effects had passed off, although we were causing each other the acutest physical sensations as our lips pressed upon one another's super-sensitive members. At last Jimmy raised himself up and we both proceeded to get into our nightshirts.

"Wasn't it just terrific!" exclaimed the Duke, his eyes sparkling with enthusiasm for the experience we had just shared.

"I should say it was—only more so!" I replied, adding; "I propose that Blackie retain the office of Master of Ceremonies permanently. He reminds me of that chap you read about in the

Roman histories—Petronius was his name, wasn't it? Who used to plan all the entertainments for Nero? Blackie would have been all right for that job, had he lived then!"

They laughed and after a little further talk we said "Good night." The light was put out, and we prepared for sleep.

IMRE
Anonymous

"From the time when I was a lad, Imre, I felt myself unlike other boys in one element of my nature. That one matter was my special sense, my passion, for the beauty, the dignity, the charm...the, what shall I say?...The lovableness of my own sex. I hid it, at least so far as, little by little, I came to realize its force. For, I soon perceived that most other lads had no such passionate sentiments, in any important measure of their natures, even when they were fine-strung, impressionable youths. There was nothing unmanly about me; nothing unlike the rest of my friends in school, or in town-life. Though I was not a strong-built, or rough-spirited lad, I had plenty of pluck and muscle, and was as lively on the play-ground, and fully as indefatigable, as my chums. I had a good many friends; close ones, who liked me well. But I felt sure, more and more, from one year to another even of that boyhood time, that no lad of them all ever could or would care for me as much as I could and did care for one or another of them! Two or three episodes made that clear to me. These incidents made me, too, shyer and shyer of showing how my whole young nature, soul and body together, Imre—could be stirred with a veritable adoration for some boy-friend that I elected...an adoration with a physical yearning in it—how intense was the appeal of bodily beauty, in a lad, or in a man of mature years.

"And yet, with that beauty, I looked for manliness, poise, will-power, dignity and strength in him. For, somehow I demanded those traits, always and clearly, whatever else I sought along with them. I say 'sought'; I can say, too, won—won often to nearness. But this other, more romantic, emotion in me so strongly phys-ical, sexual, as well as spiritual it met with a really like and equal and full response once only. Just after the close of my school-life came a friendship with an older gentleman, of striking beauty of physique, and uncommon strength of character. This early relation embodied the same precocious, absolutely vehement *passion* (I can call it nothing else) on both sides. I had found my ideal! I had realized for the first time, completely, a type; a type which had haunted me from first consciousness of my mortal existence, Imre; one that is to haunt me till my last moment of it. All my immature but intensely ardent regard was returned. And then, after a few passionate months together, my love, my teacher, all at once, became ill during an epidemic in the town, was taken to his home, and died. I never saw him after he left me.

"It was my first great misery, Imre. It was literally unspeakable! For, I could not tell to anyone, I did not know how to explain even to myself, the manner in which my nature had gone out to my *young* mate, nor how his being spontaneously so had melded itself with mine. I was still young, as I said. But I knew clearly now what it was to *love* thus, so as to forget oneself in another's life and death! But also I knew better than to talk of such things. So I never spoke of my dead lover.

"I grew older, I entered my professional studies, and I was

very diligent with them. I lived in a great capital, I moved much in general society. I had a large and lively group of friends. But always, over and over, I realized that, in the kernel, at the very root and fibre of myself, there was the throb and glow, the ebb and the surge, the seeking as in a vain dream to realize again that passion of friendship which could so far transcend the cold modern idea of the tie; the Over-Friendship, the Lánczhidove-Friendship of Hellas—which meant that between man and man could exist, the sexual psychic love. That was still possible! I knew that now! I had read it in the verses or the prose of the Greek or Latin and Oriental authors who have written out every shade of its beauty or unloveliness, its worth or debasements—from Theokritos to Martial, or Abu-Nuwas, to Platen, Michel Angelo, Shakespeare. I had learned it from the statues of sculptors, with those lines so often vivid with a merely physical male beauty—works which beget, which sprang from, the sense of it in a race; I had half-divined it in the music of a Beethoven and a Tschaikovsky before knowing facts in the life-stories of either of them—or of an hundred other tone-autobiographists.

"And I had recognized what it all meant to most people today! From the disgust, scorn and laughter of my fellow men when such an emotion was hinted at! I understood perfectly that a man must wear the Mask, if he, poor wretch, could neither abide at the bound of ordinary warmth of feeling for some friend of friends, that drew on his innermost nature; or if he were not content because the other stayed within that bound. Love between two men, however absorbing, however passionate, must not be—so one was assured—solemnly or in disgusted incredulity—as sexual love, a physical impulse and bond. That was now as ever, a nameless horror—a thing against all civilization, sanity, sex, Nature, God! Therefore, I was, of course…what then was I? Oh, I perceived it! I was that anachronism from old—that incomprehensible incident in God's human creation…the man-loving man! The man-loving man! whose whole heart can be given only to another man, and who when his spirit is passing into his beloved friend's keeping would demand, would surrender, the body with it. The man-loving man! He who seeks not merely a spiritual unity with him whom he loves, but seeks the embrace that joins two male human beings in a fusion that no woman's arms, no woman's kisses can ever realize. No woman's embrace? No, no!…for instead of that, either he cares not a whit for it, is indifferent to it, is smilingly scornful of it; or else he tolerates it, even in the wife he has married (not to speak of any less honourable ties) as an artifice; a mere quietus to that undeceived sexual passion burning in his nature; wasting his really unmated individuality years-long. Or else he surrenders himself to some woman who bears his name, loves him—to her who perhaps in innocence and ignorance believes that she dominates every instinct of his sex!—making her a wife that she may bear to him children; or thinking that marriage may screen him, or even (vain hope!) 'cure' him! But oftenest, he flies from any woman, as her sexual self; wholly shrinks from her as from nothing else created; avoids the very touch of a woman's hand in his own, any physical contact with woman, save in a calm cordiality, in a sexless and fraternal reserve, a passionless if yet warm…friendship! Not seldom he shudders (he may not know why) in something akin to dread and to loathing, though he may succeed in hiding it from wife or mistress, at any near approach of his strong male body to a woman's feminine one, however far, however harmonious in lines! Yes, even were she Aphrodite herself!

"And yet, Imre, thousands, thousands, hundreds of thousands, of such human creatures as I am, have not in body, in mind, nor in all the sum of our virility, in all the detail of our outward selves, any openly womanish trait! Not one! It is only the ignorant and the vulgar who nowadays think or talk of the homosexual as if he were an—hermaphrodite! In every feature and line and sinew and muscle, in every movement and accent and capability, we walk the world's way as men. We hew our ways through it as men, with vigour, success, honour…one master-instinct unsuspected by society for, it may be, our lives long! We plough the globe's roughest seas as men, we rule its States as men, we direct its finance and commerce as men, we forge its steel as men, we grapple with all its sciences, we triumph in all its arts as men, we fill its gravest professions as men, we fight in the bravest ranks of its armies as men, or we plan out its fiercest and most triumphant battles as men...in all this, in so much more, we are men! Why, (in a bitter paradox!) one can say that we always have been, we always are, always will be, too much *men!* So super-male, so utterly unreceptive of what is not manly, so aloof from any feminine essences, that we cannot tolerate woman at all as a sexual factor! Are we not the extreme of the male? Its supreme phase, its outermost phalanx?—Its climax of the aristocratic, the All-Man? And yet, if love is to be only what the narrow, modern Jewish-Christian ethics of today declare it, if what they insist be the only natural and pure expression of 'the will to possess, the wish to surrender.' Oh, then is the flouting world quite right! For then we were indeed not men! But if not so, what are we? Answer that, who can?

"The more perplexed I became in all this wretchedness (for it had grown to that by the time I had reached my majority)...the more perplexed I became because so often in books, old ones or new, nay, in the very chronicles of the criminal-courts, I came face to face with the fact that though tens of thousands of men, in all epochs, of noblest natures, of most brilliant minds and gifts, of intensest energies...scores of pure spirits, deep philosophers, bravest soldiers, highest poets and artists, had been such as myself in this mystic sex-disorganization...that nevertheless of this same Race, the Race-Homosexual, had been also, and apparently ever would be, countless ignoble, trivial, loathe-some, feeble-souled and feeble-bodied creatures!... the very weaklings and rubbish of humanity!

"Those, those, terrified me, Imre! To think of them shamed me; those types of man-loving-men who, by thousands, live incapable of any noble ideals or lives. And then I chanced to meet a very great and intelligent man who taught me that there was love to be had between men. True love!" And I hesitated briefly, summoning the courage to continue.

"This fine man told me of the great Oriental princes and the heroes and heroic intellects of Greece and Rome! To a Themistocles, an Agesilaus, an Aristides and a Kleomenes; to Socrates and Plato, and Saint Augustine, to Servetus and Beza; to Alexander, Julius Caesar, Augustus, and Hadrian; to Prince Eugene of Savoy, to Sweden's Charles the Twelfth, to Frederic the Great, to indomitable Tilly, to the fiery Skobeleff, the austere Gordon, the ill-starred Macdonald; to the brightest lyricists and dramatists of old Hellas and Italia; to Shakespeare, (to Marlowe also, we can well believe) Platen, Grillparzer, Hölderlin, Byron, Whitman; to an Isaac Newton, a Justus von Liebig—to Michel Angelo and Sodoma; to the masterly Jerome Duquesnoy, the classic-souled Winckel-mann; to Mirabeau, Beethoven, Bavaria's unhappy King Ludwig;—to as endless procession of exceptional men, from epoch to epoch! Yet as to these and innumerable others, facts of their hidden, inner lives have proved without shadow of doubt (however rigidly suppressed as 'popular information') or inferences vivid enough to silence scornful denial, have pointed out that they belonged to Us.

"Nevertheless, did not the widest overlook of the record of homosexuality, the average facts about one, suggest that the most part of homosexual humanity has always belonged, always would belong, to the worthless or the wicked? Was our Race gold or excrement? As rubies or as carrion? If that last were one's *final* idea, why then all those other men, our severest judges, those others whether good or bad, whether vessels of honour or dishonour, who are not in their love-instincts as are we…the millions against our tens of thousands, even if some of us are to be respected…what right do they have to cast us out of society?

"And yet, the rest of us! The Rest, over and over! Men so high-minded, often of such deserved honour from all that world which has either known nothing of their sexual lives, or else has perceived vaguely, and with a tacit, a reluctant pardon! Could one really believe in God as making man to live at all, and to love at all, and yet at the same time believe that *this* love is not created, too, by God? Is not of God's own divinest nature, rightfully, eternally—in millions of hearts? Could one believe that the eternal human essence is in its texture today so different from itself of immemorial time before now, whether Greek, Latin, Persian, or English? But I long for the day when men such as myself will gather and say in one strong voice 'Come—enough!—Be free of all!'"

I paused. Doing so, I heard from Imre, who had not spoken so much as a word—was it a sigh? Or a broken murmur of something coming to his lips. Was it—no, impossible! I thought I heard a sort of sob, strangled in his throat! The evening had grown so dark that I could not have seen his face, even had I wished to look into it. However...absorbed now in my own tenebrous retrospect, almost forgetting that anyone was there, at my side, I went on:

"You must not think that I had not had friendships of much depth, Imre, which were not, first and last, quite free from this other accent in them. Yes, I had had such; and I have many such now; comradeships with men younger, men of my own age, men older, for whom I feel warm affection and admiration, whose company was and is a true happiness for me. But somehow they were not and, no matter what they are I had not yet found love. Of that eternal, mysteriously disturbing cruel emotion, which so vibrates sexually against my hidden Self.

"How I dreaded, yet sought that love! How soon was I relieved, or dull of heart, when I knew that this or that friend was not enough dear to me, however dear he was, to give me a greater sexual stir and sympathy, an inner, involuntary thrill! Yet I sought it ever, right and left, since none embodied it for me; while I always *feared* that some one might embody it! There were approaches to it. Then, then, I suffered or throbbed with a wordless pain or joy of life, at one and the same time! But I learned from my experiences how I could feel toward the man who could be in his mind and body my ideal; my beloved. Would I ever meet him? Meet him again? I could say to myself—remembering the love of my schooldays.

"At last I sought the help of a doctor who simply told me that I would be 'cured' if I were to marry. Suddenly, I was lighthearted. I paid the man and went in search of a wife—my cure!

"Marry! Well, that was easily to be done. I was popular enough with women of all sorts. I was no woman-hater. I had many true and charming and most affectionate friendships with women. For, you must know, Imre, that such men as I am are often most attractive to women, most beloved by them…I mean by good women…far more than through being their relatives and social friends. But alas! it is the irony of our nature that we cannot return love to any woman, except by a lie of the body and the spirit; marriage with any woman could have meant only a friendship.

"But now I had my prescription, and I was to be cured. In ten days, Imre, I was betrothed. Do not be surprised. I had known a long while earlier that I was loved. My betrothed was the daughter of a valued family friend, living in a near town. She was beautiful, gifted, young, high-souled and gentle. I had always admired her warmly; we had been much thrown together. I had avoided her lately however, because—unmistakably—I had become sure of a deeper sentiment on her part than I could exchange.

"But now, now, I persuaded myself that I did indeed return it; that I had not understood myself. And confidently, even ardently, I played my new role so well, Imre, that I was deceived myself. And she? She never felt the shade of suspicion. I fancied that I loved her. She loved me; and she would have given herself wholly to me, as my bride.

"The date for our marriage was set. I tried to think of nothing but it and her; of how calmly, securely happy I would soon be, and of all the happiness that, God willing, I would bring into her young life. I say 'tried' to think of nothing else. I almost succeeded. But...nevertheless...in moments....

"It was not to be, however!

"One evening, I was asked by a friend to come to his lodgings to dine, to meet some strangers, his guests. I went. Among the men who came was one...I had never seen him before...newly arrived in my city...coming to pass the winter. From that instant that set me face to face with him...that let me hear his voice in only a greeting...that put us to exchanging a few commonplace sentences...I thrilled with joy and trembled to my innermost soul with a sudden anguish. For, Imre, it was as if that dead lover of mine, not merely as death had taken him; but matured, a man in his beauty and charm...it was a if every acquaintance that ever had quickened within me the same unspeakable sense of a mysterious bond of soul and of body. Out of the slumberous past, out of the kingdom of illusions, straying to me from the realm of banished hopes, it had come to me! The fires of passion were not to be quenched, that subjection of my whole being to an ideal of my own sex...that fatal 'nervous illusion', as the famous doctor's book so summarily ranged it for the world...all had overtaken me again! My brief flight of peace was momentarily shattered—if ever I had had true peace. I was lost with it!...

"From that night, I forgot everything else except him. My former, unchanged, unchangeable self, in all its misery and mystery reverted. The temperament which I had thought to put to sleep, the invisible nature I had believed I could strangle—it had awakened with the lava-seethe of a volcano. It burned in my spirit and body, like a masked crater.

"Imre, I sought the friendship of this man, of my ideal who had re-created for me, simply by his existence, a world of feeling; one of suffering and yet of more delight. And I won his friendship! Do not suppose that I dared to dream, then or ever, of more than a commonplace, social intimacy. Never, never! Merely to achieve his regard toward myself a little more than toward others;

merely that he would care to give me more of his society, would show me more of his inner self than he inclined to open to others. Just to be accounted by him somewhat dearer, in such a man's vague often elusive degree, than the majority for whom he cared at all! Only to have more constant leave to delight my spirit in silence with his physical beauty while guarding from him in a sort of terror the psychic effects it wrought in me. My hopes went no further than these. And, as I say, I won them. As it kindly happened, our tastes, our interest in arts and letters, our temperaments, the fact that he came to my city with few acquaintances in it and was not a man who readily seeks them...the chance that he lived almost in the same house with me...such circumstances favored me immediately. But I did not deceive myself once, either as to what was the measure or the kind of my emotion for him, any more than about what (if stretched to its uttermost) would be his sentiment for me, for any man. He could not love a man so. He could love...passionately, and to the completing of his sexual nature...only a woman."

In the gathering darkness, I swallowed and proceeded: "Did I keep my secret perfectly from him? Perfectly, Imre! You will soon see that clearly. There were times when the storm came full over me...when I avoided him, when I would have fled from myself, in the fierce struggle. But I was vigilant. He was moved, now and then, at a certain inevitable tenderness that I would show him. He often spoke wonderingly of the degree of my 'absorbing friendship.' But he was a man of fine and romantic ideals, of a strong and warm temper. His life had been something solitary from his earliest youth...and he was no psychologist. Despite many a contest with our relation-ship, I never allowed myself to complain of him. I was too well aware how fortunate was my bond with him. The man esteemed me, trusted me, admired me...all this thoroughly. I had more; for I possessed what in such a nature as his proves itself a manly affection. I was an essential element in his daily life all that winter; intimate to a depth that (as he told me, and I believe it was wholly true) he had never expected another man could attain. Was all that not enough for me? Oh, yes! and yet...and yet....

"I will not speak to you more of that time which came to pass for me, Imre. It was for me, verily, a new existence! It was much such a daily life, Imre, as you and I might lead together, had fate allowed us the time for it to ripen. Perhaps we yet might lead it... God knows!...I leave you tomorrow!

"But, you ask,—what of my marriage-engagement?

"I broke it. I had broken it within a week after I met him, so far as shattering, it to myself went. I knew that no marriage, of any kind yet tolerated in our era, would 'cure' me of my 'illusion', my 'nervous disease', could banish this 'mere psychic distur-bance', the result of 'too much introspection.' I had no disease! No...I was simply what I was born!—a complete human being, of firm, perfect physical and mental health; outwardly in full key with all the man's world: but, in spite of that, a being who from birth was of a vague, special sex; a member of the sex within the most obvious sexes; or apart from them. I was created as a man perfectly male, save in the one thing which keeps such a 'man' back from possibility of ever becoming integrally male—his terrible, instinctive demand for a psychic and a physical union with a man—not with a woman.

"And of my dear friend, at last I could not contain my feelings for the man and one late evening I told him all! I confessed to disengaging from my betrothed because upon meeting him, I realized that not only could I love men alone, but that I loved him!

"He heard my confession through with ever more hostile eyes, with an astonished unsympathy...disgust...curling his lips. Then he spoke—slowly—pitilessly: 'I have heard that such creatures as you describe yourself are to be found among mankind. I do not know, nor do I care to know, whether they are a sex by them-selves, a justified, because helpless, play of Nature; or even a kind of logically essential link, a between-step...as you seem to have persuaded yourself. Let all that be as it may be. I am not a man of science nor keen to such new notions! From this moment, you and I are strangers! I took you for my friend because I believed you to be a…man. You chose me for your friend because you believed me…stay, I will not say that!…because you wished me to be…a something else, a something more or less like to yourself, whatever you are! I loathe you!…I loathe you! When I think that I have touched your hand, have sat in the same room with you, have respected you!…Farewell!…If I served you as a man should serve such beings as you, this town should know your story tomorrow! Society needs more policemen than it has, to protect itself from such lepers as you! I will keep your hideous secret. Only remember never to speak to me!…never to look my way again! Never! From henceforward I have never known you and never will think of you!—if I can forget anything so monstrous in this world!'

"So passed he out of my life, Imre. Forever! Over the rupture of our friendship not much was said, nevertheless. For he was called to London a few days after that last interview; and he was obliged to remain in the capital for months. Meantime I had changed my life to meet its new conditions; to avoid gossip. I had removed my lodgings to a suburb. I had taken up a new course in professional work. It needed all my time. Then, a few months later, I started quietly on a long travel-route on the Continent, under excuse of ill-health. I was far from being a stranger to life in at least half a dozen countries of Europe, east or west. But now, now, I knew what it was to be a refugee, an exile!

"And yet, involuntarily, sub-consciously, I was always hoping… seeking—something. Hoping…seeking…what? Another such man as I? Sometimes I cried out as to that, 'God forbid it!' For I dreaded such a chance now; realizing the more what it would most likely not offer me. And really unless a miracle of miracles were to be wrought just for me, unless I should light upon another human creature who's sympathies, idealisms, noble impulses, manliness and virile life could fill, and could wish to fill, the desolate solitudes of mine, could confirm all that was deepest fixed in my soul as the concept of true similisexual masculinity...oh, far better meet none! For such a miracle of miracles I should not hope. Even traversing all the devious ways of life may not bring us face to face with such a friend. Yet I was hoping—seeking—I say: even if there was no vigour of expectancy."

And with my last ounces of courage, I did conclude: "Or, how easy to meet such a man, he also 'seeking, despairing' and not to recognize him, any more than he recognizes us! The Mask— the eternal social Mask for the homosexual! Worn before our nearest and dearest, or we are ruined and cast out! I resolved to be content with tranquility...pleasant friendships. Something like a kindly apathy often possessed me.

"And nevertheless, the desires that still so stirred my nature? The man that is...inevitably...to be loved, not merely liked; to be feared while yet sought; the friend from whom I can expect nothing, from whom never again will I expect anything, more than calm regard, his sympathy, his mere leave for me calling him '*barátom*'—my brother-friend? He, by whom I should at least be respected as an upright fellow-creature from the work-shop of God, not from the hand of the Devil; be taken into companionship because of what in me is worthily companionable? The fellow-man who would accept what was good in me is like the rest of men, nor draw away from me, as from a leper? Have I really ceased to dream of this grace for me, this vision—as years have passed?

"And then my hope returned when I met you, Imre.

"Met you! Yes!" My voice strengthened and I began speaking in the familiar terms of Magyarország with its soft archaic thee's and thou's. "Now I have met thee. Thou wert *to be*; somewhat, at least, to be for me! That thou wast ordained to come into the world that I should love thee. That I believe! But, see! Fate also has willed that thou shouldst be Magyar, one of the Children of Emesa, one of the Folk of Arpád!"

"I cannot tell thee, Imre,...oh, I have no need now to try! What *thou* hast become for me. My Search ended when thou and I met. Never has my dream given me what is this reality of thyself. I love this world now only because thou art in it. I respect thee wholly— I respect myself—certain, too, of that coming time, however far away now, when no man shall ever meet many intelligent civilization's disrespect simply *because* he loves another man! But—oh, Imre, Imre!—I *love* thee, as men can only love. Once more helpless, and therewith hopeless! But this time no longer silent, before the Friendship which is Love, the Love which is Friendship.

"Speak my sentence. I make no plea. I have kept my pledge to confess myself tonight. But I would have fulfilled it only a little later, were I not going away from thee tomorrow. I ask nothing, except what I asked long ago of that other, of whom I have told thee! Endure my memory, as thy friend! Friend? That at least! For, I would say farewell, believing that I shall still have the right to call thee 'friend'—even—O God!—when I remember tonight. But whether that right is to be mine, or not, is for thee to say. Tell me!"

I stopped.

Full darkness was now about us. Stillness had so deepened that the ceasing of my on low voice made it the more suspenseful. The sweep of the night-wind rose among the acacias. The birds of shadow flitted about us. The gloom seemed to have entered my soul—as Death into Life. Would Imre ever speak?

His voice came at last. Never had I heard it so moved, so melancholy. A profound tenderness was in every syllable.

"If I could…my God! If I only could!…say to thee what I cannot. Perhaps…some time…Forgive me, but thou breakest my heart!…Not because I care less for thee as my friend…no, above all else, not that reason! We stay together, Oswald!…We shall always be what we have become to each other! Oh, *we* cannot change, not through all our lives! Not in death, not in anything! Oh, Oswald! that thou couldst think, for an instant, that I—I—would dream of turning away from thee…suffer a break for us two…

because thou art made in thy nature as God makes mankind—as each and all, or not as each and all! We are what we are!…Forever! Forever, Oswald!…

"Here, take my hand!" whispered Imre, and in the gathering shadows, he touched my fingers and took my trembling palms into his own.

His words were so beautiful to me, and yet still at this late moment their source, this man Imre, struggled with the vast doubts of tangled fears and passions. And yet I stayed my own listing hopes and mounting fears to listen, to hear Imre as if these would be our last moments to share together on Earth:

"As long as I live…and beyond then!" cried Imre. "Yes, my God above us, my God in us!…Only, only, for the sake of the bond between us from this night, promise me that thou wilt never speak again of what thou hast told me of thyself—never, unless I break the silence. Nevermore a word of—of thy—thy—feeling for me. There are other things for us to talk of, are there not, my dear brother? Thou wilt promise?"

And yet despite these words, after only a single moment's pause, dream to my dreaming, Imre leaned forward, and kissed me on the lips. Our moist flesh met, and the single spark released of the true and bottled passion we shared ignited and set ablaze the chaotic, terrifying darkness within which I had been whirling about as I had spoke. All the darkness of my endless, lonely search was suddenly vanquished with the brilliant flare of reciprocated desire. My emptiness dissipated as Imre's lips filled every corner of my heretofore perceived being. As he leaned into me and met my lips with his, I felt my physical being change and metamorphose. His touch was almost exact to the sensation of his caresses in my dreams. He held me fiercely, he held on to me in the dark, so close to his quaking chest, and I joyfully returned the passionate kiss.

Our tongues touched, entwining hungrily, deeply within this, our very first kiss. We caressed one another, moving our hands to one another's temples, cheeks, shoulders and arms. I moved on our bench in an effort to be nearer to Imre, and he clutched me till we broke into a frenzy of mutual discovery. Surely we had been starved, deprived of this intimacy for so very long, and now we nearly tore at one another's flesh in this devouring embrace. We stayed, our lips, our tongues pressed together for what seemed to be a timeless expanse. Our kiss had moved through a languor that gave way to a violent search, as if somewhere within this kiss could be found our very souls. Kissing Imre was like tasting the most magical, the finest of all the wines in the world. I was intoxicated.

I moved my fingers through Imre's jet black hair, a single action about which I had spent many waking moments fantasizing, and found it to be as soft to the touch as it was to the eye. His fingertips traced the outline of my neck, of my breast within the confines of my shirt. He traced delicate little circles around the sensitive aureole of my nipples through the soft, thin fabric. They became erect, and my chest seemed to thrust forward, pushing into his touch, of its own accord.

Imre began to furiously unbutton the ivory clasps of my blouse, as I continued to kiss his lips. I put my nose to his hair, to his skin to inhale the scent of his natural perfume. It was an appealing musk, one that I had smelled frequently upon his clothing, upon his neck when he leaned in to whisper some comment at a café table; but now I fairly swam in his smell, I breathed and drank in the smell of Imre. My member strained impatiently at my breeches, responding to his passing caresses with aching desire. I slowly reached between Imre's muscular thighs to find that he too had become fully erect at our impassioned embrace.

I could feel his hot breath against my chest as he pushed my shirt aside to slowly kiss me there. He put his trembling lips to my nipples, wetting them, drawing them into his mouth, forcing me to shudder with excitement. With a delicate strength, he then slid his hands to my sides and and moved me back, that his hungry mouth could be drawn down over my abdomen, and when his kisses reached the sensitive flesh low upon my belly, my cock leapt with uncontrolled passion.

In turn I undid the buttons of his officer's blouse, thrilling to the feel of the bronze and silver pins that were his lieutenant's bars and medals, as well as the rough planes of stitching that were the signifying patches of his regiment and battalion. But then, my desire to feel his naked skin against my own became single-minded. I tore away the crisp fawn fabric of his fatigue blouse, and swiftly broke open the belt which sealed his beautiful cock and balls away from me, and soon we were locked in a wild embrace completely naked on a mossy bed of earth.

"At last," said I.

"Yes. At long last," he whispered, his velvet voice plush with desire and emotion.

His smooth tanned flesh was extraordinary to the touch and exceedingly warm, as though there were small fires burning just beneath the surface of his glowing skin. I could not resist allowing my hands to explore the wonder of his beautiful physique. His stomach was a delight of rippling muscle, which contracted as he leaned forward to hungrily take my throbbing member in his capable hands. He began to stroke me with grace and care. And as my hands continued in their travels over the majestic terrain of his buttocks, his legs, the gentle curves of his flanks and his waist, I felt that I could quite possibly inhale every particle of him, so splendid did he feel, taste and smell.

I closed my eyes, suddenly afraid that this was not happening at all, but was simply an extraordinary dream, one among many, so perfect was the fruition of my desire and passion. I wanted to taste his manhood completely. I bent down and took his cock between my lips. To my delight he had an exquisite penis, perfectly formed and throbbing with anticipation of my kisses. I took him in my mouth, and then deeper still into my throat, and as I did this I heard and felt the deep resonating moan of pleasure ripple through his body, the echoes of which were felt in my own. And then he followed my gesture, twisting atop me so that he too could taste of me.

Imre then took my painfully-throbbing cock into his mouth, and drew upon it with hunger and passion, filling me with voluptuous pleasure. As I sucked and licked Imre, his hips began to slowly, and then more rapidly pump over my face and I took him as deep inside my mouth as I possibly could, taking incredible delight from the force of his hips against my chest as they thrust with animal vitality.

Suddenly my mouth, my throat, my being, was filled with Imre's electric seed. I felt his buttocks tighten, then tremble, then contract as I wrapped my hands completely around him, swallowing every drop that he gave me as he softly moaned.

"Will you take me?" he whispered longingly, through harsh breaths. And without waiting for a response, Imre fell over to the side and offered his smooth perfect buttocks up to me as if it were a passionate plea.

I leaned over and moved upon him in a loving embrace, moving my hand to his beautiful face to gently trace the outline of his lips with my finger. Imre moved his mouth and took my finger between his lips, lubricating it with warm saliva. Slowly, I lowered my hand, and traced my lubricated finger round the sweetly puckered rim of his anus. The simple touch of his most sacrosanct anatomy, offered up to me thus, moved my heart and passion farther than any fantasy I had yet dared to dream. Unable to wait any longer, I introduced my member to the edge of that blessed abyss and then, without pause, I plunged my dagger into its' rightful sheath.

Imre cried out with pleasure, and his low cries and groans were soon mingled with mine own as I began to thrust. Slowly at first, deeply probing the moist and tight interior confines of my beloved, did I make love to Imre. And then, with swifter and swifter strokes, I plunged wildly into him, gripping his narrow hips tightly, as though I feared I might fall from the edge of the earth. We cried out, moaning into the air like wolves at the charge of our connection, the liquid fire which brought my pearlescent seed to such a boil that it exploded forth, far deep into my lover—Imre—as would a deluge, a torrent unleashed.

We fell together again in a tight embrace on the earth's cool floor and fell into a brief but opiate-like sleep. But just before we slept, Imre sighed into my hair, my face, my mouth:

"My love."

TEDDY

Anonymous

It was upon an early fall day, one of those crisp, sunny, cheerful days when New York seems to blossom in anticipation of the greater winter season; a time when all are freshly costumed; when the business houses flaunt anew all their temptations; when there are new plays in town, new faces invading old haunts; when the town in every way seems to take on added life.

Randall's employment had been transferred to the private home of the president of the bank. His duties had become progressively fewer and more important. His time was almost his own during the briefer business hours. He was even able to arrange a few day courses at the university, some early and some after business hours. With greater leisure he even found more time to give to love. He found himself thinking of Teddy between his tasks, planning everything with reference to him; Teddy wanted to see certain shows, he provided the tickets for the following Saturday;

Teddy liked him best in dark blue, he bought blue; Teddy did not care for this and did not care for that; Teddy! Teddy! Teddy!

Teddy had invented a new type of automobile. He was anxious to try it. Also, this day, he was anxious to get Randall out into the secluded romantic country where he could feel more free with him. In the city there was the ever-present crowd, at the theater, at the restaurant, on the street, anywhere. Even the halls of their boarding house were constantly being invaded and there was no opportunity to caress at ease. He knew intuitively that Randall would have to be won unsuspectingly—taken unawares.

So this lovely fall day he planned to try out his automobile and also to try out Randall. He suggested a run up the Hudson. The novelty of the thing was appealing. Randall was tingling with excitement, the thrill of his new love, the sense of novelty, the stimulation of the wonderful fall day. Life seemed glorious. He would love Teddy always and Teddy would love him and that would be all there was to it, love, love, love—purest love!

They turned from Thirtieth Street onto Fifth Avenue. Randall waved gayly to several acquaintances. Any automobile was a novelty then. He felt a pleasant sense of importance in being different from the crowd, an admired and envied something different. They passed through the park, over to the Drive and up the Hudson where the foliage was all brilliant reds, yellows, oranges and purples. Teddy's car was a success. 'Twas a glorious ride, of wonderful distance—for those days! They were far out in the country and finally arrived at an eminence where the view of the Hudson was superb. Here Teddy halted. They alighted to enjoy the scene and also to have a picnic supper.

The dead, dry grass, sunned all day, was delightfully warm. They sat down, even as the sun was beginning to redden the sky. They ate their sandwiches lingeringly and quietly. Words seemed unnecessary. Randall's face, as he gazed on the beauty about him, wore a look of exaltation. The sunlight on his short, curly hair turned it to reddish gold. A faint happy smile played about his lips.

Teddy too was affected by the scene. Also, he was experiencing the happiness which comes from satisfied achievement. He was stirred by Randall's youthful beauty as never before. Also, he had become increasingly aware of Randall's excellence. For the time being he thought himself capable and eager to renounce all other loves for the sweetness of this, the most entrancing affair of his life. There are times when sex dominates completely. Such a time had arrived!

As the sun sank, a chill wind sprang up. Teddy went to the car for robes, one to sit on, the other to wrap about Randall. As he enveloped his companion's slender body with the robes, he closed his arms about him, and meeting no resistance gave him a long lingering kiss.

"Oh, Teddy, Teddy, how I love you!" he whispered, though there was no one to hear had he declaimed it aloud. Randall almost swooned in his arms.

Teddy, to do him justice, had never been so much in love as at this moment. He kissed Randall over and over again and they made repeated avowals of their love, just as all lovers do.

The sun set in a glorious burst of flame that encompassed the whole horizon. They were alone; the world, the entire world, seemed theirs. As the sun disappeared from sight, the moon came up casting its dark blue shadows. Teddy pleaded. The almost hypnotic compliance invaded Randall. He felt no emotion other than the compulsion to do Teddy's bidding.

Before long, the two of them were nude to the world, and the cool evening air whispered across their bodies. Teddy was younger and more handsome than Mr. Fisher had been. Though pale and somewhat soft about the edges, Teddy was better fleshed, and Randall thrilled to the musculature of his upper arms and shoulders. Then they were upon each other.

The feeling of embracing a naked man in the wide open astonished Randall and he became overwhelmed with emotion. They wrestled about passionately, kissing one another in the grass, stroking and petting one another as their cocks grew large and stiff between their bellies.

"Dear Randy, I want to taste you," murmured Teddy. "Let me please you, I beg you."

"Oh Teddy!" cried Randall. "I am yours to do with as you like."

They turned in upon each other at once; their heads moved into the lower regions of one another's nudity. Randall examined Teddy's thick-headed cock only briefly before taking it into his mouth for a delicious sucking. But he was taken completely by surprise with Teddy's simultaneous reciprocation. The feeling of Teddy's lips wetly creeping over his cock nearly made Randall swoon, and for a moment, he lost hold of the member he had been nursing himself. So shocking was this pleasure that Randall cried out despite his efforts to stifle himself, and he could only but continue to rub Teddy's engorged penis with the palm of his hand. In seconds Randall was brought to a fiery climax, and he released a pitched scream as great jets of come exploded from his throbbing erection. Instinctively, Randall grabbed and pulled at Teddy's cock even as he still convulsed with passion, and, crying out with sheer joy, Teddy came fully into Randall's face.

The ride home was very quiet. Teddy was beside himself with glee. Far from feeling satiation, his experience had served to make him more truly in love with Randall than ever. On every possible occasion he stole one hand beneath his lover's robe and caressed the still-trembling cock within.

Teddy came into Randall's room to bid him goodnight. Then he took him again into his arms and gripped his new lover's body madly as if, with such viselike force, he would fuse them into one being. God! How he loved him!

"Teddy," Randall whispered, "you do love me, don't you?" and when Teddy answered that he loved him more than ever Randall begged, "Then don't let me ever forget my better self again!"

Teddy laughed as he said, "Oh, you've been there before. You're too good at it."

"Stop, stop," whimpered Randall. "Go away before I hate myself and you too."

Puzzled, Teddy gave him a perfunctory embrace and hurried to his own room.

For hours Randall lay awake thinking alternately of his love for Teddy and his new fall from grace, with its accompanying sense of shame. But this time he was calmer in the face of self-realization.

The next morning, Sunday, Randall felt ashamed to meet Teddy at breakfast, and planned to remain in his room. But Teddy's actions showed that he experienced no such qualms. His attitude was entirely matter of fact. He was in love with Randall and he cared not who knew it or what others thought; this was Randall's affair and his; it was for them to seize happiness when it presented itself, in whatever form, and make the most of it as and while they could. In after years Teddy was wont to relate with pride that this was the great love affair of his life. True, he was ten years older than Randall and also came from more sophisticated people. Ten years more of experience did much to develop Randall's character; at the end of that time he would have been quite a match for Teddy. Complete revelation had not yet come to Randall. To too many it never comes at all; else the world would be much more tolerant and kindly.

Teddy arose bright and early. Randall could hear him whistling in his room above, whistling gaily. What would he think of him? Would he tell on him? He had forgotten to make him promise not to tell. He was terror-stricken at the possibilities. As he sat gazing into space, imagining all of the horrors of such a situation, he was startled by a knock on the door, followed by Teddy's cheerful call, "Hello! Are you coming to breakfast?"

"In a minute!" he answered as he realized thankfully that

Teddy still desired his companionship. He put the finishing touches to his toilet, then opened the door. "Come in Teddy!"

Teddy stepped into the room and closed the door quickly, then gathered Randall into his arms. Randall did not resist but welcomed this demonstration of Teddy's continued interest in him. "Teddy," he murmured, "Promise me that you will never tell anyone about yesterday!"

"Of course not! That is for me and you alone to know. But you take things too seriously," he whispered as he kissed his ear. "Don't you wish to make me happy? Are you not happy loving me? Let us make the most of life while we can. I love you. You love me. What else matters! Now come along and eat breakfast."

So they went down to the dining room and Randall found enjoyment in the luscious late peaches with cream, the hot waffles and the coffee which Jinny, the cook, set before them. Jinny too could have told a tale of love—of loves, of many loves, in which conscience had not been the least bit troublesome to her. She had survived them and had been and still was happy. After all, we are beginning to question whether repression, with its frequent dire consequences, is the desired thing that the priesthoods of all nations would have us believe it to be.

Teddy wished to rush off at once to church so they might enjoy the music together. With their automobile, it was almost a triumphal tour to the church of St. M's, where the music and pageantry at that time were unrivaled and where the senses were lulled into sweet dreams that answered well for religious sentiments when one was too advanced in thought to accept either Judaism or any of the teachings of its many, and even more childish, Christian offshoots.

The music was exquisite. Randall was ecstatic. All through the service he and Teddy held hands under the overcoat thrown across his knees. They did not accept communion; they never did.

They dined in the Park, a special dinner in celebration of their happiness. The afternoon they spent driving up and down the avenue in the novel car, astonishing the onlookers and earning the curses of the cabbies whose horses had not yet become accustomed to the newfangled machine. At night they returned to their boarding house, tired and happy. Teddy, perceiving that he must not proceed too fast and too suddenly with Randall, or perhaps satisfied enough with his conquest, gave Randall a chaste goodnight kiss as they parted in the hallway before his door.

Except for an occasional sigh at the thought of his peccadillo of the afternoon along the Hudson, Randall was wildly happy during the following week. Teddy gave him every evidence of being in love with him, and he in turn loved Teddy—in fact thoughts of him almost excluded all others. Every evening they met for a short turn on the avenue in the new car and later they would always slip into Café Martin for Teddy's "nightcap."

Already Teddy was planning for another weekend. They would run up to New Haven in his car, see a theatrical tryout and put up with mutual friends there. He proposed this one evening as they were walking home from the old barn where he stored his automobile. Randall snuggled close to his side. He agreed that it would be delightful but added, "You must promise to be good, Teddy. Our love must be kept above all sordidness. We must keep it ideal and pure." Teddy, having never experienced the novelty, acquiesced. Joyfully Randall exclaimed, "Oh, Teddy! I never thought love could be quite so beautiful. I am the happiest person in the world." Then, "We are the happiest people in the world," he amended.

In sex matters Teddy was quite unmoral. His opinion was that what people do with each other is only their own personal concern, a tenet which seems to have become more and more a part of the teaching of the present generation, when one is likely to hear sex, normal or abnormal, openly discussed by adolescents at fashionable luncheons, or tea dances, or between dances at an evening gathering. Teddy lived for the joy of the moment.

Kindly, and certainly a gentleman by instinct, he would not intentionally have hurt anyone. He had been spontaneously attracted to Randall, and Randall was attracted to him likewise. It was all very simple. Thus he reasoned. Saturday came. Randall had never visited New Haven before. He was eager with anticipation; he almost fluttered, his movements, unrestrained, taking on the mannerisms that are so revealing of one of his kind.

It was another perfect fall day. The ride was enjoyable from almost every point of view, despite the fact that roads had not yet been improved to their present smooth stage. They arrived in good time and wandered over the campus. They visited some student friends of Teddy's, and though these admired some of Randall's characteristics, they laughed, one and all, at the unusual timbre of his voice once he was out of earshot. Perhaps Randall, a little forgetful and excited by the novelty of everything, failed to repress what his brother Bill had characterized as "that damned voice."

They had luncheon. They attended a frat dance. They hurried to the theater. The play was the premiere of a musical piece that later became famous. The young men and women of the cast had been chosen not alone for their singing and dancing ability, but also for their pulchritude. Teddy was outspoken in his admiration of the physical attractions of various members of the cast. Randall felt a quickening sense of jealousy, admitted their good points, and then gushed forth in praise of some of the wonderful Yale men they had met earlier in the day. Teddy sensed his own jealousy, and he was annoyed with himself for the ill-suppressed emotion.

After the theater, they rejoined some of Teddy's college friends and together went to a rathskeller, a haunt of the students and the theatrical people. Teddy was busy acting as toastmaster. Randall was neglected and a trifle bored. To make the time pass more pleasantly he engaged in conversation with a young instructor who was seated at his left. This man had made his own way in life, even as Randall was doing. He drew Randall out, his true self, as no one else had ever troubled to do. He was interested to hear of Randall's college extension work, of his desire to give up business and earn a degree in science. Mr. Wright, of the many men who were attracted to Randall, was drawn not by sex, but by the quality of his mind. He gave him valuable advice, outlining easy ways for the accomplishment of his ambitions.

The evening wore along. Randall did not drink. Teddy, though he carried his liquor well, was unduly exhilarated. He was sufficient master of himself to realize this and suggested that they take a long walk before appearing at his friend's apartment. They wandered out into the country. The houses were fewer and fewer. Teddy removed his hat and complained that his head was hot and throbbing. Sympathetically Randall laid a hand to his brow. As he let it drop Teddy caught it to his lips, "How sweet you are, Randy!"

They nestled close, and in but a moment their arms were about each other. Teddy's kisses were wild and furious, and he fairly tore the clothing from his companion's lean and supple body. This time Randall felt a mad desire for compliance, a conscious enjoyment. They brought their newly awakening cocks to bear upon one another and sandwiched them between their bellies. Randall felt Teddy's nipples strike up against his own, and it was as if they were electrical conduits, throwing sparks as they touched then moved away.

Randall's senses became enveloped with Teddy's body. He drew in each of his masculine odors; felt the different skin textures in his bearded face, his soft neck and his firm breast; tasted the salt of the sweat from his brow. He did the same with each part of Teddy's anatomy, and so expert were his probings that Teddy soon came with such intensity that pearlescent sperm lay across their bodies like morning dew. But then Randall moved to please himself upon his lover's body, and straddled Teddy so that he could run his long, thick member forward and back upon the supine and panting man's soft belly. As Randall abandoned himself to this act, Teddy grabbed his lean and tender thighs with terrific force, and, after a few soft swats delivered by Teddy's open palm, Randall shot come to reach the lower edge of his lover's vandyke.

More calmly they walked to Teddy's friend's apartment. As they bade each other good night Randall said almost lightly, "Teddy, we must stop being naughty."

To this Teddy answered, "We only obeyed something stronger than ourselves—instinct." He was quite sincere when he added, "I only love you all the more for it."

During the night Randall heard a stealthy tapping at his door. He understood. Without hesitation he opened it. Teddy was upon him in an instant, his dressing gown fluttering open to reveal the intensity of his passion raised between his legs. Randall was fairly knocked onto his own bed, and their bodies writhed in a tangle of desire. So lost was Randall in the sea of emotions, in excitement at the danger of their love-making even as the room's door stood slightly ajar, that he did not notice as his thighs were parted and his legs were splayed. He did not notice till it was too late what Teddy's true intentions entailed.

It was as if a lighted torch were run up the hole of Randall's backside. Teddy's cock head had pressed upon it, making it tingle and itch, and then it had started its inevitable invasion. Randall was being deflowered. He was being fucked. Shrieking with anguish and delight, Randall tore at Teddy's chest with his nails, and grabbed hold of his waist with his legs, the better to receive his lover's pounding rhythm. Again, his innate proclivity betrayed his innocence. The feeling of being so filled and refilled was more than he could have dreamed possible, and he brought Teddy to a thundering crisis, even as his own overwrought member truly burst of its own accord, sending a stream of come to run over the flat plane of Teddy's belly.

Thus began their more intimate clandestine relationship.

ARCTIC SUMMER
Kevin Killian

One July morning, George woke up alone, in the new apartment Ralph had bought for him. The bed was alive, with lumps in ticklish places. The sensitive skin of his balls itched with slow crawling strokes, and he woke up holding them tenderly, as he once had held baby birds under a tree in the backyard of his mother's Indiana house. Now he lay in the half-light streaming from the open bathroom door, conscious of the gleam of the radiator, its noise and heat. Around his waist something tickled and scratched him, tickled and scratched, until he woke up further, wary and confused, unable to recognize the walls and shadows that loomed around him. "Anyone here?" No answer, just noise from the street outside, and the hum of the new refrigerator, the ticking of the radiator. He clawed at the constriction around his waist, couldn't make out what it was. Was he tied down somehow? No, he was wearing the bottom half of a pair of silk pajamas. He didn't wear PJs as a rule, couldn't remember putting these on. Maybe someone—probably Ralph—had done it for him. They felt greasy to the touch, as if smeared with filth. Truth is, George didn't remember very much about the night before. He and Ralph Isham had paid an impromptu visit to the Gray Goose before the ballet, and had stayed and stayed— "one thing leads to another," missed the ballet, had a good time. Gallons of Manhattans later, they were ejected at 4:30 A.M. George squinted and the light that played over the ceiling wavered in intensity, like a fluorescent tube in an office. Hurt.

The alarm clock said 10:30.

"Fuck off," he said.

He sat up and swung his long legs over the side of the new bed. He stripped the dirty silk pajamas off, left them in a yellow circle on the rug. Then he tried standing up, it didn't work very well. Took a shower, thought about sex, then gave up on that. To clear his head, he decided, while dressing, to try going out for a walk. Maybe get a drink in the one bar he knew was open at this absurdly early hour. Out on the street the light of summer blasted against his ears and eyes like alien invaders with strange messages. But he kept walking, ignoring the sensory input.

He hadn't gone two blocks before he had the feeling someone was following him. Out of the corner of his eye, he spotted an average-looking man darting into shopfronts and subway stations. He looked again and the man was gone—the space where he'd been now an empty space filled with sunlit air. Some kind of optical illusion, perhaps? Like the line drawing they showed you in the army exam: are you looking at two vases or a woman's head? This time, it seemed, he was looking at two vases. But he could have sworn he'd seen this man, sandy or auburn hair, slinking behind him. Then again, maybe it was just paranoia.

"Next I'll be seeing little green men from Mars, I guess."

The sun was high, and the top of his head felt unpleasantly warm. With his knees shaking beneath him, he stood and glared with staring eyes down the sunlit pavement which lay behind him. All was quiet, as in a dream landscape. Silver sunlight and the black patches of adjacent alleys—nothing else could he see. Then from out of the silence, imminent and threatening, there came once more that low, throaty croaking, far louder and closer than before. There could no longer be a doubt. Something was on his trail, and was closing in upon him every minute. He stood like a man paralyzed, still staring at the ground which he had traversed. Then suddenly he saw him. Maybe fifty feet down the street, a man looked at a plate-glass window with minimal interest. A man with red hair, a shock of it standing on top of his head like a rooster's red comb. The man turned idly from the window display and looked inquiringly at George, who averted his head.

Determined to elude pursuit, he ducked into a restaurant he'd never been to. One way or the other, he'd get away from them all. The maître d' was stern and authoritative. "Table for one?" he asked, holding a pink finger up in the air to summon a waiter.

"I'm not really hungry," George thought; but he followed the officious man to a booth and sat down, feeling the tight friction of the leather seat against his thighs like a warning or a caress. In the center of the table, a large bouquet of red roses waved a plumy perfume in the slight breeze. He'd been seated at the last booth from one to the men's room—by no means a choice placement. Bearing a flyspecked menu, the waiter approached. What was the name of this place, anyhow? Its wallpaper was flocked with water spots that streaked through a design of mallard ducks rising up out of a reed-strewn horizon. George read from the menu, "Victoria's Canadian Tea Shop."

"Thanks, that'll be all," he told the waiter, handing back the menu. The waiter looked surprised for a second, then lapsed into a passive reverie, staring at the faded wallpaper. "I'll just have a bowl of soup—what's your special today?"

"No soup today," replied the waiter without emotion. "Too late, mister."

George took back the menu. "Ain't that the story of my life."

Then the front door opened and in walked a man—a man with bright red hair the color of fire. With a start George opened the menu and covered his face with it. Prices and entrees swam before his eyes.

"Mister, what you like?"

"I'll have the Salisbury steak," he said quickly. "Maybe a couple of vegetables. I don't know—go away and let me think about the vegetables."

But the waiter wouldn't leave. he stood there steadfastly with his palm out, like a bellboy expecting a tip in a Joan Crawford movie.

"People steal our menus," the waiter observed with a huge shrug. "I don't know why."

With a guilty start George passed the menu to the waiter, who nodded imperturbably and added, "Irving Berlin used to eat here and write his songs on our menus. The owner's got a couple of them framed in there"—pointing to the men's room, which seemed to be the heart of the restaurant. "Some men like a tearoom—it brings something out in them. Maybe you agree, mister?"

George jumped up. "I'll take a gander," he said brightly, slipping into the alcove. "Irving Berlin…'White Christmas,' right?"

"Right, mister."

George could see the red-haired man approaching the maître d' with a question in his eyes. He saw the man take a photograph out of a card case and display it. Lingering no longer, he pushed open the heavy door to the men's room and hurried in. He tried to lock the door from within, but the damn catch was broken, and dangled loosely from the clasp. What kind of fix was he in? He couldn't think. His heart was racing a little, but nothing to keel over and die from. It was all very odd—that's all.

The restroom was fairly large, about thirty feet long and ten feet wide. An elderly gent stood whistling at a sink, patting his face with some kind of green unguent: liquid hand soap. He stopped whistling when George barreled in.

"Look like you just saw a ghost," said the old man.

"The prices on the menu scared me," George said.

"Wait till you hit my age, sonny boy," said the geezer to George. "Nothing scares a man of eighty but a flu bug or a warm pussy." The old man chuckled and turned the tap with a great flourish. Cascades of faintly red water steamed out of the tap and soaked the old man's slimy green hands. George's stomach turned over, and his intestines seemed to be full of fluid—sympathy pangs, pangs of nausea. He looked away past the grinning old man to a place of safety.

Four urinals lined the wall to their right, one a little shorter to accommodate child patrons. The smell was excruciating. On the left a row of stalls stretched to the far wall, in which was set a window—one window, too small to climb through, covered with a fine metal mesh. Street noise. But no safety, no escape. Irving Berlin's lyrics to "Heat Wave" hung, framed, next to this window. Very nice. Very nice *decorative bullshit*. In a minute the man who pursued him would be upon him. And George couldn't let that happen: it wouldn't be fair, he thought obscurely. One of the doors of the toilets was ajar, and George slipped inside it.

"Yessirree," called the old man. "When you hit eighty, you're not scared of the Devil himself."

"I bet," George called, over the partitions. Then, breathless, he examined his surroundings, which were what he expected, maybe a little dingier. One door, two marble walls that stopped a foot from the floor, a toilet built into the far wall with a flush handle. The walls were covered from top to bottom with messages from other men. Just the kind of reading George preferred in lighter moments, but he hadn't the energy to peruse them right now.

Alone in the stall, George sat down on the cracked black wooden seat and put his head in his hands. He thought for a few minutes about the course of his life. The small town where George and his sister has been raised was a pleasant one, but from the time he turned ten, George had felt an insistent need to escape. His mother did laundry for the well-to-do, and during the Depression managed to make a decent—if stultifying— home for her children. He needed pictures, though, pictures more vivid than the graffiti that lined the gray marble from top to bottom. Lifting a hip, George reached back and took out his wallet from the back pocket of his slacks. He'd had this wallet since the service, and it looked it. "I'll buy you a new one," Ralph had said.

"You buy too much," George had said, holding the wallet up in one hand and flapping it at him as though it meant all his independence.

The money he opened to now had come to him from Ralph Isham. All in all, there must have been sixty or seventy dollars in the wallet. "I don't want you arrested as a vagrant," Ralph said.

Fuck him, George thought, in the toilet stall. From an inner compartment of the scuffed brown wallet, he pulled out a fistful of mementos and pictures. This was his past: somehow it felt correct to bring it out now, here, amid the scents of Lysol and men's piss. This handful of memories and expression. A subway token clinked on the damp tile floor—George let it lie, for Ralph had bought that for him, too.

"Yessir," called out the old man, "when you get to be my age, you wake up to some new terrible thing every day."

George shuffled the stack of cards and papers from hand to hand, while listening with one ear to the sound of the tap water and the old man whistling Irving Berlin's "White Christmas."

One photo showed the smiling face of his dead mother, pale and fragrant with laundry soap. He rubbed a finger over her languid eyes, then tried to forget her. "So long, sonny boy," called the old man, finally finished cleaning his old palsied hands. George heard the restroom door swish open and shut. Then, in the sudden gray silence, he pulled out a card—"any card," as the jokers in the bars tell you to—and turned it over from back to front. In his palm lay a small photo, two inches by three: a picture of Tommy

Calhoun's face. George took a deep swallow. Waves of feeling washed over him in a deep, regressive movement.

"I don't want to play none of your games," Tommy had written him. "I'm not the guy for them—find another." Tommy's face, his shrewd expression, clear unfrightened brown eyes, a "thoughtful" pose. George stood up quickly and undid his pants, pulled out his cock, sat back down again, playing with it without thinking much. He'd had the same sensation earlier this morning, in the shower, as though he couldn't concentrate on sex, couldn't will it to stay in his brain long enough for it to make an impression in his balls. His crotch smelled faintly of cigarette smoke, food, and sex. Tommy watched him through the fog of rejected pleasure that had come between them to spoil everything that mattered to George. Watched him, now, with the same sullen expression that had thrilled George to begin with, so that he'd had to seek him out and ask him to pose for him.

Tommy Calhoun who, when first seen, sat slumped on a bench at the Y in a pair of faded dungarees, the cuffs rolled up, and a sleeveless white polo shirt. Some stupid prompt had made George approach him, standing before him to breathe in his smell. *Want some pictures to give your girl?* In the boy's serious face, George saw recognition, all the exquisite pain of consciousness stirring. So he took him to his studio uptown and posed him against a snowy backdrop, telling him about his face's potential. "You take good pictures?" Tommy had asked him.

"Who cares? You do," George replied. "Now, how about you get more comfortable. What are you wearing under those jeans?"

"Not much." Tommy admitted, "but I'm keeping them on, if it's all the same to you." Three weeks later, as agreed, Tommy returned to pick up the pictures of his face and some more spending money. "I like this arrangement," he said.

"You take good pictures," George said.

But there wasn't any fag stuff. George remembered asking him, remembered Tommy's impassive refusal. His head, shaking no, his shrewd foxy face pursing its lips, no, no, George. A few drinks later, his pants were down to his knees, then George pulled them off and threw them over the folding screen he kept in the studio for medical layouts. Stark naked Tommy stood, weaving, hands folded behind his back as directed, his great long cock swinging no. "No fag stuff, you said."

"I'll make you feel so good," George had said, moving in, touching the tip of Tommy's cock with one inquiring finger.

Tommy laughed. "Forget it, okay?" And the picture George held in his hand now, of Tommy's face, was like a living reminder of everything he'd missed out on in his life.

George was standing with all his weight on one foot, clothes in disarray, his cock draped across his palm neither soft nor stiff, with its usual dead weight and perplexity, when he saw the hole in the wall. When he noticed it wink at him.

His eyes widened forcibly, as though he'd been given a jolt of electricity or shock treatments. Again he saw the wall blink, or appear to blink, its solid gray surface part and join again. There *was* a hole in the wall, and someone was standing in its light, in the next stall.

The wall that separated the two stalls was a thick slab of Carrara marble, and in its center a hole had been drilled in the ancient, sexual past; through this hole now a finger poked, nail upward, and then twisted to measure the dimensions of the space it was in. George gazed steadily at it, thinking, "Tommy Calhoun." He wondered if, when you think about someone, you think of them by name or as they actually exist.

The finger continued to probe, leaving fingerprints all over that portion of the inner wall it touched—greasy fingerprints, as if left from liquid hand soap or semen. In his fantasy that finger wanted to stretch to an unimaginable length to touch the very tip of his penis, which he held firm in his own right hand.

The finger withdrew. Next, George saw an eye staring at him, a placid green eye that blinked once or twice but otherwise made no signal. George smiled politely at the eye.

The eye closed, then withdrew. In a moment George heard the sharp sound of a zipper descending, then the soft fold of cloth. He began to tremble in his loneliness and his longing, waiting for what he knew must come. Next an enormous cock appeared through the hole, ringed in a nest of soft crisp orange pubic hair, like a birthday corsage for a little girl, a toy. Finger, eye, cock: finally George put together the various parts of the body that had been shown him, figured they were all one male. This sum of addition made George swoon. If this wasn't the man who'd followed him into the restaurant, George would eat his hat. In sexual life, he'd always had a weakness for redheads. Why not go for it? *Here I thought I was being followed. Hell! I was being cruised.*

A strip of ripped toilet paper, ringed with gray moisture, floated to the wet floor. George read the words before they could dissolve. TOUCH IT. Then they dissolved.

He raised his left hand shakily to the bobbing cock, felt its vague heat with two fingers. In response, it lifted its weight to meet his questioning touch. The ringing in his ears vanished, his headache with it, and now he heard and heard again his own voice remonstrating with Tommy—"Put your hands at your side. Look at the lens. Smile."

The cock shot forward; George put his mouth to its head and kissed it. Inside his mouth, the cock had little volume of its own, but a great suggestion of propulsion and questioning. George's nose hit the marble wall, which deflected it. "I'll make it easy for you," said the man, a low throaty baritone. *Tommy's wide, full, "go-to-Hell" mouth.* Bent in two, George sat back onto the toilet seat sideways as, from under the marble partition, two bare knees came forward, followed by the whole crotch to come squatting directly into his face. An athletic guy, obviously, confident, bouncing on his heels with his pants and underwear drawn down to his ankles. I could pick his pocket in twenty seconds, George thought obliquely, as he leaned down to the floor to suck Red's dick. Down so low his face felt damp and clammy, and the muscles in the left side of his face started to harden and contract, as he continued to suck. "Red" spoke the familiar words of praise and contempt.

"That's good, Georgie," he said. *How'd he know my name?* "That's good as a woman any old day, I guess."

An athletic guy—a mysteriously knowing guy—and a guy who really knew not only what he wanted but how to get it out of George. How'd he know my name? All in all, George had to hand it to him, but now wasn't the time or place.

He reached up through the legs and his hands passed through the light growth of hair on the thighs, till he felt the weight of the ass in his hands, then the delicate filigree of the balls. Red was so excited, he was practically sitting on the floor. "Fuck me," the voice said. "Is your dick hard?"

"A little," George replied, and the sound of his own voice frightened him. Again the hardness in his mouth throbbed, as though he were hitting a nerve. He let it slip out of his mouth, which instantly felt hollow.

"Slide under!" Red commanded, and George, oblivious to the piss on the floor, slid his crotch into the crack of the freckled butt, which glistened from exertion and summer heat. A pale hand, coated in some shiny invisible glop, guided A to B. From there on in, nature took its course.

After a while, Red rose, adjusted his clothing, and left. George lay back against the stubby toilet and panted. The contents of his wallet were spread on the wet tile exactly as they had fallen. Only one item was missing.

The picture was gone—the photo of Tommy Calhoun's face.

THE REAL THING
William Carney

Very well, we will continue, since you wish it so.

And there is at least one aspect of this regrettable business which shows you in a good light, and that is the fact that you have not lost your *public* self-control. This augurs well, since it shows that you have not only placed limits on your self-indulgence, but that you also have the strength to hold yourself within bounds. We can build upon this excellent foundation. And I do realize how upset you were. Yet remember that I am always ready to be your buffer and to receive the brunt of such displays so long as they go no further than myself. No matter the cause, nor whom it concerns, nor how violently you may feel upon any matter, write to me about it. If I am to be your guide, then we must keep in close touch. As it stands now, no one knows of your weakness—your inner weakness—save myself. It remains, so to speak, *en famille*.

And one more thing: I did not require such abject apologies as you offered in your last letter. Such effusions, coming from you, do not please me. Not now, at any rate. We do not know yet exactly where we stand, perhaps; but we do know what we are about.

So, let us now pick up where we left off before the holidays with the classification and description of this peculiar and superb fauna so that we may better understand the obligations of those on top and the duties of those on the bottom in this work.

Now that you are familiar with the various ranks and somewhat conversant with the work that is done by us in this Way, you will doubtless have noticed that not all those involved in it are engaged in the same *type* of activity. Some are more aggressive and more active than others; a few seem only to watch or to talk; others appear stricken motionless and speechless, as if they had seen a great light and been immobilized by fear and wonder on beholding it. There is order in all this. Yes, for where to your unpracticed eye the hugest confusion seems to reign, transcendent reason is at work patterning a system which is ideal, methodical, and interlocking.

You demur, and I understand what bothers you here. For it is evident in this as in other, peripheral, domains that most grab what they can when and where they find it with a mindless disregard for principles and discipline. Yet again I must remind you (and I cannot overemphasize this rule): it must be only to the excelling few that you look for guidance and examples of capability. Elsewhere all is confusion and (what follows upon it) degeneration. Just because most of those whom you will come in contact with slide insensibly into bad habits and lack the integrity and the will to sustain themselves on any level of excellence is no reason that you should follow their example or imagine that integrity and discipline are of little matter. Few become saints, to be sure; yet it is the saints who have maintained the church in the face of darkness. And so it is with us. And nothing less than the communion of the dedicated is what you must aspire to. With this in view, heed what I and others like me tell you and look to apply it, for with these guidelines to steady you you will be less prone to error when a choice presents itself and more able to recover (as you have so recently and so beautifully done) should you stumble off the straight path.

Types. These constitute the basic classification in this work. There are three of them and they are to be found fully developed only among Exemplars and the Perfect, i.e., The Real Thing. They may appear only as inclinations in the Purists. Quite simply, the type an Exemplar or one of the Perfect may be determines beforehand what you will find and what you will do with it, or, conversely, what finds you and what will be done with you. There are, then:

Masters and Slaves. These are by far the greatest in numbers, though by no means the most evident.

Cruel Masters and their Victims. These are much in demand, relatively abundant, but the hardest to find in any state of excellence.

Guides and Pilgrims, sometimes known as Shepherds and Sheep, Sponsors and Postulants, Executioners and Martyrs…; the designations go on, seemingly numberless. These are, by their very nature, the rarest and the most difficult to spot, to arrange, or to get to know. Because they move in darkness they are also sometimes referred to as the "Shining Ones."

I will cover each of these types separately as I have time in future letters, but for now I will close with the admonition that you become absorbed once more in this work. Lose yourself in it. Excel in it. Following the precepts I have given you, you will choose the right partner, adopt the proper course of action, and thus eventually find that joy which comes to one when this Way is followed correctly and this work is well done.

I cannot tell you how pleased I am that you have come to your senses and have decided to go on with it. I congratulate you!

February 8, _____

Masters and Slaves. What a lot of nonsense has been written under this rubric!—all the flap one hears about freedom and equality: the verbal sewage of publisher and politician concerning human oppression. All this goes against the grain, and if our work did no more than to repair in however small a way the harm being done in the world by these misguided fools who refuse to understand human nature for what it is, then its justification would be assured. And in nothing more than in this does our love of order, restraint, and discipline mark us as humanists.

For there is found in all men a need to serve and to obey, to suffer abjectly beneath the yoke of the more fortunate, and to complain about it incessantly. There is, moreover, as a corollary to this, a countertendency to dominate and to exploit the fellow creature whenever the occasion permits and its weakness warrants it. The joys of commanding and serving, threatening and cringing, humiliating and enduring it, are among the most superb and constructive to be found in the human psyche.

This category represents a privileged situation where there are rights and duties to be found. The Master has an absolute right to the body of his Slave to do with it as he pleases, and the Slave's sole duty is to submit to his Master's will. There are all kinds of Masters and as many varieties of Slave to fit their mold. Some of the former are overbearing, others love to tease; some strike suddenly and in anger, others do so at leisure, coolly; there are some who enter into an easy camaraderie with their vassal, and a few even who never utter a word to them, but communicate by signs and slaps and scraps of paper; some are insulting, some are petty, and not a few are truly noble in their relationship. Slaves can be fawning, proud, or may smolder with resentment (a type very much in demand); some are savages in chains or geniuses denied their calling; they are handsome, ugly, well or badly formed, merry, long-suffering, jittery, calm, soft, tough, lazy, industrious, dangerous, milksops, or crybabies. There is a place for everyone here. The ethos is submission, the gesture is the *osculum infame*, and querulousness constitutes the mood.

Now, what is a Slave but someone who waits upon others. They are shackled at night and kept busy during the day. Ideally they sleep on the floor beside their Master's bed or outside his door, or at any rate within call, if it be only by telephone. Paltry pleasures are allowed them as a means of refreshing their abilities to serve rather than as a reward for anything they may have done. For what they are able to accomplish is of little importance compared with what they fail to do. They must be watched at all times and never allowed a moment to themselves lest they rebel, or sneak off, or go to sleep from boredom, or allow themselves to be lured away by an interloping Master. Insult rather than injury is what is needed, for the idea here is not so much one of punishment as of degradation—or rather, the punishment takes the form of degradation. Tasks (often disagreeable or disgusting ones) are required of them for the most part. To be sure, a good beating now and then is never amiss, but with this type the sudden trouncing is more appropriate. This accounts for the black eyes, the bruised jaws, and broken teeth you occasionally notice among the crowd.

Slaves are nourished with contempt and bloom under a steady rain of vituperation. To be put down is their great and sorrowful joy, and akin to it is their need to be betrayed by someone they trust. By nature a garrulous lot, they are forbidden to speak unless spoken to, and while doing so it is not permitted that they look their interlocutor in the eye. When accompanying their Master in public they walk on his left, when, indeed, they are not following at a respectful distance in his wake. They stand just behind him in company ready to do his bidding, and they laugh whenever he does. Otherwise they attend in silence, maintaining a deferential downward gaze, unless given permission to talk or perhaps to wander. Their body not only does not belong to them but it may be loaned or offered as a gift by the Master to whomever it pleases him to favor in this manner. A Slave may not look up in the presence of his own or any other Master. A breach of this rule constitutes insolence and calls for immediate correction, usually in the form of a backhand to the cheek. The penalty is automatic and there are no mitigating circumstances. I once saw a devoted Slave save his drunken Master's life one evening after the bars had closed by grabbing him in time as he was about to step off the curbing into the face of oncoming traffic. After thanking him for his timely intervention, the beautiful bully knocked his benefactor into the gutter and kicked him roundly for having spoken out of turn and for daring to look up in public.

What, then, must a Slave expect of a Master? Besides finding in him an inexhaustible reservoir of inventive vindictiveness and an unpredictable source of rage and humiliation, the Slave also requires him to be a comforting shield, a protective taskmaster, and a guardian against the twin dangers of boredom and abandonment. He will expect and receive, after he has absorbed sufficient abuse, just that amount of tenderness and forgiveness necessary to reassure him of his Master's fundamental approval, which will no doubt encourage him to fuck up once more in order to provoke new reprisals. And so it goes, like the beautifully lubricated mechanism that it is. As long as the Slave can find a good Master, his life will have meaning and nothing else (worse) will get him. Good Slaves, it should be noted, are not hard to find. The advertising columns of special publications devoted to this quest are full of them, and even the larger dailies give them coded listings.

Good Masters, however, are rare. Few can stand the strain

of constant vigilance which such a calling demands. If you do not care for children or animals or restive adolescents, then this is not the type for you. For a good Master must look after his Slave; he must see that he is well-fed, properly attired, exercised, and trained. He must teach him the private signals and expressions that are so much a part of this particular work—the secret language of command and acquiescence to be used in public—until he learns to heel and fetch and cower like a dog.

Bad Masters lose their Slaves. A few have even been killed by them. But more on this at another time.

Most Masters and Slaves are born to their roles; their problem is one of finding their partners in the crowd and then holding on to them. This is an entertaining spectacle, and one of the delightful things about this type of work is that it is the only one which can be carried on more or less openly and thus be enjoyed by all, the instructed as well as the ignorant, for no one is so dense as not to notice who it is that calls the tune and which one dances to it.

So, if you think you are a Master, I suggest you get to know a few first and learn from them how to be stern yet just, inflexible yet occasionally forgiving, and how to handle opposition in a recalcitrant lackey. If a Slave is your calling, then make yourself worthy of some good Master and enhance your value by the correctness of your conduct and your willingness to obey, no matter what he may command. And since you are in all other respects so fine a specimen, it is well to bear in mind that you may sometimes be sold.

February 13, _____

Next: Cruel Masters and their Victims.

The former put the question to the latter and are therefore the teachers *par excellence* in this work. So dramatic are their sessions, so richly are their arrangements overlaid with tradition and ceremony, and so popular are they among all ranks and routes, that they have come, in untutored circles, to usurp the whole meaning of this Way to themselves. And even among those who know, whenever someone is mentioned as an S or an M without further amplification, he is understood to belong to this particular type.

Here is an art of gesture, trickery, and bedazzlement played against a background of formal commentary and illuminated with flashes of mannered violence: controlled implacability on the one hand, and passive obstinacy on the other. The captor seeks to make his victim plead, and the bound prey attempts to seduce his questioner at last by a spectacle of helplessness. Its ethos is the hunt, while the mood is one of surpassing vulnerability; the gesture is penetration.

This is tricky work and demands great subtlety if it is to succeed. For this reason it is the preferred field of the Exemplar, and hasty candidates for this rank fall quickly by the wayside when it comes to being tested. To survive and flourish, a Cruel Master must possess imagination, patience, and strength, while his Victim must be responsive, endurant, and tough. Stamina may serve both in place of strength or toughness. Proof of this is to be found in the remarkable way women bear up under the strain of this kind of action. I once knew a lesbian who—but our concern here is not with them.

Now, as I pointed out, the great danger for Masters and Slaves is boredom. The danger here is something far more serious. Panic. This type of work may be likened to a voyage into charted but peril-strewn waters, where the threat of foundering or mutiny is always present. Because of this it demands a longer apprenticeship for top men. Skill with instruments, with knots and locks and many kinds of mechanical devices is required, as is a more-or-less-detailed knowledge of anatomy, particularly of nerves and the soft parts of the body. It is not surprising that many doctors are found in this type of work.

Self-knowledge is demanded to a superlative degree if you

are to be the top man here and not succumb to the pitifully appealing wiles of your adversary. For never imagine for a moment that simply because you have your victim bound and helpless before you that you are in no danger from him. You will be in great danger, particularly if you let him look at you. Note also that you will seldom encounter an absolute neophyte in this, yet the less your victim knows the greater will be the onus upon you to perform well, since in this case you risk botching the work either through leniency or by a premature severity. Besides knowing yourself, you must be able to gauge your partner, too.

As you have by now gathered from these remarks, there is a great deal of ritual, paraphernalia, and protocol connected with this type of work. In addition, all the elements of classic venery are found here: the lure or chase, the trap or ambush, the trussing of the quarry when he's caught, the flaying, the gutting... *mentula in culo*. In fact, so appealing is its presentation it risks becoming popular. Only conservative methodology and a strict regard for technique have saved it from being vulgarized ere now. And this safeguarding is due in most part to the fact that its secrets and its ceremonies are in the keeping of uncorrupted Virtuosi.

I would have you read over what I have just covered and study it in the light of what took place between you and J. last December. Knowing what he is and the role you (unwillingly?) played, would you still return to him on these terms?—that is to say, the only terms on which he will have you?

What have you been doing lately? There was a singular lack of news about yourself in your last two letters. Why don't you surprise me sometime soon? I am sure you are capable of it.

February 19, _____

The Others?

Yes, they are sometimes called this. They are called all sorts of things. This because they remain so shadowy, so hard to be precise about, save in one thing. And while you probably will not be concerning yourself much with them, I agree that you ought to know something about them, if for no other reason than to be on your guard. I can only, however, give you a few general observations on them as a type, since each of them is more or less unique.

The work they engage in is the ultimate, since beyond it one cannot go, and the practice of it is confined to the Perfect, except when accidents occur in one of the other two types of work just described. This happens whenever somebody panics or gets careless.

Guides and Pilgrims slip like ghosts from role to role, easily and convincingly adopting the manners and the work of other types. This they do as a recruiting measure, and not only in this work, but in all other domains are they to be found.

It is said that many, if not a majority, of this type do not realize their calling until they have been working this Way for many years, while others (very few, but outstanding) are suddenly enlightened right from the first. Be this as it may, the fact remains that, due to the nature of their work, they are generally known too late. For this reason many during their whole career are limited to a single accomplished act. There is, therefore, a strong element of self-immolation here, or, as some call it, heroism— in the ancient sense of the word. They are like sacred kings whose bloody triumphs lead inevitably to their own fall. A few (but only a very few) have been able to combine their profession with their calling. Even here, however, they tend not to be ostentatious, so that the enigma remains. The jailer, doctors of one sort and another, the man weaponed by the state, the hunter… Who is and who is not? Who might be, given the occasion?—and there are always occasions.

A further impediment to spotting them is the fact that they blend, as I have indicated, into other types and categories in order to contemplate the work before them, to choose, and (who knows?) simply to keep their hand in. Over a period of weeks, months, years even, they may plan and work with one candidate in view and one object in mind for that candidate. If, for instance, one of the Others should consent to the mechanics of slavery, it would only be in order to prepare his Master for the role of questioner. Many must be led to see their calling. Or again, if one of them should practice torment on a Victim, it would mean that he is enticing his treated exponent of restraint and violence toward martyrdom, that mystery which is the only joy and so often the single glory of the Perfect.

These Others (also called Helpers, because of the work they do) are latter-day anchorites, periodically emerging from the waste places of the mind to make forays into the throng. Such advents bring in their wake conversion and a strengthening for all those who go this Way. They also loosen up the flow of fear— the cold lubricant of this work. They are legendary, appearing with a somber glitter from the mists of disbelief, lessons to the believer and to the scorner alike. They are the only type for whom consent is not required, because they are thought to be deaf to what is said. They know in advance and are the soul of patience; the mood of their work is the unexpected, the gesture is the flaming hand.

I cannot advise you as to any relations you may have with them. Indeed, no one can advise you—not even one of them. If this is to be your type, you will know it and you will be your own guide in finding the Other whom you need.

Now briefly to other matters. The reason I have not answered your questions concerning your brother is that I do not think it is time yet for that. Besides, I am not sure he would have wanted me to discuss such matters with you. If certain people have told you certain things about him, they may very well know what they are talking about. On the other hand, they may not. I will tell you that I was in close touch with him from the time he was discharged from the service and came here to go to school until he flunked out and returned…to his mother. More than this I will not say at present.

Which brings me to my first query. Why have you started seeing H. again?

Secondly, I should like to know why you have not applied some of the teaching I have thus far given you to these adventures you have been having? What good is learning if it is not put to use? And such drivel! You work on someone, they give you the slip, and then, as if to justify your ineptitude you tell me "…anyway, I don't think he knew what he was looking for." It was your business to know, even if he did not, what he was looking for. After all, you were the top man here, if I read you right. Instruct him!

Let me know about this business with H.

THE MOTION OF LIGHT IN WATER
Samuel R. Delany

39. An autumn night on Central Park West:

I walked uptown on the small hexagonal pavings. The trees flickered bare branches before the street lights. There wasn't anybody sitting on the benches beside the park's wall—it was too cold. Somewhere ahead, a man was coming forward, unsteadily. He had no overcoat. As he got nearer, he looked like a hefty Hispanic business man in his late thirties, black hair, blue suit, white shirt unbuttoned and tie loose. One hand was in his open fly. When he saw me, he came over. I could smell drink. He stopped in front of me and shook his head, steam coming from his nose and mouth: "Please, please, man...you know where I can get a blow job?"

I was surprised. I was also a little frightened. But his desperation was a turn-on.

I looked around. There wasn't anyone else in sight. "Come on," I said.

He said: "Huh...?"

"Come on."

He followed me while I walked toward the nearest park entrance. Just behind the wall, I squatted down. He came up to me, and, it seemed, only now realized what was going on. Afterwards, when I stood up, he kept both his hands on my head. "Oh, man. Thank you," he said, blinking at me. "Thank you, that was great...I didn't know what I was gonna do, if I didn't find someone to suck me off. I just didn't think I was gonna make it." Then he put his arms around me and hugged me tightly.

I patted his back. "It was nice. I like it, too."

He stepped back, got his clothes together, then we went out, him to continue downtown, me to walk up. But he was the only person I met that night.

39.1. One early November evening, I told Marilyn I'd probably be out for the night and left our Sixth Street apartment to wander over to the docks. One of the people I had to do with that evening was a thin, hard, little white guy, older and shorter than I, in engineer's boots, jeans, a garrison belt, denim jacket and cap—at a time when not everyone wore baseball caps. He had a pockmarked, good-looking face. Slight as he was, he still had very big hands, and, though not a nail-biter, he must have recently been doing some manual work so that his hands were quite rough. The sex? After some necking, I blew him. Then he blew me. What was notable was that, though I'd had many hundreds of sexual encounters by then—a hundred of them probably in the previous six months— this was the first time I'd ever cum in somebody's mouth.

But he had been patient enough to do the job sensitively and with lots of extra body contact; and, for his effort, he had gotten the prize. My twenty-one-year-old response was to fall, indeed to splatter head-first, silently and hopelessly in love. We talked a little afterward. I think he suggested we go for a beer. We found a bar a couple of blocks up from the docks, roomy, dark, frequented mostly by truckers. It wasn't a (particularly) gay bar— though seven or eight years later it changed hands and became one. Back then, beer came in twenty-five cent draft glasses. After your first three, the bartender would "tap" you one—come up to you, rap his knuckles on the wooden counter, and give you your next glass free. Thereafter, every five or so, he'd tap you again.

I'd never encountered the custom in the Village bars, with their tourist trade and their mugs rather than draft glasses. But in the Irish working men's bars, in the truckers' bars, and in most neighborhood locals it was commonplace—though Phil had to explain to me what was going on. He told me he was twenty-eight. (A couple of years later, he confessed that he'd lied. He'd actually been thirty-one—not that I could have cared less.) He had an easy southern drawl—was, like my father, from North Carolina. He was very sharp and had numerous quirky opinions about numerous unusual things. That evening, as we sat on the worn leather stools, I learned Phil had lots of information about where to find sexual action, for which I was always hungry. He told me about various movie theaters and about the Soldier's and Sailor's Monument up on the West Side. He said he lived fairly near it.

Finally, at his suggestion, we exchanged numbers.

There at the bar, I wrote his down in my notebook, which I carried pretty much wherever I went. But by the time we parted and I was walking home back along Fourth Street, I'd memorized it.

A couple of days later, I phoned him. Yeah, I should come up. I did. And in his tiny bedroom off the hall of his Upper West Side apartment, we had more sex. It was extraordinary. In the conversation around it, I learned more about him. He was a bastard, had been orphaned at about five, and had been in an orphanage in the South. But from about eight on, he'd lived largely with a foster family with whom he was still close. He had a straight roommate named Hal—who, while Phil and I were sitting naked in the living room, walked in in his suit, tie, and winter raincoat, said "Hi," like someone who often found two naked men drinking beer in his apartment on a November afternoon, and retired into his bedroom.

Phil said, "See how I've got him trained?"

Phil was deeply into sado-masochism and was a little worried that he drank too much.

A while ago, he explained, sitting back down in the brown overstuffed chair and using a can opener with a green wooden handle to pry off the top of another beer bottle, between thighs that looked so very smooth, with hands that looked so very rough, he'd brought home some guy for an S&M session he'd picked up in the park. They'd both been drunk. As part of the scene, the man had bound and gagged Phil, naked, in the bathroom, to the toilet pipes. Then—not part of the scene at all—he'd decided to rob Phil.

Hal happened to be home, reading in his room. Phil managed to make enough noise so that Hal figured maybe something was wrong.

Though Hal was a junior stockbroker down in the Wall Street area, he was a stolid bear of a guy—with impressive shoulders and a curly blond beard (not that common, back then, among stockbrokers). He'd wandered out into the hall and pushed open the bathroom door. I don't know how familiar Hal was with Phil's S&M shenanigans, but from Phil's squirming, Hal realized something was amiss. "Don't you think it's time for you to leave?" Hal said to the man.

Who put down the pilfered objects and did.

Then Hal unbound Phil.

Phil was a bit worried about sex getting him into this kind of trouble.

My own experience of S&M had been minimal. I'd had one two-week S&M "affair" (if you could call it that) with an NYU English instructor (also met at the docks), which had left me pretty confused and unclear about why various things went on—though my view at the time was that I was hugely sophisticated about all such matters. After all, I'd at least *done* it—in a world where most people could hardly imagine it.

I said something like, "Oh, yeah. I've tried that. But it's nothing I'm very interested in." I wouldn't be surprised if that's what brought Phil's and my sex to an end for which I'm still sorry today. The truth was, I'd have happily beat Phil within an inch of his life and called him every kind of humiliating name conceivable as often as he wanted if we could have gone on sleeping together—but I was young and (he knew by now) married, which probably made me a less likely prospect.

Anyway, we never slept together after that.

Before I left, Phil showed me a journal he kept of his sexual encounters.

Its thousands of pages were stored in thick black or green spring binders on the shelf above his bed. From each day's activity, he made handwritten notes. Then, a couple of times each week, or possibly each month, he typed them up in fuller versions which would go into the binders. He let me browse through the earlier volumes.

Though some of the entries were only notes, many were beautifully written, dense with detail and observation that far outweighed mere prurience. This was before the days of *Straight to Hell* and *First Hand*; before Stonewall and Gay Liberation. Neither D. H. Lawrence, the Marquis de Sade, nor Henry Miller was then published in the United States. (But I'd read the Olympia Press edition of *The 120 Days of Sodom* and *Black Spring* Barbara had brought me back from Europe years before.) I was reading, I knew, an astonishing document on gay sexual patterns in New York.

That first afternoon, Phil wouldn't let me see the most recent volume in which he'd described our own dockside encounter.

I went home.

After a while, when I didn't hear from him again, I called

once more. Rather lamely, I suggested he might like to go to the Metropolitan Museum with me. Yeah, he said, that sounded good. We're talking here about a twenty-one-year-old kid who was crazy-sick with lust after this guy—and absolutely unsure of how to express it.

We met on the wide gray steps of the Met that Friday, and went in to wander the museum for an hour.

It was a nice afternoon.

I don't know whether Phil picked up on my quivering, tongue-tied ephebic rut—it was probably hard to miss. As we were leaving, though, he said, well, he had to go see some friends now—and abandoned me, in front of the museum, in the darkening afternoon. I went home and was probably rather uncommunicative with Marilyn that evening. I didn't see Phil again for another three or four months.

But I had memorized his phone number.

At home I turned back to my writing.

39.2. Near midnight on November 21, 1963, I finally took the one thousand fifty-sixth page of *Voyage, Orestes!* from the typewriter. In the concluding six-page epilogue, the young black hero (working as a cashier in a barbecued chicken store—where, for three weeks at the beginning of the autumn, my musician friend Dave had gotten me a job) and the white, folksong-playing heroine wandered down the empty November beach at Coney Island, long for something that would change the world; and the book was complete.

I'd promised to deliver the entire manuscript as soon as it was done to Bobs (at Bobbs-Merril). The next day, I called her to see if I could bring it up. Sure. Why didn't I aim for two or thereabout. She'd be back from lunch. At a little after one, I set off, carrying the entire thousand-plus pages under my arm, against my notebook, over to the Astor Place subway station in front of the Cooper Union. I went through the turnstile and stood, waiting for the subway, beside the news kiosk, its sides and counter slick and heavy with new red paint, rows of girlie and muscle magazines racked along its back, the science fiction and astrology digests stuck up behind rusted wire holders. I heard the black radio at the counter's corner say (my attention came around with the words): "...is dead, it's now been confirmed. Governor Connolly is in serious condition at the Dallas General...." Then the train came.

I rode uptown, wondering at the fragmentary newscast. Who was it that could possibly be dead? And Governor Connolly? I tried to remember which state he was from. But Dallas, certainly, was in Texas....

There was no receptionist at the desk of the Bobbs-Merrill offices, and I had been in the offices proper enough times by then to feel it was okay just to go back to Lorn's desk and give him my manuscript to pass on to Bobs. When I walked through the archway, I saw people were walking all around the office, talking excitedly, and looking like anything but the staff of an efficient New York publisher. One middle-twentyish woman in a gray-and-white knitted suit turned to me and simply said:

"...want to know is President Kennedy still alive?" as though she were finishing a question that she'd begun to someone else. "That's, of course, what everybody wants to know!"

Though I hadn't heard the name on the newscast, all the pieces suddenly came together. "He's dead," I said. "It's been confirmed. I heard it on the radio at a newsstand when I was in the subway, coming up here."

The young woman turned around. "He's dead!" she called out. "President Kennedy is dead!"

The news bubbled through the chaos. And seconds later Lorn stepped up and, a moment later, Bobs. They said hello, took the manuscript—they would get back to me as soon as they could. But I must understand, of course, that today....

39.3. The year was almost up. And the first of the year meant another birthday—my twenty-second—was only three months off. With very little pause I took out the manuscript of *City of a Thousand Suns* and began to work on it once more. The new chapters came as easily as the opening one—and, I fancy, with as much energy. The handwritten draft was finished on the last day of February; at once I began giving it its two obligatory passes through the typewriter. The first took me well into March: that's when I added the postscript that has accompanied it ever since. The second, once again, lapsed over into April by a couple of weeks.

39.4. Nor did the sense of voice desert me. A few days later, I called Bernie at his office. How was he coming with *The Ballad of Beta–2*? Well, he'd put the first half-dozen pages through the typewriter again, but really, he'd had no time to do anything else. Nor was he sure when he could.

What about if I took it back?

Fine, he said. Come up and get it.

I did. He gave me my original and the few pages he'd rewritten. Reading them on the subway downtown, I decided that I could more or less ignore what he'd done and work from my own version. Over the next two months I finished it and retyped it. I even held off submitting *City of a Thousand Suns* for a while. Ace published double books. Occasionally both books were by the same author. Perhaps they would put this small novel on the back of *City of a Thousand Suns*. A chance call from Don about something else entirely, however (another fan letter had arrived about the just-issued *Towers of Toron*; did I want to come pick it up?), made me decide to turn it in anyway.

Then *The Ballad of Beta–2* was finished.

Apparently Don liked *City of a Thousand Suns* a lot; at least he was far more enthusiastic than he'd been over the trilogy's first two books. "It rounds the whole thing off very nicely. For a while there, I wasn't sure if you were going to be able to do it. I think we'll give this one a volume all its own," he told me.

And when he read *Beta–2*, he said, "It's a nice little story. It'll make a good short side on a double. Of course, you know, we only pay seven fifty for those...."

39.5. When it began to grow warmer, I gave Phil another call. Yeah, why don't you drop by. So I did. At his apartment he played me some wonderful old Folkways records. Friends were staying with him that week, Jim and Jamey—a gay couple, heavily into S&M, who'd been together ten years and were, respectively, a nuclear physicist and a sometime journalist. They'd left New York to live in Washington when Jim (the elder and physicist) had gotten a government advisory job. There was another funny story about Hal, of course.

Jim, Jamey, and Phil had met in an S&M encounter, several years back, where they'd become good friends. Now, whenever Jim and Jamey came to New York, they stayed with Phil. In memory of whatever scene had brought them together, when they came to visit Jim would piss in a couple of empty beer bottles and leave them in the refrigerator for Phil. Nobody considered possible problems, but one day Hal had gone to the icebox, seen an open bottle, and thought, well, it wasn't there this morning, why open a new one? I'll just finish this one up, unless it's completely flat—

"Jesus Christ, Phil! What the hell have you *got* in here...?"

This had occasioned an apartment-wide discussion, involving not only Hal and Phil, Jim and Jamey, but also Hal's girlfriend, a twenty-five-year-old lawyer named Lilly. Magnanimously, Jim proposed that, from now on, he would leave the piss on the *left* side of the refrigerator and the beer would be clearly separated from it on the *right* side....

Hal's response? Fuck that! For the duration of Jim's and Jamey's stay, he'd do his beer drinking outside the house in bars, thank you!

Telling me this, Phil laughed. "For a straight guy, Hal's pretty tolerant—some of the things that go on here...well, how we stay friends, sometimes I really don't know." Minutes later, Hal—with lawyer Lilly—came in from work. Jim and Jamey came in only minutes on. At the time, Jim was about forty-five years old and regal in black leather: pants, vest, boots, jacket, and cap. Phil had cooked something for dinner and there was enough for everyone: so we all sat in the living room and ate it. And I found myself for the first time in a conversation I've had many times since when straight people and gay men talk about sex together—which, somehow, we began to do.

"Given the comparatively huge amount of sex available to homosexual men," I asked Hal and Lilly, "I still don't understand how heterosexuals survive within the institutionalized scarcity system imposed on them by society."

Their answers were not very clear or sure. What exactly did I mean?

Well, did Hal and Lilly realize, Phil asked, taking the topic up, that any of the four queers in the room could walk out of the apartment and, within fifteen minutes, find someone to have sex with, to orgasm, without even having to pay bus fare?

"Well," leather-clad Jim said, over his beer, "say forty-five minutes—for those of us a little older."

I was by then within weeks, one way or the other, of twenty-two. And though Jim was more than twenty years my senior, I was (back then) sure he was exaggerating.

It was a long and interesting discussion, with Lilly—in her smart orange number from Bonwit's—saying lots of very sharp things. Hal did a lot of listening and, now and then, asked a pertinent question. I probably did a lot of talking. And when, around ten-thirty, I got ready to go home, Phil walked with me into the hall.

As I started down the steps, he took my shoulder. "I'm really glad you said those things you did tonight—and that we all talked about what we did. They needed to hear that. That was very good. Thank you."

I was a little surprised. Since Phil and Jim and Jamey had all seemed so open about *being* queer around Hal and Lilly, I just assumed they'd always been equally open about talking of the realities of their homosexual behavior—which, apparently, was not the case. But there you have at least one scene from gay life—I have no idea how common such discussions were—in pre-Stonewall New York.

39.51. The sexual was—sadly for me, as far as I was concerned—out of my relationship with Phil. But Marilyn had articulated the rules for this kind of situation: I forced myself to function, refused to let myself go to pieces over it. And I suppose if you act a certain way long enough, it kind of seeps in. Now Phil came down to dinner with Marilyn and me; he and Marilyn took to each other right off. A couple of times Phil had both of us up to his house for dinner. Along in there somewhere Phil was out of work for a while. Marilyn introduced him to our friend Bernie; and for some six months, when Bernie was running International Authors' Representatives from Mrs. Cavanaugh's cubicle on the nineteenth floor of the ancient office building between the movie houses, at 220 West Forty-second Street, Phil was Bernie's secretary.

39.6. My best friend that year was a guy named Dave—sometimes, especially later, we called him Big Dave. (Don't confuse him with my composer friend Dave from high school.) I'd first met him as a boyfriend of Ana's, when Marilyn and I still lived on Fifth Street. But that affair had fallen off. Now his two passions were handball and playing the guitar. He'd been born on the Lower East Side and lived in a fourth-floor apartment around on Avenue B. With a group of neighborhood boys (Bobby, Billy, Dapper...), he'd grown up there and only left home a couple of years before. He'd shown me photographs of himself from a few years back, at the end of a pear-shaped, pimply adolescence. But with all the handball, his hips had slimmed, his shoulders had broadened, and a final, late, two inches of growth had brought him up to six feet, to make a well-above averagely attractive twenty- or twenty-one-year-old. Over the same time, his halting guitar technique had improved till it rivaled mine; and, through concerted practice, he'd strengthened his voice from a faltering baritone to a firm, pleasing tenor. (Anyone hearing the two of us would pronounce him the far better singer.) Exploring his own hetero-sexual map, Dave was trying to adjust to the fact that fat, smart women were far more sexually attractive to him than women who met more ordinary beauty standards—an adjustment that took some real self-examination and maturing for a young man whose looks I'd heard more than three people describe, when he was not there, with the cliché "like those of a Greek god." For a while Dave worked at a place called Bob's Bargain Books on the north side of Forty-second Street, just west of Sixth Avenue—a walk-in vastness of secondhand men's magazines and soft-core porn.

Once he'd got me a job there, and for six weeks I'd worked behind the cash register for balding, cynical, cigar smoking Bob. Dave and I did a lot of talking over that time—I have no memory of first telling him I was homosexual. But I know when I did, he already knew it.

One of the reasons it didn't bother him, he explained, was because two of his best friends, Joe and Paul, were a gay couple who lived in the rear apartment on the first floor of his own building. They were both from Philadelphia. They'd gotten together when Paul was seventeen and Joe was twenty-three. Now Paul was twenty-three and Joe was twenty-eight. They'd lived here in New York for several years now. Paul kind of stayed home and kept the house together. Joe was a truck driver, with his own minuscule trucking company in partnership with another New Jersey driver. Joe was away a lot. But whether Joe was in town or off hauling something, their apartment had become the social center of the building. Dave volunteered to introduce me. I said, sure, I'd like to meet them, but it didn't happen for a while. If anything, I think I was scared.

Once, going to visit Dave, I saw that the door to the first floor back apartment (where I knew Joe and Paul lived) was open. The sound of hammering came from inside. By angling my step a little on my way to the stairs, I got a glimpse through. A white guy in his late twenties wore workman's greens, his short sleeves rolled up over muscular arms. With very thick fingers, he gripped a hammer's handle, pounding at a nail on some up-ended table. He was bent over it so that you could see his brown hair was pulling away from his temples and thinning over a coming bald spot.

A slenderer guy in jeans and a short-sleeved shirt was just bringing him a cup of coffee.

Though I figured the one hammering was Joe and the one bringing the coffee was Paul, I didn't recognize who Joe was right away. Still, instead of going on up the stairs to Dave's place, I moved to the door's edge, out of the line of sight, and stood listening for ten minutes to the quiet conversation of two men who were clearly fond of one another, who hadn't seen each other for a week, the returning one of whom, at the request of the other, was fixing something that had lain long broken in the house. But when, invisible to me now, Joe said playfully, "You really want me to finish this up? I'm too tired. You work on it for a while," I realized I knew the voice.

39.7. On Central Park West one spring night, a lanky, nail-biting Englishman picked me up. Seems he was a painter named Kevin. At his West Side apartment, the conversation ranged from his dog, a friendly Irish setter who kept bounding into bed with us, to Andy Warhol, an acquaintance of Kevin's who'd just left advertising about a year back to go into "serious art."

We two became friends. As had happened with so many others, sex left the relationship early. Soon Kevin was coming down to dinner, and a little later showed Marilyn and me a novel he'd written.

The text seemed totally confused—how could we tell him it needed rewriting? When we finally did, though, he explained he'd rewritten it already—five times! On a hunch, I asked to see one of the earlier drafts. I chose draft three:

It was a perfectly acceptable novel, with one or two simple structural faults.

It was a major lesson in the dangers of overworking a text.

Since then I've rewritten novels of my own many more than five times. But there's particular work (orchestrational, organizational) appropriate to the first two or three drafts. And there's another kind of work (stylistic, small expansions and small cuts) appropriate to later ones. To undertake the wrong task at the wrong time in the compositional process is not the way to craft the best book.

39.71. I write of "voice," "dictation," and the "energy" that resulted from it. But whether you characterize the phenomenon with metaphors from speech or writing or production, it came at quite a price.

39.8. The acrophobia I mentioned parenthetically in the June walk we'd taken across the bridge in '62 had grown more and more intense in the first months of the year, so that by the time I finished *Voyage, Orestes!*, and a few months later *The Fall of the Towers* trilogy, I could not have taken that walk again. Even to be in a room with windows more than three or four stories above ground level was disturbing, physically painful. The muscles behind my knees would clamp in pain. My breath would grow shallow. My head would become dizzy. At the same time, another fear, metamorphosed distressingly and magically from the first, had grown up that I would, first, fall under a subway train and, shortly after that, that something inside me was compelling me to throw myself under an onrushing subway car. But general anxiety was rising all through my life.

Two or three times that spring I woke at three or four in the morning to leap from the bed and stand, shaking, naked, in the middle of the room, unable to breathe, my heart pounding, a red film over everything that, as my breath came back, would swirl clear in patches. Shivering, I would lie back down, unable to explain what had occurred to Marilyn who now tried harder and harder to ignore my stranger and stranger behavior.

39.9 A winter's night on Central Park West:

I walked uptown on the small hexagonal pavings. The trees flickered bare branches before the street lights. There wasn't anybody sitting on the benches beside the park wall—it was too cold. Hands in my pockets, I trudged from the kiosk at Fifty-ninth Street, up by the great named apartment buildings on the far side of the street, the San Remo, the Dakota, past the semicircular plaza with Humboldt's bust, and the great, gloomy façade of the Museum of Natural History, all the way to Ninety-sixth, where the cruising was always pretty slim. Then I walked back. Then I walked up again. And back down once more. "Within fifteen minutes...", I thought. Sure. But there was nobody out. So I went home.

TEMPLE SLAVE
Robert Patrick

There came a pounding, pounding at the door. I hadn't realized it was locked. Joe strode forth and opened it, and a huge Rubenesque red-haired woman entered screaming with laughter and practically carried him back to his table. "Stormy!" people called. She was attended by a tall, bald young man, his fluttering bangled arms full of costume bags. "Stormy!" people cried, "Larry! Close the gates, Mickey!"

Mickey was already padlocking the rusty folding gates to seal us in. The jukebox was emptied, and Larry jammed in records he'd brought. Stormy hugged and kissed Johnny and chatted with Joe in Italian. Nate had some Handsome Actors shove tables together in the middle of the room. Brassy music blared. Stormy hopped onto the tables with surprising agility and threw off her fur coat to release billowing hoop skirts. "She's still in costume from *Traviata*!" someone roared.

"She sings?" I asked the air.

Cameo, sticking close to me, muttered, "She's an extra." (Look who's talking!) and "Larry's in the corps de ballet. Relax."

Joe and Johnny stood in the front row, beaming up at Stormy. Wayne gave her dark-red lights with patches of pulsing blue, like coals in Hell. To shouts and rhythmic clapping, she undid her bountiful billows. She took it all off and threw it to Larry, except for what must have been her own rose-festooned garter belt, framing her flame-red bush.

Amid her applause, airy Larry hopped onto the tables as she hopped off. While Stormy washed her face in the punch bowl, Larry improvised a wild, wiggling solo to *Scheherazade*, replete with backbends and whirls, during which he managed to peel down to a dance belt. Despite enormous encouragement, he retained the dance belt and leapt down to boos and booze, whining, "It's too cold. Gimme mah britches!"

"Johnny, Giovanni," the crowd chanted. With a shoulder-sagging sigh, Johnny stepped easily up onto the tables, which were held together only by the crush of the crowd. Some fool put on Ravel's *Bolero*. Johnny laughed, looking up into a creamy yellow light not a foot from his face. He spread those airplane arms, shrugged again, and began to dance.

Most people dancing to the *Bolero* would stick to the rat-a-tat-tat drumbeat, getting silly and frenzied as it accelerates. Johnny danced to the swaying strings and reeds, sounds like camels lumbering over yielding dunes. He moved his feet less than his shoulders, his hips less than his horse-thick hair. He used his arms only to balance his towering self. Halfway through, he knelt, reached out, took Joe's hands to lift his lover onto the stage. There was a startled flutter of fresh applause, like bats wakened in a cave.

"Johnny shouldn't do that," I heard Kurt cluck.

"Joe hasn't danced in years," Nicholas whispered. However long it had been, clearly less of Joe had gone to fat than one might think. There was much muscle in that cookie-jar form, and he was a man who lived very much in his muscles. Almost a foot shorter than Johnny, he moved even less, and more as if beset by deep subterranean tremors than moved by mere music. Johnny and Joe wove, without touching, a webwork of twitches and poses that suggested they both were stuck in some arabesque of energy that could not escape from a magnetic field of force involving them. Climactically they stood buckling simultaneously, eyes closed, faces pinched, until Johnny collapsed at Joe's feet like a sacrifice.

The crowd cried, "Olé!" and sweaty-shirted Joe circled the fallen god like a toreador, a gladiator, plump fists held out, plump thumbs up.

Then he hopped down and could not be bullied to encore. The crowd groaned. Wayne's blue hand hung over his levers. Johnny lay panting. Was it over? Hardly. Another piece started. What, I can't remember. And Johnny, eyes closed, gave an almost-malicious chuckle and began to peel.

Stormy and Larry observed with professional approval, everyone else with glassy fascination. Lying on the tables, Johnny unclothed like a snake sloughing his skin. Everything that had been whispered about him was true, okay? We're used to grotesque muscle-men now; Johnny had the body of a dancer, a worker. There were no purely cosmetic clumps of muscle making a rococo joke of his long, lean lines.

Nude and honey-hued by watchful Wayne, he extended his pythonlike arms, and someone on each side handed him candles. With flaming stars in his hands, Johnny rose.

He held the stars as high as the low ceiling let him. He tilted them to trickle lines of colored wax down his body, like lava leaking from Wayne's fiery lights. Revolving like a maiden in her bath, he carefully defined his form with the lines. He was handed other candles of other colors. He crisscrossed the lines, winding himself in a flexible net of red, yellow, purple, pink, white, black, blue.

He handed the empty stars to ready hands, knelt, and leaned

first this way, then that. Fingers reached from the throbbing dark to peel wax away from him, mine among them. He was beginning to swell into an erection.

Up front, Mickey slightly opened the door and gate to allow those who chose to, to leave. All the women left: Veiled Ladies, Stormy, the actresses, some others. Amon Jones walked out with dignity, looking back briefly at his boys in the crush being fondled by Handsome Actors, in turn being nuzzled by Nate. Careful Kurt tiptoed out with yet another Handsome Actor.

Mickey was about to seal the gate, but held it ajar to admit a slight, unfamiliar silhouette which slipped in and paused a moment behind Cameo behind me to watch Johnny being peeled, then slipped to the light-nook to whisper to Wayne. Wayne shushed him violently and concentrated on lowering lights in a pulsating rhythm.

Cameo concentrated his pulsating pants against my burning buns and reached over me to strip a thread of wax from Johnny's thigh. Mickey closed the gates. Johnny reached out for Joe's curly head, then raised himself slowly and thrust his long dong gradually into Joe's mouth. Tears of effort oozed from Joe's eyes.

The lights dimmed to near-darkness, and there began a general urgent gentle move rearward, not to the left behind the counter into the curtained Back, as I expected, but past the light nook, where Wayne's friend's silhouette backed away to avoid being swept down the little narrow rear central corridor and past the dressing room to an unnoticed little door that opened onto a softly lit concrete courtyard, where a small house sat unillumined.

As soft hands urged me into the escape, I glanced back into Cameo's leering teeth. Past him I saw Johnny's shape among others, and up front Wayne and the slight shadow exiting together. I never broke Wayne's piñata. I think a lot of candy curdled in there.

Hardworking Mickey locked the gate for good behind them,

closed the doors, then scuttled to catch up to the rest of us, whipping-off his sequined shirt.

We spilled down two steps into the dizzying air. With hot breath on my neck and strong hands kneading my buns, I was nudged with the whispering revelers across the courtyard and into the little house.

The house was lit only by the spill from the courtyard.

No furniture. Mattresses on the floor, scattered sheets.

Clothes rustled away, shoes clomped. The soft spill lit hasty caresses. We collapsed onto mattresses. The Handsome Actors manipulated the Pretty Boys into unlikely positions. Grinning Nate swung among them and other lambent figures. Naked Nick, even his bush white, fucked the still-garbed Winston Smith's toothless mouth. Cameo and I and others plugged one another in every hopeful opening. Larry rolled from group to group to grip and grope.

Joe and Johnny made love. Johnny reached out and cupped other buttocks, other balls, wagged other staves, sometimes craned his neck and licked, sucked, kissed anything near, all the while modeling Joe under, over, around him like God creating man. Now and then he would tug a dickhead down to swab it around in Joe's mouth, wipe a Pretty Boy's behind across Joe's face, spread sweat or come from someone over Joe's hairy hard stomach-hummock or enormous firm breasts. Joe endured everything. Once, as Cameo had me on my belly fucking me languidly, Johnny lifted my head by my hair and blotted my mouth on both Joe's rock-hard nipples.

Joe never opened his eyes, never objected, never added to the hoarse chorus of "Wait," "Now," "No," "Easy," "Harder," or gave an order like, "Fuck me," "Take it," or "Suck his dick." He yielded to be used and fused as Johnny chose. But whenever allowed, he had his hands, his mouth, his full fine hairy ass on Johnny's long, strong, straight, smooth, and calmly indefatigable cock.

Others would interweave themselves with Joe and his Johnny. No permission was needed, no intrusion denied. Once Mickey stood astraddle Joe, fucking Johnny's indifferent mouth as Johnny fucked himself on Joe's barrel-shaped cock. Larry and a Handsome Actor, eating their way up Johnny's whang, met at the top and kissed with his planetoid glans penis choking their conjoined mouths. Larry motioned me to lick Johnny's high-riding balls, which Larry held in his hands like jewels. But somehow, unless forced, I couldn't touch the sacred pair: Joseph and John.

I could touch anyone else. I was like a glass prod. This was the first orgy that had meant anything to me but popular mechanics. I came and came again. Even after coming, I stayed hard. Hardworking Cameo despaired of diminishing me. After a long session of wormy squirming where I stood firm, he lifted one leg in a divinely gross posture so people could see me jammed in his join. "I can't get this thing down," he complained. "Somebody else jump on it for a while." Somebodies else did.

After Joe finally groaned and collapsed under jockeying Johnny, and Johnny fell forward to squeeze foam onto Joe's face, a lot of people came on the puffing couple.

I fell asleep with Nate's crew cut tickling my thighs, Larry's tit in my mouth, Winston Smith's finger up my ass, and Cameo's leg lobbed over my waist, his poor worn-out opening flexing and unflexing as he snored. All around, other vague bundles snorted and shifted for slumber in the gloom, variously suggesting custard and pasta. It was an hallucinatory spectacle before I ever had a hallucination; but until I passed out, I had my eyes on gigantic Johnny, sticky and gleaming, sliding sleepily around on the snoring, comatose Joe.

In the morning, one of the Pretty Boys and I, apparently the sole participants with regular daytime jobs, pulled ourselves from the clammy, crusted mass like sailors emerging from a shipwreck. I thought he was robbing the Handsome Actor, but he only wanted a sunlit look at that wallet-photo. Incredibly, we both felt like sex again; but, despite vibrant erections, we hadn't time. I never found my yellowbird sweater. My office clothes were like something used to clean stables. I had to ride all the way to 77th Street for fresh ones.

Al was almost dressed when I entered our bedroom. "Jesus, where have you been?" he asked. "You look, and—whew!—smell like a stockyard."

"I was at a party with some friends," I said, peeling. On the bed was a crumpled Kleenex. I felt so sorry for him.

"Bob, you're covered with hickeys," he admonished.

I looked at both of us in the mirror. I looked pearly and polka-dotted. "I may have them tattooed on," I said. "Is my ass red?" I turned my back on him and spread my chafed cheeks.

"Bob!" he said. "You're encrusted with come!"

"Not enough," I said. I jerked his pants and Jockey shorts to his nervous knees. I made him sit on the bed and blew his accusative early morning hard-on.

"Wellll," he said, flushed and pleased as he reached for more Kleenex. "That was rude. What's happened to you?"

"I'm in love!" I yelled from the bathroom as I turned-on a roaring shower.

"With whom?" he asked from the sink, recombing his hair.

"Ooooooooooh," I pondered under the steaming stream and finally said, "With a waiter, I guess."

So I started an affair with the cameo waiter, a Black Irish welder from Brooklyn named Oscar—not for Wilde, but for some obscure political martyr from the Auld Sodde. My Oscar Weld and I wrote a lot of poetry to each other. He read his at literary evenings; I read mine to him. He hadn't my penchant for puns or humor (aside from sly sexual wooing-wit like the poem he'd done at the Buono; such caprices, he said, could be indulged only underground). He was annoyed by my running gag, when he'd gouge himself into me, about "getting Oscar for my performance." But we managed an impassioned heavy-breather for several months.

Not long ago, preparing some papers of mine for a museum, I came across a fragment of erotic macaronic, probably to Oscar, probably doodled while waiting for him near one of his welding gigs—not, however, so near that his work-buddies might see us together. It's entitled "My Wait for Your Weight," and it begins, "Sittin' on a fireplug, thinkin' of you."

Oh, well, everyone should have one love affair. At work I could have been rising had I cared to exert myself against the tired methods and rampant nepotism that ate at the fraying firm. Under weak management, the company's mistakes were so repetitious that I was able to do my assigned job with five rubber stamps and three form letters, which was good, because I spent most of my eight hours tracking down fantastic careless errors in filing or accounting. Only after a raging fight with the dyke who ran the Orders Department with a fervor which equaled mine was I allowed to extract ignored payment-forms from her sacred files and save the company from losing literally a million dollars in Kansas textbook sales. I might have gotten a raise for that in a rational universe, but my boss had to cover up the whole thing or he might have gotten canned. He said.

Possibly, of course, he took the credit and got the raise.

It didn't matter. All that mattered was the Buono and, oh, yes, of course, Oscar. He was often around filling in for Wayne, who was off lighting tours for traveling dance troupes from whom he stole the Buono's lights. Whenever the troupes played nearby, Wayne would pop in to design lights for the week's play, leaving them to be run by Johnny or Mickey or Oscar, or even little ol' me.

It was accepted now that I would appear at the door by ten or twelve minutes after five, shop, sweep, help with whatever was in the works.

Mickey had come to accept me, but always thought I moved too fast. "Just don't go through anything," he'd plead. I hoped he hadn't a cleaver.

The regulars, who had considered me furniture for some time, made jokes about my speed, energy, availability, and general ditheriness. I still felt shy with them, even after the Great Orgy. I no more felt that that gave me entrée into the elite than it did for the vacuous Pretty Boys.

THE MOTORCYCLIST
Phil Andros

I guess I'm what some people would call a tough guy. I don't exactly know why they do. Something about the way I look, I reckon—or kinda tighten up my eyes when I talk. Mebbe it's a kind of reputation I already got—some guys pass me on to others, if you know what I mean. There was a pansy in Kansas City who said afterward he'd been scared to death pickin me up, accounta the sideburns scared him. And there was a boot queen in San Francisco—you know, one of them queers likes to have you rub your boots in their faces and make 'em go down on you—who said he thought I was tough accounta the way I wore my motor-cycle cap.

Anyways, why it is I don't know, but traipsin around over these here United States, I sure been able to get what I wanted everyplace I been. Cunts, sure—plenty of 'em, I affect 'em just like I do the pansies. But after bein on the road, and a coupla years in San Quentin for a bum rap, I don't get much kick anymore outa cunts—they're too damn loose. They get so hot with me suckin' their tits or muff-divin a little that they come fore I'm anyways near ready. In San Quent I had me a coupla gobblers, damn cute kids. One of 'em knew more tricks with his mouth than any bitch I ever ran into. Christ! It was wonderful! He'd run his tongue round the end of my cock, or he'd make it kinda quiver on the head of it, or he'd take it clear back in his throat until you could feel it begin to go down. That'd set me wild. I'd grab his head and push him down on it till he'd gag. Once I pushed too hard and tore that there skin at the back of his throat. Goddamn, he sure looked sick! But the next week when he was outa sick bay, he was right back askin for more of my old eight inches.

Yeah, that's what I got. Not much more'n parlor size, huh? But I kin do more tricks with it than forty feet of grapevine. Sure, Mac...you can buy me a drink—bourbon, straight. Yeah, I was in the navy for a while, too. You guessed it from my sayin "sick bay," huh? You were, too? Well, my name's Jack. I'm 6'2", 190 and my hair 'n' teeth are my own. Twenty-eight, free, white, and single. I just got in town this afternoon.

Well, I hadda *lot* of adventures on the way. All kinds—whadyuh want—men, women, or what? Sure—I don't mind stickin it in a nice clean one—only you gotta watch out or they'll get ya. A man? Christ, yes—I had a dozen on the way from St. Louis.

Well, there was that kid I met in Kansas, f'r instance. It was about three weeks ago, middle of August, and I was hightailin it along the highway—goggles on and all—and had made about 350 miles that day, counta I got a late start. Got tight in St. Louie and didn't get up till noon. Well, my old ass was gettin tired, and ridin there in Kansas is sure monotonous with them long, straight roads goin off in the distance far as you can see. The wind kept me pretty well cooled off, but I was kinda itchy—you know how it is. Us wheelers calls it road-burn—your old cock gets all knotted up and hard from all that ridin, and Christ, you think you're gonna go nuts. I'da liked to had a good blowjob right there, and I'd had that damn road-burn all afternoon, my old John a-layin there on the motorcycle seat, tensin up and sorta raisin his head to look around—you know what I mean? By God, it sure is wonderful how they seem to got a life of their own, ain't it?

Well, I'd been keepin my eye peeled on the fields a-lookin for a calf, even though it ain't exactly the season of the year for them—and I'd seen a storm a-comin up from the south. I sorta figgered I'd have about a half hour more afore it hit me, and I'd oughta been able to find a place to run in in that time. But I reckon I miskalkelated, cause after about ten minutes I felt a coupla drops, and Jesus, there wasn't no shelter in sight nowheres. I was just beginnin to goddamn it, when I round a buncha trees (only ones I'd seen for miles) and there standin right by the roadside was a farm kid with his thumb up hitchin a ride, I don't generally like to give rides, cause usually it's too much chance to take on balancin—and if a guy ain't never rode a wheel afore, he's likely to throw you off when you're hittin a curve or doin' eighty. Man, that's fatal. So generally I don't stop, but this time I did because I thought maybe the kid knew someplace wheres we could go to get outa the rain, cause the drops was gettin bigger.

So I pulled up beside him.

"Hi!" he said. "Gimme a lift?"

"You know howta balance?" I asks.

"Sure," he says. "I rode one of them things lots."

"Anyplace to get outa the rain?" I asks.

"Yup," he says, "bout a mile down on the Stafford farm. Old man Stafford's got him a storage barn about two miles from his farmhouse, but we can get in it on account I know how."

"Okay," I says. "Hop on."

He was a good-lookin kid, about two inches shortern me, about six feet, and he had curly blond hair and a good tan. I kinda envied him that on account my goggles leave white circles around my eyes. All he had on was one of them combination overalls with a bib up front, you know, the kind with straps over the shoulders, and he was built like a brick shithouse, no kiddin. I thought I had a good build, but his was better. And them coveralls fit him like a glove. I felt ole Betsy begin to move about in my pants when I looked at that cute little ass of his—bet he was tight as anything, and I could just see me sorta partin the cheeks of it like as if it was cabbage and socking my old dong right down to the heart of it. I could see from the front he had quite a piece a baloney himself—big bulge down there atween his legs.

He hopped on and then he stopped a minute. "What're you waitin for?" I growls. "Grab aholt of me, around me, and let's get goin—it's gonna rain like hell in a minute!"

He pressed close to me, and then he kinda put his arms around my middle like as if he was half-afraid to, and I remembered I had my shirt open clear down to my belly button and he'd have to touch my hairy chest and belly "Fer chrissake," I says, "a little hair ain't gonna hurt you—grab aholt tight." With that he did, and those big forearms crossed in front of me and held tight. The kid smelled like hay—kinda fresh and good—and we lit out for the barn.

Not soon enough, though. Bout a half mile from it, the rain began to come down in buckets. I was afraid the damned motor would flood on me, it was that bad. I kept holding her down, and I could hear the kid kinda gasping behind me because he dint have no goggles and he was half-blind with the rain. Finally he yells in my ear, "There she is!" and I rattled up to the barn door skidding the gravel in a hailstorm up agin the wood. He jumped off and ran around the corner, and in lessn a minnit he opened the door from the inside. I wheeled the bike in outa the rain.

The both of us was soaked to the skin. The water was running outa my jeans and would of got into my boots ifn I'da had 'em tucked down in the way I usually ride. The kid was kinda laughin and tryin to get the hair outa his eyes, and his overalls was soaked clean through except for a big dry spot right on his front where he'd been huggin me close from behind.

"Looks like we gotta dry these things out," I says.

"How?" he says. "They ain't gonna be any sun till tomorrow, and we can't light a fire in here."

"Okay," I says. "Looks like we're stuck here for the night or until it stops rainin."

"Yeah, I guess so," he says. He looks kinda worried. "What'll my folks say?"

"Bout what?" I says, kinda sarcastic. "Spendin the night with a strange man in a barn?"

He turned red as fire. "Naw," he said. "They jest might worry." He began to unbuckle his shoulder straps, and then he started to peel off his overalls. Peel's the word for it. Being wet made it tighter, but he managed to get it off. Meanwhile I'd took off my own jeans, soppin wet, and hung 'em up, but I left my cap and boots on. He was standin with one foot up on a box and tryin to wipe the water off him with his hands, and shiverin a little. He kept his back turned to me, bashful-like, but that was okay, that was the part I liked lookin at. Jesus, it was a good back—and real muscled legs, but mostly I liked that tight little ass. It looked hard as rock. And I could just see me spreadin the cheeks apart with my hands like you'd open an oyster and gettin' in there where it was nice and hot. Thinkin like that made me begin to get hard, and so to stop it and not to scare him to death, I opened my kit and pulled out a towel and flung it to him.

"There," I says. "Wipe."

"Gee, thanks," he said.

He took it and wiped his hair, and then gave himself a good rubdown with it. But he still kept sorta turned away from me as if he was bashful about showin his cock. I pulled a pint of licker outa the bag and took a good stiff snort of it. Then I said, when I got my breath back, "What's yer name, kid? Can't spend the night here without we interduce ourselves. Mine's Jack." I stuck out my hand. He had to turn around on that, and I looked down at his cock.

"Ed," he says, "Ed Johnson." Then he saw where I was lookin and he kinda made to cover it up, but then he musta thought that was silly because he took the towel away.

I still had the bottle in my hand. "Drink?" I said, and grinned at him. That grin had knocked more cunts over than you'd think, and he fell for it, too. He kinda grinned back and reached out for the bottle.

"Whiskey?" he said, sorta uncertain.

"Oh, no," I says, sarcastic. "Mother's milk. Good for you. Won't get pneumonia."

He began to collar up agin, and then he took the pint and put it up, and jesus, he swallered about half of it. Just straight, runnin down his throat with him not swallering. When he stopped he handed it back to me and grinned.

"Ain't you outa breath?" I asks. He dint even gasp which is moren I could do after that bigga drink.

"Hell, no," he says. "Us farm boys're raised on corn likker. Pop's got hisself a still, and I sneak some every Sattiday night. Good stuff...Jack," he adds, friendly-like.

In about fifteen minutes we killed the bottle, and he's sittin there naked with that big john dangling down atween his legs—he was hung almost as big as I was. And I saw for all his braggin' he wasn't as used to whiskey as he made out. He began to yawn a little, and purty soon he went over and picked hisself out a nice pile of hay and sorta laid back in it and closed his eyes.

The rain hadn't let up at all, and I was beginnin to get sleepy myself. The barn was hot as hell, and the cool air dint come very far in the door. So I yawned a coupla times and he never stirred.

"I think I'll hit the hay, too," I said, and sorta chuckled on account it really was hay this time, and he kinda mumbled and moved an arm back. He was layin there wide open, his cock sorta swollen but not standin up, so I flops down on another pile of hay just the other side of him, and lays back and shuts my eyes.

Goddamn, it wasn't moren a minute till I heard his feet comin across the floor from his pile of hay. And then he musta kinda sat down near me on account I could hear him breathin hard and short. I just kept my eyes closed and my hands behind my head, pertendin to be asleep, but I sorta arched my ass forward, sexy-like, and knowin the kid was right there beside me made me begin to git hard. I felt it risin slow and easy-like until it was standin straight up, and I knew the kid was watchin it because he was holdin his breath, until all of a sudden he couldn't hold it anymore, and he let it out in a kinda gasp, and then began to breathe hard and fast again. I could hear him even above the rain on the barn roof. Well, by then I was real stiff, stiff and standin straight up, and I made it throb just once so that the head swelled real big and red, as I knew. He saw it because he kinda gasped once.

Kids are funny, especially farm kids. Course they know all about sex, but they ain't had much experience with people. I could guess he admired my cock because it was big and clean and hard, and it kinda fascinates anybody who sees it, let alone gets a taste of it, on account I know how to use it okay. I may not got so many brains, but I sure have learned how to fuck. Lotsa practice.

Anyway, after about a minnit, I felt his hand on my cock, just a kinda light little touch, like a feather, and then he musta jerked his hand away agin. I made 'er jump agin, and sorta stirred, you know the way you do if somebody lays a hand on your cock while you're sleepin. All that's malarkey about people goin down on you while you're asleep—ain't nothin wakes you any quicker than somebody's hand or mouth on your cock.

Well, purty soon he puts his hand back on my cock. This time he took a good holt on it, laid his thumb up alongside it, and got it around the bottom with his fingers, and he sorta squeezed it a coupla times, and I answered him by makin it jump in his hand. He swallered hard and kept on workin it, and it was hard as a rock. But I kept my eyes closed until he began to feel sure I wouldn't wake up. Then it began to feel good, real good, and I thought, Christ, I don't wanna come with him just jackin me off, so I opened my eyes wide without movin and looked right at him.

He dint see me at first. His lips was kinda parted and his eyes shinin, and he was watchin my cock while he jacked it off. His own cock was hard, too, and standin up straight, the head as red as could be, and I could see a little sweat on his shoulders and back from the excitement.

Then I says, quiet-like, "Kinda like it, do yuh, kid?"

He jumped like he was shot and looked at me with big scared blue eyes. But he dint let go of my cock. He wet his lips a little and said, "You sure got a big un."

I stuck my hips forward even more and strained aginst his hand. "Yuh want it?" I said, kinda lazy-like and lookin at him with my eyes half-shut and me half-grinnin, and he swallered agin and nodded, and said, "But wotta I do with it? I'll jack you off, huh?"

That did it. I swings my arms around from back my head and raised up. "Any ole day," I says, tough as I could. "What the hell you mean, jack off? That's for babies. Gimme a blowjob."

"Blowjob?" he says, kinda puzzled. "Like this?"

Honesta God, if the sonofabitch dint blow on it! Yeah, kinda gentle! I swore. "Goddammit," I said, "aincha never hearda blowjob? Go down on it suck it, put yer mouth on it and suck it! Blow's just... just an expression."

He let go of it. "I ain't never done nothin like that," he says, scared-like.

I jumped up offn the hay. "By God," I says, "you ain't gonna be able to say that after today!" I says, and I grabbed him by the shoulders and twisted him around so's I had my left leg agin his chest and my cock was jumpin there about six inches under his nose, and then I grabbed ahold his left wrist and at the same time grabbed his head with my left hand and shoved on it so's he was clamped there and couldn't move. Then I began to push him down to the head of my cock. He sure did fight back against me with his neck muscles and try to break away, but I held him fast.

He tried to talk me out of it, and his voice sounded scared. "Jack… please! Jack, please don't! Honest, I ain't never done nothin like this before. Please, I'll jack you off—lemme do that."

"Nothin doin," I said. I kept forcin his head toward my cock. His neck muscles stood out and he was squirming like hell, tryin to pull loose. I laughed at him. "Christ, Eddie boy, what's a little cock gonna hurt you? You'll like it soon's you getta taste of it and feel it jumpin down yer throat. Ain't nobody ever been hurt by swingin on a good clean cock." His lips were clamped tight shut, but I'd got his mouth down to bout a inch away. He kept twistin his head, and once he got it turned sidewise and looked up at me kinda beggin-like. He whimpered a little.

"You'd call me a cocksuck—" he began to say.

Just then, when his mouth was open, I gave a hard shove on the back of his head, and the whole head of my cock jumped right inta his mouth. I could feel his teeth close down, and I knocked the back of his neck with my elbow. "Goddammit!" I said. "You bite me, and by Jesus, I'll beat your brains out. C'mon now—suck!"

The size of it and me pushing it was cuttin off his wind every time I hit the back of his throat. I could tell, and his eyes was waterin, but I sorta shifted position and got my left boot around his back and pushed him down on his knees and arched my old ass forward so's he could get the benefit of all eight inches. I got both hands onna back of his head, and Christ, it felt good as hell. I was sockin it away and he was takin it without much complainin when I felt a kinda change in him. He stopped pushing against me with his arms, and slid one hand in atween my legs and started to play with my ass and grabbed my left leg around with his other arm, and then he got one finger in my asshole and did I go wild! God, anybody sticks his tongue or finger in my ass, I bout go off my nut.

He was beginnin to like it—that's fer sure. Just as I was bout ready to come, feelin that thrill all up and down my legs and in my belly, I saw a box bout ten feet away, and I yanked my cock outn his mouth and pulled him to his feet.

"What for?" he says. "You mad? I'll—I'll finish you," and he makes like to get down on his knees again, but I takes him by the shoulder and shoves him over to the box. "Git down on that," I says.

He looks at it. "How?" he says, puzzled.

"Git your back on it," I says, "and lay there with your head back. I'm gonna give you some reverse English." He did like I said. Then I stood t'other sidea the box and straddled his head and he opened his mouth, and began to push my old whang into his mouth like that. That's my favorite position—it kinda opens up a guy's throat, and you seem to be gettin in a lot deeper and further. I grabbed his head and kinda took holda his jawbones, where I could dig my fingers in along the sides. Then I started to fuck his mouth, slow and easy at first, and payin no attention to the stranglin sounds he made. They got me even hotter than I been. He got his arms kinda in atween my legs and around my back and kept pullin me inta him steada trying to push me off.

I was beginnin to pump faster on him and my cock was swellin larger and I was about ready to blow. So was he, I guess. I saw his cock was purple at the head and kinda angry red and its veins popping, and then—guess what! All of a sudden he came, without me layin a hand on his cock, shootin right straight and up, all over his belly, gobs and gobs of come, and his body jumped and quivered, and a big blob of come hit me right on the shoulder. I leaned over and licked it off, and just then I began to feel myself

coming—and Jesus!—what a wad I shot inta him! I couldn't stop
comin—he gagged on it and his mouth filled up, and it ran out the
sides and down his neck and back over his shoulders. I ain't shot
such a load in a long time. And my butt muscles wouldnt stop
working or my legs tightenin up, and me bent over holdin tight
on his chin. He began to try to get up. I figgered he was gonna spit
out *my* come!—and so I rammed my cock deep as I could and
grabbed him under the chin, and one hand around the throat
chokin him a little, and I says, "C'mon, damn you, swaller it,
swaller all of it," and then I heard him swaller and it all went
down. So that kinda satisfied me, cause nobody's gonna spit out
any good come of mine if I know about it, so I began to take my
cock out, real slow. He kinda slumped down from the box onta the
hay on the floor, and he laid back against the box, pantin and
outa breath, and his face wet from the tears I'd made come when
I was forcin it in. His yaller hair was all mussed up, and I kinda
felt sorry for him account the poor kid really hadda kinda rough
time, specially this being his first experience. Sometimes I forget
how big my cock is when I get hot—well, you know how the
sayin goes, a stiff prick ain't got no conscience. So I goes to my
kit and takes out a piecea rag and goes back to him with his chest
still heavin and his eyes closed, and I begins to wipe the come offa
his belly. His old cock was still dribblin all right; it was sorta
bendin in the middle but still puttin out blobs of come. I guess I
really dint wipe him off good with the rag, just spread it around
to make him feel sticky and then have it tighten up when it got dry.

"Worn out, kid?" I asks him, on my knees in fronta him. He
kinda opens one eye and nods, on account he still can't speak. The
way he was sittin, with his legs up, sorta brought up the cheeks of
his tight brown little ass so's I could get a gander at 'em, and so help
me God if I dint start to get hard agin. Mebbe I never even stopped.

"Aw, you ain't had nuttin yet," I says. "That's just a little appe-
tizer. I'm gonna give you the real thing—the real meat course."

Both his eyes popped open like as if he'd been goosed, wide

open, but he dint look near as scared as he had been the first time. He kinda smiled. That was enough for me. I reached over and grabbed his two legs and threw 'em up in the air, and then caught him along the thighs afore he came down. That sure showed his asshole. There it was shinin out at me like a little brown eye, small and clean, and sorta squeezin itself together— y'know what I mean? Like as if it was waitin for what was comin and was still kinda scared of it. So I puts my face down between those two soft cheeks—and me not shaved, it musta scratched hell outa him—and he was hard again in no time. I stuck out my tongue and tasted that little hole. First I ran it all around the edges and watched it kinda jump back in, and then I really buried my face there, breathin hard, and rammed my tongue in as far's I could stick it, and wiggled the tip of it. The kid liked it. He was moaning with pleasure and groanin and also pushin his ass hard agin my face. Then I took my tongue out and licked his asshole the way you usta lick a lollipop— long, slow licks up and down against it. Christ, he liked it!

He grabbed ahold my boot and pulled hard. That upset my balance and I kinda fell backward and his legs came down. He laid there pantin and kind of relaxed. I got up and put my hands under his armpits and gave a big heave-ho and lifted him up on the box. He just laid there kinda easy, one arm hangin down on the side. Well, I pushed his right leg aside, and lifted th'other one up on the box, and then I kneeled down agin and licked his asshole some more, only this time I lefta lotta spit laying there and also took my fingers and laid some more spit along my cock. Then, aholdin his legs apart, I went in.

Nothin hard at first, y'understand—real easy-like, givin that ole muscle a chance to relax without no trouble. He groaned once but kept his head down and his eyes shut.

Christ, man—you ever browned a boy? You have? Jesus, it's great—lots better'n a woman, ain't it? Boys always stay tight on your cock, no loosenin up like a cunt when she comes. Man, that kid was tops! I ain't ever found a tighter cleaner little asshole.

My cock fit in there like as if it'd been tailor-made for it. I pushed it in slow, like I said, same speed, but makin sure it was all in, all eight inches, afore I stopped. I musta hit that gland in there cause all of a sudden his body twitched like he was gonna come agin. But he dint.

It was kinda like layin it in warm leather, that got wet and shrunk down till it squeezed you real hard. Then I began to fuck him—long, easy strokes. I'd bring it clear out almost, just to the tip, and then shove that big head as far in as it'd go. And I'd watch it as I drew it out, and see that hole expandin and squeezin tight like as if it didn't want to let go of it.

Gradually the spit dried offn it and—jeez, what a sensation, goin in dry! I knew I was hurtin him, but hell—by now I dint care. His head was turnin from side to side, and he was groanin.

I can't come standin up like that, so I finally took my cock out, and then picked him up and held him—he kinda held onta me, too, and I sat down on the box, and then I pulled his back against my belly, so's he was sorta settin in my lap with his ass above my prick. I got one of his legs doubled up and my arm under it, and then I reaches around him to squeeze his tit, and with the other hand I grabbed ahold of his cock. Then I kinda eased him down until the head of my cock was just kissin his asshole. Then—wham! I pushed him down real hard on my cock—jeez, he hollered and threw up his arms and grabbed one wrist and threw his head back—but I kept right on pushin, dry, as it was, until it was inta the hilt. Man, how he was squeezin me in there!

Then I started rockin him—y'know? Me settin on the edge a the box and usin my leg muscles to rock him up and down. And I was jerkin him off the same time. I gives about three passes on his prick with my hand and whammo! Damned if he dint come again! Musta shot about eight feet in the air. And the squeezins his asshole gave my cock when he came made me come, too, and my come inside him made the head of my cock all hot, hot as hell as it kept spittin out the last of it.

Then he just kinda fell apart, and I got up— quite a job, husky as he was, and I sorta staggered with him—my cock still in him, y'understand— over to the hay, and eased us both down on it. He was plumb tired out. I pulled my cock out real slow—it made a kinda hollow suckin sound, and wiped it offn a fistfulla hay. Then I laid down aside him and put my arm around him, and musta snoozed a minnit.

Anyways, when I woke up, by God, iffn he dint have his head down there atween my legs, suckin me off for good and all, and seemin to enjoy the taste of his own shit on my cock. His old dong was right up by my face, and I no more started to lick it till bang! Off he went agin, all over my face. And just then I let fly, too, all over him.

Right then I happened to look up at the hayloft and whaddyuh think? Be damned if there wasn't another guy up there, jerkin hisself off all alone! Been watchin' us all the time. "Hey!" I hollers up to him, "c'mon down and join the party!" So he gets up and starts downa ladder...

Huh? What's that? Ain't you feelin' well, Mac? Oh, you can't take any more of it? Thought you liked to hear dirty stories. Jesus, just when I was gettin goin good...

Oh, you mean—not hear it here, in the bar? Naw, I don't mind. I'll go along with you. What kinda partment you got? Far? I gotta be back down at the Y sometime—get an early start tomorrow. By 7:00 A.M. fer sure...

Hell, Mac, do I sound like as if I cared if you're queer. I'm itchy agin, mister—itchy all the time. What dyuh like to do? Okay, then—everything. Mebbe even a little piss inna mouth, huh? Good fer the digestion.

Okay, Mac—let's go.

THE SEXUAL ADVENTURES OF SHERLOCK HOLMES
Larry Townsend

In the year 1878 I took my degree of Doctor of Medicine from the University of London, and subsequently the course for army surgeons at Netley. Attached to the Fifth Northumberland Fusiliers, I was sent to the front in Afghanistan, where I was wounded soon after my arrival. I then spent a memorable several weeks in the hospital at Peshawur, under the care of some exceptionally attractive orderlies, before being returned to England. Still in a poor state of health, I was discharged from the army on a small, monthly stipend. Though a young man of less than twenty-five, I now found myself in a singular situation of being a retired gentleman, trying to live on a tiny government pension at a time when prices were soaring and decent accommodations were not to be had at a price within my means.

Consequently, I had taken up residence in a small hotel—not the sort of lodgings to be recommended for any person of taste—and began spending a fair amount of time in the local taverns. Of these, I especially enjoyed the Criterion, because of the many handsome men who went there. While sitting at the bar one afternoon, I had the good fortune to run into a young fellow named Stamford, who had been a dresser under me at the front. We had engaged in a brief affair, and I remembered him particularly for his truly extraordinary rectal structure—his ability to relax and contract the sphincter muscles as if they were under a totally voluntary control. Quite apart from these unique talents, I was naturally delighted to encounter any former comrade-in-arms in London. I immediately removed to a table and asked Stamford to join me.

"My dear fellow," he said, after we had been drinking for several minutes, "I do not wish to pry, but although I am delighted to see you again, I am distressed to note a certain…er…lack of prosperity in your appearance, sir."

"Ah, Stamford," I sighed, "you eye is keen as ever. Yes," I admitted, "I am rather up-against-it." I went on to explain my present circumstances, and being somewhat in my cups I omitted nothing of the dilemma which faced me.

"Poor devil!" exclaimed Stamford. He hesitated then, watching me closely before going on. "I greatly fear I may be misunderstood if I suggest what comes most readily to mind," he continued at length, "but while the initial suggestion may shock you, I think sober consideration may produce quite the opposite reaction…."

He eyed me quizzically, and I shrugged, wondering what exactly he had in mind. I had already noticed the expensive, overly stylish cut of his suit, and also the clever bit of tailoring about his crotch. Well, I thought, Stamford was certainly never lacking in that respect, either. The memory was a pleasant one…large, deep-ruby colored genitals…thick, wide penis with veins that twined about its shaft like the vines on a wall of brick…bollicks of a bull with the heady aroma of manhood aroused…

I sighed at length, smiled despite my apprehension and this reminder of my distressing circumstances. "I am desperate enough to try almost anything," I admitted, "but my health precludes maintaining even a minimal practice."

Still speaking under obvious strain, and in an almost apologetic tone, Stamford admitted what I was already beginning to suspect, that he was actively procuring young men for various and sundry activities, supplying these to persons of means who could pay for whatever their particular tastes required. "But you must understand, Watson," he continued, "I am not a protector of male harlots, nor what is called a 'pimp' in the common vernacular. I am, rather, a broker. I charge a modest fee for bringing together two gentlemen of similar persuasions. If the one who is better able pays the fee, this is something I do not question. Nor can I control what may subsequently pass between the two persons once I have introduced them...."

"You are not suggesting...?" I began in horror.

"Now, now...wait a moment, my dear friend," he urged. He seized my elbow in a firm but gentle grasp to prevent my standing. "Really, Watson, I recall you were not above an occasional dalliance, and unless your wound is excessively disfiguring I see no reason why this body of yours—this body which has already caused you such distress despite your youth—should not be put to use to remedy the deprived situation in which you presently find yourself."

"I find the idea outrageous!" I replied indignantly. But despite my offended tone the prospect was remarkably intriguing. Nor was my shifting attitude completely hidden from young Stamford. After all, it was his business to detect the subtle nuances on another's features, and to interpret these for his own advantage. A faint smile crossed his lips, and he gestured for the waiter to bring us another round of drinks.

"I think you will find the gentleman I have in mind very much to your liking," he continued, as if I had already agreed to join his stable. "The fellow is a chemist, of sorts, but actually quite a brilliant student in several varied and diverse areas of scientific endeavor. In short, he is a man of your own class, who is simply in more fortunate circumstances."

As Stamford rattled on, I found myself increasingly attracted by his proposition. Habit and decency fought a fierce though losing battle within my conscience. In the end, I agreed to meet the man he had in mind—and without saying so to Stamford, I had more or less decided to follow through with the rest of his suggestions. Thus it happened I was introduced to Mr. Sherlock Holmes that very afternoon.

Stamford sent a boy to inquire when we might come by, and the lad returned a short while later. "Mr. Holmes says you should come straight round," he told us with a knowing grin. "He seemed quite anxious to make the gentleman's acquaintance," he added, brazenly winking at me.

"There, Watson!" said Stamford with a chuckle, "your problems are over—at least for the present."

"I hope they're not just beginning," said I.

Holmes received us in his laboratory at the hospital, where he was conducting a series of peculiar experiments. Quite an energetic person, he bounced forward to greet us, extending a large, angular hand, much stained by his careless handling of chemical solutions. "This is indeed a pleasure!" he said brightly. His sharp, gray eyes quickly traveled the length of my body, resting momentarily at my crotch as a smile spread openly across his narrow, aquiline features. A man about my own age, Holmes was quite handsome and appealing despite his high-bridged nose and excessively slender physique. Somewhat taller than I, he was a man of obvious strength and willfulness. "You have been in Afghanistan, I perceive," he added after a momentary silence,. And before I could question this extraordinary statement, he launched into an enthusiastic description of the experiment in which he was presently engaged.

"I've found it!" he told us excitedly. "I have discovered a reagent which is precipitated by hemoglobin and nothing else!"

"That is interesting, chemically, no doubt," I answered, "but practically..."

"Why, man, it is the most practical medico-legal discovery for years! Don't you see that it gives us an infallible test for blood stains? Come over here!" He seized me by the coat sleeve in his eagerness and drew me to the table at which he had been working. "Nice," he muttered absently, as his hand slipped from my arm and grazed lightly across my hip and backside. Then he launched into a description of his experiments and their result, drawing a drop of blood from his own finger to illustrate the point. "Ha! ha!" he cried as the solution underwent an obvious reaction. "What do you think of that?"

"It seems a very delicate test," I remarked. By now I was more than minimally attracted to him, wishing he would forego his scientific endeavors and get more to the point of my visit. The hour was growing late, and I think we were probably the only people left in the laboratory portion of the building.

"Yes, yes!" I see you are impatient," he remarked distractedly. "I shall not burden you with a further discourse on my discoveries. Stamford, I thank you," he said turning to our companion. "If it is agreeable with John, here," he added, smiling at me, "I think we might hit it off just famously!"

There was a brief conversation between Stamford and Holmes, then carried on just outside the range of my hearing. Afterward, my new-found friend invited me to accompany him to his lodgings. "I have just moved into a marvelous suite of rooms on Baker Street," he remarked, "and I am most anxious to christen them." He laughed merrily, clapping me lightly on the back and allowing his arm to remain across my shoulders as he guided me toward the outer door. Stamford followed at some distance, and once outside he slipped discreetly out of sight. Holmes hailed a passing hansom, and we were soon on our way to his flat.

This was all such a new experience for me, and everything had happened in such rapid sequence, I hardly knew what to say or do. Being somewhat embarrassed, I resorted to a chattering dialogue about the people and buildings we passed. Holmes remained largely silent, although he was watching me with a friendly, almost amused expression. Had I known him better I would have been even more disconcerted, for with his uncanny ability to deduce the whole from its constituent parts, I was inadvertently baring my soul to him in a manner I would never consciously have done. At length, he reached across to me, laying his hand gently on my thigh.

I started at the sudden and unexpected contact, glancing sharply at my companion who remained completely unruffled by this show of alarm. "Nothing to fear, old fellow," he said softly, "but you are such a handsome chap, I find it difficult to keep my hands off you. You don't mind, I hope?"

"Well…er…under the circumstances…" I stammered. "No," I managed at last. "No, in fact, it's rather pleasant. Your hand is so warm…and large…."

My companion laughed aloud. "That is quite an interesting comment," he remarked. "Tell me, as a doctor, do you adhere to the belief in a correlation between the sizes of various cartilaginous membranes?" There was a definite twinkle in his eyes, now, and I realized he was alluding to that particular portion of his body that must remain presently hidden from my view.

"I have never given it a great deal of thought," I replied, "but I would suppose there is some logic to support such a conclusion. Certainly, the size of one's hands and feet do seem to bear a predictable relationship."

"Yes, indeed," he muttered. "Yes, indeed." Then, quite boldly, he permitted his fingers to slide across my thigh, coming to rest with the tips of his long, heavy digits against the growing mound between my legs. "Fascinating!" he breathed softly.

Outside, the shadows of evening had lengthened into a cloak of total darkness, with only an occasional gaslight to break the heavy gloom. Inside our hansom it was quite black, and there was little possibility of anyone being able to see us. Taking advantage of this, Holmes leaned his body against me, slipping an arm about my waist and pressing his warm, thin lips tightly on mine. Though surprised at this display of unguarded passion, I was both pleased and excited by it—my arousal only heightened by the potential danger of so public a contact. As he held me ever more tightly against himself, I felt my senses whirl into a maelstrom of lust. Only the sharp, steady "clip-clip" of our horse's hooves penetrated my awareness to remind me where I was.

We were still huddled tightly together when the hansom began to slow, and the driver's voice announced our arrival. "Two-twenty-one Baker Street!" he called.

Holmes paid the driver and conducted me into the house. We proceeded immediately up the stairs; and, although a tall, rather dour-appearing woman looked her head out of a door in the lower hall, my companion seemed to take no notice of her. This, as I would later learn, was Mrs. Hudson, the landlady—or so she called herself. But that is another story! Holmes opened the unlocked door on the upper landing and motioned me inside.

The sitting room was large and comfortable, although my host had obviously not finished his unpacking. Boxes tied with string were stacked against one wall, and several bales of books were piled in a distant corner. Two doors led off the chamber, apparently connecting to a pair of bedrooms. These joined, I discovered, through a bath. There was no kitchen or any sort of cooking facility, for the landlady served breakfast, supper, and afternoon tea as a part of the monthly contract.

In keeping with Holmes' direct and positive nature, he said very little after he closed the door behind us. There was a subtle glow of heat and reddish light from the hearth, but other than this the room was quite dark. Not even taking time to ignite a gaslight, my companion turned to me and encircled my torso with both his arms, drawing me against his slender body with a degree of strength I would hardly have credited to him. Once again, his lips crushed on mine, and this time he forced my mouth to open as his tongue darted between my teeth. There was the heavy, pungent sweetness of aromatic tobacco on his breath and a musky maleness about his body that sent my senses reeling. I returned his embrace with all the urgency of my being, and this response encouraged a fresh surge of passion from him.

It was a delirious moment for me, a deeply absorbing exchange which affected my inner senses as no previous meeting ever had. Thus, from the very beginning, my affair with Sherlock Holmes took on an urgent significance that presaged its ultimate development. I found myself standing loose and helpless as my companion's long, deft fingers worked loose the buttons on my waistcoat, pushing this over my shoulders along with my jacket. He quickly plucked the stays from my shirt, working from the collar down, passing quickly over the center of my body to unfasten the front of my trousers. I was grateful for the lack of fuller illumination, for to be perfectly honest my undersuit was old and rather frayed.

I hardly remember how it happened after this, but my clothes were soon stripped completely from me, and within seconds, it seemed, I was standing stark naked in the middle of the sitting room. His dry, warm palms traced their patterns across my musculature, and his lips made a series of soft, sucking sounds as he explored the contours of chest and groin and midsection. At the time, of course, I was quite young, as I have previously noted, and my body was extremely well-defined. Being blond, I had little hair except at head and pubis, and what there was held so light a hue and so downy a composition it hardly showed under even the brightest lamp.

"Magnificent!' said Holmes in a soft, breathy tone. His lips caressed my shoulder, where the dark scar from my recent wound still showed against the milky skin. Then he dropped his mouth to my left nipple, where he proceeded to draw and knead the flesh while spasms of delight coursed through me. I was quite beyond any recall then, and likewise past caring what circumstances had brought us together. His every motion across my flesh was electric, so fiercely arousing that it left no room for other thoughts. One arm lingered about my waist, the rough tweed of his sleeve serving to emphasize my nakedness as opposed to his own state of being fully clothed. Yet even this produced a certain thrill of expectancy, a sensation of raw and almost savage surrender.

Without disengaging his lips from my nipple, where they continued to cast forth the wildest, most furious waves of euphoric warmth, my companion allowed his free hand to wander gently across the firm ridges of my belly, finally coming to rest upon the full hardness of my penis. Adoringly, almost reverently, his fingers explored the width and extension of my member, grasping the shaft within his palm, and seeming to measure its dimensions against the breadth of his hand. "Marvelous!' he whispered. "John, you are truly an exceptional boy!"

"Hardly a boy," I replied. "I am almost five-and-twenty."

"You still retain the sweetness of youth," he murmured. His lips still worked against my teat, and his voice vibrated through me in heated, thrilling waves. He stood, finally, and crushed me against him, holding me full length across the nubby fabric of his hound's-tooth coat. Through the lighter material of his trousers, I could feel his own responding hardness. From this, as well as from the deeply drawn breaths against my face and neck, I knew he was fully as aroused as I.

Slowly, he began guiding me across the darkened room, toward the door to the left of the hearth. Glancing down, I could see the patches of redness reflected to outline the rigid planes of my body, the shadows delineating each well-formed thew and sinew. Standing proudly erect, above the apex of my legs, my cock arched upward, bobbing in stiff, almost defiant salute in response to the motions of my walking. Protruding through the thick folds of foreskin, the crown glistened in moist evidence of my arousal.

My bare feet soon touched the richer carpet of Holmes' bedchamber, as we continued our progress toward the wide, four-poster bed that stood against the farther wall. With a quick flick of his wrist, my companion stripped the counterpane and blankets, gently pushing me down on my back, upon the cool luxurious satin sheet. This room was even darker than the other, although there was a soft, silvery aura from the street light outside the window. Lying quietly in the darkness, I watched as Sherlock Holmes stood beside the bed and removed his clothes. Carelessly, he tossed these aside until he was down to his undergarments, at which I noted he was wearing one of those new, two-piece sets of vest and drawers. I must have gasped, because I had always thought this somewhat extreme for a gentleman of good taste.

Holmes chuckled when he heard me, and muttered some remark about the greater freedom such undergarments gave him. "Lets the prick and bollicks swing," he added. "Keeps one ready and alert."

His entire body was now exposed to my view, although the forward portions were largely in such heavy shadows that I could not clearly see the form. While unquestionably lean and slender, my companion displayed a far more symmetrical physique than I would have expected. Deeply corded muscles covered his chest and abdomen, while the definition of his arms and legs was really quite exceptional. His erection, while a trifle smaller in circumference than mine, was of phenomenal extension. As I subsequently discovered by actual measurement, it attained to slightly over nine inches from base to tip—this statistic being achieved along its upper lateral.

As if aware of my admiring observation, Holmes stood motionless for several seconds, staring down at me. Totally naked, his hard-flexed frame was softly outlined in lights and shadows by the glow from the street. Watching him, my entire body seemed to burst into flame, and I experienced a passionate desire,

unmatched by any remembrance of previous sensation. I think
he smiled, though this was difficult to discern in the uncertain
light, and abruptly cast himself upon me. Hungrily, he buried his
face against the muscles of my chest and shoulders, applying his
teeth to my flesh as if he indeed intended to devour me. This
generated such a fierce response within me, I lost all awareness
of time or place, and simply clung to him while mounting lust
forced a series of animated groans and protestations of affection from my lips.

I could feel the powerful pressure of his lengthy member
between my thighs, and as he continued to gnaw and suck at my
skin his lips undulated in a steady rhythm, driving the rigid shaft
against the underside of my crotch. My own cock as pressed
between us, crushed and rubbed in tantalizing confinement as the
hard wall of his lower belly moved against mine. Finally I could
restrain myself no longer, for the wild pleasure deriving from his
ferocious assault was exciting me beyond endurance. Using all my
strength, I placed my hands against his shoulders and forcibly
lifted his torso away from me. Twisting quickly, I brought my
head about until my lips lay within grasp of his singular manhood.

I closed about the willowy lance, and Holmes seemed suddenly
to weaken. His body collapsed half upon me, his arms falling
upward above his head as he slowly settled onto his back. His legs
still rested upon my thighs, so I had to bend myself double in
order to maintain my grip about his cock. I began working my
lips up and down along the solid column, drawing him into me
until I choked and sputtered in an effort to force the enormous
projection down my throat. All this while, Holmes reclined with
hardly a movement of his body, silent except for an occasional
groan and the deep, shuddering gasps of his heavy breathing.

My hands grasped the sides of his waist, holding the lean,
hard flesh in place as I ground my face against the coarse, wiry
bristles of his groin. My chin grazed the heavy orbs of his testicles, where they hung in the deeply suspended sac, cradled

between the lower curve of his arse and the bed, itself. The heady aroma of his arousal rose in waves of moist warmth from the depths of his crotch, bringing with it his essential maleness.

At length, his hands moved to stroke the back of my head and neck, and his hips set up a regular, driving pace to propel the slick, hard-risen cylinder against the membranes of my hals. I was trembling with excitement, then, and felt a like response in my companion. Expecting he would achieve a climax at any moment, I quickened my possession, sucking and drawing at his glans to provide the maximum stimulation. Holmes, however, had other ideas.

With an abrupt shifting of his position, he sat up on the bed, yanking his swollen prick from my grasp. Shoving me flat upon my back, he knelt astride my thighs and ground his mouth fully down the length of my penis, taking it totally and completely into him without pause or hesitation. This sudden warm, wet enclosure caused such a spasm of thrilling delight to course through my veins that I dropped my head backward on the pillow and arched upward from my hips and a belly. This drove my questing column more deeply into him, which only seemed to intensify the pleasure he took in its possession. I felt his strong, broad hands close about the cheeks of my arse, lifting me so my pubic hairs were flattened against his nose and cheekbones.

I wanted to shriek with delight, but contented myself with thrashing my head from side to side, and wrapping my legs about him. My calves were shoved tightly into his armpits, my toes touching in the middle of his back. Then he released my penis and dropped his lips to touch my anus, grazing the scrotum with his tongue as he descended. This organ now probed gently at my puckered canal, dabbing hotly, wetly at the tight-closed opening as if asking permission to enter. Finally he inserted the tip, parting the sphincter as his tongue glided within, moistening and lubricating the passage as wave after wave of unbridled passion swept through my body. I was so weak from emotion that I could have denied him nothing, and while I knew he was preparing me for an unaccustomed assault, I did not protest.

Nor did Holmes ask for my consent. After a considerable time, spent probing and preparing the channel, he simply raised his upper body, spat upon his hands, and applied the lubricating film to his lengthy protuberance. Centering the crown against my anus, he adjusted the position of my legs across his shoulders and began to ease himself into me. Because his shaft tended to be slender, the initial penetration was accomplished without undue difficulty. My body responded to him, and I felt the first, pleasurable sensations as his glans slipped past the grip of my muscle-ring.

He paused, then, allowing me to adjust to his possession. I had closed my eyes, so my awareness consisted almost completely of the glorious, swelling euphoria occasioned by my impalement. Gradually, he continued to enter me, pressing his groin ever closer to my willing, unobstructed passage. I was so completely beyond any possibility of retreat by then, I actually pulled him further into me by tightening the pressure of my legs upon his shoulders. He great length slid forward until tiny fingers of pain expanded through my viscera and blinding flashes of light streamed before my eyes. I whimpered softly, begging him to take me, and finally experienced the ultimate joy of feeling his bristly pubic hair collide gratingly against my sac.

Again, Holmes hesitated, permitting both of us to savor the fullness of our joining. Gradually all elements of discomfort subsided, until I was ready for the pounding assault Holmes now began to deliver. I opened my eyes, gazing up at his face in the darkness. He smiled at me tenderly, and bent his neck to kiss me lightly on the lips. "John!" he whispered, simply. "John ..." He said no more; but the expression in his eyes, even the little I could discern in the gloom, denoted a depth of feeling which transcended the basic lust of our interaction.

As he resumed his gentle, pumping motion, rocking and grinding his loins into the cradle of my legs, I seized the hardened shaft of my own penis and began massaging its length in time with the motion of Holmes' body against me. The dual, combined pleasure—his penetration and the flesh stirring in my testicles that resulted from my masturbation—cast me once again into the throes of renewed desire. I shoved my lower body upward to meet his every thrust,—writhing, moaning, trembling as I felt his manhood swell within me. Emotionally, I was just as affected as he, and while I would have denied the possibility prior to our initial meeting, I suddenly realized that it was the first thrill of love that made this moment so complete.

"That a bit of buggery should so completely change one's life!" remarked Holmes several days later. He smiled at me, reaching out to grasp my arm in a firm, warm grip.

"A change for the better, I hope," I returned his adoring look, and placed my palm on top of his, squeezing it gently.

He bent to kiss the back of my hand and chuckled softly. "Very much so!" he whispered.

We were sitting side-by-side on the divan, in what was now our front room. Holmes had insisted I move in with him, and had refused even to consider my sharing the rent. "When you are fully recovered from your illness," he told me, "we can discuss your financial contribution. For the moment, just having you with me is all I could ask."

"I feel rather a fool, not pulling my own weight," I replied.

"Nonsense!" Holmes retorted. "But if it will make you feel better, we shall maintain appearances by telling the world we split all expenses down the middle. In the meanwhile, you can owe me your half, and as this will keep you eternally in debt to me I shall never fear to lose you. An honest fellow like yourself would never think of departing when there is a sum owing his house-mate, right?"

"Right," I admitted.

And so my long, fulfilling relationship with Sherlock Holmes began. To the rest of the world we were a pair of bachelor gentlemen sharing quarters because it was convenient and economical to do so. Between us, once the door at 221B Baker Street was closed against the world, we shared such moments of blissful contentment I doubt anyone outside ourselves could have understood or believed, even if told.

TODD
James Colton

In the hush of the corridor, which still smelled new, his key clicked in the lock. He rushed the door, reached inside, touched a silent wall switch. Quiet light dropped from handsome lamps over handsome furniture. The color plan was charcoal and sand: masculine and brand new. No one had had these rooms before him. They still looked as if no one lived in them. He slept here, bathed here, dressed here. But not often. Box-pleated floor-to-ceiling curtains masked one wall. He touched another thermal switch. A small motor whined. The curtains parted. The wall was glass. The city was out there, asleep with its lights on. Todd didn't take the man's coat—he didn't wear a coat. Just slacks, jacket, crewneck sweater. Todd nodded at a hi-fi rig on glossy modular shelves with a stiff rack of records still in their cellophane.

"Music?" He hoped the man would know how to work the thing. He, Todd, didn't. For weeks it had sat there silent. Not gathering dust, no. There was maid service. Dust hadn't found this building yet. But the components looked lonely, reproachful. They were built to sing and he never let them. When he was here and not asleep, he watched the shifting colors of the television set in the bedroom, watched without seeing. The man who'd bought him the stereo had made it work once—working Todd's cock at the same time. That man had also stocked a kitchen cupboard with liquor. Todd didn't think he himself had ever set foot in the kitchen. He went there now, shedding his topcoat. "I'll fix us a drink."

The kitchen was copper and waxed brick. When he opened the refrigerator, it glowed at him like a scrubbed idiot. Empty. But moronically at work. The ice cube bin was full. He found untouched glasses in an untouched cupboard. From the unopened bottles he chose Jack Daniels and made the drinks strong. He walked with them, into a wash of music. Piano. Chopin waltzes. He'd never looked at the albums, otherwise he'd have thrown that one out. A Chopin waltz was what he'd failed to play the night he'd betrayed his mother, the night Brice had betrayed him. He set the drinks down, jerked up the smoked plexiglass cover, lifted the tone arm.

"I'm sorry." The man turned from the window where he'd stood staring out. He came toward Todd. "I thought you asked for music."

"Not that," Todd said, "not that." Tears scalded his eyes again. The man mustn't see them. He went fast into the bedroom. "Pick out something else. Anything. I'll be right back." In the bathroom's sterile glare, he splashed his face with cold water. But he hadn't shut the door. And when he raised his head, the mirror was there and in the mirror he saw the man. He reached for a towel, making himself smile.

"Don't smile," the man said. "You don't mean it. The crying is what you mean. You're very beautiful, and very sad. That's a combination I find hard to resist."

Todd dried his face and dropped the towel. "Don't resist,

then." He turned, slid his hands under the lapels of the man's jacket, moved them outward on the hard shoulders to take the jacket off. The man stepped away from him. He went back through the dark bedroom into the living room. Todd followed, found him tasting his drink by the record player, staring down at the now naked turntable, moving it with a finger. Todd asked, "What's wrong? Have you changed your mind about me? Look, don't worry about the tears. It's part of my routine. They go for it every time."

"Oh, shut up." The man said it harshly, and his look was harsh. There was a lot of the hawk in him at that instant. "Don't act like a cheap faggot. You're hurt and the hurt goes deep. It was on your face in the piano bar. I didn't need the tears. And you don't need them either, and you don't use them. That's a cheap lie. It's beneath you."

Stung, Todd lashed back, "I've had a lot of things beneath me and I've been beneath a lot of things. What the hell are you? Some kind of saint?"

The man set the drink down. "All right," he said quietly. "My error. Sorry. I'll go."

"Don't go." Todd hadn't known he was going to say it. He didn't know why he said it. He reached out. "Please. Stay. I want you to stay." The man's back was to him. He stood, head bowed, hand on the doorknob. Through the bays of shadow between the lamps, Todd's voice went begging. "Don't leave me alone." He yanked loose the knot of his tie, jerked the tie off. He unbuttoned his shirt. "I'll do anything for you." He threw the shirt away. "What do you like to do?" He unbuckled his belt, tottered, prying off his shoes. "You want to fuck me? That's all right."

He pushed trousers and shorts down his legs in the same motion. "I bet you're really hung. Can I swing on it? You want me to suck you off?" He balanced first on one leg, then the other, tugging off his socks. "You can suck me. Man, I'd come buckets if you sucked me." He walked naked toward the man, kneading his cock, squeezing, tugging, to get it stiff. It got stiff. "Look," he said, "it's on for you. Really on."

The man didn't look. He leaned his head against the door. "Dear God," he said, "will you stop that?"

And Todd knew he should but he couldn't. His mouth went on yammering. "I'll be good for you, man. We'll have great sex, the greatest. You'll see." He grabbed the man's shoulder to turn him. "It'll be wild. You'll never forget it. Ask anybody in town. I—"

The back of the man's hand struck him hard and sudden across the face. The blow turned him around. He hit the couch, fell across it, sprawled on the floor. For a second he lay stunned. Then he rolled over and sat up. He stared at the man. He rubbed his face where the knuckles had stung. He got shakily to his feet. "Get out," he said.

"No." The man shook his head. "You need me."

"I don't need anybody," Todd said.

"Of course you don't." The man took off his jacket and laid it across the couch back. "That's why you've had everybody in town."

"You shouldn't have hit me," Todd said.

"Somebody had to," the man said, "and I'm the only one here." He came around the couch. His look was steady and very gentle. He came close to Todd. He waited. They both waited. Then he took Todd in his arms. Through the rough knit of his pullover, Todd felt the warmth of him, felt the beating of his heart, firm and slow and strong. The man stroked his back. Todd shivered. It felt so good. It was so like Brice all over again. It mustn't be like Brice. He pulled away.

"Leave," he said. "Please leave."

"After you've told me why." The man went back to his drink at the stereo. Tasting it, he looked down thoughtfully, nudging with his boot Todd's crumpled clothes on the sand-colored carpet. He looked up. "What's it all about? The tears tonight. The wound I can't see, the wound you keep tearing open so you can watch it bleed."

"I—" Todd shut his mouth, shut his eyes, shook his head. "I can't. I've never told anybody."

The man chuckled. It was like Brice's, that chuckle. He had the same deep, kind voice. "That's sort of an Alice in Wonderland reason, isn't it?"

"What do you care what hurts me?" Todd said. "I'm a pickup, a trick, something dirty you do when you're out of town you'd never do at home. Something you'll forget all about before your plane touches down in Des Moines."

"Los Angeles," the man said.

"You don't even know my name," Todd said.

"It's under your picture on the poster outside the bar, remember? It was that picture that made me go in. Your picture. Beautiful and sad. Your name is Todd Rowan. I won't forget it. Not when the plane touches down, not ever. But you don't know my name and you don't know a lot of other things about me. For example, that I've never picked up a stranger in my life before."

"Jesus." Todd whispered it. "What lousy luck it had to be me." And he wanted suddenly to make it not lousy luck. His own first time had been so bad. He went to the man and took the drink out of his hand and set it down. He took hold of the edge of the man's pullover and raised it. The man lifted his arms and Todd pulled the sweater off for him. His body was as brown and hard as Brice's, the belly flat and young. Todd put a kiss on his mouth, unbuckled his pants, let them drop, knelt, and pulled the man's shorts down and pulled off his shoes, his socks. He nuzzled the man's cock and balls, felt the cock stiffening. The man's hands stroked his hair.

"I think it was wonderful luck," he murmured. He raised Todd to his feet, kissed him clumsily but with a lot of earnestness. His smile was uncertain, apologetic. "I'm afraid I'm not going to be very good. It's been a long time for me"—his hand found Todd's cock and stroked it—"waiting to find you."

"Come on," Todd said, and led him into the bedroom. He

ripped off the spread that made the bed look like something in a furniture-store show window. He folded back the clean sheets and blankets, sat on the bed's edge, drew the man by his hands to where he could take the dark, wanting reach of his sex into his mouth. Even that was like Brice's: strong, thick. It wasn't light in here. Only a narrow yellow leakage came from the living room. He looked up and couldn't tell that the man wasn't Brice. He needed to be told. With his face against the man's belly, he asked his name.

"George." The chuckle came again. "My parents weren't over-burdened with originality. George William Herbert." Todd had taken his cock in again. "Mmm," he said, "that's good. So good. But if you keep it up, I—" Todd kept it up. This didn't have to be elaborate. The man probably hadn't had it happen to him before. It could be lousy and he'd remember it with a smile, he'd jack off remembering it for years. But it wouldn't be lousy. Not if Todd Rowan did it. Todd Rowan gave good head. It wouldn't be lousy. It would just be quick. "If you keep that up, I'm going to—no, look, wait, stop. I can't—" And that was it. He came, in a shuddering flood, bending above Todd, leaning on him heavily, panting, swallowing. "Ah, Jesus," he whispered, "ah, God, how good, how good."

Todd let the cock out, licked it, nuzzled the balls, looked up, grinning. The man wasn't grinning. His face looked grave. "You did that as if I was nobody," he said. "Nobody at all."

"Aren't you?" He got up, went into the bathroom, snapped the harsh light on, pissed. "You said you'd be gone tomorrow. What do you want me to do? Fall in love with you? There's a thousand miles of nothing between Chicago and Los Angeles. Can you handle that?" He hit the flush lever and turned to face the name in the doorway. "Because I can't handle it."

"Ah." George Herbert nodded. "I see. That's what the crying's all about. Someone you fell in love with, who went off and left you."

"After he promised to take me along. He looked like you." Todd edged past George, their nakedness brushing, meaningless. In the dark, cigarettes lay on a stand by the bed. Todd lit one, shook out the match. He dropped onto the bed, sat with hands hanging between his knees, head drooping. "I was eighteen and I'd never made it with anybody." He mumbled the whole story. He finished, "And when I came back, he'd checked out. No word. No nothing." He'd hoped telling it would help. It hadn't. Smoke from the cigarette burning short in his fingers rose straight and stung his eyes. He ground it out and lay back on the bed. George sat on the bed. His hand came dark and gently smoothed the hair off Todd's forehead. It felt cool, the hand did.

"Let me make love to you," George said.

"It's very late," Todd told him.

"That's what I'm afraid of. And if you let it get much later for you, it's going to be too late forever. You'll never love anyone again. You won't be able to."

"Maybe it's too late already."

"No," George said. "You can still cry."

Todd said and meant it, "You're wise, aren't you?"

"But not skillful," George sighed. "The last boy I had told me if I'd sucked as many cocks as I've written articles I'd still be only fair at it. I haven't. I don't want to."

"Only mine." Todd said it with heavy irony. "That's possible." The man stretched out beside the boy and took him in his arms. "Don't stop believing in possibilities."

"What I've stopped believing in are promises."

"All right, I won't make any." George's mouth went, hungry and tender, down Todd's body till it found his limp cock. It took it in like an orphaned child and raised it with warm and demanding affection. It was a clumsy mouth. Todd flinched once or twice from the edges of teeth. But George knew he wasn't skilled. He didn't try long without help from his hand.

And as it had to happen, it happened.

TAILPIPE TRUCKER
Clay Caldwell

Curly slouched behind the steering wheel of the huge rig, his eyes fixed on the sunlit pavement ahead, the rhythmic throb of the motor crawling up his legs and into his crotch.

"Durn it!" he chuckled aloud. "A couple of hours on the road, and already I'm as horny as a bull in season!"

He'd been up with the dawn, leaving Trag still sleeping at the motel, hustling to the truck depot and checking out the rig, then hitting the highway for Harper's Junction.

"I wonder if Trag's still sleeping off his drunk." Curly often talked to himself when running solo, and his expression sobered. "Curly, you'd best think out things about Trag."

He fumbled a cigarette from his shirt pocket and struggled to light it, trying to keep his gaze on the roadway.

"Last night—maybe he really was passed out...but it doesn't seem possible that a feller could get plowed without knowing it. And he surely wasn't a cherry at getting his little tail rode!"

He inhaled deeply, letting the ash from his cigarette tumble down the front of his unbuttoned shirt. He checked the side mirrors automatically, then frowned.

"Could be you were wrong, Curly...about Trag's wanting to be in Steve's place yesterday. He was mighty rough with that lad, using his belt and pissing up his ass and all...but there was something about the way he acted when—"

There was a battered car creeping along in the lane ahead, and he signaled and pulled out, passing easily, checking clearance in the mirrors and swinging back.

The car's headlights flickered.

"Fruit fly?" Curly questioned aloud, then shrugged. "Nope, I reckon I'd best not take time out from this run just yet."

He lost the slow-moving vehicle in a blast of exhaust, and suddenly he shook his head, amused.

"Curly, you forgot what Trag told you about Harper's Junction! He said there's nothing there, and nothing on the way to-and-from there, either. And your little pecker is bound to get mighty hungry!" He snorted. "Trag never would've passed up that car without checking out those headlight signals!"

He held his foot steady on the gas pedal. The miles of endless pavement clipped past.

"Trag's mighty hard to understand! It's like he's ready to enjoy himself proper-like...only, then he growls about being a trucker as if—lordy, I still don't understand that feller!"

He dropped one hand from the steering wheel and cupped the masculine firmness filling his crotch. Beneath his khaki trousers, his thick-shafted cock lay clearly outlined against the lining of his thigh, and his testicles bulged potently at the base. He fingered the hidden organs for a moment, then chuckled to himself.

"Little pecker," he drawled, "I do believe you're getting fired up from thinking about riding a stud again, but part of that hardness may be that you need to take a leak!"

He let his hand stay motionless until he spotted a road sign announcing REST AREA AHEAD. He signaled and gripped the wheel securely, guiding the rig onto the access road.

A row of newly planted saplings lined the pavement leading to the broad parking area, gleaming restrooms set in a patch of sparse grass at one side. Curly downshifted and braked with sureness, landing in the center of the asphalt some distance from several parked cars. A family was trying to picnic on the lawn, and a woman was hurrying a toddler toward the concrete-block building.

"Trag was right," he murmured. "This isn't the kind of pit stop for a horny trucker!"

He swung out onto the running board, adjusted his crotch, and dropped to the ground.

He was partway up the walk when a husky teenager ambled from the latrine, and both men grinned as their eyes met.

"Howdy," he drawled.

"Hi." The stranger had wavy black hair and strong, masculine features, and his athletic physique was sharply outlined beneath his white shirt and low-slung Levi's. "Nice day, huh?"

"Yup, I reckon so." Curly continued on into the building, then stopped cold and sucked in a deep breath. "Lordy! That lad's as fine-looking a stud as I've seen for some time!"

The large room was well lit and spotless. Curly strode to one of the individual urinals at the far side. He scanned the freshly scrubbed wall for graffiti, shrugged, and unzipped his fly. His fingers dug inside to haul out his warm cock and balls together, and he frowned down at the heavy flesh-column.

"Little pecker, you behave yourself. It wouldn't be proper-like if that feller came wandering back in here and found you all fired up from thinking about how fine he looked!"

He started to piss, waiting hopefully.

No one came in.

"Durn it!" Curly exclaimed as he finished and shoved his genitals back inside his pants, leaving the fly spread open. "I must've misjudged that lad, but he surely did look interested!"

He crossed to the washbasin, splashed his hands and face with cold water, dried himself with paper towels, then stuffed his shirttails deep into his trousers and zipped up.

As he sauntered from the building, he saw the young stranger standing near his diesel, viewing it critically.

"Goddamn!" Curly whispered to himself. "Maybe I was right about that lad after all!"

The youth turned and shot him a big smile as he approached.

"Man, that's some rig you've got!"

"I reckon it does its job," Curly drawled, studying the teenager openly—gleaming black hair...handsome features... white shirt slicked to muscled torso, a tint of suntan showing through the cloth, wisps of dark silk sprayed at the open collar...crotch-bulging Levi's ...thick thighs and legs—"You're hitching?"

"Yeah." He returned Curly's gaze. "How about giving me a lift?"

"I'm heading for Harper's Junction."

"That's where I live."

"Then we might as well travel along together, lad."

"Great!" He thrust out his hand with youthful enthusiasm. "My name's Martin Nelson, but everyone calls me Mike."

"I'm Bobby-Leroy Calhoun," he answered gravely as they shook hands. Then he grinned. "But everyone calls me Curly, Martin Nelson called Mike." Chuckling, he pulled away and started to circle the truck. "Climb up into the cab. We've got some highballing to do!"

Mike was already settled by the time Curly slid behind the wheel, and he gave a pleased laugh as the huge machine rumbled and began rolling back toward the highway.

"Damn it, Curly, I'm glad you braked in for a piss-stop! I've been waiting a couple of hours for a ride."

"It seems like a fine-looking feller like you shouldn't have to wait hours."

"I could've gotten rides with different people, but I dig rolling in a rig like this." He saw Curly fumble for a cigarette, and he quickly pulled two from his shirt pocket, lit them and pressed one between the blond's lips. "I graduated from high school in June. I'm going to try driving a rig myself."

"How old are you, Mike?"

"Eighteen. I'll be nineteen in the fall."

"I reckon you'd best start out riding shotgun," Curly advised thoughtfully, then grinned again. "From the way you just lit that butt for me, I do believe you've learned a bit about highballing already."

The two men relaxed and talked easily.

From time to time, Curly glanced at the husky teenager and found him staring in return.

The miles clipped past steadily.

They stopped for lunch, then went back to the road.

The throbbing sensations from the motor and tires shivered up Curly's legs, and he felt the sex-hunger rise in his loins.

They fell silent. It was mid-afternoon when the blond trucker finally spoke again.

"Martin Nelson called Mike," he drawled formally, "I've been thinking, and I reckon it's time I spoke straight out. How come you're on the road hitching?"

"Once in a while, everything kinda builds up and—hell, it's like I've just got to hitch a ride in a rig."

"You truly enjoy highballing?"

"Yeah. It—It gets me in the nuts...know what I mean?"

"Yup." Curly proceeded cautiously. "And that brings me to another thing. I reckon you've hitched with enough truckers to know that some of us get mighty horny."

"Damn right!"

"Lordy! You sound just like my partner Trag!" He chewed his lower lip for a moment. "Speaking of Trag—if you were hitching with him, he'd expect you to do something in return for the ride."

"Shit, Curly, I know the score!" Mike chuckled easily. "If you're horny—Jesus, I sure as hell don't mind taking you off. As a matter of fact, I've been sitting here half-hard for hours, just thinking about it!"

"I reckon I've been the same way," Curly confessed. "It seems like my little pecker's been somewhat stirred ever since—"

"'Little pecker'?" Mike laughed and slid across the seat to clamp one hand on the massive bulge at the trucker's crotch. "Damn it, there's nothing little about that rod! I've been watching it swell up and—"

"Durn it, Mike! Act proper-like or I may run this rig right off the road!" He felt the youth's hand jerk back, and he sighed. "We'd best wait a bit, lad."

"Keee-rist, what for?"

"Well, I sweat something awful when I'm on the road, and I'd feel better if I was washed up beforehand." He paused and let his huge paw drop from the steering wheel to Mike's thigh. "Also, I've been thinking about playing with that fine hard-on you've been building up."

Mike watched the thick fingers roam toward the hardening ram locked inside his Levi's, and he gulped for breath.

"Curly...uhhh...you—you want to—"

"I figure on making it a two-way street between us, Martin Nelson called Mike."

"Goddamn!" He looked at the rugged blond, his expression suddenly boyishly shy. "Got a place to stay tonight?"

"Nope. From what Trag told me about Harper's Junction, I figured I might as well sleep right here in the rig cab."

"My folks're out of town. Want to stay...with me?"

"Yup." Curly's fingers traced over the powerful, rigid prick outlined inside Mike's Levi's, then drew back and gripped the steering wheel again. "I'd best concentrate on my driving."

"Some—Something wrong?" The youth squeezed his eyes shut. "The size of my dick, maybe?"

"Lordy, no!"

"The guys at school—they've said I'm kinda—"

"From what I felt," Curly drawled, grinning, "I reckon you're hung like more than one trucker wishes he was!"

"Like—Like you, maybe?"

"Yup...if that means anything."

They fell silent again, and the miles clicked past.

The sun moved lower toward the western horizon.

A highway sign marked the city limits of Harper's Junction.

"Curly...want to pull off the road? Let me pay for the ride? You know...like the other truckers?"

"Nope. It seems like you offered me a place to stay tonight, and I reckon I'll settle for that."

"Shit! Goddamn it, I—"

"You're talking trucker-style!" Curly chortled. "You've only been riding shotgun with me for the better part of one day, and already you're talking as rough as my partner Trag!" He sobered and let one hand reach out to rest against the youth's thigh once more. "Mike, if you still wish me to stay with you, you'd best show me where in Harper's Junction you live. I'll drop you off there, and then I'll dock this rig in the depot. And then—well, I reckon we both need to wash off the sweat we've been working up."

"Curly," Mike said thoughtfully, "You sure aren't like the other truckers I've met."

"'Cause I'm somewhat queer?"

"'Cause you're—you're—hell, 'cause you're nuts!"

"Lordy!" Curly exploded with a laugh. "Trag says I'm a crazy bastard, and you say I'm nuts! I do believe I'm truly just me, and that's all." He settled back, smiling. "Now, you give me the directions, shotgun."

The highway became the main street of the small town, a handful of stores bordering clean-swept sidewalks, and Mike guided the trucker down a side road to a tree-lined residential district.

"The neighbors'll crap when they see this diesel," he announced proudly as they braked to a halt in front of a handsome two-story house.

"You'd best get your little tail inside before a friendly police-man comes along and gives us a ticket," Curly advised, and he reached behind the seat for his canvas bag. "You might as well take my gear with you."

"Sure." Mike paused, studying the brawny blond. "No shit, you're the greatest!"

"You're a mighty fine lad yourself," he answered sincerely, then sighed. "But you'd best leave me to finish this run proper-like. The sooner I do that, the sooner we can settle in and enjoy ourselves."

"Damn right!"

Mike swung down from the cab, and Curly watched him hustle toward the house, then eased the truck into gear.

"Durn it!" he exclaimed to himself. "I do believe Mike's some-what special to me already!" He dropped one hand to his heat-swollen crotch. "Little pecker, you'd best behave yourself for a while longer!"

Curly had no trouble finding the truck terminal. He docked in and went through the ritual of shutting down, then checked his schedule with the traffic manager.

During the night, the rig would be unloaded and reloaded for the next day's run back to Middleton.

Finished, Curly sauntered from the depot and headed down the street past the small town's business district toward Mike's home. His leg muscles still quivered with the pounding sensations of a day spent highballing a diesel, and he thrust his hands into his trouser pockets, his fingers digging into the cloth to probe at his genitals. He felt the thick heaviness of his loosened cock and sweat-warmed testicles, and the tingle of renewed sex-hunger rose inside him.

The end of another trucker day...bull-size nuts churn-ing...take the end-of-the-run leak...strip down, cool air lapping at bared body and naked flesh... shower and wash away the grime and weariness...let the need for sex rise and become total and find release—with Mike!

The heel of his work shoes clicked on the wooden front steps as he strode to the front door of the house, and he rang the bell.

There was movement inside, and then Mike opened the door.

The teenager was naked except for a towel knotted about his trim hips, droplets of water still gleaming on his dark, wavy hair, his eyes bright and flashing. A pleased smile lit his handsome features, and his freshly scrubbed bronzed skin shone in the soft light like burnished velvet. His thick neck curved into powerful shoulders, and the hard-etched arcs of his chest were sprayed with sleek silk, his wide, dark nipples showing at each side. His stomach was taut and muscle-plated, and below the towel, his thighs and legs were molded solidly, a bulge of male strength mounded at his crotch.

"I barely had time to shower," he explained, nodding Curly into the house. "How about a drink?"

"I reckon I wouldn't mind," the rugged blond drawled, pleased at his own pulsing excitement. "I only wish I'd gotten here in time to share that shower with you."

They grinned at each other, relaxed and sure of what was to come.

"C'mon," Mike said, suddenly turning toward the stairway at the rear of the entry. "I put your gear in my room. You can shower while I fix you that drink, and then I thought we'd have dinner—hamburgers, okay?—and there's television, if you want to watch it later, and—"

Mike continued talking as he led the way up the stairs, and into a sparsely furnished bedroom. Sunset glow poured in through the windows at one side, and a large double bed stood opposite… newspaper clippings tacked on a bulletin board…a high-school pennant…sports trophies mixed with textbooks on shelves in the corner…two framed photos of diesel rigs…Curly's gear on a chair.…

"This is a mighty fine room, lad."

"The latrine's right across the hall," Mike mumbled. "Make yourself at home…you know… I—I'll go make that drink for you."

The youth darted out the door, and Curly chuckled to himself as he stretched and unbuttoned his shirt.

"Lordy, I do believe that lad's having second thoughts about bringing a trucker home for the night!" He peeled off his shirt and hung it on the back of his chair, and a sheen of sweat washed his golden-tanned torso, the scent of his own body wafting into his nostrils. "Or maybe he's having second thoughts 'cause I smell something awful!"

Still grinning to himself, he stripped completely, pawed his powerful nakedness, and sauntered across the hallway to the bathroom.

End-of-the-run leak...shower...cool water and slick soap foam... lathered palms rubbing over muscled arms and torso... heavy, potent genitals...powerful thighs and legs...wash and rinse down again....

Finished, Curly found a towel and dried himself lazily, then crossed to the shaving mirror and checked his bristly beard.

"Curly," he murmured to himself, "you'd best do the best you can at making yourself properlike for young Mike."

Knotting the towel about his hips, he found the youth's razor and shaving cream, and he grinned happily as he shaved.

Satisfied at last, he went back to the bedroom. Mike was waiting, offering a drink, his eyes shifting rapidly over the blond's rugged frame.

"Drink, Curly?"

"Thanks." He drank deeply, returning the towel-clad youth's gaze, and then he set the half-emptied glass on the dresser. "That's a fine drink, lad, but at the moment, I do believe I'm more interested in something else."

"Me, too!"

The two men faced each other and moved together until they barely touched. They stood motionless for a long moment, and then Curly put his hands on Mike's hips, loosening his towel and letting it drop to the floor. The youth gulped for breath, then stripped the burly blond. They locked together hungrily.

"Goddamn!" Curly exploded, and he held the teenager strongly, feeling his masculine nakedness and their fast-hardening pricks trapped side by side. "Martin Nelson called Mike, if you've changed your mind about shacking up with this trucker tonight, you'd best say so right now!"

"Shit, I'm just as fuckin' horny as you are, y' sonofabitch!"

"Lordy!" Curly chuckled. "That's mighty pleasing to know! You see, my poor little balls've been working overtime all day, 'specially since you climbed aboard the rig to ride shotgun with me!"

"Damn it, Curly—" Mike snickered softly. "Like I told you before, you're the greatest!"

"And like I told you, it's going to be a two-way street between us."

They shared a silent special-fine moment...the rugged, drawling trucker and the dark-haired young hitcher...naked and hard up...arms embracing each other...bodies fully met...sharing... understanding....

They eased down onto the bed, still locked together.

The curves and hollows of Mike's strong body fit to Curly's...heaving chest...taut stomach...flat, hard belly...rigid cock...pulsing testicles...powerful thighs and legs....

"Horny trucker!" Mike murmured.

"Horny shotgun!" Curly answered quietly. "Lordy—"

"Awww, shut up, y' dumb shitkicker!"

Curly felt the husky youth squirm against his broad chest...lips nuzzling the golden silk...the full-arched pecs...the wide, hard-tipped nipples, first one and then the other....

Curly was a trucker, brawny and blond and sex-hot from running the rig from Middleton to Harper's Junction. But when he'd been a young'un growing up back home, he'd traded hand jobs with the other lads and found out that it felt mighty fine to spurt his come ...and then there'd been that first feller who'd sucked his little pecker...and he'd sucked that feller in return because it was only proper-like...and so many others had taught

him so much while he was growing up and taking to trucking
and—

Curly lay back and felt the young hitcher's lips and tongue
trace downward over his nakedness toward his surging cock. It
was somewhat strange that he felt the teenager was only trying
to pay him for the ride…. Lordy, there'd been so many hitchers
he'd made suck his cock! Yup, Trag didn't know about that—
about the way he'd made hitchers suck or get fucked…
"trucker-style!" Nope, not exactly…

Curly was lying on this bed in Mike's room, and Mike was
crawling down between his legs, seeking his little pecker—and
it wasn't like being with those other cocksuckers or asslickers
or fruit flies or—Mike's mouth covered the bulging head of
Curly's hard cock.

"Lordy!"

Curly knew durn well that he was hung somewhat larger than
most fellers, and he didn't grip the hitcher's head and ram it
choking-deep on his soaring iron just to get his rocks off. He
wondered if his partner Trag would understand such feelings….

"Martin Nelson called Mike," Curly drawled softly, "I do
believe I wish this special time to last…and I do believe my little
pecker's too fired up to hold back much longer!" He gripped
the youth's head, not to slam him down on the turgid giant but
to drag him up from it. "Durn it, you stop that so we can do this
proper-like!"

"Shit, I know how to—"

"Do what I say, shotgun!"

Mike pulled up on his knees, staring down at the cock-hard
blond, then pawing his pecs with his palms. He was young—
teenaged…athletic…tanned and husky…a hitcher who'd taken
off truckers 'cause— hell, highballing in a rig gets a guy horny,
right?—and his prick was so goddamn hard and aching…and
the drawling shitkicker called Curly was lying back and grinning up at him…and the sonofabitch was so goddamn—

"Damn it, Curly—"

"I reckon highballing makes you as horny as it does me, shot-gun." He viewed the husky young'un—the strong, eager features… the muscled shoulders and arms…the heaving chest, conelike nipples at each side…the huge ram jutting iron-stiff from the thick tangle of pubic hair, thin-sacked nuts drawn up beneath the swollen shaft…thigh muscles quivering —and he felt mighty pleased. "Mike, I wish to—well, you'd best crawl up here and let me taste your pecker and balls—"

"Yeah!" He remembered another trucker who'd been so goddamn male…and who'd wanted to fuck and get fucked and—"Damn right, y' lousy bastard!"

Mike rocked forward, and his massive cock slammed toward Curly's face, the broad shaft traced with taut veins, the bulging crown gleaming with heat.

Still smiling, Curly ran his palms up the youth's tensed thighs.

"You're a mighty fine-looking lad, and I do believe you're as well hung as any feller I've known." He let his fingers creep into Mike's crotch and touch his huge testicles gently. "I figure on getting durned well acquainted with every part of you, but right now I'd say you're as fired up as I am!"

And he raised his head and caressed the churning balls with his lips.

Mike groaned with pleasure as he felt the tongue-lapping and the tantalizing suction on his throbbing nuts.

"Awwww…Curly…ahhhh…."

The burly man gripped Mike's hips for support and shifted his lips to the youth's towering hard-on—the turgid shaft…the hard-ened undercord…the wide, cleanly marked collar…the inflamed glassy crown. He took the pulsing flesh-column deep into his mouth, and the fresh, exciting taste of maleness flooded into his throat.

He looked up at the husky, naked young man looming over him, and let his hands rise, stroking the pale, flat belly, the muscle-plated stomach, the full chest, silky hair, and sharp-tipped nipples.

Mike took a deep breath, and then a broad smile lit his handsome features.

"Curly, you're the goddamnedest trucker I've ever met!"

Curly dropped his hands to the youth's waist again, then released his powerful prick and lay back, grinning.

"I truly wish to suck your fine little pecker," he drawled honestly. "But I'm not worth much when it comes to doing it when I'm lying on my back like this." He gripped Mike and rolled him over onto the bed with surprising ease, then twisted against him. "Now, you rest back and—"

"Sheee-it!" Mike exploded, almost laughing. "You said this was going to be a two-way street, remember?" And he broke into a mock drawl. "Lordy, you'd best switch around so I can take on your fine little pecker while you take on mine!"

"Durn it, if you're making fun of the way I talk—" Curly stopped in mid-sentence, and he met Mike's gaze directly, his voice losing the amused easiness. "Mike, I don't remember wishing to share this special-fine time with a lad more than I wish to share it with you. It's got nothing to do with my being a horny trucker—although I do believe that highballing a rig does seem to get both of us somewhat fired up!"

"Damn right!"

"And it'd be mighty pleasing if we shared—"

"Christ, that's what I've been trying to tell you!" Mike groaned. "Twist around so we can sixty-nine, y' crazy bastard!"

"Durn it, I'm getting somewhat tired of being called a 'crazy bastard!' That's what Trag's been calling me ever since we started out on this long-haul, and—" He chortled and swung around, offering his massive ram to Mike's lips as he faced the youth's turgid counterpart. "Young Martin Nelson called Mike, I do believe—"

"Awww, shut up and start sucking before I shoot my load in midair!"

"Yup!"

Curly looked down at the naked youth...the strong, maturing body...the handsome features...the warm lips lapping the tip of his swollen prick...sucking it base-deep...and he eased forward to suction Mike's potent ram into his mouth and throat.

When he'd been a young'un, Curly had sucked and been sucked, fucked and been fucked...grown up to be a trucker... lordy... yup....

He sucked the cock of the cocksucker who was sucking his cock...Martin Nelson called Mike...mighty fine lad...hitcher riding shotgun in the rig on the road to Harper's Junction...durn-fine young'un...durn-fine cocksucker!

Curly felt the surging desire rise in his loins, and he locked his arms about Mike's hips, cupping the narrow cheeks of his ass in his palms as he gulped on his massive iron hungrily. He heard the youth's muffled groans of growing ecstasy, and he pumped his quivering ram into the willing mouth and throat.

Together the two men raced toward the summit of climax, hovered on the precipice for an instant, then plunged into the consuming pleasure.

They clung to each other, come-spurting, swallowing, gasping and moaning, sharing the ultimate moment...hot, thick sperm gushing...swirling fury exploding...again and again...pent-up maleness unloading...slowing...lingering...finally ending.

Curly drifted back to reality, still locked up to the relaxing youth, and he swallowed the last races of come from Mike's softening prick before releasing it and settling on his back.

"Lordy!" he murmured as he felt Mike pull away from his fading cock. "That was mighty pleasing, lad!"

"Keee-rist!" Mike exploded with a laugh, and he twisted about to sprawl flat on top of the naked man. "It was the greatest!"

"Yup, I reckon so!" He embraced the young athlete and stroked his powerful shoulders and back. "I'd best warn you, shotgun—I figure on riding that fine little ass of yours before this night is over."

"Hell, I'm no cherry." Mike chuckled and broke into a mock drawl. "Trucker, I do believe I aim t' ride my little pecker int' that tail of yours, too."

"I'm willing." Curly sighed. "Durn it, young Mike, you'd best climb off of me so I can dry myself proper-like. I sweat something awful, 'specially when I'm enjoying myself as much as I am right now!"

Curly stared at the night-dark ceiling and grinned to himself.

There he was, a goddamn trucker staying overnight in a nowhere hick town called Harper's Junction where Trag had warned him there would be no action, and one of the finest young'uns he'd ever met was curled up barebutt beside him, dark-haired head on his shoulder, hand on his chest, heavy genitals pressed against his thigh.

Lordy, what a day it'd been! Leaving Trag to sleep off his drunk—maybe Trag truly was passed out when he'd gotten himself fucked last night...highballing the rig and growing so awful horny...stopping to take a leak and picking up a hitcher...Martin Nelson called Mike...talking with the lad and getting to know him...wishing to share their maleness...and having it happen so durned proper-like!

Yup, they'd showered and shaved...and young Mike had fit up to him, sure and honest...and they'd sucked and traded their juices—durn it, Mike's little pecker was somewhat large, like Trag's and Curly's...and the lad surely wasn't shy about pleasing a feller and being pleased and saying so straight out...and sharing the shower afterward so Curly could wash off the sweat he'd worked up...and laughing and joking and having dinner full-naked...and letting it all happen so easy-like, coming back to Mike's room and fucking and sucking...and...making love....

"Curly?" Mike whispered. "Are you asleep?"

"Nope." He felt the youth's fingers trickle across his hairy chest, and he stifled a chuckle. "I was just lying here wishing for a cigarette and not wishing to untangle myself from you in order to reach for one."

"Shit!" Mike bounced up, grabbed two cigarettes from the bedside stand, lit them, and shoved one between the grinning blond's lips. "I guess a copilot's supposed to butt his partner anytime, right?"

"It depends." Curly inhaled, blew a stream of smoke into the darkness, then put out one hand to touch the brawny teenager's thigh. "You aren't old enough to copilot a rig, but I do believe I'd be mighty pleased if you'd ride shotgun with me once you've finished up with your schooling."

"Honest?"

"Yup."

Mike fumbled for an ashtray, found it, placed it between them on the bed and lay back.

They finished their cigarettes in silence.

"Bobby-Leroy Calhoun called Curly," the husky teenager whispered, and his voice was honest-soft, and not mock-drawling any longer, "I've never met a trucker like you before. You're the greatest!"

"I reckon I've come to feel the same way about you, young Mike. Maybe getting to know each other while we were high-balling today helped."

"It helped get me as horny as hell—that's for sure!" Mike laughed easily and put the ashtray aside, squirming back against the burly blond. "Damn it, I bet I have a hard-on all the time when I'm running shotgun with you!"

"I'll have to break you in on running barebutt like my partner Trag and I—"

"Curly," the youth interrupted seriously, "Trag— your partner—are you guys lovers?"

"Lordy, no! We've taken turns with fellers at pit stops and the like, but Trag doesn't—" He rested on his side and put one hand on Mike's high-arched chest to stroke the slick, sparse hair against the bronzed curves, his expression thoughtful. "I sucked him off for the first time last night, so I reckon he knows I'm queer."

"What'd he say?"

"Not much. He'd been drinking, and he seemed to pass out afterward." He gave Mike a self-conscious grin. "I was mighty fired up, so I plowed my little pecker into his tail, but maybe he was too passed out to know I did it."

"Bullshit! I sure as hell knew it when you fucked me tonight!"

"And I reckon I truly enjoyed having you ride me!" Curly let his fingertips trace over the youth's tight stomach, then nodded at the huge, limp flesh-column dangling between his thighs. "I do believe that cattle prod of yours gave me as fine a ride as I've ever had!"

"'Cattle prod'?"

"That's what Trag calls my cock. Durn it, he talks mighty rough at times…about screwing a feller with a motorcycle tailpipe and such."

"I met a guy like that once. It turned out he wanted to get belted and fucked and pissed on—all sorts of crazy shit like that."

"You did it?"

"Yeah. If that's what turned him on, it was okay with me."

"I reckon I feel the same way about doing what a feller wishes to have done." Suddenly he dropped his face to Mike's chest and nuzzled the large, dark nipples with a snicker. "What turns you on, young'un?"

"You do, you crazy bastard!" He rolled against Curly and gripped the trucker's heavy, flaccid cock. "Damn it, I like playing with your cattle prod when it's soft."

"It won't stay that way long if you keep on playing with it."

"Good!"

They locked together and let their powerful rams stiffen side by side.

"Durn it, lad, we surely do seem to fit together properlike!"

"Curly...want to fuck me again?"

"Yup, I do believe that'd be most pleasing to me." He cradled the young athlete in his arms for a long, silent moment, then eased him down onto the bed. "Now, you lie there on your back this time so I can gaze on what a fine feller you are while I'm easing myself into you."

Mike stretched out and watched Curly reach for the tube of lubricant on the bedside table...big, rugged, drawling trucker... wavy blond hair...strong, farm-boy features...huge shoulders and arms...barrel chest, tanned and washed with sun-bleached silk...thick-muscled physique...massive, throbbing cock...horny goddamn trucker!

"Curly? Anyone ever tell you you're beautiful?"

"Lordy, no!"

"You are. You're the most beautiful, crazy bastard trucker I've ever known!"

"Sheee-it!!" Chortling, he shifted to kneel between the youth's spread legs, one pawlike fist pumping his inflamed iron and covering it with shining grease. "Maybe I'm getting used to being called a 'crazy bastard,' but I'm not sure I'd ever get used to—"

"Mind if I say that I love you, Curly?"

The husky blond paused, staring down at the naked youth he was ready to fuck...dark hair...honest, handsome face...maturing athletic body...durned big little pecker fired up and slapped back against taut, pale belly...fine big balls exposed....

"Nope, lad, I don't mind. I'm not much at love-talking, but I do believe I just might try to—"

"Goddamn!" Mike roared. "What're y' tryin' t' do, y' stinkin' sonofabitch? Tryin' t' queer a fuckin' trucker like me?"

"Lor-deee!" Curly howled. "You're talking trucker-style, and I haven't even finished breaking you in to riding shotgun!"

Their eyes met, and Curly's amusement settled into a gentle grin, pleased and honest...understanding.

Mike nodded and cocked his knees, exposing the cleft in his ass.

Curly gripped his folded legs and rocked him back on his shoulders, poised the glistening cockhead toward the shadowed crack...nudged it inward...found the tensed opening...thrust....

"Curly!"

"Easy, shotgun...yup, I don't wish t'—there!"

"Yeah!!"

The blond trucker's huge cockhead was locked deep in the young hitcher's straining asshole, and he hunched forward slowly, driving it deeper... deeper ...deeper!

"Mike—?"

"Partner!"

Curly was a rugged, tough trucker, and he'd plowed his massive prick into plenty of fellers, sometimes gently, sometimes mighty rough...and Martin Nelson called Mike was lying back and grinning up at him, sharing the something-special feelings, maybe....

"Yup...partners...you and me, young Mike... *Damn right!*"

"*Yeahhhhhh!*"

Curly pumped his ram into the willing youth... fast...hard...slow...almost lazy...again and again... male-proud and knowing young Mike wanted it to last....

"*Lordy, shotgun!*"

"*Now, Curly! Nowwww!!*"

"*Agggggghhhhh!!*"

Curly wrapped his arms about the writhing youth and wrenched back, hauling Mike up on his pulsing iron...sinking back on his haunches, the squirming young'un pinioned on his soaring cattle prod...both of them locked together...then—

"*Awwwwwwhhhhhh!*"

Curly clutched the muscular athlete in his embrace, Mike's thick, hot come spewing up over his stomach and chest, his own convulsing climax pouring into the youth's guts—

"*Lordy!! Lordy!!*"

"*Ahhhhhhhhhh!!*"

"Goddamn, Mike! Yeah! Shit!…Awww!… Goddamn!!"

They held together, the sperm draining, the moment of climax fading…sinking…relaxing….

"Martin Nelson called Mike," Curly whispered at last. "Still wish to love-talk?"

"Yeah…more than ever, y' crazy bastard!"

"Me, too." He sucked in a slow breath, then shivered. "Durn it, shotgun, I've worked up another sweat! I'd best shower proper-like and—"

"Not yet…let's stay like this a little longer."

"Yup." Curly let his lips graze over Mike's forehead, then found himself kissing the young'un lightly on the mouth. "Lordy, yes!"

THE HEIR
John Preston

The War had ended. There were only nine men left from one of the armies. They lay together, each with his hands and feet bound. They were in misery, not from any injuries—no one who had been wounded had survived—but from the fact that they were alive. It was somehow dishonorable to have been the only ones to have not died in battle. They were shamed.

There were over thirty survivors from the other army. In the strange way such things work, they were the victors. They sat around a campfire and, even though their families and friends were dead, they celebrated their victory. They drank and sang and thanked their god that they lived and conquered.

It wasn't that they were without sadness. There were moments when memory would creep into their words and the group would become somber. But there was hope. And, because there were more of them, they were not shamed. They had captured the last of the vanquished army. They could go on.

In the morning the thirty and more men from the winning side woke. They went to the lake and splashed water on themselves. They regathered and they relighted the fire in their campsite. They drank a beverage made from water and herbs heated on the fire and talked seriously about what they were to do.

They were young, as were their captives. There were few of either group who were as old as eighteen years. Their army had taught them to fight, but they now had to decide what other skills they had among themselves. How were they to organize? There was one who had been an officer in the army. They agreed they had no better way to pick a leader than to have him remain in control. He accepted and took over their discussion. This officer asked each one of them questions about his knowledge. The new leader told them about the weather in this place. And he said what they had already expected to hear. There possibly were no other people remaining but themselves and their nine captives.

The captives could not understand the victors' language and couldn't follow the discussion. They remained in their bondage and waited to die: They expected nothing else to be the outcome of The War. They whispered among themselves that the quicker death came the better, the shorter would be their shame for having lived while their comrades had died.

The victors had discovered a wide range of skills among themselves. One man knew how to be a blacksmith and even had some rudimentary tools with him. The men debated what could be made by the smith and one of the ideas presented a whole new concept to them. The smith could make chains and with chains they could keep their prisoners securely. They would no longer have to guard them so closely to make sure they didn't break through the rawhide thongs with which they were tied.

They also learned that one of the victors knew the language

of the captives. He could be their overseer until a single language evolved.

Their conversation about these new developments took much of the day and there were many decisions made. The smith went to work soon after, scavenging through some nearby ruins to find what he needed. He worked through the night and all the next day.

When he told the others he was ready, they went to the captives. The nine men did not resist. They looked forward to their deaths. Their shame would end.

They stood listlessly as their clothing was ripped away and did not try to run when their bonds were undone. Even if the victors hadn't been standing there to stop them, the captives would not have tried to flee. They had agreed among themselves that the truth was obvious, just as it had been to the victors. There were no other people left after The War. There was no one to whom they could escape.

Then one of the captives was grabbed by a pair of the victors and taken to the smith. His arms were held securely. The smith brought pieces of searing hot metal first to one wrist, then to the other. With quick, expert motions he hammered at the metal and then, ignoring the screams of the captive, he ducked hot metal and hands into a waiting pail of water. He moved quickly to do the same to the man's ankles and then his neck. Chains had been made or salvaged from the ruins, lengths of them were used to join the two wristbands and then the two anklebands together. The captives were astonished.

One by one, the process was repeated and each of the captives was soon standing naked with painful burns beneath the heavy metal restraints on his wrists and the collar around his neck.

They were led away by the one who knew their language. He used still another piece of long chain to link them to one another and then to an enormous tree which they could never damage with their hands, the only weapons left to them.

"You are to live," the victor explained in their language. "But you are to be slaves. There is no reason to fight us and there is no place to which you can escape. You must resign yourselves."

After he left, the captives spoke quickly among themselves. What were they to do? They did not notice that they were already speaking in whispers, anxious not to draw their masters' attention. One finally said, "We do not know what this life will be. We have no idea. We cannot all kill each other. Perhaps we are meant for this as part of our shame for losing The War. Let's wait. Let's see what this means."

In the morning, the man who had been assigned to oversee them woke them with rough shakes. He had them stand in a line and he looped the long chain which had held them to the tree between their legs, attaching it to each of their handcuffs. Now they had to stand in line and they could not lift their arms.

The victors approached them and newly made packs were hung from the backs of the captives. The packs were heavy burdens, but not one said anything; there seemed to be no cause. The victors also carried heavy packs. They were taking everything that could be moved on a long, long journey. The victors formed themselves in a circle, actually a long oval line, around the captives and on the order of their officer they began to march. The overseer had found himself a long switch of subtle birch and now used it to flick at the bodies of the new slaves, signaling them to move forward.

At first it was very difficult and awkward. The chains between their feet were a limitation that the captives had never experienced before. Nor had they ever had to move in such a limited line. But by the end of the day they had learned to calibrate their steps so they never had to fight against their restraints and they learned to move in a fashion that never brought the links up too sharply on any one man's groin.

The victors sang songs as they marched. The captives were silent and pondered the end of The War that had left them alive and in this horrible position.

They all, captives and victors, fell into an exhausted sleep at the end of the first day. They woke at dawn and started walking as soon as they had eaten a small meal from the stores in the victors' packs.

So they continued for six days, eating only twice a day, marching until they could march no more. The victors sang their songs and the captives pondered their fate in silence. On the seventh day, the victors stopped the caravan at noon. Even warriors must rest, they told one another.

They were lucky to have come to a beautiful river, one with sweet water and many fish that they were able to catch with their spears. They built a huge fire in the middle of their makeshift camp. There were still some spirits left in their packs and they began to drink.

The overseer took some small pity on his charges. Their bodies were caked with filth and sweat. He led the nine to the river and into the water that was cool and refreshing. As much as their predicament had weighed on them, they were delighted by the sensation. They became playful, as much as they could in their chains, and they splashed handfuls of the river over each other, and laughed.

They were led back to their place just outside the circle of the campfire. The long chain was once again looped around the trunk of a mighty tree and they relaxed. Their overseer brought cooked fish for them. He left it in one large bowl and the nine men shared it. They luxuriated in the overseer's largess and they talked more than they had since before the journey began.

"They treat us strangely," said one. "The birch switch has been used only once, in the beginning. They feed us as well as they feed themselves."

"Better," corrected one. "I've noticed. I paid particular attention the time they hunted. There were too many men to feed well off one boar. But they cut large pieces for us and only afterward did they themselves eat."

Another added, "And the way they march around us is strange. They needn't guard us so closely. We can't escape."

"They are protecting us," one of them finally said. "They don't want a wild animal—a stag or a large cat—to attack us. And they feed us to keep us strong. Everyone has to carry a large pack, but ours are the heaviest and as they go along they take food and provisions from their own, not ours, to make their loads lighter while ours remain heavy."

"They protect us?" another said. "You would think they would be more willing to have us attacked than one of their own."

"But we have value for them. We carry the heaviest of burdens for them. They want us to make their load lighter."

Silence descended. Then one said, "It is the price we pay for living. It is our shame made real."

"We do not have to accept this. We can find a way to die."

"We will live and pay the price in order to see if the future will be better." One of them said this with conviction and they were silent for a long, long time.

The victors had begun to grow rowdy. They sang more fervently as they drank and enjoyed their feast day. Lewd jokes were told. It seemed that each man had a story to tell about his feats of great lustfulness before The War. But now there were no more women. They did not talk about that. They told their jokes and drank. Slowly they went to the outskirts of the circle and most fell asleep.

But three had been assigned to guard the captives. They stood with their spears and laughed at their lewdness long after their comrades slept.

One of them in particular looked longingly at the naked bodies of the youths who slept in chains so close to him. He finally succumbed to the drink and told the others what he wished to do to those nine captives. The other two joked at first, making the first seem foolish. But then one said in a serious voice, "They are only slaves."

No other words were needed. They moved to the first three captives and shook them awake. They held knives to the captives' throats and told them they were to open their mouths and take the needing cocks of the victors for pleasure. All three protested and one claimed to wish himself dead first. But their chains had more weight in them than that of metal and their resignation was more intense than that of men who had only lost a war. Their mouths opened. The three guards used them roughly and quickly and then let the captives fall back to sleep.

"We will tell no one," said the first guard, being the one used to guilt and the need for secrecy.

"No one," the others agreed.

The party continued its march. The overseer had let his charges know that they were moving southward. There might be, far from the arena of The War, other people. In any case, there was warmth, less need for shelter and more likelihood of fruit and game. That was the reason the officer had told them they must go such a great distance.

The feast day had become something the victors looked forward to. The officer recognized this. So long as there would be that, he could convince his men to push themselves the remaining days. At the next feast day, they found a lake. It was wide and a deep, beautiful blue. There was a slight plateau not far from it, and this was where the officer chose to make camp. There were fish to be caught and there was game in the forest nearby. The overseer had his charges wash once more and, as he had before, attached them to a tree where they could rest under watchful eyes.

There was a great meal and spirits for the victors. When most had gone to sleep and it came time to change the guard on the slaves, there were six guards, not three; for each one of the original ones had confessed the secret of sexual release to a friend and that friend had wanted to join the guards.

The captives had never talked about this new shame among

themselves, nor had any of them mentioned it to the overseer. But as soon as they saw the six men, each with his hand on his hardening cock, the slaves knew what was to happen. They made the same protests and received the same threats. One by one they submitted to use and one or two cried in deeper shame than he had ever known before. But it was their fate and they had to do this to live.

The overseer became suspicious the next day as he led the nine captives on their march. They were more silent than before. That night at camp he discovered the truth, for once six men had used the slaves, it became something that was talked about by more and more of the victors. The overseer went to the officer in charge and explained what had happened. What was to be done?

The officer thought long and hard, "It is best to make this a part of the feast day celebration. There is no value in hiding it. It is stupid and potentially dangerous to leave this only to drunken guards. Those six will be reprimanded for their actions. Their punishment," the officer smiled, "is that they will not be able to use the prisoners for two more feast days. But the rest of the men can take their pleasure at will.

"This may be useful," the officer went on thoughtfully. "It may help us with the captives. Their memories go back to before The War, and they may harbor thoughts of freedom. If our plan is to work, they must be made subservient and compliant. This will be better than pain."

The next feast day the company found itself at the foot of a large waterfall. Their campsite was small, and the victors made their resting place closer to the water than usual.

The overseer took his charges and led them under the fall. The victors could see the slaves' naked bodies as the sparkling water fell on them. Men who had never noticed the captives as anything but enemies or beasts of burden saw them anew in the closing hours of the day. They experienced new thoughts and desires and probably would have become upset and confused if the officer hadn't called them together.

He announced a tribunal. As the leader, he announced, it was his duty to sit in judgement of the warriors.

The men's backs stiffened. Discipline, to their knowledge, hadn't been a problem. They didn't know why there should be a trial. The officer told them about the six guards and what they had done.

Tension surged through the victors as they listened. Only minutes before they had each watched the bodies of the slaves under the fall, and now their fellows were to be judged for having done just what they had thought of doing. Shame was a new experience for the victors.

But the officer explained that the actions of the guards had not necessarily been bad. What had been wrong was the way the guards had gone about it, in the dark, under the influence of spirits and selfishly, secretly keeping this pleasure to themselves when it belonged to everyone.

"It belongs to us?" one man asked aloud, giving voice to the confusion they were all lost in.

"They are slaves. Their bodies are for our use. They carry our packs and they are manacled with our chains. Why shouldn't we use them in that way as well? This should be done every feast day. It is not right that they should look forward to this day of rest as much as we do. They should still labor. But on feast days, they shall labor for our pleasure."

The overseer turned to the captives. He told them what the officer had told him to say: "Your bodies are for our use every feast day. You must resign yourself to this. You will be chained after you are bathed and they will come to you as they please. You will give them service as they request it. You will not complain. I have been good to you. Not once have I used a whip nor have I abused you. If you do not give service, I shall do these things. This I promise you."

They say, chained once again to a tree. Finally one said, "It is the price we must pay to live." They were all resigned.

They had, in fact, been resigned to this since the previous feast day. Once there had been six guards using them, they had known there would be more. A wide river had been crossed at one point in their journey. If they had chosen to, the captives could have drowned themselves. They had discussed this idea and dismissed it. They would live.

At night, even before they were drunk, the victors began to come and use the slaves. The officer was the first, making sure none of his men hesitated. He came to the line of freshly-bathed slaves and saw that one was more beautiful than the rest. The officer undid his clothing. He let it drop to the ground. The handsome slave looked up at the officer's erect penis. There were tears in his eyes. He leaned forward, not waiting for a command, not needing one, and took the officer in his mouth. Perhaps because there was daylight, perhaps because this was now the third of the victors to use him, the slave did not just open his mouth and allow it to be used. He didn't just rest on his haunches and wait to have the cock gag him and ram his throat. Instead he made the movements himself. He ran his tongue over the cock and caressed it with his chained hands as he did so. When the officer came, yelling his pleasure, the slave did not move, but let the fluid run into his stomach.

The officer put his uniform on once again. His hand rested on the handsome slave's head for the briefest of moments. Then the officer left. The handsome young captive felt more shame than before and he could not look his fellows in the eye. But he felt other emotions as well.

So all the victors, except the six to be punished, used all the slaves that feast day.

SLAVES OF THE EMPIRE
Aaron Travis

Magnus the gladiator ran the whetstone down the length of his long sword. Sparks flew from the glittering steel. Whetting blades was work for one of the attendants; but before a match, Magnus preferred to tend to this necessity himself.

He set the whetstone aside and pressed his thumb against the sword's edge. The blade could not be keener. Magnus sprang to his feet and swung the sword above his head, thrilled as a child at the sharp slicing wind of its passage through the air.

Magnus heard the distant roar of a thousand voices cheering. The sound erupted from the short hallway that led from the gladiators' quarters into the arena, signaling that the bout between Tardis and Urius had been decided. From the enthusiasm of the crowd's response, the victor had been the mob's favorite, the tall, fair-headed Urius.

Magnus frowned. He despised Urius. The young gladiator was hardly twenty, four years younger than Magnus, his smooth, sun-bronzed flesh as yet unscarred by the ravages of the arena. Urius was blond, with a shaggy straw-colored mane of hair cut on the Vandal style, square-jawed and clean-shaven with high cheekbones and heavy lips. He was handsome as Apollo, and a genius with the net and trident.

Urius was the new darling of the mob. The plebeians had begun to cheer for him almost as loudly as they cheered for Magnus—and to bet on him almost as heavily. The nobility had taken to inviting Urius to their private feasts; not long ago, only Magnus, of all the gladiators, had been accorded that privilege.

Though they often attended the same orgies, the two gladiators never spoke to one another, and never drank from the same passing wine cup. When they occupied the same room, they kept conspicuously apart, radiating opposing energies from their opposite corner: Urius was light and Magnus darkness. They had both been favored by the gods; in a crowded room, the eyes of all others went back and forth between them. Urius was taller, but Magnus was more massive, his trunk and limbs as hard as hammered bronze. Urius' features were lean and classic; Magnus' face was broad with large, striking features, framed by the tangled curl of his hair and his beard. Where Urius was smooth as glass, jet-black hair washed over Magnus' broad chest and bristled across his massive forearms.

It was not the envy of a plain man for a handsome one that had made them enemies, it was their difference as men.

As Magnus had judged from the tumult of shouting, Urius had won his match. The young fighter came swaggering in from the arena and stood for a moment framed in the stone doorway of the gladiators' quarters, his trainer's arm reaching high to circle his broad shoulders. His arms and legs were covered with dust. A victory wreath was set about his sweaty brow, pressing the dark blond curls flat against his forehead. His bronze breastplate, molded to match the genuine contours of muscle and flesh, even to the details of nipples and a navel, was spattered with blood.

The other gladiators looked up from their chores and hailed him. Urius smiled wearily. He stood still and raised his arms as his trainer unlatched the straps of his breastplate. The heavy shield of bronze fell to the ground with a clatter, exposing his heaving chest. His broad, hairless pectorals and the deeply etched muscles of his belly were glossy with sweat; the golden flesh shone as smooth and hard as the sculptured plate of bronze that had protected him from Tardis' sword, and now lay in the dust covered with Tardis' blood.

His trainer withdrew. Some of the gladiators went back to their work, overseeing the slaves who were polishing their armor, exercising on the dusty floor to loosen their muscles; but most, like Magnus, continued to watch Urius, knowing what would happen next.

Urius pulled his lips into a thin smile, showing a glint of straight white teeth. His eyes narrowed; his nostrils flared. A single bead of sweat clung to the tip of his broad nose.

He clutched the sheer, pleated skirt wrapped around his hips and tore it from his body. Beneath the skirt he wore only the leather cup that had protected his genitals during the fight. He unlatched the narrow straps of hide that circled his waist and threw the cup aside.

Urius then stood naked, except for the brown thongs wrapped around his forearms and hands, the sandals on his feet, laced tightly to the knees, and the victory garland tangled in his long blond hair. His smoothly sculptured chest began to rise and fall, his eyes became glazed, as if he were in the heat of battle. His thick pale shaft, freed from the leather cup, at first hung heavy and bloated between his thighs, then began to jerk and stiffen until it stood upright, its blunt tip grazing the muscular depression above his navel.

"Zenobius!" he shouted.

Magnus run his thumb down the blade of his sword and watched. One of the slaves who attended the common needs of the gladiators, a Syrian boy with black hair and olive skin, sprang up from polishing a shield and ran to the naked gladiator.

The slave Zenobius wore a very brief chiton, cut to reveal half his chest, and a chain around his neck. "Yes, lord," he said. His voice shook.

Urius narrowed his eyes and looked down at the boy. One corner of his mouth twisted into a smile. He took the base of his shaft between his forefinger and thumb and bent it down, pointing to a space on the floor before him.

"Kneel down, little pig."

Zenobius fell to his knees. He stared upward with wide eyes at the slick, rippling mass of Urius' torso, then dropped his gaze to Urius' shaft, now upright in the gladiator's fist. The long, pale sword of flesh was incredibly thick; Urius' hand could not encircle its girth. Zenobius stared at the shaft, and a shudder ran through him.

Magnus watched, as did all the gladiators, and clenched his teeth.

Urius tensed his body. A hundred muscles drew taut and quivered beneath the glaze of sweat. He ran his hands over his chest, coating them with sweat, and clutched his shaft with both fists. He closed his eyes, threw back his head and began to stroke himself.

The Syrian boy groveled at his feet, staring upward at the gladiator as if he beheld a god. He pursed his lips and pressed his thin brown hand between his legs, shaking with excitement. His eyelids flickered. His narrow chest began to rise and fall in time with the man who towered above him.

Urius roared like a wild beast. He pulled his hands away from his groin. He opened his eyes and looked down at his shaft. The massive pole of flesh shuddered. A jet of white cream bolted from the tip and landed with a liquid slap across the slaveboy's face, from his forehead to his chin, some of the liquid entering his open mouth. Zenobius writhed in the dust, eyes barely open, eyelashes clotted with white, as the gladiator's mallet danced in the air and painted his face with semen.

Urius smiled broadly and planted his fists on his hips. His chest heaved. His body glistened with a fresh sheen of sweat.

"Kiss it, pig."

Zenobius moaned. He leaned forward and touched his lips to the tip of Urius' rod.

"Little pig," Urius muttered. He slapped the boy's face. He drew back his hand, wet with semen, and slapped the boy again. Zenobius moaned and clutched the gladiator's thighs.

He leaned forward and kissed the tip of Urius' shaft.

Urius struck him again. The boy was knocked to the ground. He whimpered and crawled forward on his belly to kiss the gladiator's feet. Urius kicked him aside and strode toward the trough of water at the end of the long chamber. His shaft swung before him, slapping heavily against his thighs.

"Come, pig, I'm not done with you yet," he called, crooking his finger over his shoulder, not bothering to look back. "Come clean the sweat and dust from my body. Come and lick me, little pig!"

Zenobius rose shaking to his feet and followed in a daze.

Magnus clenched his teeth and curled his lip. Urius disgusted him. All the gladiators needed sexual release after a death match. Magnus knew the sensation well enough—the red haze of lust, the erection that would not subside, the overwhelming need to feel himself swallowed in flesh. After a kill, most of the gladiators had the modesty to retire to one of the private cubicles that lined the quarters, where they could be as demanding of the attendants as they wished without subjecting the boys to the added humiliation of being watched. Urius insisted on doing it in front of all the athletes, as if demonstrating that the power of his shaft were another part of the performance. He would probably do it in the arena, Magnus thought, spattering his semen on the corpse of his victim, if the gamemaster would allow it.

Urius was an exhibitionist, vulgar and conceited. He liked nothing better than for all the gladiators to see him, naked and smeared with blood, his muscles swollen from the exertion of the fight, with one of the boy attendants at his feet, groveling before his shaft.

Urius was large between the legs; larger than any of the other athletes, including Magnus. He was vain about his body—the sculptured mass of his arms and legs, the breadth of his shoulders and chest, the stonelike hardness of his belly—but even vainer about his shaft, aware of the edge it gave him over the other men. He displayed it proudly; he called attention to it constantly. He was often naked in the gladiators' quarters, usually more erect than flaccid, reaching down to stroke himself in the middle of an ordinary conversation, keeping his shaft big and swollen, observing with a smirk the intimidation he could achieve with a subtle reminder of the thing he carried between his thighs.

Once Magnus had asked him, in the first days of their acquaintance when he did not know Urius' nature and still thought they might become friends, when he preferred the trident over the sword. "My sword is between my legs," Urius replied, licking his lips, smirking lewdly as he gently raised his hips and touched himself. "It hasn't yet killed a man—but it has drawn blood, more times than I can count." His shaft was almost instantly erect.

That was the way Urius thought of his shaft, and the way he used it—as a weapon, to punish, to penetrate, to command. It was a potent weapon. There was no denying that. Even now, Magnus could hear the sounds of gagging from the far end of the room. He did not bother to turn and look. He knew what he would see: Urius, sitting on the edge of the trough with his massive thighs spread apart, holding the Syrian's curly head in his hands and spearing the boy's throat with his newly hardened shaft.

Magnus heard the bark of the announcer's voice from the arena. He listened, glad of the distraction. Cleon and Philip, the two

Greeks, were next. He watched them gather their weapons and head for the arena. Magnus liked them both. It was unfortunate that one would have to die today.

After that match, there would be a wild-beast spectacle; the gamemaster was ready to debut his latest acquisition, a rhinoceros from upper Egypt. There was a rumor, probably untrue, that a woman would be forced to copulate on its horn.

Then the sand would be swept clear for the chariot race; and after that, Magnus would be called for his match with the Nubian, the climactic fight of the day, the event that everyone had come to see. The Nubian was new to Rome, an import from Alexandria, where the crowds were said to adore him. Magnus had had only glimpses of the challenger; the Nubian was being kept apart, in his own quarters. All Magnus had been able to see was that the man seemed to have been hewn out of black marble, hard and smooth and shiny everywhere, even on his shaven head. The Nubian was tall, even taller than Urius. Magnus was confident, but apprehensive; they would both be using swords, and the Nubian had long arms.

The sound of rhythmic slapping, quick and sharp, drew Magnus back to the present; Urius was slapping Zenobius' face with his shaft and laughing. Magnus wished that he had been scheduled to fight Urius, instead of the Nubian. Then Urius would be dead today, an end put to his vile strutting and crass displays.

It would be at least two hours before he would be called to fight the Nubian. Magnus closed his eyes and clenched his fists, wishing the time would fly, wishing his own erection, cramped and bent inside his leather cup, would subside. His staff was always hard on the days he fought, from the moment he woke, even without the stimulus of watching Urius torment the Syrian slave. He knew, from long experience, that it would remain hard until the fight itself, when all his lust to pierce and penetrate would be drawn from his shaft into his sword.

A few times, he had given in to the need to relieve the tension between his legs before a match. Such indulgence was dangerous; it drained him of energy, and of the drive to stab and kill. On those days he had fought poorly, and once had come very close to being killed himself. It was better to wait, despite the burning need. Afterward, there would be relief, in the mouth or ass of one of the attendants.

Which of the slaveboys would he use today? Certainly not Zenobius, though he had used the boy before and been pleased. The Syrian would be half-dead by the time Urius finished with him. Magnus could hear the slaveboy now, groaning loudly. He turned, unable to stop himself from looking.

Zenobius was on his back in the dust, naked. His chiton had been ripped from his body and lay in tatters beside the trough. His lean brown legs were in the air. Urius was atop him, driving his shaft into the naked boy with long, vicious strokes, holding the boy's head up by the chain around his throat, slapping him and spitting in his face, laughing crudely. A small circle of gladiators stood and watched, groping themselves and exchanging lewd comments.

Magnus looked more closely. There was a strange, shifting expression on the slaveboy's face, vacillating from slap to slap between utter submission and intense shame. His face was like a clay mask, battered by Urius' hand. At one moment, the mask showed pain and humiliation—then Urius would strike it as he stabbed the boy with his shaft, and the mask was reshaped into an expression of craving and worship. Over and over Urius slapped the boy, until Zenobius' face began to twitch out of time with the blows; to draw tense and fall slack; his lips were broken, his cheeks were dark with bruises. The mask became unreadable, hardly human, almost frightening.

Urius suddenly pulled his shaft from the boy's ass and stood. His legs shook, his chest heaved. He looked down at the hard, glistening mass of his sex and smiled.

Zenobius remained for a moment on his back with his legs in the air, panting, staring hard at the gladiator's shaft. Then he lowered his legs and rolled forward onto his hands and knees. Urius retreated, taking small backward steps, flexing the muscles in his groin so that his shaft bobbed obscenely in the air. Zenobius crawled after him, his bruised mouth open wide, whimpering with lust, never taking his eyes from Urius' sex.

Urius stopped his retreat. Zenobius caught the waving shaft between his lips and drew it down his throat. Urius pursed his lips and hissed with pleasure.

Magnus looked away, disgusted. The boy was ruined for him. He could never use the Syrian again. Urius had polluted him. Magnus turned his back on them both, clutching the swollen mass inside his leather cup.

A crowd, larger than the group surrounding Urius, had gathered at the entrance of the gladiators' quarters. The rhinoceros had been led into the passageway. The beast was stamping its hobbled feet and snorting. A frantic Egyptian, evidently the animal's master, was shouting for the crowd to step back. The athletes, trainers, and attendants, overcome by curiosity, ignored his warnings.

Suddenly the rhinoceros thrashed its head, swinging its powerful horn within a hair's breadth of smashing the Egyptian's skull. The crowd gasped and scrambled back. Magnus laughed, glad again for anything to distract him from thoughts of sex.

Then a figure stepped through the crowd: a short, very muscular young slave with blond hair. The boy seemed oblivious to the commotion surrounding the rhinoceros; he appeared to be looking for someone in the gladiators' quarters.

Magnus recognized the young slave, and his thoughts were instantly wrenched back to the ache inside his leather pouch.

It was Eskrill—or Erskin, Magnus could not tell which—one of the twins owned by the Senator Marcellus. It was said that the twins had been Germanic princes, warriors of the dense Northern forests, captured and enslaved by the general Silvius in his spring offensive. On his return to Rome, the general, knowing but not sharing Marcellus' sexual tastes, had given the boys to the senator as a gift in return for his political support of the war.

The two youths had excited great comment when Marcellus had presented them at a dinner party earlier in the season. Magnus had been a guest at the party. He remembered quite clearly the moment he had first seen the twins, kneeling at either end of the senator's divan, feeding their master grapes and quail's eggs with their fingers.

The brothers were identical, exactly, matched in every feature. It was almost unthinkable that two faces could be so extraordinarily beautiful. There was innocence in their pale blue eyes and perfectly regular features, in the softness of their sunbrowned cheeks; and something about their mouths, wide with sensuous, deeply colored lips, that could tempt a man to spoil that innocence. Their hair was blond, that pure yellow tint seen only among the Northern races, falling across their smooth foreheads in tight curls.

That night, at Marcellus' party, the boys had been virtually naked, decorated rather than dressed— chokers of gold around their necks, golden bracelets on their ankles and wrists, small pouches of blue silk tied about their genitals with gold wire. They were rather short, but dramatically proportioned, with broad, square shoulders, thickly muscled arms, flat bellies, and narrow hips. Their pectorals were naturally large and sharply defined, thick slabs of muscle with a sleek, hard cleft between.

Their calves and thighs were unusually developed, flowing upward into large muscular buttocks, smooth as white porcelain, full and round with a deep crevice between. Their posture, when they stood, invited every shade of lust: shoulders back, chests raised, legs apart—the high, hard shelf of their pectorals predominant in the front, the smooth, spherical thrust of their asses predominant behind.

Magnus had ached to touch them that night, to fill his hands with their firm breasts and cheeks, to taste their large brown nipples with his teeth and explore with his fingers the deep shadow between their buttocks. But the party had not offered the opportunity; Marcellus had kept the boys to himself. They had not been seen in public since that night, but Magnus had thought of them often.

Now one of the boys had entered the gladiators' quarters. He stood in that seductive posture, back arched, arms at his sides, scanning the chamber with his eyes. He wore a blue chiton, cinched at the waist by a thin leather cord, cut from a fabric so sheer that Magnus could probably have held the entire garment crumpled in one fist. The chiton left the right side of the slave's chest exposed, and was barely long enough to conceal his testicles and the bottom curve of his ass. The golden bracelets that marked him as Marcellus' slave were tight around his throat and wrists.

The boy's eyes fell on Magnus. He averted his gaze and approached the gladiator warily. Despite his reserve, it was the boy who spoke first.

"You are Magnus the gladiator, property of Harmon the merchant?" The boy's Northern accent was atrocious.

"Yes. And which one are you?"

The boy looked at him blankly, as if his Latin were not sufficient for him to have understood.

"What is your name, boy?" Magnus said sharply.

"My name is Eskrill. And you are the gladiator Magnus?"

"I am."

Magnus could not resist the urge to reach out and touch the boy's naked pectoral. He cupped the hard slab of muscle in his hand. The boy's flesh was smooth as silk. He lightly pressed his thumbnail against the boy's nipple.

Eskrill winced slightly, but did not draw away. Magnus was puzzled—and intrigued—by the display of sensitivity. He ran his fingertip around the aureole and discovered a ring of faint scabs, almost healed. Curious, Magnus pushed the strap of the chiton from the boy's shoulder.

The garment fell silently and the slave stood naked above the waist. The boy's nipples were out of symmetry. The one left bare by the chiton was marred but healed; the one that had been hidden was freshly molested, swollen and flushed, the skin mottled with patches of pink.

Magnus felt a surge of lust, an impulse to pull the cord from the young slave's waist and let the chiton fall, so that he could see him naked. But if he did that, he would be unable to resist proceeding further—his energy would be spent, the boy's owner would be furious. Magnus withdrew his hands. The boy began to pull the strap back into place across his shoulders, but Magnus gently deflected his arm; he wanted to look at the boy.

"My master would speak with you," Eskrill said.

"Now? What does Marcellus want with me?"

The boy looked at him warily, "My master sent me to fetch you," he said cautiously, as if he were afraid the words might give offense. Again, he attempted to cover himself; again, Magnus knocked his hand away.

"Where is he?" Magnus said.

The boy gestured with his chin: above, in the stands.

Magnus looked at the boy's swollen nipple. Some of the marks suggested the smooth curving bite of fingernails; others might have been the impressions left by a man's teeth. Where else had Marcellus left his marks on the boy? Eskrill's reserved manner was certainly not that of a young warrior from the barbarous North. A few weeks in Marcellus' thrall had rendered him submissive and subdued. There was no imagining the indignities the boy had been subjected to. Gladiators, Magnus knew, were known for the cruelty of their natures, the harshness of their sex; but there were those among the senators, each the petty tyrant of his villa outside the city, whose appetites were far more savage.

"Very well," Magnus said. "Lead me to him." He allowed the boy to pull the strap of the chiton over his shoulder.

The boy turned. Before he could take a step, Magnus took up his sword and gave the slaveboy a playful, impulsive slap across the cheeks. The boy jumped and looked over his shoulder with startled eyes. He reached behind and rubbed his hand over the place where the sword had stung him.

Magnus laughed, but the boy's expression stopped his laughter. There was a look of hurt in Eskrill's blue eyes, together with a passive acceptance that make Magnus' thoughts run wild. The boy's face reminded him of Zenobius' face when Urius had slapped him—not nearly so wild and uncontrolled, but the shame was there, and the craving as well, mixed together into an alloy that was both saddening and seductive, corrupt and irresistible.

"Go on!" Magnus barked. If he had to look at the boy's face for another instant, he would not be able to stop himself.

Eskrill led him through the crowd still gathered around the stamping rhinoceros, down one of the side corridors, and up a flight of steep, narrow steps that led upward into sunlight. Magnus watched the muscular workings of the boy's sturdy thighs and calves as he mounted the stairway. From his place behind and below, he could see beneath the hem of Eskrill's chiton.

Marcellus had beaten the boy, perhaps as recently as that morning. A thatch of welts ran across the lower portion of each pale cheek, the marks of a wooden cane or a thin strop of leather. Magnus' fingers flinched with the impulse to reach up and touch the marks, to trace the raised pattern they made across the firm, silky flesh. The welts looked fresh enough to still be warm.

They were alone on the stairway. It would be easy for him to push the boy to his knees on the steps, pull the chiton up over his ass and take him. He pictured the boy like that, crushed against the sharp stone, thighs spread apart, his face turned back in fear—teeth clenched, gasping as Magnus entered him....

†††

The fantasy clouded his mind—then they were clear of the steps, standing in sunlight and surrounded by the noise of the spectators. The boy turned and led him along the walkway that ran between the inner wall of the arena and the lowest tier of seats.

Magnus heard his name, spoken and shouted by the mob. Eskrill, too, was noticed—"and look, he's with one of Marcellus' new toys! The senator is a fool to trust Magnus with that one." There were whistles, laughter, shouts of "Hail, Magnus!" from the more serious spectators, and a drunken voice that yelled, "Fuck him, Magnus! Show us how you fuck the boy!" Magnus saw the Eskrill was blushing; his ears and the back of his neck turned deep red.

They walked a quarter of the way around the coliseum, past a file of soldiers and into the section reserved for the titled classes. The senator Marcellus sat alone in the third row, near the aisle, with an empty seat on either side.

Eskrill walked up the steps and past Marcellus, taking the seat at the senator's right. The short chiton pulled up as he sat, so that his welted buttocks pressed naked against the cushion.

Magnus waited in the aisle. "The slave says you wish to speak to me, Senator."

Marcellus did not look up, but indicated the cushion to his left. Magnus sat.

The senator took a sip of wine, looking shrewdly at Magnus above the mouth of his goblet. Marcellus was a large man. The formless toga he wore did not conceal the immense breadth of his shoulders and chest. His body was still hard from his years as a general of the legions in Spain. His short black hair was touched with silver at the temples. His nose was large, but did not dominate his face. People remembered his eyes, gray and piercing, his large, square jaw, and his mouth, a straight grim line that seldom changed expression.

Marcellus lowered the goblet. "Would you like some wine Magnus?" Even when asking a question, he sounded as if he was issuing an order; his cultured, brassy orator's voice had been hardened to steel by his years as general.

"You're generous, Senator. But I must refuse. Not before the fight."

Marcellus nodded. "Of course." He looked away, into the arena, where the match between Cleon and Philip had been decided. A boy was being carried out. Magnus could not tell which. The rhinoceros was being led in.

Marcellus looked again at Magnus, and seemed almost to smiled. "I trust my slave had the good manners to introduce himself to you."

"Yes," Magnus said. Below, the Egyptian and several assistants were removing the hobbles from the rhinoceros's legs. "He seems to be quite well mannered, for a barbarian."

"Thank you. It was not easy training him, I assure you. He and his brother were very insolent when I received them from Silvius. They seemed to think they were still warriors—lazy, disobedient, much too proud. They tended to glower at me; it was not an expression suitable for their handsome faces, so I decided to change it to something...more pliable." He took a sip of wine.

"It tried my imagination, Magnus, thinking of ways to prove to them that they were no longer free men, no longer men at all, really, but slaves. *My* slaves. I don't think they knew what the word meant; perhaps their tribe does not practice slavery—that is sometimes the case among the lower races. I explained to them that I owned them, just as I might own a horse—but that I would expect much more than an occasional ride upon their backs."

Marcellus placed his hand upon the boy's thigh. Eskrill flinched and remained tense. Marcellus' voice returned to a lower pitch.

"They have other strange habits in the North. They dress themselves in trousers and furs, the men as well as the women. For the cold, of course; but it is insanity to cover legs like these, don't you think? Polished metal and nude flesh are the only suitable clothing for a boy such as this. They did not take to nudity. They found it unnatural and embarrassing." Marcellus shook his head slightly and took a sip of wine. "So selfish with their bodies—so many things they swore to me they would never allow, so many acts they simply would not perform. All that is changed now. I'm sure the details of their conversion would only bore you."

Magnus glanced beyond the senator, at the boy, who sat stiffly, staring down into the arena. The rhinoceros had begun stamping about the field, smashing through barriers of wood as thick as a man's chest.

"You speak of the slave as if he were not here."

"He understands very little of what we say. I'm afraid that he and his brother, beautiful as they are, are not very bright. The Latin language is to complex, too sophisticated for them. But I have managed to teach them to recognize certain words, to obey certain commands, as one might teach a dog. Their speaking vocabulary is limited, but interesting. They have learned how to beg. And they don't need Latin to whimper."

The grim line of his mouth twisted at the corners. The senator was smiling. "I was afraid the little mule would bring me the wrong gladiator. But I see that my instructions were specific enough. Fetch me the tall, dark, handsome one, I told him. The one with the thunderous shoulders and soulful eyes."

Magnus shifted in his seat, frustrated by the senator's monologue, by the nearness of the boy with Marcellus between. "Did you call me here to pay me compliments, Senator?"

The thin smile faded, but Marcellus seemed more amused than before. "I called you here to discuss this slave, and his brother. I have a proposition to put to you."

"Yes?" Magnus' heart quickened in his chest. He glanced at Eskrill again and squeezed his leather cup without thinking.

The boy continued to stare into the arena. The agitation of his eyes belied the tranquillity of his profile. He knew he was being observed and discussed; clearly, his grasp of Latin was greater than Marcellus acknowledged.

"The Northern stock, despite its backwardness, produces on occasion extraordinary specimens of masculine beauty," Marcellus said, "Eskrill is proof of that, don't you agree?"

"Yes," Magnus said. His mouth was dry. He thought of taking Marcellus up on his offer of wine, then decided against it.

"His nipples," Marcellus said, returning his gaze to the slave-boy. "Have you noticed how large they are, how they protrude, soft and swollen, from the hard slabs of muscle beneath? They are extremely sensitive, as sensitive as a girl's." He lowered his voice, almost to a whisper. "One night…one night I tied his arms behind his back, and Eskrill and I made love, the two of us, using only my hands and my teeth, and his nipples. He was unaccustomed to the pleasure. He spat at me. He twisted in his bonds and cursed me in his crude tongue. Slowly the curses turned to babble, then to whimpers, then to screams, and finally to weeping. He cried until his face and chest were wet with tears. Finally, he begged me to stop, but he was begging for the wrong thing. By morning I had only to breathe upon his nipples to make him weep. That was the night he learned to call me lord. The night he learned to beg for my shaft in his mouth."

Marcellus touched his fingernail to the tip of Eskrill's nipple. The boy stiffened, drew his eyebrows together and parted his lips.

"He has a large mouth, don't you think? But his throat is tight. His ass…" Marcellus did not finish the sentence, lost for a moment in thought. "They were both virgins when Silvius gave them to me. Neither had so much as taken a woman. Perhaps a goat." Marcellus laughed drily. "They will never know a woman now, unless I decide to breed them. It might be pleasant, having their sons to amuse me when their own beauty grows dim.

"They had a curious revulsion for their own sex. They swore to me that no man's rod would ever pass their lips. They were astonished when I explained that it was not their pretty mouths which interested me most."

Marcellus put his middle finger into his goblet and pulled it out, red with wine. Eskrill stiffened. Marcellus slid his hand between the cushion and the boy's buttocks. Eskrill gasped softly as the finger entered him.

Marcellus turned to Magnus. "I had to break them. I had to strip them naked, chain them, put collars around their necks, beat them, starve them. They were very brave, my little princes. But in the end, it was their loyalty to one another that proved their undoing. I learned that neither could bear to see the other in pain. Their love for one another finally crushed their resistance. It was sad to break the spirit of a wild, beautiful boy, almost tragic; but a greater tragedy to let such perfection go to waste."

He turned back to Eskrill and spoke into the boy's ear in a low voice. "Tell me, slave, what do you think of this gladiator?"

Eskrill did not speak. He sighed as the finger churned inside him.

"Magnus is a great man," Marcellus whispered. "He is a slave, like yourself, but he is the idol of many a free citizen, envied even by nobles. A few years ago he was a mere galley slave on one of the trading vessels owned by the merchant Harmon. That explains the massive strength of his shoulders and arms. Then, so the story goes. Harmon caught a glimpse of the thing between Magnus' legs, and decided that Magnus was better suited for ploughing than for rowing. So the merchant took the galley slave into his home, and Magnus became the old man's stud. Are you listening to me, boy?

"Eventually Harmon turned Magnus out of his home—there was a scandal, I believe, something about a pregnant daughter—and put him to work as a gladiator. He has killed more than forty men in this arena and received hardly a scratch in return. He is young, though not quite so young as you; handsome, as handsome as you. Magnus is a slave, but he is also a man. The hair is thick on his chest. There is not a woman in Rome who would refuse him in her bed, and many a man who would gladly kneel in worship before him. They say his shaft would not look out of place on a horse—very potent, very thick. Would you like to be used by this man?"

Eskrill bit his lip, then quickly released it, trying to hide his distress as another finger was pushed into his ass.

"Answer your master, slave." The words were cool but threatening, spoken through clenched teeth. "Or do I have to beat you for the second time today, here before all Rome?"

Eskrill sighed and closed his eyes. "Yes, lord, I would like to be used by this man."

"Would you like him to use your mouth? To choke you with his sex? Think of it. Think of its thickness in your throat."

"Yes."

"And your ass. Your beautiful ass that you force me to cover with welts because of your stubbornness. It would make you happy to take this gladiator's rod in your ass, to have him mount you and ride you like a squealing pig?"

"Yes."

Marcellus nodded gravely and smiled his grim smile. He pulled his fingers from Eskrill's ass and wiped them across the boy's lips. Eskrill wrinkled his nose and jerked his face away.

Marcellus' smile vanished. "You will be punished for that," he said flatly. He turned back to Magnus.

"That is my proposition to you. I have wagered a great deal on your victory in the match with the Nubian today. Because of that—and for certain other reasons—it is very important that you win the contest. Win it, Magnus, and I will give you a night with this slaveboy and his brother."

Magnus looked from Marcellus to the boy. "Both of them, together?"

"At my villa, tonight."

"Alone with them?"

"The three of you in a sealed room. You will own them for the night."

There was something suspicious about the senator's offer. Bribes were sometimes offered to a gladiator to lose a match, when the stake was not death; rewards were regularly given to encourage the athletes to continue fighting. But it made no sense to offer a bribe to win a death match. Magnus would be fighting for his life; there could be no greater inducement.

"You seem doubtful, Magnus. Perhaps you do not want the boys."

Marcellus lifted the skirt of Eskrill's chiton and folded it back, exposing the boy's genitals. Eskrill's hands flinched, but he did not move to cover himself.

Magnus stared. The slave had been shaved between his legs.

Marcellus ran his fingers lightly over the denuded flesh, smooth as glass, at the base of the boy's shaft. Eskrill began to grow erect. His eyes were tightly shut, his brows drawn together. The silky, hairless flesh of his groin and inner thighs, like his face, blushed deep red.

Eskrill's short, slender shaft lengthened and rose from the cushion. Marcellus ran his thumb over the moist tip and around the fold of foreskin. He flicked the knob with his forefinger.

A young woman in the row ahead, bored with the rhinoceros, glanced over her shoulder and saw the boy's erection. She raised her eyebrows, covered her mouth, tittered, and looked away. Her chaperone, a middle-aged matron wearing emeralds and a painted face, glanced back to see what had amused the girl. Her mouth fell open and she looked away quickly.

"Disgusting," she muttered.

Marcellus laughed. He removed his hand from the slave's shaft, but left the chiton folded back.

"He is at that age," Marcellus said. "Always hard. Well, Magnus?"

"I want him."

"What man would not? Win the fight, and you will have him. You will have them both, together. Now go, and fight well. Eskrill and I shall be watching."

Magnus left them, his mind spinning. When he reached the file of soldiers who marked the boundary of the nobles' sector, he heard from behind him a burst of laughter and screaming. He spun about and looked back.

The rhinoceros had caught the Egyptian on its horn and catapulted him into the air. The man's body had been thrown clear of the arena and lay writhing and broken astride the inner wall, bleeding in great spurts from the gaping hole in his chest. Two soldiers broke from the file, rushed down the aisle, and threw the offending body back into the arena.

The painted matron, who had been so scandalized by the sight of Eskrill's erect, denuded shaft, was clapping and shrieking with excitement, oblivious of the blood spattered across the hem of her gown.

Magnus turned and hurried on.

THE ROPE ABOVE, THE BED BELOW

Jason Fury

Although the weather was brutal, I still enjoyed my walk along Broadway toward the Ritz.

Just within a few blocks of each other was probably the largest concentration of gay hangouts in the world. And I knew them well.

I was never a bar person, so I never frequented them. But when I first came to Manhattan two years before, I loved going to the David Cinema, at 236 East 54th Street and living in the orgy room, where men were packed over the weekends. You could suck cock until your jaws were sore or lean against the wall and let men do you until you could come no more. Now Jack Wrangler was appearing in *New York Construction Co.*

Just a block away was the swanky little 55th Street Playhouse, where *Joe Gage's Closed Set* was packing them in. Behind the screen was a wonderful make-out area. I couldn't count the orgasms I'd enjoyed back there, especially the night Al Parker appeared for the gala opening of his new triple-X-rated classic, *Inches*. Men were doing each other in the auditorium and especially back behind the screen.

The Broadway Baths was at 218 West 49th Street. For the price of a towel, you could enjoy wall-to-wall sex. It was a favorite spot for many of the dancers and Ritz fans to go after the show and let off steam. A favorite room was the "sling" chamber, where men would put their legs and arms into the slings and let themselves be fisted.

The Big Top Cinema was at 1604 Broadway at 49th Street, and *In Search of the Perfect Male* was enjoying record business. Never mind that the gay flicks rotated from theater to theater and you could still find the same titles playing a year later. To most of the patrons, watching the movies was of secondary interest. They wanted some hot action.

I paused to study the marquee of the swinging, wild little Ramrod Theater, also on 49th Street, which was still advertising Marathon Disco Fever and featuring in person Keith Anthoni in his notorious one-man show, "You Will Not Believe Your Eyes." It wasn't every day that you saw someone sucking his own cock onstage. *Christmas Time* was the main movie being shown with Big, Big Sly, plus Joey, Mike, and acts of passion. That last was a code word to the savvy that you would also see live sex onstage.

The Night Shift at 777 Eighth Avenue at 47th Street offered nearly everything a sensualist needed for erotic release: "glory holes…slings…lounges…bunkrooms and our new mirror room."

Between 45th and 46th was the shadowy Eros Cinema, which was not only having the premiere of the movie, *Grease Monkey*, but was featuring "live onstage" the film's lusty young stars: Lee Marlin, Nick Rogers, and the very popular Kip Noll.

I still loved dropping in occasionally at the Gaiety Burlesque at 201 West 46th Street, just around the block from the Ritz. That night it was advertising DYNAMIC MARATHON WITH 12 BOYS!

and was showing that ever-popular *Boys of Venice* and *The Destroying Angel.*

Just down the street on Eighth Avenue was the world-famous Adonis Theater, immortalized in the movie, *A Night at the Adonis.* That night, it was showing a Kip Noll double-treat, *Westside Boys* and again, *Boys of Venice.* Around the block, the best blowjobs in town could be found at the dismal little hole-in-the-wall King Cinema, which was showing *The Portrait of Dorian Gay.* In winter, there was no heat, and I could imagine the bleak scene inside the theater. But for some strange reason, it attracted a loyal clientele. Usually the men sitting in the back rows were ferocious cock-suckers. You just stood behind them, dropped your drawers, and they would take over. One of my favorites was a slender, bald man who always wore a ski cap.

He had a fantastic technique of tonguing the slit and taking all the cock down to the pubic bone, regardless of its length. One night I watched him taking on two men at one time, going from one hard-on to the other, passionately sucking and wanting more after the guys came.

And probably the Ritz's biggest competitor was the wild and woolly Show Palace at 670 Eighth Avenue, near 42nd Street. Their ads screamed: PINBALL! CRUISING! MORE! KINKY! BIZARRE! They, too, offered an Amateur Night competition with the winner winning $100. That was how I got my start a year before, and I was on my way. The Palace was also featuring a "turkey gobble" onstage and veterans quickly picked up on its meaning: the strippers would be sucked on stage.

I glanced at the other "legit" theaters as I hurried along. *9 to 5* had just opened with Jane Fonda and Dolly Parton, and the very hunky William Hurt was starring in the sci-fi movie, *Altered States.* An Australian movie had just opened to good reviews, too: *Breaker Morant* which I heard featured some handsome, beefy boys from Down Under.

Maybe someday I'd have a chance to see some of these movies, but I was too obsessed with my world at the Ritz, which gave me everything I wanted. Within that beautiful old theater which Matt Dempsey had renovated with red carpets, cushioned seats, crimson and gold lamé curtains, and a sound system second to none, I had everything I wanted.

Fame, money, and sex with the most handsome men in the world.

"Hey, look who's here! Brett, the Body Beautiful!"

"Hi, you sluts! Hey, get that hard-on out of the way. You know how easily I shock."

"They're horny out there tonight, Brett! Looka that kid on the front row! He's buck naked, and he's been jerking his meat for the past hour! Ain't it shocking?"

"Just another night at the Ritz," I drawled. Our backstage banter at the Ritz before a show was raucous, brutal, and fun. Especially on Friday nights when we made our "nut"—that big block of money which more than paid the bills and gave us our fancy salaries.

It was scuzzy and cramped behind the stage as dancers wandered around, smoking, sipping mineral water and Cokes, and snacking on M&M's, chips, and oranges. Matt Dempsey, our handsome millionaire theater owner, had fixed me up a dressing room the size of a broom closet. I loved it, though. It demonstrated that I was at the top of our very transitory profession. I realized only too well that today's Kings of Burlesque could be tomorrow's weekend strippers—those handsome guys who take their clothes off only on the weekends to make some easy money.

I began putting on my Ivy League outfit: sweater, slacks, boots, which would all hit the floor in front of nearly eight hundred men. Armand, the golden-bodied Frenchman, flopped down in the chair next to my table. He wore just a white G-string. His lean muscles danced as he grabbed a handful of jelly beans from my candy bowl.

"Where's that gorgeous stepbrother of yours?" he cooed.

"Don't worry, slut, he'll be here at midnight sharp. He doesn't want to see his stepbrother doing such evil things like getting blown or sucking cock."

Teddy, another handsome dancer, wearing only a black bikini stuck his curly head in the doorway. "Your stepbrother needs to get his dick deep-throated and that beautiful butt rimmed."

"What do you guys think I've been trying to do for a month? He only lets me jerk him off."

"You beat his meat?" squealed Pepe, the Mexican cutie who wore nothing. "*Mamma mia*, tell us about it."

And so while Al Parker was fucking some lucky stiff on the movie screen behind us, I shamelessly filled them on every facet of Steve's orgasm, including the way his muscles rippled during eruption.

Pepe, who had just finished sucking his own cock to the delight of his fans out front, was pulling on his meat again. Teddy, who had no inhibitions either, fell to his knees and began blowing the dark-skinned Pepe, who leaned against the door frame. Some of the other dancers paused to study this familiar scene.

"Pepe," I joked, "how many times have you come today? Look at Teddy's face! It's all purple! He must have your cock in his throat."

Pepe rolled his eyes comically and nodded his head, causing us all to burst out laughing. He tapped Teddy's head and the sucker pulled back, just in time to watch Pepe unload. I grabbed a paper towel just in time as he spurted a thick puddle of semen into it.

Teddy remained on his knees, panting, his face flushed and looked around. "Come on, let me suck some more, you guys! Whatsa matter with you all?"

"We've got to save it for the fans, stoopid!" I explained. "Go into the john. I'll bet Mr. Dickhead is in there."

"Say, you're right!" Teddy grinned, getting to his feet. "I blew him for an hour this afternoon, but I hate kneeling down on that sticky floor."

We all knew who Mr. Dickhead was. He was a regular who never missed a Saturday. He was a young guy, probably a college kid, who installed himself in one of the johns, stripped naked, and offered his sturdy cock to all who wanted it. I had blown him once out of curiosity and found him delicious. But, like Teddy, I hated having to kneel on that piss- and come-sticky floor.

Matt Dempsey stuck his handsome head in my doorway, glanced at Teddy, who was tugging at his erection, and frowned. "Teddy, damn it all, how many times have I told you to have your sex onstage? Anyway, all of you are invited to an orgy at the Plaza Hotel after the show. Some rich Texas big-wig is putting on the dog for you sluts."

The others whooped, but I shook my head. "Sorry, but Steve's coming by and—I know, I know, I should bring him along but he's still a real innocent and he's lonely, too. No, we're going home, get in bed and—"

"So when's your stepbrother going to strip butt-naked on my stage? I'll give him $500. And if he loses his virginity to one of you guys with everybody watching, I'll add another $500."

The others gasped—not just at the money, but at the idea of Steve actually getting fucked on-stage.

"Say, now you're talking, Matt. He'll decide that. I'm not forcing Steve into anything. Uh-oh, it's my number they're playing. Teddy, don't brush your cock against my pants. Your cock's drooling all over the place!"

Ruth Brown was wailing the old classic, "Daddy, Daddy," my theme song, and I listened as Eddie, our midget deejay with the velvety voice announced me.

"And now, we are proud to bring you our star attraction, the body beautiful you've all been waiting to see, not to mention his big dick and beautiful ass! the Ritz Male Follies now brings you—Brett, the Body Beautiful!"

The theater erupted into screams and applause and whistles. My faithful fans were certainly out there, including a healthy sprinkling of tourists who had heard about the wild goings-on at the Ritz. They would now have plenty to report back to their buddies in Boise, Montgomery, and other Bible Belt cities.

The other dancers always wanted the latest disco hit to perform by, but I much preferred those sexy old rhythm-and-blues classics and anything by the great Ruth Brown. I swiveled out into the gold spotlight, my blond curls gleaming, and gradually stripped off everything but a blue silk bikini.

The naked kid in the front row was jerking his cock, grinning at me, glancing down at his hard-on with an inviting look. Suck me, suck me, he seemed to pant. I recognized old Petey, the little gay man and his boyfriend, a tall, dour German. They were always sending me small gifts of cologne, scented soap, sweaters.

The body I worked so hard to keep in top condition was now completely nude. I watched a ripple of excitement pass over the audience. It was now time for me to find some lucky partner and actually do it!

My eyes had become used to the darkness now, and as I fell to my stomach and wriggled out onto the runway which went into the audience, I saw the face I was looking for.

Sam O'Brien sat right next to the runway, completely naked, stroking his hard-on, and now he winked and grinned at me. Sometimes I struck out with my random selection of "partners." The guys who looked so hot performed poorly onstage, overcome with temerity and nerves. Occasionally I would strike solid gold with some lusty, uninhibited sexualist.

Faces were so close to me as I continued crawling and wriggling along the wooden walkway that I felt mouths kissing my ass, stroking it, hoarse words: "I love you! God, you're beautiful!"

When I finally reached Sam, who was causing some excitement among his neighbors because of his smashing good looks, I draped my legs over the edge of the runway. Without hesitation, he pulled my thighs around his neck and crammed my cock into his mouth.

There was more heavy breathing from all those who watched him suck. Eddie had trained the spotlight on us so that everyone could see. Now and then, Sam would pop my cock out of his mouth and let everyone see how thick and big it was. I wasn't just feigning my sexual writhing. Sam was incredible.

I felt my come boiling for eruption and tapped Sam's bouncing head. Reluctantly, he took my hard-on out just in time. Three long streaks of whiteness jetted out among the audience, which cheered and whistled.

But Sam wasn't finished. He joined me on the runway and lay over me, thrusting my thighs around his back. His hard-on was a sight to behold—purple and furious. Without any lubrication, he began to inch it up into me.

The dancers were cheering Sam on, and I spotted many men in the audience either jerking themselves off or bending over the lap of a neighbor. Sam's body was gorgeous, too, as he continued to fuck me. It wasn't every day that we dancers found someone as handsome, big, and uninhibited as Sam.

Suddenly, he pulled out and aimed his dark erection at the audience. The lucky ones were dappled with thick gobbets of sperm.

We kissed and he laughed softly, "That was as great as I knew it would be." He shook his cock and sat back in his seat, still nude, still playing with his cock. I watched a young man in the adjoining seat bend down and take it in his mouth as I dashed behind the stage.

The other dancers praised me for my "performance," and they all swore they wanted to use Sam in their sex routines. I showered quickly and threw on a robe. I didn't want to miss a second of the act following mine.

Although I was the star of the Ritz, Matt Dempsey liked hiring a "guest star" for the busy weekends. He had to pay plenty to get the notorious but very popular Bruno from the Show Palace. Bruno's act was so wild that everyone— including me—had gone to see him. Now I wanted to see whether he had toned his act down for the classier Ritz.

"Good Times" by Chic pulsed through the theater. A red spotlight hit Bruno dressed in his favorite costume: a black biker's cap with skull and bones, black leather jacket, and pants, and boots. Besides my stepbrother and Sam O'Brien, he had one of the sexiest bodies I had ever seen.

A dark stubble gave his boyish face a rough edge, along with the sunglasses. He threw off his jacket. Powerful pecs gleamed from sweat. Each nipple was pierced, glittering with metal rings. Without even attempting to dance, he just strolled around the stage as though he were in the privacy of his bedroom.

Making no pretext at dancing, he peeled off his leather pants quickly. A gasp went up. His cock was huge and as dark and mean looking as Sam O'Brien's. Glinting in the long snout of his foreskin was another metal ring.

From his hips, he bent down and took the ring between his teeth and kept it there as he straightened up, stretching his fleshy overhang to an incredible length.

He removed the pin and ripped his skin down so the rosy tip popped out like a small tomato.

Walking down the walkway, clad just in his boots and cap, his beautiful butt swung to and fro and he kept digging fingers into his foreskin, spreading it out like dough. He was looking for a partner. From around his waist, he removed a long length of black leather which he swirled over his head like a cowboy's lasso. His eyes searched the gaping fans and settled on Sam O'Brien. One man was bending over Sam's shoulders, pulling at the thick nipples. Sam's cock was still being worked on by his neighbor.

The leather rope fell over Sam's head. A cheer went up. Sam pushed his sucker aside and bounded onto the runway. Obviously,

Bruno had liked the way Sam partnered me. Judging from the Irishman's turgid, dark hard-on, he was ready to go again.

Bruno fell to his knees and crammed Sam's hard-on into his mouth. His ability to deep-throat was legendary and we watched him relax his throat as he swallowed the dark, hard organ slowly.

Sam, standing there with his legs apart, shivered as we watched the rest of his dick vanish into the wet mouth until—finally—Bruno's mouth was pressed against Sam's shaven pubis.

We could hear Bruno's wet, strangled gulps. His head trembled as his throat went to work on Sam's hard-on. Sweat began popping out on Sam's beautiful white body. His fingers plucked at Bruno's dark curls until, finally, he tapped him on the head.

Reluctantly, Bruno released the glistening thick tube. Sam gasped as his fists milked out a huge orgasm which covered Bruno's face.

Frantically, the dancer fell on his back and raised his thighs back, pointing toward his asshole. I didn't think even Sam had enough energy to do it, but my neighbor grinned and fell on top of Bruno.

We all watched him work his still-oozing dick up into Bruno's ass. For several minutes, we watched Sam's shapely butt rise up and down as he dug deeper into Bruno. Then, once more, he pulled out to spatter the floor with his male elixir.

But Bruno was only getting warmed up. Two of the dancers brought out a low dais, covered with leather. Taking Sam's hand, Bruno went up to the sturdy table and lay down on his back. Another dancer, Calvin a butch marine type, came out completely naked. In one hand he had a big can of Crisco.

He began packing the greasy stuff over Bruno's butthole and casually popped four fingers into the cavity. Then, expertly, he slid his hand, then his wrist up into Bruno's hungry ass. Sam slathered more Crisco over Calvin's arm, all the way to the shoulder. We were spellbound to see Calvin's entire arm vanish up into Bruno's butt.

The swarthy dancer was joyous, grinning and grunting his pleasure. Calvin pulled his arm out and then clasped Sam's hand in his. Together the two fists vanished up into Bruno again, then their arms.

It was like watching an enormous dildo swivel back and forth as Bruno's butthole was stretched to an incredible degree. This ritual seemed to turn on both the fist-fuckers. Calvin's cock was standing straight up while lubricant was dripping from Sam's ever-ready phallus.

Finally the two men withdrew their fists. Towels were handed to them to clean their arms while Bruno wiped his ass.

He went to the edge of the stage and an-nounced: "Anybody who wants to fuck me, come on up! I won't turn away anybody who's healthy and clean and wants to come! Come on, you studs! Let me do some sucking while you do the fucking!"

The naked kid on the front row jumped up on the stage, and other men, completely naked, hurried down. Soon Bruno was flat on his back again, sucking a cock and getting fucked again.

Calvin propped Sam against the wall and fell to his knees, cramming the Irishman's cock into his mouth. As Alicia Bridges sang out, "I Love the Nightlife," the other dancers, all bareass and horny, came onto the stage and their fans fought to fall down on their knees and pay them oral homage.

I caught Sam's eye. His body trembled from Calvin's ener-getic blowjob. He winked and whistled, as if saying: this is heaven.

Oh, how I wanted to get out there and orgy, too. But it was midnight, and Steve was waiting for me.

His eyes were wide as he beheld the sight onstage and out in the audience. Some of the dancers were worn out, though, and wanted to watch the action. They fluttered around Steve, who blushed and grinned.

"Wouldn't you like to come and join the fun?" cooed Johnny the Cowboy as he rubbed his hand over Steve's crotch. Just as he began unbuttoning my brother's jeans, Steve moved back.

"It looks like everybody's having fun," he smiled. Turning to me, he said quickly, "You ready to go?"

We were passing Bruno's dressing room, where we noticed a crowd watching something within. Steve and I were just in time to watch Sam O'Brien slide his flushed-looking cock up into Bruno's asshole.

"Push it in deeper, Sam!" Bruno squealed. "I like it rough!"

Sam had taken Bruno's leather lasso and draped it over his neck. He pulled on it as he began to fuck. Bruno's face turned red as he gasped for breath.

"Not too hard, Irishman! I want to be alive when you fuck me!"

As Steve and I left, we heard Sam slapping his partner's butt with loud, stinging blows.

And I looked down to see my stepbrother bulging out in his jeans. He had been turned on by all the wild, raucous activity. It was just another Friday night at the Ritz Male Follies.

THE MISSION OF ALEX KANE:
SWEET DREAMS
John Preston

Alex Kane was sprawled over the bedspread. Night had come to Boston; the bright autumn sun had disappeared. As Kane stared out the windows of his room, the reflection of the city's lights came to play. He paid them no attention.

Farmdale did it to him every time. It had been ten years, but he couldn't see the man without memories rushing into his mind and taking it over. The old man had left more than six hours ago. It didn't matter. Kane had exercised to the point of inhuman pain. The screams of his body hadn't driven away the memories. An expensive room-service dinner hadn't done it either. Nothing would.

There was nothing to do but let the thoughts wash over him, the way they always did. As he had to every time he saw Farmdale, Kane let the whole thing play itself out. He was forced to look at his past and see it all...the hope, the loss, the unbearable loneliness of the present.

It had begun in Vietnam. So many stories did. His own started when he was a grunt, straight out of boot camp at Lejeune. Eighteen years old and ready to fight for America and everything he held sacred.

His unit landed at Da Nang. They came charging off their amphibious troop carrier right onto the beach. Gung-ho and green, convinced they could take on Ho Chi Minh single-handedly—probably only take 'em a week, maybe two.

Along the beach was a line of seasoned veterans, the marines who had already seen the horror of the war that would never be won. They had scoffed at the untried jarheads. They had watched the enthusiasm with deadened eyes, barely able to remember when they, themselves had last had faith in this god-forsaken war.

One veteran had stood out from the rest. He hadn't been as cynical as the others, nor as quick to put down the new men. He was a tall, handsome blond officer, a first lieutenant. His eyes evaluated the new troops in a way that seemed different from the rest.

There was something about that measurement that made Alex feel very uncomfortable. He couldn't quite put his finger on the cause of the sensation, but he knew that there was a way the officer was examining him that was different, alien from the way Alex was used to men looking at him.

Yet he had to admit there was something different about the way he appraised the lieutenant as well. Alex and the rest of his class at boot camp had measured themselves against one another, noting the growth of muscles while they went through their rigorous training, sensing the way each one was able to expand his endurance. There was a coolness to the way that the men had stood themselves against one another. It hadn't been cold, it wasn't cruel, but it was distant. The men appreciated each other's bodies the way they would have acknowledged the possession of a great car. Alex knew that he was doing something more than just that when he looked at the lieutenant. He saw the way the man's cammy pants slung low on his hips, showing off the firmness of his butt. He saw a thin line of skin that was naked between the bottom of his shirt and the top of his pants. Alex could even see the indentation of the lieutenant's navel, and found it disconcerting in some way he didn't understand. Why should he care if the man showed off that little piece of skin? Why should Alex Kane even notice it. But Alex *did* pay attention to it and was worried that the image was going to make its way into his dreams.

Later, when Kane had found his quarters and was walking around the ancient city of Da Nang—once the playground of the French colonists, now the most armored fortress in the world—he had found some old friends who had preceded him. They all went for a beer in one of the many dives that had sprung up to serve the American military men.

"Hey, guys, I saw this First Loot on the beach. Big guy, blond with a beard that was so light it looked white. Know who he was?" The image of that officer had struck Alex Kane with some power he had never experienced before. Ever. He was lucky. His friends did indeed know who the man was.

"Meanest son-of-a-bitch in the corps," Gerry Maxwell said. "Just mean."

"Didn't look it," Alex had responded.

"He is. Drives his men harder than any other officer here."

"Fairest, though," Tony Andrews admitted.

"Yeah," Gerry added, " but fair in a way that's going to get some people killed."

"What do you mean, killed?"

Gerry looked down at his beer for a minute. "Look, Alex, you haven't been here long. You don't understand. Men here aren't just fighting an enemy, they're trying to survive. It's got so the only thing anyone cares about is getting their asses out of here in one piece. Well, the only way to do that is follow Headquarters' Command. It's real simple. 'If it's dead and Vietnamese, it's Viet Cong.' You shoot first and ask later. Kids could be Viet Cong. Young kids. And women, too. You don't trust no one here if they're gooks.

"Well, Farmdale's got all these ideals, see. He won't let his men do that. Protects the civilians like they were Americans or something. Even learned to talk their lingo. His men are going to get it bad some day."

"Yeah," Tony agreed. "But hell, you can't take away that man's courage. He's led some patrols——"

"Well, that's another thing," Gerry interrupted. "He's a hotshot. He's a real, honest-to-God hotshot. Wants to win medals and all that shit. Thinks he's going to win the war and win it with something he calls honor. Let me tell you, honor died in Vietnam about a hundred years ago. This is a game of survival."

Alex had let the man talk some more about the rigors of war in Southeast Asia. The incredible heat was already evident to him. It would always be like this, so hot you couldn't tell the temperature. It didn't matter if it was 100 degrees or 110 degrees—it was too hot.

Out of nowhere, Alex Kane announced something to his hometown pals. "I'm going to join up with him. Get a transfer to his platoon."

"Whose?" Gerry asked incredulously.

"Farmdale's. Honor's the best word I've heard since I got here."

Then it began.

Farmdale was a mean son-of-a-bitch all right. But as soon as Alex was part of the group he saw that Farmdale might be the most respected officer in the whole of Southeast Asia so far as his command was concerned. He held a special control over the men. It sometimes seemed as though his disappointment in them would have been the worst thing they could have experienced.

Alex understood that. He had never needed to make someone respect him as he did with this guy. He volunteered continually, and for the most dangerous assignments, especially if he knew Farmdale was going to lead the troops himself. He took risks that were barely short of insane. Farmdale would often reprimand him, but with an expression of pride in Alex's courage that took away any sting to his words.

When an army is in battle, promotions come fast, very fast. It's a combination of the deadly attrition rate and of the opportunities battle offers to a foot soldier to prove himself. Kane was an exceptional soldier, an exemplary jarhead. Anyone could see it. He shot up through the ranks.

In only a matter of months, he was a sergeant, proud of his stripes and anxious to continue to earn his lieutenant's ongoing praise.

One day, after a particularly hazardous and successful patrol, Farmdale had announced they were up for R&R. Ten days out of the jungle. They were all wild with excitement at this break from the constant fatigue and ever-present danger of the war—but none more than Alex. Alex was euphoric because the lieutenant had privately invited him to spend the R&R with him.

They had flown down to Bangkok on military transport. Farmdale had arranged for himself and Kane to go separately from the rest of the men. Alex didn't understand why, but he didn't question the reason. In Bangkok he had expected they'd go to a hotel. There had been rumors about the Loot's being rich, maybe it would be a good one. But Alex was totally unprepared for what had come.

They didn't just go to "a hotel." They had the same suite in the best hotel in town that the General Staff often used to house visiting senators. When Alex saw the opulent surroundings, he felt suddenly and completely inadequate. His longing for R&R

with its private time with Farmdale was no longer something he was desperately looking forward to; it became a trial.

Farmdale saw discomfort on Alex's face and laughed at him. Then he did the most amazing thing. He just walked up to Alex and kissed him on the mouth. Not just a peck, nothing that could be explained away as a joke. It was a long kiss, one where his tongue invaded Alex's mouth with its wet length and lingered there, as though Farmdale wanted to taste every drop of Alex right away.

Kane wondered why he hadn't hit him or something. That would have been the jarhead thing to do. But he hadn't. Alex Kane, big bad Alex Kane from Portsmouth, New Hampshire, just broke into tears. The big brute of a First Loot had uncovered some need in Alex Kane that no one—not even Alex, really—had ever known existed. He needed the love of a man. He had wanted the love of this man. It had been a carefully hidden need, one that showed itself only in shadows in Alex's mind, but now James Farmdale had given that need a body and a personality.

Kane had hoped he'd never have to admit it to anyone—even himself. But that kiss ripped away the covering and exposed Alex as naked and needy and lonely as any man should ever be. And that kiss meant it was going to be all right.

Farmdale led Alex into the enormous bathroom and undressed him. He put Alex into the shower and then stripped himself and joined him. Alex had never felt another man's body, certainly not this way. The touch of James Farmdale's cool skin and the feel of his hard and heated cock sent the young Greek-American into an unexpected ecstasy. The men embraced, wrapped their arms around each other, felt their erections slip and slide against one another's bellies.

The taste of a man's mouth, the feel of a man's beard, the intimacy of a man's cock all combined to let Alex know that this was the most perfect thing in the world. This was something he had always wanted but hadn't been able to even think about. He could have been happy with that one moment, just that one embrace, but then the lieutenant slowly began to move downward. Alex was bereft when James's mouth left his. Then he felt Farmdale's smooth lips close over one of his nipples. Those perfect white teeth began to nibble at Alex's chest, sending never before felt waves of electricity through Kane's body.

The lieutenant's mouth moved farther downward just when the pressure on Alex's nipple was reaching a crisis point. What more could there be to life than this? What more could there be that was worthwhile? Alex found out when James sucked in the head of Kane's painfully swollen cock.

There was such warmth! There was such excitement! The shower water ran down over Alex's body, forming rivulets that broke onto James's head, making them part of the same flow of passion and completeness.

Alex pushed the lieutenant back, away from the cock that was close to exploding. He had never sucked another man before, but he knew he had to do it. He had to taste Farmdale in his own mouth. Alex got down on his own knees, and then the two of them sprawled out on the floor of the luxurious shower. James wasn't going to give up his own trophy, he wasn't about to let go of Alex's cock. But now they could both find the impossible: the gift of total pleasure as they formed a masculine sixty-nine figure on the enamel. They weren't just hungry, they were starving. They weren't just anxious to find satisfaction, they were driven. Their equally hard and equally needing flesh dove into each other's throat. When they finally came—together, at the same time, at last—they drank each other's fluids as though it might be the last liquid in the world.

They collapsed apart from one another, the shower water still rolling down over them. Speechlessly, they stood up. The lieutenant finally turned off the shower and took one of the thick towels. He began to rub down Alex Kane's muscled body, tenderly drying off Alex's testicles, roughly rubbing the cotton against the nipples that Alex had only just discovered were capable of providing such immense pleasure.

Before James could finish, Alex was hard again. He had to have it again. James smiled his patrician smile while he held on to Alex's thick cock with a marine's defiant manner. "Fuck me," James said.

Alex was shocked once more. He hadn't thought about it clearly, but he'd assumed that he'd be the one who'd have to take it up his ass. The idea of stuffing himself into the lieutenant was still another step into still-more-unthinkable territory.

Then Alex thought back to the first time that he'd seen James, on the beach, when the lieutenant's ass had bothered him so much, when the idea that he was even noticing another man's ass had sent him off balance. He remembered something else, that glimpse of James's navel. He found it in himself to stretch to be able to run his tongue through James's belly button.

Now that James's ass was naked to him, Alex was able to really appreciate what a fine set of buttocks the lieutenant had. They were covered with a slight film of thin hair, just enough to make them smooth to Alex's touch. They were shockingly muscular, much harder than Alex expected them to be. They felt as powerful as the lieutenant's hard abs. But in between the solid mounds of muscle, Alex found the soft vulnerability of James's hole. That such a tiny responsive opening existed between those powerful buttocks amazed Alex. It somehow made him want the lieutenant even more.

James wasn't about to let Alex worry about symbols or roles. He knew what he wanted, and he was used to getting it. He took a thick glob of grease from a jar in his kit and smeared it on his butt. The lewdness of the act frightened Alex a little bit, but the image of this handsome blond man preparing his asshole for fucking turned him on even more. He let James lead him by the hand back to the big bed. The lieutenant hadn't even dried off, his skin was still moist from the shower.

Alex fell on top of James. Wasn't this supposed to be unnatural? Then why did his hard and anxious cock find its way right to the center of James's ass? How did James arrange his legs so perfectly around Alex's back? How could it be this easy for Alex to slip into the small, tight hole that James offered?

Forget the questions, remember the answer—the answer that consumed Alex as soon as he began to fuck his attractive officer. The answer was in the act of merging their bodies. If Alex had thought that their sixty-nine had been wondrous, he was totally unprepared for the extraordinary sensation of fucking another man. James took it like the marine he was. He might have winced the first moment that Alex's column shoved into him, but he didn't ask for it to be removed. He seemed to force Kane's cock to go into him deeper, farther, as though it would reflect on Farmdale's honor if he kept Alex from having anything but complete penetration.

He knew he loved this man. They'd already shown their love for one another in so many ways. Now it was time to show their passion. It was easy for Alex to do. His cock had never been in a man's body before. He had never felt the viselike grip of male sphincter muscles clamping down on him. He had never had another male's hairy chest rubbing against his. All of it was new, exciting, incomparably compelling.

Alex couldn't figure out whether he was conquering the lieutenant by fucking him, or being enslaved by this introduction to such completely new erotic power. But inquiry wasn't the point here, not at all; entry was, and that was accomplished. Alex's powerful hips began to thrust, propelling his hard belly against the softer warmth of James's buttocks.

A primeval animal began to take over Alex's soul, some animal that came from his Greek heritage, some obsession that had to have been in him all his life. He was a great warrior-lover now. He was calling on some ancient role from his past. He wasn't just making love to James, he was claiming James. And, even as Alex's torso became a living piston, a machine pounding away at James,

Alex knew that he was going to reciprocate. He looked down at the wonder of James's body and saw that the other man's cock had expanded again, once more proving itself an even match for Alex's Greek column. Alex wasn't sure which was more exciting: this sensation of fucking James Farmdale, or the knowledge that James Farmdale was going to be fucking him soon.

It didn't seem to be soon enough. Alex felt his insides burst out through his cock and into the safe haven of James's gut. Alex's body convulsed with mighty heaves as he shot into the other man's ass. The intensity was so great that Alex wasn't sure that he could retain his consciousness. How could any man survive this potent pleasure?

He collapsed on James when he was done and felt the rivulets of sweat run between their bodies. The lieutenant didn't pull away or push away, he held Alex in his arms as the sergeant's inexperienced cock gratefully, lovingly began to recede. He finally fell out of the clutch of James's butt.

That was when Alex felt James's powerful arms gently guiding him over onto his stomach. A wave of fear went through Kane. He knew what was coming. Part of him wanted to give his new mentor all the pleasure he'd just received himself, but much of him was devastated by the idea of the fleshy invasion he was going to suffer.

James was smart, though; of course he was. He knew that he had to handle this new conquest with exquisite care. He didn't assault Alex with a bludgeoning. He didn't make this offering of Alex's virginity into the kind of lewd act that he himself had just enjoyed provoking.

James was careful to begin by lathering his fingers with the grease. He slowly inserted just one of his fingers into the virginal sphincter. Alex gasped at the sensation, but he willed himself not to withdraw. It was so alien for him to have anything up his butt, certainly anything that had to do with another man. He finally began to relax into it. He conjured up the image of James's navel again, the slight slit of flesh that he'd seen when he saw the lieutenant on the beach that first day. The vision translated the invasion into something warm, incredibly affectionate. Instead of the beginning of pain, Alex started to feel heat coming out of his ass and the simple pleasure of a finger that had begun to slowly massage him.

Just when Alex was beginning to relax, James slipped a second finger into the jarhead's butt. This one was easier to accept. There was hardly any discomfort at all when it first went in, and that sensation turned to a higher degree of heat in a short time. Alex was astonished to discover his hips beginning to rotate in some elementary response. He saw himself in his mind's image again, now as a dancing man swiveling his hips to provoke an onlooker. That was the moment when Alex was completely lured into James's world. That was when he realized that getting fucked wasn't going to be a simple and straightforward act of reciprocation, it had turned into something that Alex Kane understood he needed.

The realization burst through what remained of Kane's reserve. He began to move his hips more quickly, lifting them up in a seductive motion that opened his ass and let still a third finger move into his opening. Just when that added pleasure was registering, Alex felt James withdraw from him quickly. A loud moan rose up from Alex who felt suddenly abandoned. That didn't last for long, because James simply shifted his body to poise his hard cock right at the entry to Alex's ass. He let the engorged head of his dick play with the tender protective muscles for just a moment, and then moved forward.

Alex had learned to love the fingers—he even had learned to crave them in the short time they'd explored the inside of his body—but that hadn't prepared him completely for the immensity of the onslaught that he experienced now. It wasn't just the size of James's cock, it was the sensation of that long, thick shank of flesh passing into him. This was what it meant to *get fucked*. This was what it meant to have a man's shaft up your butt.

Alex bucked, first in an involuntary attempt to repel James's assault, but it soon changed into something else. Alex swiftly went through the same process of moving from pain to accommodation to ecstasy over James's cock being inside him. The passion that shot through his body startled him and frightened him. He was bucking his hips in the air in a violent physical manifestation of his lust. His movements weren't attempts to repulse the way his and James's bodies were merging, they were unplanned responses to the extremity of what Alex was experiencing. Alex could actually feel James's cock expand as the lieutenant began to approach his orgasm. The other man suddenly stopped his fucking motions, trying to prolong this first encounter, but Alex would have nothing of it. The naïve New Hampshire boy who hadn't even thought of getting fucked by his aristocratic officer now began to articulate desires he hadn't even known he had. "Fuck me, Loot, fuck me good," Alex demanded. James couldn't hold back when he heard those words. He began to slam into Alex's ass with harsh stroke after incredibly harsh stroke.

Alex thought his insides would burst. He thought it was impossible that he could survive many more of the masculine thrusts into the center of his body. Just when he thought he had gone too far, just when he wondered whether he would be defeated, James reared up, lifting his chest off Alex's back and shoving his cock even deeper inside the jarhead's butt. Alex swore he could feel the wave upon wave of James's fluids as they splashed inside of him.

"Fuck me, Loot, fuck me good…"

That's how it started. And once they had started, they vowed they would never stop. Not until one of them died.

It wasn't too difficult to arrange everything. For one thing, Farmdale was up for rotation to a desk job in Saigon. He had been planning to refuse it; now he wouldn't. It was simple for him to use his ever-present "influence" to get his new lover transferred to the capital city as well.

They had a bungalow. They spent every spare moment together. "I'd been waiting for you," James had explained once when he took a break from sucking Alex's cock, something James never seemed to get enough of. "I'd expected you to come along sooner. But that's okay."

"What do you mean, me? Sooner?" Alex didn't understand.

"Waiting for the right man to fall in love with. It didn't happen at Annapolis, and I was tired of the city games. That's why I volunteered to come to 'Nam. I figured you'd be a jarhead, so…" James would smile and go back to the pale Greek cock he never tired of.

James tutored Alex, not so much to teach him as to wash away a lifetime of prejudice and an education that blocked real thinking. Alex was a willing student. He read everything that James gave him; he listened carefully to the explanations of the cuisine they were eating; how to do little things to produce great pleasure. And he learned to have sex.

There was nothing that James didn't want Alex to try. They dressed in Shore Patrol uniforms and had sex in dark alleys. Once James had Alex tie him to the bed posts and slide ice cubes all over the lieutenant's body, finally letting the nearly melted ice slip into his ass. Another time he positioned Alex on the bed, his face down in the pillow, his ass high in the air, and James had run his tongue along the crevice of Alex's ass. At first James just teased Alex with the tip as he licked at the small opening, but then James began to tongue-fuck Alex, sending him into still further orbits of pleasure.

Alex's old prejudices made it difficult for him to give into this bliss, but there really was no way to fight it. He had to accept the ecstasy James's mouth could create. In no time Alex was swiveling his hips in primal delight, shoving his hips backwards to let James's mouth greater access to his ass. Alex was never sure how long they went on that first night, he just knew that his butt was so wet with the wild and abandoned spittle that James had left that the lieutenant was able to fuck him without a bit of lubricant. And then, when that was finished, Alex knew it was his turn to discover that particular joy. No one would ever have thought that Alex Kane would end up eating ass, but James's butt became one of his favorite delights.

Their rotation in Saigon lasted for six months. The war was picking up; the omens weren't good. Farmdale could have kept them out of battle; he could have gotten them back to the States. But he explained that it wouldn't be honorable. "When you have power—and my family does," he explained to Alex, "then you can't misuse it. Ever. You certainly can't misuse it to become a coward, to protect yourself. You and I are marines. We chose to be marines because we believed in something. It's hard to find that something in a hellhole like Vietnam, but the last thing we can do is let the rest of them define what's right and what's good. That has to be what we know it is and we have to hold on to it hard.

"Right and good aren't easy things to know. Not at all. But they're there and they're important, Alex. People back in the States are as bad as the crazies over here. It's as stupid to think you can protect right with speeches and marches on the Capitol as it is to think you can keep it alive by killing innocent women and children. The right thing for a soldier to do is to protect what's good … however he has to do it."

So they went back, back into the rotting, stinking jungle. They went back and they marched their patrols again. "The lieutenant and his sergeant" was what they were called. Alex Kane was proud of that. The other men didn't have to know just how much Farmdale owned Kane, his body and his emotions. They were careful to make sure the physical acts they had to have were done in private. Sneaking off into the jungle in their camouflage uniforms only added a sense of excitement to their activities.

There was another sergeant in the platoon who hated these men, even if he wasn't sure just exactly what they were doing.

Sergeant Johnson, a big, beefy man from North Dakota, was jealous of all the things that he did know went between the lieutenant and "his sergeant."

One day Johnson came into the tent where James slept and found out just why he was cut out of so many of the private conversations between Alex and James. James was on his knees, Alex's pants open, his long, thick penis hard and stabbing the air. "You faggots!" Johnson sneered.

James had told Alex to forget it. Forget it ever happened—he'd have Johnson out of there within a week, and the man had been warned to keep his mouth shut. It made Alex nervous to think about it, but he took James's word.

There was a sudden enemy movement. They had to go on alert and out to patrol a particularly dangerous sector. They were willing and ready—as ready as men in Vietnam ever were.

At a point a few miles from their camp, they were attacked. Bullets shot through the air and whined death close to them. Alex and James were face-down in the damp, stinking Asian dirt. they fired their M-16's with deadly accuracy. The enemy dropped back. It seemed as though the fight was over. James lifted his body up slightly to check out the position. One single bullet sounded its call. James jerked up, then fell onto the ground.

Alex was mad with concern. He laid his body over his lover's to protect it from where the sniper's position was. He felt the weakness of James's breathing and screamed for a medic.

But his panic collapsed all at once. He had looked down at the body beneath him and seen where the bullet had landed, in James's back, right at the spinal column. He had been shot from behind. By an American. With zombielike determination at what he was seeing, Alex stood up. He looked back and saw that sneer on Johnson's face and he knew. *He knew.* Alex lifted his own M-16 to his shoulder and sent his own mortal round of bullets tearing through Johnson's chest. The sneer disappeared forever.

Then he went back to James. There was a hint of life, just a hint. He rolled the lieutenant over and held James in his arms trying not to let his sobs jostle the dying man.

James Farmdale knew he was going to die. He lifted one hand to Alex's face with great, painful effort and rested it on the sergeant's cheek.

And then First Lieutenant James Farmdale, U.S.M.C., left this world.

Kane knew that something was going on when he went before his court-martial. The charge was the murder of Sergeant Edward Johnson. The defense lawyer the marines had given him had said it was hopeless; he begged Alex to plead insanity.

"Never."

But when they went in front of the court-martial, Alex didn't see faces of men who would be willing to send him before a firing squad. The judges were nervous, more frightened than he ever thought they would be. They called the lawyer up to the bench and had a whispered conference with him.

The young attorney returned to Alex's table with a shocked expression on his face. "The trial's closed; they have orders. From way up. *Way up.*"

The proceedings lasted minutes. In one of the fastest trials in the history of the United States Marine Corps, Sergeant Alex Kane was dishonorably discharged from the service. But not for murder. For some trumped-up charge that let Kane off easy. The judges walked briskly out of the room, embarrassed by something. Tough Shore Patrol members stood beside Alex, and each took one of his arms. He looked at them. "Follow us."

He did, right to the airport, where a transport was being held for him. The guys inside figured it had to be a general at least— who else could have kept a plane that big sitting there so long? But it was only a sergeant, one with black hair and a look of uncommon sadness, even for this part of the world where sadness was omnipresent.

They hadn't even had time to process his papers in 'Nam. But the documents were waiting for him when he landed in California. He took them and all his back pay and caught a bus to San Francisco.

Alex Kane, the lover of James Farmdale, a hero of the war in Vietnam, landed in the Tenderloin and began a battle like no other he had ever fought: a battle to drown himself and his hurt and his anger in an ocean of booze. He nearly won.

He still couldn't remember whole days, weeks of the hell he put himself through. The sleazy bars, the nameless bodies, the rancid bathhouses all blurred together in a haze of self-hating sex and self-destructive drinking.

Finally, one day, there was no more money. He woke up, and there wasn't any body next to him either. The flophouse was even dirtier than most. *So this is the end of the line*, Alex had thought. He looked around the room. He had thought it would be someplace like Vietnam, or else someplace homey and comfortable like his grandparents' house in New Hampshire. He had never really thought that it would be like this. But if this was his fate, then so be it.

Suddenly the doors burst open, and three strong men stormed into the room. They grabbed Alex; when he tried to resist one of them knocked him out cold with a roundhouse punch. They made no sense to him, not in the little time he was conscious of them. He did remember one thing. *So this is the end of the line*.

When Alex Kane woke up the next time he thought maybe his prediction had been correct. He was still naked. He was clean, though, and so was the bed he was resting on and the sheets that covered him. There was something wrong with his body. Was this what heaven felt like? This slow lethargy and all this comfort? But then he knew that the sensations were more commonplace. He had been drugged. He was just dehydrated, with a chemical hangover.

He staggered out of the bed and stretched. The room was luxurious, and he could hear surf crashing on the shoreline somewhere nearby. He went to a set of doors that opened onto a patio and, beyond it, an Olympic-sized swimming pool. There were no clothes around. But there appeared to be no people, either.

A few laps were just what he needed to clear his head. He walked over to the pool and dove in. He drove his out-of-shape body as much as he could, until he could swim no more. He stopped and hung on to the edge of the pool to catch his breath.

Then he saw an old man in an immaculate suit sitting close by. The man was studying him intently, silently.

This makes no sense, Alex told himself. *What is this?*

Then an answer came to him, and he laughed out loud. "Jesus Christ, man, you went to a lot of trouble for a piece of rough trade."

The old man didn't smile. He just stared and said finally, "I am James's father."

MIKE AND ME
Eric Boyd

Mike lay in bed the next morning with a faint layer of perspiration on his body, and his thick, aching arms behind his head. Even though it was only October, his mother had the furnace cranking out heat like it was the middle of January.

He only had one sheet covering him, and it was pulled up just to his waist. He was completely nude, and his cock was outlined clearly under the thin fabric. He had lost his jock-strap somewhere in Scott Gorseth's yard last night. Reaching a hand down under the sheet, he fondled his rapidly hardening cock as he recalled the events of the previous evening. He still couldn't believe what had happened between him and his best buddy, John Wallach.

Fuck; to think that all this time Johnny-boy had been just as interested in his dick as he was in John's. Well, as soon as John got back, they'd be making up for some lost time.

And then there was Kevin and his buddy, Scott. Shit, they were a couple of hot little fuckers. Fuck! Little was hardly the word for them. His cousin's dick wasn't quite as big as his own, but it was big enough, and he still couldn't get over the impressive piece of meat that Scott had between his legs. They were sexy dudes. Between his thoughts of them and his thoughts of John, Mike found himself stroking a major hard-on.

He pulled the sheet away, exposing his rock-hard cock as he pulled himself up against the bed's backboard. Spreading his knees apart, he lavished full attention on his dick. He stroked it languidly as he thought of what he and John would do when John got back. He closed his eyes and imagined John's tautly muscled torso with beads of sweat clinging to his tanned skin. The two of them would just be standing there, face to face, totally naked, staring into each other's eyes. John had the darkest, sexiest eyes Mike could imagine, with thick, masculine eyebrows and delicate, long, almost feminine eyelashes. Their cocks would be rock hard and twitching slightly against each other in the midst of their trembling excitement.

Mike held the image in his head as his hand slid up and down the length of his stiff cock. God, he loved beating off! Even with John, Scott, and Kevin to fool around with now, he couldn't even imagine not sneaking off to be by himself occasionally, to play with his dick until it shot a load.

Every muscle in his body began to tighten, and he involuntarily found his body rising off the bed as he neared his climax. He moaned as he felt the sperm churning in his balls as he continued to pound on his cock. And then, with one final deep, throaty grunt, the undeniable release came as load after milky load shot onto the tight muscles of his chest and stomach.

As the last faint bursts dribbled from the flared head of his prick, Mike reached for the towel beside his bed and used it to wipe the sticky mixture from his torso.

When he was done, he jumped out of bed, wrapped the soiled

towel around his waist, and headed for the shower. His still-partially-erect dick showed plainly through the tightly wrapped towel as he walked down the hallway. When he made it to the bathroom safely, he pulled the towel off, letting his dick flop free, and tossed it down the laundry chute. It never dawned on him that his mother knew exactly what was going on every time she pulled one of those sticky towels out of the hamper in the basement. Between him and his houseguest cousin, she'd seen plenty of them.

After a quick shower, Mike went back to his room and pulled on a fresh jock-strap, running shorts, and a tank top. Over all that, he pulled on a pair of red sweatpants and a hooded sweatshirt, and he finished off his day's wardrobe with sweatsocks and running shoes.

"So I'm gettin' a slight beer gut, huh?" he murmured to himself in his mirror, as he pulled his sweatshirt tight around his torso and gave his stomach a few probing jabs. Only the slightest hint of softness was noticeable through the fabric. His appraising eyes caught the barest swell of baby fat over the muscles of his belly, and he could still pinch the last vestiges of those off-season love handles that had sneaked around his sides; nothing more. Still, it was noticeable enough for Scott and Kev to tease him. "Well, we'll see about that!"

Finally, he went downstairs and into the kitchen, where his parents would see him post-blowjob for the first time.

Richard and Marge were sitting at the table reading the newspaper, dad sipping coffee and silently nursing a hangover.

"Hi, Mom. Hi, Dad. Has Kevin gotten home yet?"

"No," said Marge, "he called and said he was going to spend the day over at Scott's."

Mike laughed to himself as he thought about what those two horny fuckers would be up to all day.

After downing a quick glass of milk and a couple of raw eggs, he headed for the door. "I'm going out to run a few miles. I'll be back in a couple of hours."

"That's nice, honey," his mother said without looking up as he slipped out the door.

Mike made his way to the old airport road a few miles south of town. It was a lonely stretch of highway about three klicks long that used to bring short-hop commuters to the county's rusting municipal airport. The airport had been torn down about five years ago when funding came through for the completion of a brand new state-of-the-art airport on the other side of town, and all that was left now was a deserted stretch of pavement that nobody ever used. Even weekend dragsters had abandoned the road after the local sheriff's department placed highway patrolmen out there on the odd Saturday night.

Of course, that's what Mike loved about this piece of road. As he ran down the center line, he felt like he was the only person in the world. This blue highway was all his and he could do whatever he wanted here. His Saturday morning runs were special, and almost nothing could keep him from them. It was his chance to really cut loose; to feel the potential of his body as the miles pounded beneath his feet. It all felt so physical, so powerful, so fucking wonderful.

As he neared completion of his first mile, he began to really sweat. Even though it was a cool, early-October morning, the sun was beating directly down on him and he was getting uncomfortably hot. Without slowing his pace even a little, Mike pulled off his hooded sweatshirt and tossed it to the side of the road as he continued to run.

The sweat was visibly running down his broad shoulders, soaking into the thin, ribbed material of his muscle shirt. The sudden feel of the cool air gave him a burst of energy, and Mike ran faster. It would only take another minute of running before he stopped noticing the temperature, and the sweat on his shoulders and chest was only beading now, evaporating in the cool air.

As he approached the end of his second mile, he slowed down

to a jog as he loosened the drawstring around his waist. With a few quick steps, he had his legs free of the sweatpants and was tossing them to the side as well before returning to full speed. He could feel the strain of exhaustion beginning to creep into his legs. His powerful thighs and calves bulged and relaxed with every stride he took. The hair on his legs was matted down with sweat, and his socks grew damp over his lower legs, where the hair grew much thicker. As he pushed himself harder, the silky black material of his tight running shorts began to creep up the crack of his ass, exposing the leg straps of his jock and the lower portion of his hard, powerful leg muscles.

Now the sun was beating fully on him as he moved to within half a mile of his goal. His exertion forced sweat once again to stream freely from his body. With one quick motion, he slipped off the muscle shirt and tossed it behind him. For the last half mile, he was nothing but mindless physicality. His muscles were pumping like engines, and perspiration washed down his torso.

As the road curved around a thicket of trees to its completion at the old airport field, Mike was suddenly jolted back into reality and came to a complete stop. Sitting at the end of his racetrack was a parked van. Its back doors were open, and someone was sitting there watching him as he closed in on the finishing line.

At first, Mike was furious. Who would have the nerve to invade his running track? Soon enough, though, he caught his breath and calmed down a little. This was hardly private property. Besides, there was something awfully familiar about that van, and even more awfully cute about its owner.

Jason Carmichael got up to give Mike a lonely ovation for crossing the invisible finish line. What would the golden, rich dude be doing out here on a Saturday morning?

"Hey, buddy, how's it going?" Jason called to Mike as he made his final approach.

"I'm doing fine, man. What are you doing out here?"

"I just came out to think. I do that once in a while, you know—

think?" He grinned. "But fuck, dude, you gotta be just about freezing to death."

It suddenly dawned on Mike that he was pretty cold. With no more exertion, the sweat on his body had dried, and now he found himself half-naked in the cool October air.

"Climb in and I'll shut the doors."

Mike did so, and Jason locked out the cold behind them. Typical of his rich-boy status, Jason's van was luxuriously furnished with plush carpeting, big comfortable pillows, and a refrigerator. Mike leaned back against a stack of cushions and scanned his surroundings. Jason sat down opposite him and pulled an envelope from behind the driver's seat.

"Here, dude, this'll warm you up," he said as he pulled out a joint and lit it. He took a deep toke and then passed it over to Mike, who accepted it gratefully and took a long, slow hit. As one would expect from Jason, the dope was first rate.

As he passed it back, Jason reached into the refrigerator and pulled out two cans of Budweiser. He took the joint and held it between his teeth as he opened one of the beers and handed it to Mike.

Still stinging from Kev and Scott's beer-gut jab last night, Mike considered not accepting the Bud, but then thought better of it. "Thanks. Nice custom job."

"You think so, man?" Jason said as he took a swallow and handed the joint back to Mike.

"Yeah." Mike took another drag. "I'm just trying to imagine all the wild things you could do with a set of wheels like this."

"You name 'em, buddy, and I've probably done them."

"Really," said Mike, grinning, his still-thumping heart racing the THC throughout his system. The wild stuff Jason was referring to couldn't possibly come close to what he was thinking.

"Yeah, man, I mean really kinky stuff!"

Within a few short moments, Mike realized he was getting really stoned. The beer and the grass had loosened him up, and now he was sitting there, half-naked across from the best-look-ing senior on the gymnastics squad as he talked about sex. He started to get a hard-on.

"What kind of kinky stuff, man?" Mike said half suspiciously, so as not to sound too eager.

Jason looked squarely into Mike's sexy blue eyes and slowly licked his lips. "You ever suck on another guy's dick?"

Mike's cock went totally hard. This guy wants me. He fuckin' wants me! "N-no, man," he lied. "Have you?"

"Yeah, a few times," Jason said with a mischievous look in his eyes and a shit-eating grin on his face. "Judging from the hard-on in your shorts, I'd say you've thought about it a few times yourself."

Mike looked down at how obviously his cock was making a tent in his shorts, and then looked back up at Jason. By this point, he'd determined that Jason was seriously interested in him. He could see the huge piece of meat snaking down the leg of Jason's sweat-pants, and it looked hard!

He coyly looked back at Jason. "I'll suck yours if you'll suck mine."

Jason started laughing. "Far out, dude," he said, and without further delay, he leaned over and pulled back Mike's tightly packed shorts and jock-strap and slid them down Mike's furry, hard, muscular legs. Jason began stroking his rock-hard piece of meat as he looked at Mike's entire naked body. It was clear he admired it. "You've got a hot-looking dick," he said in a husky whisper.

"Thanks," Mike half moaned as he closed his eyes and began to thrust his groin up and down into Jason's talented hands.

"In fact, your whole body is pretty fucking hot. I think it's time for me to have a taste of it."

"Go for it, dude."

Jason, still fully clothed, held himself over Mike's reclining body by his powerful arms and then slowly lowered his mouth to

Mike's chest. He began kissing the space between Mike's large pectoral muscles, licking up the sweat that had dried there. From there, he moved slowly from one nipple to the other, sucking on each of them, playing with them with his tongue, and lightly biting on the little rock-hard nubs with his teeth. Mike had never had this done to his tits before, and it was making him harder than he ever remembered being.

After giving a last lick to the nipples, Jason chewed his way down Mike's firm abdomen, nibbling and tasting the lightly salted flesh. The flavor got him hungry for more, and he moved lower down Mike's belly, digging his teeth into the hard, rippling muscles that lay partially obscured beneath that last, slight layer of baby fat. Approaching the gently puckered meat around Mike's navel, Jason was delighted to discover the faint trace of hair that started there and quickly expanded to become thicker, as he munched his way closer to Mike's throbbing penis.

It was definitely getting hot in the close quarters of the van, so before continuing, Jason leaned back on his haunches, and, after freeing his T-shirt from the waistband of his sweats, pulled it off in one quick motion. Mike, who was half gone with lust, just stared up at the hot-looking senior.

Jason's body was not quite as husky as Mike's but possessed much finer definition. The hair under his arms was a bit darker than the short, dirty-blond hair on his head, but that was about all Mike had time to notice before Jason dived down and engulfed his dripping cock with his flesh-hungry mouth.

Mike moaned with pleasure as he watched the mouth of the guy every girl in his school lusted after slide up and down on his dick. He leaned back in the pillows with his arms behind his head and enjoyed the incredible blowjob he was receiving. God, this was too good to be true, he thought. Maybe he'd picked up a scent last night—a hot pheromone that made the men of his dreams starve for his thick meat. Or maybe, he mused, he simply had what it took to get guys like Wonder Bread super-jock

Carmichael to bend a little and give it up. Who knew? And who cared!

Jason took Mike's entire cock in his mouth and plunged his head up and down its entire length a couple of times. He'd stop for a while with just the head in his mouth so that he could taste whatever pre-cum he had worked to the surface, and then he would repeat the whole process again and again. It seemed to be having the desired effect. Mike was so close to coming that his stiff cock was practically drooling now.

"Stop it, man. I don't want to blow yet."

Jason let the spit-soaked cock slip out of his mouth and leaned back on his haunches again. Perspiration trickled down the valley between his chest muscles. Raising himself to a kneeling position, he smiled sweetly as Mike, driven by sheer, overwhelming lust, crawled toward him. Sliding his hands around Jason's athlete's body, Mike kissed him full on the lips. Their tongues, dried by the pot smoke, playfully touched and slipped over one another. He took a firm hold of Jason's waist, dropped his head into his lap, and began to gnaw at the drawstring of his sweats with his teeth.

"Fuck, man," Jason said as he took this all in, "you can't wait to suck my cock, can you?"

Mike was silent as he undid the sweats and started to pull them down. The first thing he saw was Jason's thick bush of pubic hair. Jason wasn't wearing any underwear. Then came Jason's monster dick. It was at least the ten inches in length Mike had imagined it to be; and, right now, it was definitely all hard. He stifled a stoned giggle: how do these horse-hung studs stay conscious when so much blood rushes out of their skulls and into their nearly foot-long dongs!

"Go ahead, suck on it," Jason coaxed, apparently wide awake.

Mike needed no further encouragement. He lowered his mouth onto the flaring head of Jason's cock, and immediately tried to take the whole thing in his mouth, but started choking at the halfway point.

"Easy, man, you're not a sword swallower, yet," laughed Carmichael.

Mike pulled up and instead gave his full attention to the fat head. He snaked his tongue around it, feeling the ridge where it met the stalk. Jason's piss-hole had begun to flare, and Mike playfully jabbed his tongue into it.

"Fuck, man, you sure suck cock great!" Jason moaned. "Are you sure you haven't done this before?"

Mike just smiled as he gave one last lick to the head of Jason's dick and then turned his attention to the furry balls hanging below.

"Oh, yeah, suck on my nuts!"

Mike licked at them until the hair was soaked and matted. Then he turned to lie on his back, nodding and pushing his face up under Jason's balls as he licked his way toward the crack of his teammate's ass. Before last night, he never would have believed he'd be doing something like this; it just had never occurred to him in all his fantasies. How simple they had been! But that ass bath Kevin gave him last night had felt so incredible! The sheer variety of things that was possible made his heart triphammer. Jason softly moaned, as if in agreement. Gurgling, whispering unintelligible words, he then leaned over and began sucking madly on Mike's dick.

As Mike's tongue neared Jason's tight asshole, the musky smell drove him into an even higher state of frenzy, giving him no choice but to push himself through yet another dare. He used his fingers to pry the muscle open and darted his tongue inside.

Gasping, wriggling, Jason simply went nuts, and he pulled his mouth from Mike's cock. "Oh, God, that's great! Now stick your cock in. I gotta have you fuck me."

Mike was taken aback for a second. He had stuck his own finger up his ass lots of times; other things as well on occasion: pencil erasers, cleaned carrots, one of his father's plastic cigar casings. But quite honestly, it had never occurred to him that one day he might have a whopper of a cock knocking at his back door. Butt-fucking or getting rammed had not been a part of Mike's fantasy life; but then again, here was Jason Carmichael begging him to deliver it up his chute. The thought made his cock twitch, and with only those few seconds of hesitation he pulled himself out from beneath Jason.

Jason just stayed there on his hands and knees with his ass pointed in the air, "Yeah, Mike, stick your hot cock up my ass!"

Mike stroked his dick a few times. It was still wet from the blowjob Jason had been giving him. What the hell, he thought. The rich dude really does want me on top. Let him have me on top!

He held the tip up against Jason's tight hole and, after pressing against it a bit, slowly began to slide it in. He was amazed at how easily the muscle gave way, as the fat head of his cock pushed through the threshold of the sphincter.

"Oh, yeah, Mike," sighed Jason. "Slide it all the way in."

Mike did so until his pubic hair was pressed close to Jason's ass crack, and then simply held it there, allowing himself to indulge in the silky tightness of Jason Carmichael's ass. What an incredible feeling! It was as if his big cock were being grabbed and roughly squeezed by a soft, wet, muscular hand. Jason's ass seemed to be sucking Mike up by his dick all by itself. It would have been scary if it hadn't felt so damned good.

"Fuck me! Fuck me hard!"

Pulling out, then pushing back in, increasing the speed with each thrust, Mike looked down at Jason, who was moaning crazily now, sweat running down his muscular back. Their perspiration washed and mixed where Mike's lower belly wetly slapped against Jason's firm butt cheeks, raising a pungent, masculine smell out of their union. Leaning his chest against Jason's back, tenderly biting the nape of his neck, Mike reached his arms around to grab onto his teammate's nipples and raging hard-on. Nipples were pinched and cocks were teased and pulled upon, until the pair could barely take it any longer. Both college studs lost all sense of reality as their sweaty bodies pounded against one another and they both neared their points of no return.

Mike shot first, unloading what felt like gallons of hot cum inside Jason's tight ass. When he felt the searing heat washing into his bowels, Jason shuddered and called out, making a valiant effort to steady himself before shooting his own great wad. Mike felt it just as it started to erupt and he increased the speed and pressure of his strokes on Jason's cock. Carmichael shot three powerful blasts of sperm onto the carpeted floor of the van before finally turning his head to face Mike. A brief kiss to Mike's lips broke the spell, and then they both began to laugh.

As they stopped and picked up Mike's clothes on the drive into town, all Mike could think to himself was that Jason Carmichael had thought enough to kiss him when they were done.

MIKE AND THE MARINES
Eric Boyd

Mike stared out the window of the bus as it sped down Interstate 35 toward Des Moines. Mile after mile of cornfields passed him by as he thought back over the reactions that the news of his enlistment had caused.

His mother had been irritated. She had sent him to the mall to pick up her catalog order from Penney's, not to join the Marines. His father had seemed proud of him, but that could also have been the four cocktails that he'd already consumed after work.

His cousin Kevin thought it was an incredible idea—especially after Mike told him about his experiences with the recruiting officer. He immediately made his own plans to have a talk with Lance Corporal Stenson.

Mike's fuck buddies, Jason Carmichael and Dave Sommers, were disappointed to be losing him and his hot dick, but wished him the best, regardless. They also promised him a going-away party he'd never forget.

Only one person was really upset with Mike: his best friend in the world, John Wallach. John couldn't understand why Mike would want to leave him and go thousands of miles away. Mike tried to explain that it had nothing to do with him. At twenty years old, he just felt that he wasn't ready to settle down yet. John didn't take it well, though, and ended up storming out of Mike's house.

Luckily, Mike had so much to do in preparing for his departure that he didn't have time to spend it dwelling on his fight with John.

On the Monday night before Mike was to leave in early July, Jason and Dave kept their promise and invited him over to Jason's house for his going-away party. Mike called Ryan, who was also preparing for his departure, and invited him along. The two future Marines arrived to find Jason's parents gone and the whole basement laid out with wrestling mats. As they came down the stairs, they found Jason and Dave standing there stripped, coated with baby oil, and stroking their massive hard-ons. The two muscular studs were not alone, however. Off to the side, already going at it, were Mike's cousin Kevin, and none other than Corporal Randall Stenson.

It seemed that Kevin had been going to the recruiting office almost daily for the last week, always with a new question to ask. In that time he had managed to become very good friends with the Marine Corporal.

Anyway, Mike and Ryan were stripped and oiled up by the four horny studs. They spent the next six hours in an all out orgy.

At one point, Dave and Corporal Stenson were locked in an intense sixty-nine when Ryan came up from behind and shoved his oily dick all the way up to the hilt in Dave's tight ass. Jason proceeded to do the same thing on the other side, jamming his ten-inch-long monster up the Marine's hot hole. Not wanting to be left out, Kevin straddled Dave and Randy and guided Ryan's hungry mouth onto his throbbing cock. Mike just leaned back and watched the hot sight as he stroked his hard dick.

The best part for Mike, though, was when halfway through the orgy, who should arrive but John, his best buddy. The two lovers kissed and made up, with Mike promising that he would come back again. With that settled, they retreated to a corner of the room for their own private session.

By the end of the orgy, every one had been fucked at least a couple of times and had come even more.

That might explain why Ryan had slept the entire ride stretched out on the two seats behind his own, Mike thought to himself as his mind returned to the present.

The bus was headed for Des Moines, where they would rendezvous with a Marine Corps bus. That bus would then take them all the way to Parris Island, South Carolina, picking up other recruits along the way.

Finally the monotony of the countryside got to Mike, and he dozed off in his seat. He must have slept for at least an hour and a half, because when he woke up, the bus was pulling into the Des Moines terminal. He turned around and reached over the back of his seat and shook Ryan's shoulder.

"Hey, Ryan, wake up. We're here. It's time to switch buses."

Ryan got up groggily and tried to get his bearings.

"We're in South Carolina, already?"

"Not even close, dummy. We're in Des Moines. C'mon, grab your bags."

As they stumbled off of the bus along with the few regular passengers who had ridden with them, the boys were stopped by the bus driver.

"You young men will want that military bus parked over by the south fence," the middle-aged man pointed. "It's the one painted olive green."

They spotted it immediately and thanked the bus driver for his help. Hoisting their duffel bags, the two boys headed towards the khaki colored bus. It was only 8:00 A.M., but already the temperature stood at eighty. Halfway across the open lot, both young recruits began to perspire. Stopping to wipe his brow, Mike realized that it was only going to get hotter. As they neared the bus, they saw that it had United States Marine Corp. painted in black letters along its side, and an older Marine sitting inside it.

When he caught sight of the two young men approaching, twenty-six year old Corporal Matt Carlyle hopped out of the bus and strode toward them.

"Hey, guys. You must be Mike Belson and Ryan Miller."

The two were surprised to be recognized.

"Yeah, I'm Mike," Mike replied, "and this is Ryan. But how did you know our names?"

"It wasn't very difficult," the Corporal laughed, "I'm only scheduled to pick up three people here in Des Moines, and I've already got one of them on the bus."

He flashed a dazzling smile at the two boys and reached for both their duffel bags. "My name is Corporal Carlyle, but you guys can call me Matt," he said over his shoulder as he led Mike and Ryan onto the bus.

The heat in the bus was stifling. Matt tossed their gear onto the first row of seats and turned back around to face the recruits. "Sorry about the temperature in here, but you might as well get used to it. The heat in South Carolina is going to make this feel like air conditioning. It'll get better, though, once we get moving. So go ahead and make yourselves comfortable. We've got a long road ahead of us."

As he spoke, Corporal Carlyle began unbuttoning his short-sleeved shirt. Ryan and Mike were hardly aware of what he was saying as he slipped off the shirt, exposing a muscular chest, barely hidden behind the ribbed fabric of his white tank top. His dog tags seemed to almost disappear in the dark tangle of chest hair that was hidden in turn, by the cotton fabric.

Tossing the shirt aside, he swept his arm out over the rows of empty seats. "Take your pick. Except for the last row. That's already been claimed by Watson." Both youth's looked to the back, but they didn't see anyone.

"Who?" Ryan asked.

"Watson," Corporal Carlyle replied. "Hey, Watson, wake up!"

"Huh! Wha' zat!" said a sleepy voice from the back row.

Mike and Ryan watched as a handsome, young face topped with mussed-up reddish brown hair emerged from the last seat of the bus.

"Come up here and meet your fellow grunts," the Marine Corporal barked.

Mike couldn't believe his eyes as he watched the redhead rise from his seat. He was at least 6'3", and built like a brick shithouse. Mike guessed his weight to be 220 pounds, minimum.

Fully awake now, Watson strode down the aisle and thrust out his bearlike hand to the new arrivals.

"Hi! Bill Watson's the name. It's great to meet you."

"You, too. I'm Mike Belson," Mike said as he shook Bill's hand firmly. "It's definitely a pleasure."

Mike grinned as he looked the redhead right in the eyes, letting his handshake linger a few seconds longer than needed.

Bill grinned back, never breaking eye contact with Mike.

"So where are you boys from?" Bill asked as he ran a hand through the floppy bangs that had fallen over his forehead.

"Edison, Minnesota. How 'bout you?" Mike replied.

"Elk Point, South Dakota. I got here about two hours ago, and I figured it would be a good opportunity to catch up on my sleep from last night. Me and my buddies had quite a going-away party."

"Yeah, same with us," Mike laughed. "Ryan has slept the whole trip so far."

"And if you don't mind, that's what I'm going to continue doing," Ryan said as he picked out a row of seats to spread out on.

"That's right," Corporal Carlyle added, "why don't you all

find yourselves seats. It's going to be only the four of us until we get to St. Louis, so we might as well get started."

The Marine sat down in the big chair behind the wheel and started the engine as Mike and Bill headed down the aisle of the bus.

"So you gonna go back to sleep," Mike asked, "or do you want some company for a while?"

"Company. Definitely!" he said, turning back and giving Mike a killer smile.

Mike followed him to the back row of the bus and sat down next to the husky redhead.

As the bus pulled out of the station the two recruits began to tell each other about themselves.

It turned out that Bill was twenty years old, just like Mike. He had been a star football player in high school, which was no surprise, given his size. And he had figured out realistically that there wasn't a hell of a lot of opportunity in southeastern South Dakota. So here he was, off to join the Marines.

As Mike relayed his story, minus the juicy parts, it became apparent that both of the young men had a lot in common.

About a half-hour into the trip, the bus had not cooled down at all, and both of them were perspiring.

"I've just about had enough of this fucking heat!" Bill cursed. "I've been sitting in it for almost three hours now. You mind if I take my shirt off?"

"No problem, man," Mike replied, "I think I'll do the same."

As both boys pulled their sweaty T-shirts over their heads, they couldn't help noticing that each of them was trying to take a discreet look at the other's body.

Tossing their shirts into the row in front of them, the two young studs sat back in their seats. Bill put his thick hands behind his head as he sat back, allowing Mike a great view of his sculpted torso.

His chest looked huge even as he stretched out his muscles. The light sprinkling of hair had a copper hue to it. No doubt he had spent his last month of civilian life out in the sun, just as Mike had. His skin was a beautiful bronze, which Mike guessed was unusual for someone with that complexion. The hair continued in a light trail down over his rippled abdominals before disappearing into what looked to be a packed pair of jeans.

"That's some bod you got," Mike whistled as he punched Bill's arm playfully.

"Thanks, man. You, too," Bill responded as he took the opportunity to wrap his big hand around Mike's thick right biceps. "How'd you develop such an awesome build?"

"Gymnastics. How 'bout you?"

"Football and farm work. I spent every summer working for my uncle on his farm outside of town."

"Well, shit, man, it seems to have done wonders," Mike replied as he reached over boldly and placed his fist on Bill's impressive chest.

Bill just smiled as Mike began to feel him up. Without saying a word, he reciprocated by running his own hand up and down Mike's tanned, hairless torso.

With all pretenses aside, the two studs soon had both their hands roaming up and down each other's muscular flesh. Mike couldn't get over the size of this guy. His hands could hardly reach halfway around Bill's upper arms, and his chest seemed to overhang his stomach by a few inches.

But what really impressed him was the size of the bulge he saw expanding in Bill's already-packed jeans.

Reaching down to rub it through the thick denim, Mike guessed its length had to be at least ten inches.

Deciding there was really only one way to find out if he was correct, Mike undid the top button and pulled down the zipper.

The zipper almost undid itself as Bill's monster cock, still hidden behind his underwear, pushed its way out of the confines of his pants.

Bill kicked his shoes off and raised his butt up to slip his jeans completely off.

All the while, Mike couldn't take his eyes off the exciting bulge in Bill's white Jockeys. He ran the palm of his hand back and forth across the rockhard piece of meat.

"Go ahead and pull it out," Bill whispered in his ear.

Mike didn't need any more encouragement than that, so he pulled back the elastic waistband of Bill's underwear and reached in to grab hold of the farm boy's dick.

His cock was beautiful, Mike thought to himself. He held it up straight, jacking it slowly with his left hand while pushing Bill's underwear past his knees with his right hand. He was correct about it being at least ten inches long, and it was just as thick as it had felt in the confines of his pants. It had a slight curve to it as it reared up toward Bill's flawless abdomen and a fat, perfectly shaped spongy head with a flaring piss-slit. His pubic hair was a dark brown, with only a hint of the reddish tinge that the hair on his head possessed. His balls were impressive-sized globes that hung down low as they rested against the seat of the bus.

Mike licked his lips instinctively as he slowly stroked up and down on the massive dick.

"Go ahead," he heard Bill whisper. "No one's watching."

Mike looked up toward the front of the bus. Corporal Carlyle seemed to have his eyes glued to the road. Six rows farther up from the horny twenty-year-olds, Ryan was already fast asleep, stretched out over his own row of the bus.

Without a second look, Mike leaned over and took the ten-inch cock halfway into his mouth.

"Oh, fuck, yeah!" Bill moaned as he closed his eyes and let his head fall back. "Suck on that fucking prick!"

Mike threw himself into it as his head bobbed up and down on the rigid pole, covering every last inch of it with his tongue and coating the whole thing with a thick layer of his saliva.

He couldn't get enough of this huge dick as it filled his entire mouth, the soft head pressing against the back of his throat.

Letting it slip out briefly, he held the base gently as he stared at the slick, beautiful ramrod. Nothing is hotter than sucking on a sexy guy's hard cock, he thought to himself. After only a quick, deep breath, he was back to work, taking the entire ten-inch cock all the way into his mouth and burying his nose in Bill's musky pubic hair. He breathed in the intoxicating mixture of sweaty crotch and Ivory soap while his taste buds identified a saltiness that could have been either from his skin or from the precome that was beginning to ooze out of the head of his dick.

Mike thought he was going to pass out from a combination of the sensory overload and the heat in the bus. Finally relinquishing the hot cock for a moment, he sat back up. Both boys were dripping with sweat.

"You are one fantastic cocksucker, Mike!" Bill enthused as he ran a hand through the reddish brown hair that was beginning to hang down in his face. "Now I want to see what *you've* got hidden in your pants."

Without hesitating, Mike undid the buttons of his 501s and pushed the pants all the way to his knees. He wasn't wearing any underwear, and his fat eight-and-a-half-inch cock snapped up against his tight belly just a couple of inches above the dramatic line separating his tanned torso from the pale white skin that had been hidden the last couple of months by his swimming trunks.

"Nice dick," Bill responded, obviously impressed.

"Go ahead," Mike urged as he finished slipping off his shoes and pants. "See what it tastes like."

Bill hesitated only a second before bending over in the seat and taking Mike's rigid cock into his mouth.

"Yeah, you like a nice hard dick sliding in and out of your mouth don't you?" Mike whispered as his hands guided Bill's head up and down on his shaft.

Bill gave a muffled assent as his head went back and forth on Mike's thick cock.

Without warning, Mike pulled his dick out of Bill's greedy

mouth and began slapping the spit-soaked staff against the farm boy's sweaty cheeks.

Bill loved the treatment as he nuzzled his face deeper into Mike's crotch. With Mike's heavy balls right in front of his mouth, his tongue flicked at the sparsely haired sacs.

"Oh, yeah!" Mike said, a little bit louder than he should have. "lick my nuts, man!"

Bill took one of the furry sacs into his mouth and rolled it around on his tongue. Meanwhile, he brought one of his hands up to the base of Mike's balls and started to slip a finger underneath, towards the former gymnast's sweaty asscrack.

It didn't take Bill long to find his target, and with only a little effort, he slipped his index finger up Mike's wet asshole.

"Fuck, yeah!" was all Mike could add.

He soon forgot about his balls as they slipped out of Bill's mouth. All attention was now centered on his butt. His eyes closed in pleasure as he used his muscular arms to lift himself up and down on Bill's thick finger. His dick seemed to grow an extra half-inch from the excitement he was feeling.

"Oh, yeah, man, you've got me now. I'm not going to be happy till I've got that hot, fucking cock of yours sliding up my ass."

"If you can take it, man, it's yours," the hunky ex-football star promised.

"I love a challenge," Mike said as he turned to look toward the front of the bus. The Marine still seemed oblivious to anything that might be going on in the back. "You stay seated and let me try sitting on it."

Mike swung around to face the handsome farm stud. With his arms behind him, braced on the top of the seat immediately in front of them, Mike got his feet onto the edge of their own seat and squatted down on the twenty-year-old redhead's lap. His rockhard dick twitched with excitement just inches from Bill's face. The horny hunk couldn't resist taking another lick at it.

In position now above Bill's towering monster, Mike began to lower himself. His anticipation was incredible as the moment of contact approached. And then it happened. The fat head of Bill's cock pressed up against Mike's greedy hole.

Mike's descent stopped, but only for a moment. With a slight grimace, the head forced its way through the tight muscle and Mike's 175 pounds carried him down upon the ten-inch shaft.

The boys were both so sweaty at this point that the stream running down Mike's back to his asscrack was more than enough lubrication for the monster that was now forcing its way up his hole.

Mike shivered from the sensation as inch after tantalizing inch pushed the walls of his asshole aside, allowing him to sink deeper and deeper onto Bill Watson's monster cock.

"Fucking fantastic!" Mike rasped breathlessly as he came to rest on the farm boy's lap, all ten inches of Bill's amazing dick stuffed into his ass.

Mike sat there stunned for a moment as he took in the reality of the fat rod filling his tight hole. He rocked from side to side to let the hard shaft rub against his ticklish prostate gland.

Letting Bill take his entire weight, Mike shifted his hands from the seat in front of them and wrapped his muscular arms around the sweaty South Dakotan. With his own rigid dick now trapped tightly between their two flat stomachs, Mike leaned forward and locked lips with Bill in a passionate French kiss.

Without breaking their kiss, Mike began to slide his ass up and down on the farm boy's cock while his own eight-and-a-half-inch dick rode back and forth in the sweaty valley between Bill's big, flat, blocky pectorals.

Finally breaking their kiss, Mike threw his head back, lost in the sublime intensity of their coupling. For almost five minutes he continued that way, sliding slowly up and down on the ten-inch dick, oblivious to anything around him.

When his eyelids finally drifted back open, he was surprised to see Bill's hazel eyes gazing off toward the center aisle of the bus, a grin spreading over his face.

Turning to see what he was smiling at, Mike was shocked to see Corporal Matt Carlyle standing there naked, except for his dog tags, stroking his own rockhard cock.

"Far fucking out!" Mike laughed as he reached over and began stroking on the Marine's eight-inch dick. He never missed a beat as his hand slid up and down on Matt's cock at the same pace that his own ass was riding Bill's fat dick.

"Yeah, play with that Marine dick," Matt encouraged Mike as he reached over and ran his hand over Mike's smooth, sweaty chest. "Nice body, kid. You'll do just fine in the Corps."

Mike let go of the Corporal's cock and instead used his free hand to explore Matt's awesome torso. His fingers entangled themselves in the hair on his chest as they roamed freely over the muscular landscape.

Matt raised his right arm as Mike worked his hand up into the Marine's hairy armpit and then beyond onto his smooth triceps. He flexed the muscle for Mike's benefit as the blond tried in vain to cover the entire surface with the palm of his hand.

"Yeah, feel those muscles, boy, while your buddy shoves his hot cock up your ass."

Mike was feeling too confined by his present position, so, without saying a word, he stood up straight and let Bill's hard dick slide completely out of his butt. He heard the stiff piece of meat slap back against the farm boy's hard stomach as he stepped down off of the seat into the center aisle of the bus.

The handsome, hairy Marine was now directly in front of him, and without saying a word he dropped to his knees and took Matt's twitching hard-on deep into his mouth.

"Oh, fuck. Suck on my fucking dick, man!" the Corporal moaned as Mike proceeded to give him one hell of a blowjob.

Bill also moved out into the aisle behind Mike, and crouching down behind the former gymnast, shoved two fingers deep into his greedy hole.

Mike was thrilled by the attack from the rear as Matt continued to assault him from the front. The Marine was really getting off on yanking his dick out of the blond's mouth and slapping it back and forth across his face, leaving trails of his spit across Mike's cheeks.

When he stopped for a moment, Mike took the opportunity to take the fat dick back into his mouth and swallow it all the way down to the Marine's dark, coarse pubic hair. Meanwhile, in the rear, Bill had removed his two fingers from Mike's ass and was in the process of aiming his ten-inch cock at the Minnesotan's upturned bubble butt.

His mouth was too full of Matt's dick to do much else but grunt as the massive tool slid all the way up his ass in one swift thrust.

"Yeah, boy," Corporal Carlyle laughed as he continued sliding his cock in and out of Mike's eager mouth. "We're filling up every hole you have. You like taking both these big dicks at the same time?"

Mike mumbled his assent as he reveled in the piggish position in which he found himself.

Both of the hung studs began sliding their tools into Mike's greedy holes in unison, pulling out and slamming in at almost exactly the same rhythm. Meanwhile, the hunky blond reached down and began stroking on his own rigid cock. It was about as hard as he ever remembered it being as his right hand flashed up and down, bringing him closer to his inevitable release.

Then—without any warning—Matt yanked his dick out the hungry stud's mouth.

"That ass looks too hot not to have a go at it," the husky Marine said as he stepped over Mike to get behind him.

Mike almost cried out as he felt Bill's massive cock being withdrawn. But he stayed down on all fours in anticipation of what was to come next.

Matt's cock was plenty slick from the blowjob Mike had been giving him. That, combined with the loosening up Bill had done, and the sweat pouring off all of them, should have made it simple for the Marine to slide his dick up the former gymnast's ass. Even with all that lubrication, Mike winced as the Marine forced his lance up his ass. It wasn't as long as Bill's, but it definitely was thicker.

Little by little, though, Mike relaxed and he found the Marine's dick sliding in to the hilt. When it was all the way in, the hunky Corporal leaned forward and wrapped his thick arms around Mike's smooth, muscular torso. His furry chest tickled Mike's back, and the cool spot he felt where Matt's dog tags were pressed between them seemed particularly incongruous in the stifling heat of the bus.

With his body anchored firmly around Mike's, Corporal Carlyle began thrusting his fat dick in and out of the blond's tight butt.

Watching the hot sight from behind, Bill decided what his next move would be. Getting down on his knees he placed his hands firmly onto Matt's sweaty, pistoning asscheeks and spread them apart, exposing his puckered hole.

Without hesitating, he leaned forward and started to lick at the sensitive opening.

"Oh, yeah!" the Marine moaned, letting his enthusiasm be known. "Lick that fucking ass, man. Let me feel your tongue up my butt."

Bill went to it. He drove Matt crazy with his probing tongue, while Matt continued to push Mike right up to the edge with the steady thrusting of his hips.

The only thing keeping Mike from shooting his load right there in the aisle of the bus was the fact that he had to use both his arms to support his and Matt's weight. As a result, he had no hand available to work on his own straining dick.

Matt was going nuts from the asslicking he was getting, but it was nothing compared to what he felt when Bill pulled his tongue away from the dark-haired Marine's ass. Without any warning, he got up on his haunches and pressed the head of his ten-inch monster up against the Corporal's sensitive hole.

"Oh, yeah!" was all the horny Marine could whimper just before he felt the beefy farm boy's dick slide all the way up his ass.

"Fuck, boy. Do it to me just like you did earlier."

Well, Mike thought to himself, that explains the setup he fell into.

Bill slammed it into the hunky Marine who let out a string of unconnected expletives, thrilled by the experience of being simultaneously both the fucker and the one getting plowed.

Matt couldn't handle the intense situation for long. The next time Bill jammed his cock all the way up his ass, Matt did the same to Mike. And, letting loose another string of expletives, the handsome Marine stiffened all of his considerable muscles and shot his hot load deep into Mike's ass.

"Fucking! Shit! Goddamn! Motherfucking! Cocksucking! Assfucking! Sonofabitch! Take my scumsucking load!"

Mike felt about four powerful blasts of heat, and then the Marine relaxed his muscles and began to breathe deeply.

But only for a moment. Before Mike knew what was going on, Matt pulled his still-hard dick out of the blond's ass and began barking orders.

"On your back private. I want to swallow your scummy load."

"Yes, sir!" Mike replied, not needing to be told twice.

As he turned over and laid on his back, Mike's raging hard-on popped up rigid as a rocket, aiming straight at Corporal Carlyle.

The Marine leaned forward and took the entire length of Mike's cock in his mouth and proceeded to give the young stud the most incredible blowjob of his life. Meanwhile, without even a break in the action, Bill continued to slide his dick in and out of the Marine's still-willing ass.

The sight of this hunky hot Marine swallowing one guy's cock while taking another one's dick up his ass was just too much for the South Dakota farm boy. He slammed his dick up to the hilt in the Corporal's ass and let loose his own load of searing balljuice.

Mike couldn't take it anymore, either. Matt sensed the twenty-year-old stud's impending orgasm and slid his mouth off all but the fat, spongy head. Letting out one final moan, Mike shot a huge load right onto the Marine's waiting tongue. And then another load. And then still another. Matt's mouth was flooded with the sticky, salty-sweet, scummy load of sperm. He swallowed it as fast as he could, never losing a drop.

When he was sure he had it all, he let Mike's dick slip from his mouth and got up on his knees. Letting out an unintelligible howl, he jacked on his still-hard cock, and in a matter of minutes, let out another scalding load of jism all over the floor of the bus.

All three of the spent studs collapsed for about ten minutes as they recovered from their intense encounter.

"Goddamn!" Corporal Carlyle exclaimed as he stood up, "that was one hot fucking scene!"

"Fucking-A!" Bill agreed. "But I guess that's probably the last sex we'll see for a while."

"Are you nuts?" Matt countered as he slid his pants back up over his still-semierect cock. "This is just the beginning. You're going to be stuck in a barracks for thirteen weeks with a hundred young, horny guys and no women in sight. What do you think is going to happen?"

"Hey, it's why I joined up," Mike added.

"You won't be disappointed, dude. Hey, even the guys who are completely straight start thinking twice about fooling around with another guy when they get really horny. Just make sure you don't get caught. Even though everybody knows it goes on, they don't deal well with it when it's obvious. So just be careful, and you can do all the hot studs you could ever want."

"Wait a minute," Bill said with a frown. "Did you say 'thirteen weeks'? My recruiter told me basic training would last only nine weeks."

Matt just laughed. "They'll do or say anything to get you to join up. Hell, he probably even let you fuck him, I'll bet."

Bill just blushed, and Mike shrugged his shoulders as he put his shirt back on. "Oh, well, I was told nine weeks, too. Who cares, though, if I'm in the midst of a bunch of hot guys?"

Matt just laughed as he headed back up toward the front of the bus. "Time to get this crate moving. We've got a load of guys to pick up in St. Louis."

As the old bucket of bolts started up, Mike heard a sleepy voice from behind him.

"Hey, are we there? Did I miss anything?"

Mike turned around toward Ryan, who was just rising from his seat, and laughed. "No, man, you didn't miss a thing."

BOY TOY
Derek Adams

I fell fast asleep after my exertions and did not wake until the van turned off the highway. The dawn was lighting up the eastern sky and I began to watch my surroundings, trying to determine where I might be. The narrow road was lined with tall fir and cedar trees that rose high on either side. After about half an hour, the van stopped at wrought-iron gates, flanked by stone pillars surmounted by elaborately carved lions. A man stepped out of a small cottage tucked just inside the gates. He studied the van briefly, nodded, and approached the gates. He turned a key in the massive lock and pulled the gates back to allow us to pass.

Once inside, the van wound up through more trees as we climbed steeply. I saw a stream off to the left, crashing down through rocks and fallen timbers and more than once saw deer feeding by its banks. The incline gradually leveled off and we began to cross a broad, treeless plateau tucked into the heart of the mountains. As the sun rose over the peaks, I got my first glimpse of the Brentwood Academy.

It was a huge, Gothic pile, constructed of stone the same color as the surrounding mountain peaks. With its spires and towers, it appeared to have grown out of the rock it stood on. As we approached, several things struck me as peculiar about the place. There was no landscaping near the big house, not a tree, a bush or a clump of flowers. In fact, there was nothing growing higher than a few inches over the entire expanse of the plain. I had seen enough alpine meadows in books and on the television to realize that this was not a natural state. Then, there were the bars on all the tall narrow windows of the house. These were not delicate flights of Victorian Gothic fancy, but thick, strong steel bars—prison bars.

The last, and most disturbing, discovery was made when we stopped at a distance of about five hundred feet from the front door of the Academy. Our way was blocked by what I at first took to be a natural crevasse. Closer inspection revealed that this crevasse ringed the building, cutting into the rocky earth in a large, regular arc. The walls of this moat—it could be nothing else, really—were perpendicular, curving in slightly at the top, making escape impossible for anything—or anyone?—who was unlucky enough to fall in.

I heard a faint whirring sound and discovered what we were waiting for. What appeared to be a steel shelf was bridging the moat, pushing out from just below the rim of rock. I heard a sharp clang as the bridge slipped into its niche on the opposite side of the moat and the van rolled forward. Once we were across, the bridge began to retract again, leaving us isolated on our remote stone island.

The van pulled up to the doors of the house and stopped. Doctor Vandeveer got out and the dark man opened the rear of the van, motioning me out as well. I stepped out onto the drive and looked around. No cover for as far as the eye could see; no other habitation; no signs of life of any kind. Nothing but gray rock, moss, and sparse clumps of mountain grass.

"Come, Brendan," Doctor Vandeveer said, putting his big hand on my shoulder. "I know you will do very well here." He turned me toward him and stared for a long time at my face. "Very well. Excellent. Yes." His hand slipped down to the small of my back and he pushed me gently toward the steps.

As we waited for the door to be opened—even the doctor couldn't enter without permission, it seemed—a wind blew around the corner of the old house, bringing with it a bitter chill. I shivered, my near-naked torso popping out in goose bumps. Doctor Vandeveer saw me and pulled me toward him, covering my shoulders with his suit coat. I huddled close, my arms wrapping instinctively around his waist for warmth. The man's waist was narrow and his belly was like a wall of rock. It was not what I had expected of a man near my father's age. But then, my experience was very much limited. I longed to touch more of him, run my hand up his chest and down along his thighs, but I did not dare. If my presence stirred him, he gave no sign, just stood there silently until the door opened slowly inward.

"Welcome home, Doctor Vandeveer," the man at the door said, his voice a deep-chested rumble.

"Mr. Black," the doctor replied, nodding at him. "This is Brendan. Mr. Black is one of our instructors." I looked up at the big man, awestruck. He was naked, except for a band of white linen wrapped around his narrow hips that passed between his legs to cup the bulging knot of his genitals, leaving his muscular, hairy ass bare. His torso flared from his small waist, up to a chest of massive proportions and shoulders a yard wide. His arms bulged obscenely, the triceps and biceps twitching and jerking every time he moved. A tattooed dragon twined around his left arm, wrist to shoulder, its jewel colors somewhat obscured by the dense black silk that curled on the mass of his forearm. More of the luxuriant black growth feathered over his collarbones, swirled around his nipples, and spilled down the concave washboard of his belly. His thick thighs and bulging calves were similarly, sexily obscured. As I stared at him, I couldn't help wondering what sort of teacher he might be.

Mr. Black looked back at me, his expression skeptical. "You have your work cut out for you, Doctor Vandeveer."

"As do you, Mr. Black. As do you." The teacher shrugged, turned on his heel and stalked away from us. As he crossed the large, paneled room, his gorgeous ass flexed temptingly, two perfectly muscled globes of flesh, festooned with springy curls like dark, soft moss. The man who dared to touch his ass would be fortunate indeed.

Doctor Vandeveer led me across the hall and opened a door for me. "Do as you are told, Brendan. Good-bye." The door shut behind me and I was alone in a large, empty room. Everything was white—the walls, ceiling, carpets, the drapes covering the tall windows. The only contrast was a small, ornately carved wooden chair that stood between two of the windows. I sat down to wait.

I didn't have to wait long. A door opened opposite me and a man—like Mr. Black, naked except for the strip of linen— appeared and motioned for me to approach. He had flaming red hair, his pale, tightly muscled torso sprinkled liberally with freckles. The man's pale nipples were enormous, standing out from the sleek curve of his chest like pink candy kisses. His fat cock was outlined behind the thin fabric covering it, appearing to be coiled like a snake. The thick rim of the crown was clearly visible, as were the fat lumps of his balls. Evidently, all the teachers at the Academy were cocked like stud bulls.

"Brendan?" He smiled at me, immediately putting me at ease.

"Sir?"

"Come with me, please." I followed him through a door and into a large tiled room. He motioned me over to a desk in an area that was set up like a doctor's office. I stood beside the desk, hands clasped over my groin, waiting for instruction.

"Take off your clothes, Brendan." He watched while I stripped, his expression betraying nothing. When I was naked, he began taking measurements—chest, arms, hips, thighs, calves—carefully noting the data in a manila file. After he had completed his survey of my body, right down to the length of my cock and the circumference of my balls, he sent me to the opposite side of the room to shower. As I soaped myself, I saw that the red-haired man was leaning against the front of his desk, observing me. I couldn't help but wish that there was more of me for him to look at, but there was very little meat on my bones, as Jeffers had often noted. At least I still had some of the sun's color on my skin, which made me look a little less like a garden slug.

When I had washed and dried myself, the man motioned me back over to him. As I stood in front of him, hands at my sides, he opened one of the desk drawers and removed a strip of linen. He passed it around my waist and through my legs, tucking the ends together in the back. This, obviously, was the school uniform. A very strange sort of school, indeed.

Once my loins were girded up to the man's satisfaction, he went to a small refrigerator in the corner and removed a beaker of cloudy, gray-green liquid. "Drink this," the man said, holding it out to me.

"What is it?" I asked, eyeing it apprehensively.

"An herbal concoction of mine," he replied. "Drink it. It's good for you. Builds your strength." I took the beaker from him and sniffed at it. My nose wrinkled at the smell. I held the beaker, looking at it, not drinking.

"Come, Brendan." The man took the beaker and drank from it. "You see. I have no wish to harm you. No one here does." I tried again, but the bitter brew gagged me. The man smiled at me patiently and stepped so close that I could feel the heat rising off his body. He tipped back the beaker and filled his mouth, then slipped one arm around my waist. Our bellies slapped together, the fat knot between his legs pressed against my groin and his thick chest brushed mine. He inclined his head and our lips touched. I understood and eagerly opened my mouth. He pressed forward and the bitter liquid began to trickle from his mouth.

Almost immediately, I felt dizzy. I couldn't judge if it was caused by the liquid or the touch of the man's body, so I continued to swallow the bitter brew as he spit it into my mouth. He broke our kiss only to refill his mouth, continuing to feed it to me until the beaker was empty. When I had licked the last drops from his lips, his hand slipped away from my waist. I didn't move away.

"There, Brendan. That wasn't so bad, was it?" I nodded, too dazed to speak. I was beginning to distinguish the effects of his concoction. My body was tingling from head to toe, warming, buzzing as the herbs did their work. "You will drink twelve ounces of this three times a day, Brendan. I promise you will be pleased with the result." I nodded again, wondering if the red-haired man would administer them in the same fashion every time.

Once he had finished with me, the man led me into another room, this one paneled in dark wood, furnished with plush couches and chairs, clustered in small conversational groupings. The man told me to wait, that someone would come for me and show me to my dormitory. I chose a couch near the blazing fireplace, sinking into its cozy softness.

A few minutes later, I heard a door open and close softly behind me. I turned and grunted in surprise. The man standing at the far end of the room didn't appear to be a teacher. Judging by his face, he was no older than I. His cheeks were rosy and his brown hair curled softly over his forehead. With his full, pouty lips and his long lashes, he looked like a choirboy.

The eyes were not those of an innocent choirboy, however. There was a predatory look about his pale blue eyes that reminded me of the watchful eyes of a beast of prey. They locked on me where I sat beside the fire and he licked his lips.

Although he had the face of a boy, his body was a man's. His shoulders were heavy with muscle and his arms were as big as Mr. Black's, the teacher I had met upon my arrival. Thick veins snaked up his forearms and over the massive curve of his biceps, swollen almost to the bursting point. His chest jutted out aggressively, the bulging mounds of his pecs capped by thick brown nubs. The hollow of his chest was clustered with soft brown ringlets like those on his head, long and luxurious.

When the fellow stepped to the center of the room, I gasped audibly. Hanging between his muscle-knotted, hairy thighs were the biggest balls I'd ever seen. They were the size of large lemons, sagging heavily, pulling his scrotum down toward his knees. More long, silky curls clustered on his bag, making it appear even more massive.

The most enormous hard-on I had ever seen rose from his crotch. He was bigger than the mighty Lefkos, my benchmark for big dicks. It appeared to be thicker than my wrist, the juicetube running along the underbelly as big as my thumb. It towered far beyond his navel, the flaring crimson cap almost brushing his sternum. He saw me staring at it and thrust his hips forward. He ran his fingertips up the sides of the shaft and gleaming, sticky drops of cock honey oozed out the tip and slowly drooled down the long, bloated tube of flesh.

"I'm Brendan," I said, feeling the need to say something. The fellow walked toward me, his balls smacking heavily against his thighs. As he rounded the end of the sofa where I sat, I stood up and stuck my hand out to him. Instead of shaking it, he gripped my wrist and pulled my hand down toward the fat knob perched on the end of his prick. I cupped my palm around it, feeling the sticky heat pump out onto my skin. The man made a sound that resembled purring.

"Do you have a name?" I queried, my fingers curling around the pulsing stalk of his mammoth erection. "I'm Brendan." I repeated my name, hoping he'd take the hint. The was something far from normal about him.

"Joel," he said hoarsely. "Joel." I looked up and smiled. He licked his lips, his nostrils flaring. "Fuck?" I shook my head, startled. "Fuck!" This time it wasn't a question.

I tried to step away, but his arms shot out and locked me in a Herculean embrace. The lush curls on his chest tickled me and his hard-on seared the flesh of my belly. I gripped his arms—they were like warm rocks. I rubbed my cheek against the hard curve of his chest— he smelled like sex to me, musky and rich—then looked into his eyes.

"Joel, please," I whispered, "don't hurt me." He looked at me, that shy boyish look again, and shook his head. His big hands slipped down my back to my ass. He impatiently tugged at the linen strip and it fluttered to the floor. Then he began pulling my asscheeks apart, his fingers probing my asspucker. The feeling made me groan, reminded me of the long hot days in the garden at my home. I pressed my face against Joel's thick chest and my cock sprang to life, pushing up alongside his own stupendous schlong. He felt it rubbing against his belly and we both looked down at the hard sticky things pressed between our bellies like boys who were discovering sex for the first time.

Suddenly, Joel's hips stopped pumping and his eyes flew open wide. I felt his cock flex against my belly and looked down. The head swelled, the comehole gaped and jism started gushing out of him like hot lava. The first blast caught in the cluster of curls in the center of his chest and hung there like a liquid rope. The next shot arced high above our heads, spattering down on my shoulders like hot rain.

Joel's hands dropped to his sides and I stepped back to watch him come. His muscular body contracted as he pumped another gusher of cream high in the air. It hit his chin and dripped down his neck. He went limp for a brief instant, then his biceps flexed, swelling like cannonballs as another mighty contraction shook him, sending another spout of white goo pumping high in the air. He'd been squirting for more than a minute, and the jism was still bubbling out of him, rolling down the column of his cock in thick white streams.

He held his thick arms open and I stepped back over to him and leaned against him. My tongue shot out and I began licking at the white drops that quivered on his neck and shoulder. His come tasted sweet, making me instantly hungry for more. I dragged my tongue over the curve of his chest and sucked the spicy gunk out of the curls that split his mighty torso in half. When I had swabbed his belly clean, I began licking his cock, milking his juicetube, coaxing yet more hot sperm out of him. I sucked him clean, and he showed no signs of losing his hard-on.

"Fuck!" he said coaxingly, pulling me to my feet. I nodded, suddenly overcome with lust and he pushed me against the back of the sofa. I leaned forward and Joel began licking my crack, driving his hot tongue up my hole. I gripped the plush cushions and spread my legs, willing to risk being split open by him so that I could feel his mighty hardness plunging deep into my bowels. The sensation of having his tongue in my hole and his hot, snorting breath on my cheeks, coupled with the smell of him, was driving me beyond the bounds of reason.

"Fuck Brendan," he murmured, standing up and pulling me back against him. I could feel his dick pressed against my spine, halfway to my shoulder blades, and those huge, come-bloated balls slapping against the backs of my thighs.

"Fuck easy," I groaned, trembling as his muscle-corded forearms pressed against my belly. He kissed my neck.

I felt his dick sliding down my spine and between the cheeks of my ass. Then the blunt, sticky tip slipped into place against the quivering, tightly puckered lips of my asshole. He began stroking my belly, his hips pumping slowly and tentatively. I strained to open my channel for him, grunting when his fat knob popped through my sphincter. Joel growled softly and licked my neck.

He slipped one hand down along the back of my left thigh and coaxed me to hook my leg over the back of the sofa. I did so and

he began to sink into me. I reached back and pressed my fingertips against the shaft of his cock, mentally counting off the inches
of his cock, ready to tell him when he began to hurt me. I waited
as inch after inch slipped up inside me, but there was never any
pain. I felt incredibly full, and the heat that radiated through
me made me sweat, but I never had the least sensation of discomfort. It was with some shock that I felt my fingers tangling in the
silky floss of his pubes. Reaching down, I cupped his balls and
realized that he had impaled me to the hilt.

"Good?" he whispered. By way of answer, I gripped his wrist
and pushed his hand down along my belly to my rigid prick. He
wrapped his fingers around the shaft and squeezed tight. "Joel
fuck now," he muttered, seeming to have difficulty stringing the
words together. I craned my neck around and kissed him on the
jaw. He pressed his cheek against my shoulder and started to
fuck me.

Feeling his enormous, rigid manhood sliding in and out of
me made me hot all over. I could sense the fullness when his
hips were pressed tight against my ass, then the gradual emptying of my channel, allowing the stretched-out tissue to collapse
in on itself. I flexed my asshole, gripping his spike, making him
whimper. In and out he plunged, his strokes punctuated by the
slapping of his heavy balls against my leg.

I felt him come the first time, shortly after he started. There
was a flexing deep in my gut and his hard chest pressed against
my back. Judging from the intensity of the heat in my ass, he was
shooting as heavily as he had done just minutes before. The
mere thought of all that hot goo pumped into me made me shiver
in excitement. Joel didn't even slow down, just kept riding me,
fucking my ass with long, steady strokes.

By the third time he had unleashed his sticky flood up into me,
I was full to overflowing. I could feel the jism oozing out of my
ass and running down my leg. I reached down and pressed my
fingertips against my asshole. His dick was still pistoning, still

hard, almost hot enough to burn. His bulging knob battered against something tucked up in my ass that caused me to quake with pleasure. He drew out and thrust forward, battering it again, and then again.

I beat my fists against his thighs as I let fly, shooting jism out over the sofa onto the hearth beyond. Joel held me, his cock pistoning in my guts, prolonging the sensations of orgasm till they were almost painful. Once drained, I collapsed against the cushions, kept from falling only by Joel's mighty spike, driven up into me like a second spine.

He had come again when I did—I had felt it gushing into me—but still he would not stop. I struggled to break free, but his grip tightened and he began babbling that he would be gentle, would be still, wouldn't hurt me. He was gentle—as gentle as a man his size could be—but my poor bruised ass channel needed rest from his relentless pummeling.

I laid there, taking deep breaths, trying to relax my muscles, but the discomfort increased until his horny attentions seemed less like sex than punishment. Finally, in desperation, I balled my hand into a fist and lashed out at him, striking him on the hip. It was like beating a brick wall and had about the same effect. His grip tightened and his breathing became increasingly harsh as he continued fucking me.

"Aaahh!" I screamed in desperation, frantic to get through to Joel that he had to stop. The shrill sound was still echoing in the big room when I heard a door open and the mutter of voices. Joel's incessant pumping stopped instantly and he climbed off of me. He uttered a shrill squeal of fear, ran to the far corner, and cowered against the paneled wall. I turned and saw two men, big men, moving rapidly across the room.

They were tall and muscular—as everyone here seemed to be—wearing skin-tight black leather pants and heavy, knee-high boots, molded to fit their bulging calves. They were naked from the waist up, except for leather harnesses that criss-crossed their chests and wide leather armbands that cinched their right biceps. Each man carried a thick black club in his right hand. They glanced at me contemptuously, then bore down on Joel.

"Want to fuck?" the blond one snarled, waving his club menacingly in Joel's face. Joel shook his head, obviously terrified by the two men. His big shoulders were hunched and he was cupping his balls in his hands protectively. His hard-on had wilted for the first time since I had seen him and hung limply between his thighs. "I asked you if you wanted to fuck," the blond barked, pressing the end of his club against Joel's right biceps.

"No!" Joel cried. Then his body jerked convulsively and he staggered away, holding his arm. The other man approached from the opposite side and pressed his club against Joel's left thigh. Joel looked at him pleadingly, shaking his head. The man laughed cruelly and Joel dropped to his knees. I saw the spark arcing on his bare thigh and realized that the men were attacking him with cattle prods.

"Stop!" I cried. "Don't hurt him. I'm alright." They didn't even acknowledge my existence, just closed in on Joel, touching the prod to various parts of his body. The setting seemed designed less to stun than to cause pain. After a jolt to the tip of his big dick, Joel broke through the men and dashed across the room. They leaped after him, raising their clubs and beating him about the head and shoulders until he dropped to the ground. Then they began prodding him again until he staggered to his feet and stood passively between them.

"Fuck?" the blond roared. Joel nodded his head miserably. He bent forward and spread his cheeks. The blond guard smacked his ass with the club, then crammed half its length up into him with one brutal thrust. Joel moaned but didn't move. The other guard grabbed Joel's hair and pulled his head up. He pressed the tip of his club to Joel's lips and his mouth opened. He gagged as the guard pushed the club down his throat, but still made no effort to get away. Then the guards began thrusting the clubs in and out of his body, gradually increasing the current until Joel was jerking around in agony. His muscles were all knotted and the sweat was pouring off of him.

At last, in desperation, he spat out the stick in his mouth and stood up, his arms high above his head, fists clenched. The guard who had been pounding his throat with the club began beating him about the rib cage with it, the blows landing with sickening thuds against his muscle-slabbed sides. Joel jammed his elbow into the ribs of the man standing behind him and the guard let go of the club. It popped out of Joel's ass and rolled under a chair. The man he had struck roared out his rage and lunged at Joel, knocking him to the floor.

Before he could rise again, the two men were on him. One pinned his arms behind him and the other repeatedly smashed his fists into Joel's face and body. After a brief struggle, Joel slumped into unconsciousness. They dropped his lifeless body to the floor, kicked him a few times, then began dragging him away by the arms. I looked on in horror, powerless to stop them, wondering yet again what sort of place it was that I had come to.

I sat on the sofa for the next half hour, pondering the implications of the scene I had just been witness to. What had brought Joel to the state he was in? Why had the guards taken such delight in beating him when I had not been harmed and he had presented no real threat to them? Would I, too, be beaten for my part in what had taken place? What was this place, and what was really going on?

I already knew that this was no ordinary boarding school—yet I couldn't quite determine what it was. It appeared to be a cross between a clinic and a male brothel, based upon what I had seen so far. Mr. Black and the red-haired man who had examined me were hardly my idea of what teachers should be—unless, of course, I didn't yet understand the curriculum of private schools.

And then there was Joel. His body seemed highly improbable for a man of his age—I was still convinced that he was no older than I. Such mass and definition would, I was certain, take a man years of constant effort to acquire. And there was the matter of his sex drive, which seemed insatiable. Surely, all the students couldn't be as sexually charged as he. Or could they?

I was still brooding over all of this when I suddenly sensed that I was no longer alone. I looked up and gasped out loud. A man had materialized, standing no more than five feet from me. He appeared to be a man in charge. In the first instance, he was clothed— dressed in white pants, a white T-shirt and a white lab coat. He carried a clipboard and had a stethoscope around his neck. The baggy pants and the flowing coat obscured most of his body, but the torso under the tight shirt outlined the physique of a man in good, but not awesome physical shape.

I looked into his eyes and my apprehension abated somewhat. The man's smile and the warmth in his brown eyes were reassuring to me. His hair was an unruly mop of chestnut curls, falling down over a high forehead. His strongly sculpted jaw was rough with dark stubble and he had a small scar on his left cheekbone. As our eyes met his smile broadened.

"Brendan Callan?"

"Yes, sir," I replied, my voice slightly shaky.

"I am Doctor Marriot. I will be in charge of your regimen while you are here."

"My regimen?" I looked at him curiously. He put a hand on my shoulder. It was warm.

"Yes. I'll be in charge of your health and well-being, Brendan. I will administer your injections and work with your instructors to suggest the best programs to achieve our goals for your mental and physical perfection. I will monitor your progress while you are with us. If anything troubles you, please confide in me, Brendan."

"But...but, Doctor Marriot, I don't understand. Perfection? Injections? I...I..." I broke off, fearing that I was going to burst into tears. For the first time since I had arrived, I was afraid.

Doctor Marriot sensed my fear immediately. He knelt in front of me and cupped my face in both hands. "Don't be afraid, Brendan. I'll watch over you. My techniques have been perfected. You are all mine, Brendan. You will be my masterpiece." He leaned forward and kissed me gently on the mouth. Many questions remained unanswered, but in that moment, my fear evaporated.

Doctor Marriot took me by the hand and led me out of the room and down a long corridor that led to his office at the rear of the huge house. He ushered me inside and closed the door, locking it behind us. The room was in sharp contrast to what I had seen of the academy up to this point. The walls were lined with bookcases piled high with books, magazines, loose papers, and various rock and plant specimens. The floor was covered with an Oriental carpet, much stained and worn. There were two leather armchairs in front of the fireplace. Unlike the rest of the great house, the heat here was much less than tropical. I shivered involuntarily and the doctor looked at me with concern.

"You are cold, Brendan?"

"A little, sir," I replied, my shivers caused more by the way my name rolled off his tongue than the air. He knelt and lighted the fire that had been laid in the grate. He motioned me over to him and I stood in front of him, facing the fire as he began stroking my torso.

The doctor's hands were huge, the backs corded with tendon and veins, sprinkled with short, crisply curling brown hairs. As he rubbed my chest and belly, I pressed back against him, feeling the muscles in his own body flex and shift as he chafed the warmth back into me. Within minutes, with the help of the doctor and the fire, my skin was glowing a ruddy pink.

"There. That's better, isn't it?" I turned around and smiled at him, my hands touching lightly against his chest. He smiled back and didn't push me away. "Come, Brendan. We will begin."

I followed him across the room to an examining table in front of a bank of three high windows. He drew back the drapes and the sunlight flooded down onto the worn leather surface of the table. I sat perched on the edge while he tested my reflexes and examined my ears and throat. Then he had me lay back and began a thorough examination of my body from head to toe.

"Perfect skin," he muttered, rubbing his hand on my belly. "Soft as silk and not a trace of hair. We'll keep it that way, Brendan," he continued, his hand splayed on my chest. "When I have finished, you will be irresistible. Total and complete perfection." I looked into his eyes. They were gleaming with inspiration—or madness. Still, I had to trust someone in this strange place, and the doctor was so kind, so understanding—so handsome.

He walked over to a tall cabinet at the end of the table. When he turned around, he held a syringe in his hand, needle pointing up. He pushed the plunger until a few drops spurted out the tip of the needle, then walked over to me.

"Do you fear the needle, Brendan?" I shook my head in the negative. He smiled at me. "Make a fist." I did as he asked and he stuck the needle painlessly into my arm. No sooner was the needle withdrawn than I began to feel a prickling sensation along my arm that soon spread to the rest of my body.

"I...I feel strange, Doctor Marriot."

"Nothing to worry about, Brendan. Just the drug entering your system. No harm will come to you. Remember, I promised. Just relax now." I laid there while he injected another syringe in my other arm. The prickly sensation increased and I felt incredibly energized. The doctor stood beside me and stroked my body until I purred.

"No!" I shouted, sitting up abruptly and covering my crotch with my hands. "What are you doing?"

"Brendan, please be calm. I promised not to hurt you."

"No shots there," I replied, looking at him apprehensively. He had been preparing to inject something into the shaft of my cock—some pale blue liquid in the syringe he held in his right hand. Instead of becoming angry, Doctor Marriot merely shook his head and put the syringe back on a tray at the foot of the examining table.

"Let me show you something," he said, standing near the table and unfastening his pants. They slipped down over his lean, tightly muscled thighs and my eyes grew wide. "I was the same size as you before I began treating myself, Brendan. You see, I wouldn't use anything on you that I feared to use on myself." He had the most beautiful cock, a long, thick cylinder of flesh that hung heavily between his legs. The shaft was easily twice the width of mine, and twice as long as well. A fat vein shot down the center of it, splitting in two near the head, one branching into his foreskin, the other curving around the massive tube and out of sight. A pair of fat balls dangled behind it, drooping almost to the tip.

"You did that with your drugs?" I asked, amazed. He nodded and leaned forward slightly, the back of his dick brushing lightly against my thigh.

"Yes, Brendan."

"Can I touch it?" He nodded and I reached down and traced the vein from his bush down to his comehole. The doctor groaned and his eyelids fluttered shut. He reached down, scooped his massive tool up in his hand and let it flop on my thigh. It landed heavily, pulsing hot against my flesh.

"Let me show you how easy it is," he murmured. He picked up the syringe and injected its contents into the fat vein pulsing along the back of his piece. It twitched and began to stiffen, growing thicker as the blood rushed into it, making it rockhard in seconds. "Now will you let me inject you?"

"Yes," I gasped, watching, fascinated as the crimson head began pushing out of its cover, pressing hot and sticky against my skin. I felt a slight prick, and then my groin was flooded with warmth. My dick began to go hard and was soon hovering above my belly, swollen full and tight.

"The erection is the only side effect," Doctor Marriot explained, his voice suddenly hoarse. "It only lasts until you ejaculate."

"I can help you," I offered eagerly, suddenly overcome by my lust. The doctor nodded and I scrambled onto my hands and knees, swallowing his mammoth hard-on in one gulp. He thrust his hips forward and began stroking my head and shoulders as I sucked frantically on his cock.

The doctor shrugged his lab coat off and peeled out of his T-shirt, revealing a sculpted torso with no body hair to hide any of the exquisite detail. He was muscular without the bulk of the other men I had encountered, his faintly bronzed skin gleaming with vitality. Veins ran up across his forearms, over his biceps and up onto his squared shoulders. Another pulsed over the rippled wall of his washboard abs. I traced it with my fingers, from his glossy pubes up to the rise of his chest. I brushed the thick point of his left tit and the doctor's cock knob swelled so big it almost choked me. I came up off of him and looked up into his face. His eyes were closed and his mouth was open, obviously savoring every little wiggle of my tongue.

"Doctor," I asked after I had licked my way over every surface of his throbbing mantool. "Will you fuck me?" I blushed when I spoke the words, but the mere thought made my asshole tingle in anticipation.

"Whatever would please you, Brendan," he replied, scooping me up off the table in his arms and carrying me across the room. He tossed a pillow off one of the chairs and laid me down on the carpet. I rolled over and thrust my ass up, frantic to feel him pistoning his prick inside of me. The doctor got down on the floor with me, straddled me and braced his hands on either side of my head. I reached back and grabbed his stiffer, guiding it to the target.

I peeled his knob bare and pressed it against my hole. The doctor sighed softly as he sank deep into me. He hesitated more than once to skewer me to the hilt, but I kept thrusting my ass up, impaling myself deeper and deeper until his bush was scratching my asscheeks and his huge nuts were rolling against mine.

"You're so tight and deep," the doctor whispered, nuzzling my ear. "You will conquer any man who comes in your path, Brendan. Any man." He pressed his lips to my neck and began pumping, fucking me with long, slow thrusts, plumbing the depths of my channel, then pulling out till I was gaping and empty, whimpering for him to put it back in me and fill me up.

I lay there passively, staring into the fire's glowing coals, savoring his weight on top of me and the delicious friction in my ass. I wasn't just feeling it in my bowels or in my cock and balls— I felt it all over. My whole body tingled, thrilling with the ecstatic little rushes that shot through me whenever his big dick raked against something up in me, something that curled my toes.

"What is it, doctor?" I groaned, trembling as his crown raked the spot again. "I feel it all over when you do that."

"Your prostate, Brendan. A man's pleasure spot, guaranteed to be connected to every nerve in your body." He chuckled softly and began battering the place he'd named, making me jerk and twitch under him. At one point I reared up under him, lifting him up onto his haunches, leaning back against him, and pulling his arms tight around me. My own strength surprised me.

Then I fisted my cock and felt another surge of surprise. Perhaps it was my imagination, but it felt bigger to me, the shaft thicker, harder, filling my palm, making me squeeze tight to get my fingers to meet on the other side. I began jerking it, matching his rhythm inside of me.

He was pumping faster now, deep, jarring thrusts that lifted me up onto my knees. I pushed my ass back, wanting to feel all of him up in me, not wasting even one throbbing inch of his power.

The doctor began groaning, squeezing me so tight I could hardly breathe. His breath was hot on my back, the slapping of his pelvis against my asscheeks becoming louder and more frantic as he pushed himself over the top. His big balls slapped against mine one last time and I felt the heat shooting out of him, pumping his potency up my hole in thick, hot waves. I started shooting as well, striping the carpet with my jism. It seemed to pump out of me faster and longer than it had ever done before. I laid at least six lines on the rug before I started to dribble, the last of my spunk puddling between my tensed thighs.

When we were done, the doctor just held me, rocking slightly, his dick still thrust in me to the hilt. My head rolled back against his shoulder and I closed my eyes, perfectly content, feeling no need to be anywhere but in his strong, comforting arms. For this moment, at least, the Brentwood Academy seemed a much less frightening place.

DIARY OF A VAMPIRE
Gary Bowen

The many men, so beautiful!
And they all dead did lie:
And a thousand thousand slimy things
Lived on; and so did I.

—Samuel Taylor Coleridge

Baltimore, 6 October 1991

Every evening when I wake I am always a little surprised to find that once again Death has stayed his hand. Blood stirred in my veins, my lungs inflated. Slowly the coldness passed from my limbs. Bit by bit memory returned and with it came the loneliness of another day. I lay bleakly staring at the wooden canopy of my bed wishing for the uncertainty of natural life. Other men might die peacefully in their beds; not me. Murder was the only thing that would send me down to Hades.

Voices. My lethargy evaporated in an instant as adrenaline surged through my withered veins. I threw off the covers and crouched on the bed desperately extending my senses to locate the intruders. Nothing. I could hear their voices but I could not touch their minds. Like a cat I dropped lightly from my bed and padded to the closet. With a speed no mortal could match I donned jeans and a navy turtleneck to camouflage my pale skin. I would ambush the intruders while they thought I slept. A coil of hunger stirred in anticipation of the hunt.

My clothes chafed and restricted me and I realized I was melting into cat-form without conscious thought. I balked, and the transformation stalled, leaving me caught in the intolerably uncomfortable positions of being half man and half cat. With concentration I regained human shape. As effective a hunter as a cougar might be, I needed my intelligence to reconnoiter the situation and choose the best course of action. A hungry cat will kill whatever prey crosses its path. Rat or man made no difference. Blood was blood.

No board squeaked and no footfall sounded as I prowled quietly through the upstairs hall. Even in man-shape I was faster, stronger, and more ferocious than any human. I grinned in feral delight: I liked hunting. I slunk down the dark stairway with all senses alert and muscles coiled to spring.

Flickering blue light bathed the living room and spilled into the hall. Several voices bantered bad jokes about a football game, then the lilt of voices gave way to inane music. Television! I was stalking electronic ghosts.

In chagrin I crouched on the lower landing to watch Michael. He was slouching on the sofa, his head drooping and his legs splayed before him as he stared at the television. The television had lulled him into mindless passivity verging on sleep. No wonder I had not been able to sense him, there was no mental activity to detect.

My eye fell on the dirty dishes he had left on the cherry butler's tray. Chagrin turned to indignation. The dishes would scratch the fine cherry finish. I fumed. A butler's tray was normally used for carrying dishes; technically Michael had done nothing wrong. It had remained inviolate throughout the years of my ownership because I did not eat. I used it as a coffee table.

The wooden floors gleamed gently and smelled faintly of oil soap. They were not waxed, but washing away the accretion of years had freshened them considerably. The green, rose and ivory of the draperies and rugs glowed cleanly against the dark wood. Made of good materials and protected from the light they had survived in respectable condition. A faint odor of naphthalene perfumed them and preserved them from attack by silverfish and moths. Light softly reflected from the curvaceous legs and heart-shaped backs of Queen Anne chairs. Already two centuries old when I bought them, fifteen years of neglect had not noticeably aged them.

Michael had cleaned the house as thoroughly as soap and hard work could manage, and I was grateful. I could forgive some scratches on the butler's tray. My nephew had done his best to erase the deterioration of the years.

James had failed me. Before going to sleep I had arranged with him for the upkeep of my property. He was duty bound to see the house cleaned and the lawn mowed on a regular basis. He had not. The absence of vermin (animal, insect, or human) suggested that he had made some effort to carry out his obligation, but the peeling wallpaper bespoke minimal concern. He had control of my money, there was no reason for him to stint in the maintenance of my property. Worse, he had not wakened me when I failed to appear on schedule. We had planned on a short sleep, four years at most. He had let me rot for fifteen years! Michael did not even know me, but he respected the bond of kinship between us. He had worked hard on my behalf. James was bound to me by all the ties of emotion and law that I could manufacture and still he had failed me. Truly blood was thicker than water. Convenient or not, Michael was kin. I had to help him.

Michael yawned and stretched, his clean white tee shirt pulling tight across his chest, biceps bulging then relaxing. From his battered cowboy boots to his tight jeans with the silver belt buckle he was a prime hunk of American youth. His skin was smooth except for the five o'clock shadow of beard, and his muscles were supple and firm. The features of his face were regular, even pretty. But his eyes! They were large, dark and lustrous with long thick lashes. He had everything I liked in a man: Good face, good body, and good personality. Maybe not too bright, but from my viewpoint that was a bonus.

Sleep, I silently commanded him.

Emotions flitted across his face as he tried to follow the news and failed. His eyelids fluttered, the long lashes brushing his cheeks.

Sleep, I urged again.

His eyes closed and his breathing deepened as he succumbed to my slumberous influence. I watched the rise and fall of his chest in fascination as each inhalation stretched the thin fabric and briefly outlined the small bumps of his nipples. I crawled closer to crouch beside his legs, felt the heat of his body radiating from the jeans, and yearned to slide my hands under his shirt, tweaking the nipples hard, making them stand up, then lowering my mouth to each of them in turn, kissing turning into biting.... The ache in my teeth brought me back to reality. I enjoyed looking at Michael's perfect body, but my fantasy was impossible. I had promised Papa that I would not harm the family, and I had kept my word. I lifted Michael's hand to my lips and kissed it good-bye, then let go and rose. At least, that was my intention. Instead my fingers tightened their grip. My other hand slipped between his legs, pulling his thigh against my groin. A thrill of pleasure went through me to feel the hardness of his body against my soft sex. I would lie in his lap and his heat would warm me as I drank his blood.

No. Not now. I was too hungry; I would kill him.

But I want him! Blood and sex and death, I want him! I was acting like an idiot; I had friends I could go to, there was no need to throw myself at the first warm body that came along.

I want him.

I crawled into Michael's lap, my legs straddling his while my hands walked up his chest. He stirred under the strange weight, eyelids twitching with the effort to open.

No! Do not look at me! His body went limp, consciousness gone. I should get up, leave him, not molest him as he slept.

But I liked the feel of his groin between my legs, liked the feel of the blood pulsing through the arteries of his lower body. With my fingertips I traced the blood vessels to the great heart that fed them all. My hand curled as my fingers tried to bite into his chest. I wanted to crack his ribs and devour his voluptuous heart. With horror I realized that my fingers were pressing hard enough to bruise, fingernails biting into the thin fabric of his shirt. Whether I wanted it or not, the hunger would glut itself on anything it could catch, and it had caught Michael.

I dropped my head and sank my long teeth into my own forearm. The sleeve tore, and a widening stain of wetness seeped through the fibers, the blood a blacker darkness than the color of the fabric. Pain shot through my arm, but numbness quickly followed, then a pleasant tingling as the analgesic injected by my fangs took effect.

A rush of energy swept through me. Mortal blood always gave me a glow, but my own blood was like lightning. It tasted salty like mortal blood, but sweeter, and it made the room spin. I lost my balance and toppled over, falling into the narrow space between the coffee table and the sofa, scarcely aware of the impact of my limbs upon the floor. Such pleasure! No wonder it was taboo for immortals to prey on one another. We would destroy each other, or worse, deliberately beget more like ourselves to enslave for their blood.

After some moments the room ceased its spinning and I was able to rise. I had drunk enough blood to distract the hunger for a while, but not so much that I had done myself any real harm. The hunger would not destroy its host. It diminished me to know that I was the pawn of a force I could not control, but what could I do? Death or hunger, and neither was an option. Yet with hunger I could hold Death at bay, and so my course was clear.

I bent and kissed Michael's brow in gentle apology, then betook myself to the stairway, letting loose my hold on his mind.

He stirred, limbs tightening as he regained conscious control of them again. Would he remember any of the nightmare that had visited and nearly consumed him? I doubted it. Yet one hand retraced my touches on his chest, while his eyes slowly opened. He pinched his nipples lightly, catching his breath sharply at the sudden pleasure. His fingers moved slowly over and around the bumps in the fabric, then he licked his dry lips and stripped off his shirt in a sudden movement. His chest was hairless, the pectorals clearly defined. The abdominals were hard and smooth. Two little brown nipples stood erect.

He caressed his nipples, then his hands slid across his washboard belly to leisurely rub the length of flesh lying along his thigh. After a moment he stood up and slung his shirt over his shoulder with casual grace. He turned off the television and the house darkened. In the gloom of the hallway I was almost invisible, but to be sure he did not see me I stepped into the music room.

As his tread sounded lightly on the steps I slipped behind him, my eyes following him every step of the way as he sauntered up the stairs. His back was just as gorgeous as his front with his shoulder blades composed of strong triangles of muscle and bone, and his spine a subtle valley between the long muscles on either side. Helplessly I followed him up the stairs, lured by the temptation of his fresh, young flesh.

The library door closed between me and him. A hollow thump was followed shortly by a second as he doffed his boots. I plastered myself against the door, ear pressed against the wood so that I could hear every creak of the leather sofa, every soft breath.

And became aware of the growing lump of flesh between the door and my usually quiescent groin.

Immortality had its price: loss of sexual potency. I often became hard while necking, but it was only the blood lust, the desire to sink my teeth into firm, hot flesh. And when that consummation came it was far more intense than the orgasm of mere sex.

Yet I envied Michael. It was such a normal male thing to wake up horny and do something about it. Sadly I peeled myself away from his door and retreated to the bathroom. I had to make myself presentable and catch myself some dinner before the hunger recovered from the trick I had played upon it.

Michael's car keys were hanging on the hook in the kitchen. I pocketed them. He had not asked my permission to enter my house so I did not bother asking permission to use his car. Besides, if I spoke to him about the car then he would wonder why I wanted it, and I did not want to explain either my dietary habits or my sex life.

The car was an aging gray Corvette parked next to a fire hydrant. A ticket fluttered forlornly under the wiper while a freezing rain spit down from an ugly sky. I pocketed it to pay later. Anyone who hopes to escape the attention of the law should be scrupulous about upholding it in trivial matters.

I slid into the driver's seat, accidentally knocking off my fedora, but snatching it out of the air before it had fallen more than a few inches towards the runny pavement. I tucked my trench coat around me and slammed the door shut, then discovered that duct tape held the upholstery together and fast food wrappers carpeted the floor. After several complaints, the car grumbled and coughed, then roared to life. The dash lights came on and told me the gas tank was nearly empty, while the oil pressure light flickered on and off. The windshield wipers streaked, and only one headlight worked. The brakes went all the way to the floor. In short, it was a rolling death trap.

I nursed the car over to Billy Town, the white working class neighborhood on the eastern side of the city. When I was within a few blocks of my goal I eased it into the first open service station I found.

"My car needs some work," I said.

The bored mechanic was ready to go home. "Sorry, the pumps are open but the garage is closed." I opened my wallet and took out a hundred dollar bill. "I would be happy to pay overtime for you to stay and fix it." A crisp green hundred dollar bill works a special kind of magic. People will do things for one that they would not do for five grubby twenties.

"If it needs any work it'll cost more than a hundred," he said.

I pulled another Franklin out of my wallet. "Whatever it takes."

"You got it."

I stayed on the sidewalks as I cut across the damp and windy expanse of Patterson Park. The weather was vile, nobody would be cruising tonight, though perhaps a desperate john might be hanging around the men's room. I had been here often in the past; the anonymous sex and men without names had provided a regular part of my diet. But tonight I had another goal in mind: Clement.

Dodging puddles I wended my way through a twisting dark alley to the back of a shabby apartment building. A stick propped open the back door in blatant violation of the faded sign that said, For Your Own Protection, This Door To Be Kept Closed And Locked At All Times. I stood looking at the building in trepidation. Was it more decrepit than I remembered, or was that the additional effect of fifteen years of neglect? A miasma of decay oozed from the place, making my skin crawl. But I had to go in, had to at least look and see if Clement still lived here. My stomach turned to think that I was seeking out a creature that could abide such filth and dilapidation. But I had no choice; I needed to eat, and I needed Clement's special skills.

I slipped carefully through the sagging door to avoid snagging my trench coat or dirtying it by contact with the building.

Unidentifiable brown splatters marred the dingy beige of the walls while the odors of sour laundry and stale marijuana smoke permeated the air with a stench that clogged my lungs. It was hot inside, a temperature I normally relished, but the air was stifling, hardly relieved by the open rear door. I unbuttoned my coat, but did not remove it. It was my armor against the filth of the place.

I picked my way down the corridor, its threadbare carpet stretching over a hump running the length of the hallway. The carpet was the same dirty brown carpet that had been there fifteen years ago, the additional stains blending perfectly with the ancient decrepitude I remembered. Door number fourteen was surrounded by posters announcing the resident's political opinions: Anti-war, anti-government, pro-feminism, pro-ecology. Many of them dated to the time of my last visit more than fifteen years ago. A few posters of more recent vintage but similar sentiment had been added. Clement obviously still lived here. I rapped on his door with a black-gloved hand.

"Come in, the door's open!"

I pushed the door open as wide as it would go. It stuck on some dirty laundry. A skinny, gray-haired form I recognized as Clement turned in his chair, his mouth opening in a silent O of amazement. On my right a woman was sitting smoking Kools on his rumpled, sagging bed.

"Good evening, Clement. I have business with you." I tried to suppress the sound of disgust in my voice.

"Angel," he said in a choked voice. "I thought you were dead."

"That was naive of you."

I turned to the female on the bed. She had limp brown hair and wore a black tee shirt advertising a rude rock band. "If you will excuse us, Clement will make it up to you later."

"Hey, he's supposed to take me out to dinner tonight!"

Knowing the kind of females that associated with Clement I knew it was the loss of a free meal, and not the loss of Clement's company, that concerned her. I took a twenty dollar bill out of my wallet. "Get yourself some dinner." She snatched the bill.

"Hey, thanks mister. Take your time." I closed the door behind her and locked it.

Clement looked at me nervously from under shaggy brown hair streaked with gray.

"So what's with the suit, man?"

"This is a business call." He flinched, but his eyes glittered with the memory of what I had to offer.

"Whatcha want?"

There was no place that I dared to sit. Books and magazines were piled everywhere. On top of the refrigerator, on chairs, on the floor, on the counter beside the sink, over the rack where a few presumably clean clothes hung—no place was devoid of printed materials. The center of the room had a small clear space to enable him to reach his bed, his computer, and his refrigerator. I stood there.

"Do you still work for the university?"

"Yeah."

"I need a college transcript. Tonight."

"It'll cost you."

I opened my wallet and took out a hundred dollar bill. That was his usual fee for altering a grade.

His eyes fixed on the greenery. "More," he said. He was perpetually short of cash because of the way his mercenary girlfriends spent it. I pulled out a second bill. He licked his lips and kept watching. I pulled out a third bill. His lips parted and he started to breathe harder. I pulled out a fourth bill and his mouth worked in soundless protest. I pulled out a fifth bill.

He looked up at me. "How come you always have so much money?"

I fanned out the five hundred-dollar bills and held them in front of him. "Do you really want to know?"

He emphatically shook his head "no." He took the bills with a trembling hand.

"I want you to fix the records tonight. I'll be calling tomorrow for transcripts."

"No problem. What years?"

I thought about it. I had allegedly graduated from high school in '83. That would mean college graduation in '87—too many years to fill between then and now. "Eighty-five to '89." He typed, the ineffable numbers and letters scrolling past, then asked, "Name?"

"Rafael Guitierrez, Junior."

"How do you spell that?"

I spelled it.

"This you?"

I tensed. I had not wanted Clement to know my real name, but there was no help for it. "Yes," I said reluctantly.

"Birthday?"

"December 27, 1965."

"You're older than that. You're at least as old as I am."

"You're aging prematurely." He winced.

We filled in all the personal information, then proceeded to fill in the details of my education. It took hours of looking up classes in the on-line catalog, and then cross referencing them to make sure they had not been dropped or changed. Once we had the classes picked and grades assigned, it would be a number of more hours for Clement to enter them into the record and make sure it agreed with all the other records. I was running out of patience. "Make sure all my bills are paid," I grumbled.

He laughed. "No problem. Want to join a club or anything?"

I reflected a moment. "A big club. Anything musically oriented, or artsy, or literary. But big enough that nobody would remember a shy guy who never said anything."

"Theater?"

"Too cliquish."

"Movie club?" Lots of bodies sitting quietly in the dark, reviewing obscure foreign films, with discussion afterwards.

"Perfect."

"Anything else?"

"I think that finishes the education part." His weasel eyes swept over my suit and tie. He was not used to seeing me like this, and it made him nervous.

"You have something else in mind?"

Food.

It was too late to go elsewhere. The hunger would not allow it.

"Blood."

"You know what you have to do to get it."

I knew. I had done it with hundreds of men, preferably men I did not know, but Clement's hobby of computer hacking had come in handy often enough for us to get to know each other rather well. Or to put it more accurately: We knew one another's vices well.

I dropped to my knees before him as he unzipped his beltless beige polyester pants. I hated him for the way he smelled, hated myself for needing such a repulsive specimen of humanity. I did not remove my gloves as I pulled the pants down his legs. He pulled down his dirty underwear, the sight of which made my stomach turn.

I took his flaccid flesh in my black-gloved hand and fondled it. With the leather of the glove between my hand and his flesh I could almost pretend it was not what it was. It felt like overripe fruit. Then it hardened, and juice dripped from the tip, making a shiny spot on the black leather.

I put my other hand on his thigh, caressing it, while avoiding looking at his face, or his crotch, or his room. I closed my eyes; self imposed blindness was the only way to get through what I had to do. I bent my head into his lap and took his flabby little hard-on into my mouth. The taste of his dripping juice aroused my hunger, and I sucked him hard.

"Oh God that's good!" he said. "Nobody does that as good as you!"

I sucked him eagerly, wanting the hot liquid of his body squirting in my mouth. I clasped his hip in one arm while I cradled his balls in my other hand. I went down hard on him, sucking him down my throat, massaging his cock with my tongue, squeezing his balls with my fingers, wanting the consummation of my need as fast as I could get it.

Clement grabbed my hair and thrust his cock deep into my throat. I gagged, my nose buried in his smelly pubic hair. He liked fellatio; why would he not perform the elementary courtesy of shaving? But that was too much to ask of a man who wore the same underwear for a week.

I pulled his hands off my head and tried to sit up, but hot sour fluid oozed from his cock into my mouth, and my resistance melted. My need latched me tight to his flesh while he raped my face with violent strokes. He was going to come soon, and I was going to get what I wanted and be free of his filthy embrace.

A sudden eruption of sour liquid filled my mouth, and I sucked eagerly, devouring every drop of the liquid of life he let me have—and craving more. My fangs extended, brushing against the sides of his cock, making him whimper in fear. I lifted my mouth and sank my teeth savagely into his thigh.

"Ow!"

I was not gentle with him; no tender embrace to reassure him that I cared for him and would not harm him, no soft sensual sucking like a baby at his mother's nipple, no sensual communion of blood and desire; only the animal feeding upon his prey.

I wanted to kill him, wanted to wipe out his witnessing of how my need overrode my self-respect, the way it dragged me to the lowest levels of humanity, the way I would pay any price to keep myself alive. And most of all, I wanted to destroy him for understanding nothing but that he could exploit my lust to gratify his. Better that he should die than humiliate me this way.

He beat futilely at my head, whimpering and moaning in fear. He could not hurt me; he was a spineless geek. I could drain the blood from him like a giant leech and he was powerless to stop me. I could bloat myself with blood, fill myself with so much blood that I would not need to eat for a week.

But only for a week. I would have to eat again—the hunger never ended. If not Clement, then somebody like him. A drunk at a nightclub, a bum sleeping in the park, a prostitute; these were the inevitable companions of my hunger.

I sat up abruptly, his blood dripping down my chin. I rubbed it with my gloved hand before it could spot my white shirt or stain my expensive suit. Clement stared at me, the fearful confusion in his face showing that he sensed but did not understand the danger he had barely escaped.

I rose and went to his filthy sink and ran the water. I put my gloved hands under the flow and washed them clean with plenty of melting green soap, then washed my face and mouth. I washed them again, then washed them a third time. I rubbed clean a circle on his grimy mirror and inspected myself carefully. Satisfied that my clothes were unspotted, I put my gloves under the water and washed them again. I would never feel clean.

At last I turned to him. He had righted his clothes and was crouching on the far corner of the bed, as far away from me as he could get in the chaotic confines of the room. He was pale, and had one hand on the wall to keep his balance.

"I'll apply for transcripts and a copy of my diploma tomorrow. The records had better be ready by then." He nodded compliance with my will.

I stalked out of the claustrophobic room, retracing my steps to the cool, fresh air of the park. Loamy smells of decaying leaves and the perfume of ever-present frostflowers cleansed my nose of human pollution. I leaned against a leafless tree for a long time with the rain beating down and dripping from the brim of my fedora.

SWIMMER'S BODY
Pat Califia

"**T**ime for morning laps, Surfer Boy," Gary told himself. "No dawdling. Well, maybe a few extra deep-knee bends, just to show our bronzed and God-like body to the stolid Swede in the far lane. Wonder if he can see the crack of my butt in this new suit—or do the leopard spots (which make Coach Bassett cluck his tongue) camouflage the dividing line between my buns, which have been unbuttered for far too long?" He did an imitation of Coach Bassett's cluck. "A young man, so much promise, so little—what? Let's just say he wouldn't marry the boss's daughter, Coach."

The outdoor pool was perfectly smooth turquoise Jell-O in a white, Olympic-sized trough. Gary thought (peeking between his toes) that it might really be like diving into a thick gel, and he would simply flounder, unable to pull his smoothly shaved torso through it, no matter how long his reach. It would be a fitting end to these deadly dull two months (and two still to go!) at the Little Dixie training camp.

As always, he was in the water before he knew his body had decided to throw him into it. It was a good dive, and the shock of pleasure he felt at his own skill made him lose consciousness of the need to time arm-strokes, breathing and kicks. Instead, it felt as if a wave flowed down the whole, single muscle that was his body, propelling him smoothly, without thought or strain. Then he rolled (toes brushing the electric eye that timed his laps) and kicked harder, suddenly furious to be done with it. He had hoped, when he sent in his deposit, that the heat and isolation would make it easier for him to stay in the water here, building his peak for the spring matches.

But he hated swimming when he was only training, hated it as much as someone who wasn't any good at it. It was his ticket to college, to something other than obscurity and a desk job in a medium-sized city. He loved competing—the adrenaline rush, the knowledge that, win or lose, you didn't dare hold anything back. But everybody in the pool came ready to win. You had to train, and it never got easier for him, only harder, and he was so upset with himself that he took in a lungful of water instead of air and had to haul himself up on the rim of the pool, choking like a little kid in his first Red Cross swimming class.

The Swede finished before he did, and Gary passed him in the shower on his way to his locker. Larsen was bigger than Gary. His muscles looked like slabs of pale stone when he was in repose, but in the water he was a shark. His impartial, careful hands applied soap evenly to his body, completely unaware of the beauty of what they touched. Gary made the clucking noise again. He couldn't imagine anybody snapping a wet towel at his ass in this locker room, much less waving anything more interesting around.

Back in the dorm, Gary saw a small stack of mail on his cot. He immediately cheered up. Under a letter from his mother and a letter from his "roommate" Aaron (the return address had only a discreet initial before the surname) was a big gray envelope. *The Advocate* had finally caught up with him. He had debated whether it was wise to notify the paper about his temporary change of address, then figured he would go nuts without a little contact with gay life. Since nobody was in the dorm, he slit the package and skimmed the magazine. The letters (even Aaron's) would be safe to read at lunch. This was not.

They had sent him the East Coast edition. He chuckled at the restaurant reviews for New York City and Washington, D.C. No excuse not to have a swinging weekend now! Probably nothing in the classifieds either, but what the hell, he didn't want to read the opera review or a feature about gay involvement in the anti-nuke movement. There were four whole columns of ads from California. Unbidden, his eye picked out Aaron's post office box and flipped up to read the ad ("Straight-appearing young executive looking for summer fun, no strings, no games, no fats, fems or downwardly mobile types"). Well, they had agreed there was no sense in Aaron coming home to an empty apartment every single night. Feeling a little pain behind his sternum anyway, he flipped to the end of the classifieds. Well, what do you know—there was actually one entire ad running under his state. "Fine mind in a swimmer's body seeks same. Let's make a big splash!"

He couldn't stop laughing. He ripped the ad out, stuffed the magazine back into its envelope, and on his way to the cafeteria, as he buried it under a bunch of trash in a big oil drum, he was still laughing.

Over lunch, Coach Bassett stopped and handed him a thick packet. "What're these?" he said, around a mouthful of salad.

"Publicity photos. Pick out the three you like the best. You can keep the rest or pitch 'em."

He had forgotten all about the photo session last week. Surely this was an omen. He fanned them out on the table and picked one of himself on a stand, with his arms up and tense (showing off the deep armpit, his beautifully proportioned lats). His quads stood out nicely. Unfortunately for the newspapers, so did his basket. But the anonymous advertiser (read "geek") would appreciate it. Before he went to the track to run his laps there ("Are you a man or a merry-go-round, Surfer Boy?"), he stopped at the dorm again for an envelope and stamps.

"This is a real swimmer's body," he wrote on the back of the photo, "and if you can match it, drop a pic c/o," and the address of the camp. "If not, don't bother."

Three days later (three days during which training seemed less arduous), he had a snapshot of a man (still young, but older than Gary, with a nose that looked as if it had been broken) treading water. Even wet, his dark hair curled. His thickly furred chest was so broad that Gary wondered if it didn't churn up too much water resistance to make good time. But those biceps and forearms looked burly enough to drag the Titanic to safety. He reluctantly conceded that in this case, the phrase "swimmer's body" had not been just a euphemism for "90-pound weakling." He turned the picture over and read, "All this, and I have my hair," and a phone number. He ruefully rubbed his shaved skull. He was so used to other swimmers' faces, he had forgotten how odd his pale blond eyebrows and bare pate would look to anybody who wasn't in training. Cocky fucker. Where was the pay phone?

It was a brief call. Something wrong with the connection. He even had trouble making out the guy's name—Marvin? Martin? But it turned out he lived just a bicycle ride away. Gary explained his situation at the training camp—so many days of working out, followed by a break day—and received a standing invitation to come over any time during his "off-day." Tomorrow, as it turned out.

That night, in his sleep, the lumpy cot turned into the chest and thighs of the well-built stud in the photograph. He lay face-down on him, his hands pinned between them, searching for the other man's cock. He knew it would be thick, the foreskin like folds of silk, the balls heavy in a sac covered with crinkly black hair. The whole flexible, flaccid shaft could be cupped in one hand until he began to squeeze and massage it, then it would slowly add inches until it protruded beyond his fist.

Instead, he woke up, and realized it was his own cock that was thrusting in his grip. He took a deep breath, listened. Nobody else was awake. Then the urge to come was so sharp, a pain in his lower stomach, that he said, "So what?" out loud and took himself over the edge. The splashes of cum felt good on his knuckles, hot, and the tangy smell made him realize he had not jerked off since his first night here.

He made himself eat the next morning, made himself wait. He read a newspaper that was two days old and started a letter to Aaron knew he would not finish. But it was only 9:30 when he got his ten-speed out of the shed and pedaled away from the training camp, a note with directions he had already memorized tucked carefully into the pocket of his T-shirt. He was only on the macadam for twenty minutes before he peeled off and went down a dirt lane. A pheasant broke cover and beat frantically across his path. He swerved, then realized it was already safe in the brush at the other side of the road. The sweat between his T-shirt and skin reminded him of the shape of his own body, how it had felt to rub his palm across his nipples, last night, and pinch one of them gently to make himself come.

He heard the creek before he saw it. The bike bumped across a wooden bridge. Then the road took a turn to follow the creek, which rapidly became a river. Even after the water was hidden from view by thick growths of willow, he could hear it laughing to itself. According to the odometer between the handlebars, he must be almost there. Yep, the road forked here, and there was a lightning-struck oak, so he took the right-hand branch, away from the water (twinge of disappointment), and there was the house, "set back from the road a piece," as Marvin or Martin had promised, under shady trees. The yard was overgrown and the house looked uncared for. He knocked on the front door, got no answer, and walked his bike around to the back. A note was pinned there. "Gary, I'm down by the lake. Just follow the trail. Hope you left your Speedos at the camp. Martin."

He grinned, leaned his bike against the steps, and loped down the trail. It was a few hundred yards down a slope, and there was the river again, feeding a medium-sized lake. A homemade dock ran into the water. This must be where the snapshot had been taken. But he didn't see anybody. Oh, well, the water looked good. He skinned out of his cutoffs and T-shirt and strolled to the end of the dock.

"Dive in! It's deep enough," somebody called. There was his host, treading water thirty feet away. How had he gotten so close without making a sound? Gary shrugged and slipped into the lake. It felt good.

Then it felt better. A hand that was a great deal warmer than the water had circled his shaft, and was measuring him slowly, up and down. Taken aback by the lack of preliminaries, he tried to reach for the other man's body, but Martin evaded him. "Let me take you out further," he said, and had him in a towing hold before he could protest. Gary could have sworn they didn't stop until they were in the center of the lake. Martin let him go, then began a weird game of sexual tag. He was swimming around Gary in amazingly quick, tight circles, and he would dart in just often enough to administer a caress (and keep Gary afloat). Sometimes it would be his mouth instead of his hand that would enclose Gary's cock. He trembled, trusting the hands under his buttocks to keep his head above water. It had been too long since he'd felt so good. He was eager to reciprocate, but no matter how hard he tried, he couldn't grab hold of Martin's dick, although a couple of times he felt it brush his stomach or thigh, and knew it was as hard as his own.

"Let me touch you!" he finally cried, exasperated, near tears, and Martin (behind him) pulled him close, wrapped his hands around Gary's aching, over-stimulated rod, and thrust his own cock in between the muscular cheeks of the other swimmer's ass. He timed the caresses to his thrusts, giving Gary the giddy sensation of simultaneously fucking and being fucked, though he knew Martin's cock remained outside his body. He did not realize they were still swimming until he saw swirls of semen lost behind them and the familiar piers of the dock.

He was pushed toward the ladder before he could turn and kiss Martin, who had darted away, back to deeper water. "You go inside, lunch is on the table. Don't wait for me to eat. I want to swim a little more."

Gary felt as if he would collapse if he stayed in the water. The intensity of his orgasms made his limbs shake. How often had he fantasized about sex in the water—weightless, streamlined sex— with another athlete whose stamina and physique equaled his own? He dragged himself into the house and ate cheese and fruit. He even made himself a thick sandwich out of forbidden coldcuts. This morning had made him feel better than months of coaching, lectures on nutrition, sprints and power-lifting. When he was done eating, Martin still had not come out of the water. He wandered into the living room and fell asleep on the couch. His dreams were disturbing.

He had read about Vietnam vets who had been injured by a particularly nasty kind of land mine, one that jumped to waist height before exploding. The men who survived usually lost their genitals as well as their legs. (In his sleep, Gary protectively cupped his drained, tender cock and balls.) These men had a powerful incentive to participate in a government experiment with human DNA that might restore the lost parts of their ruined bodies. While a carefully crafted virus went to work on their genes, the men sat patiently in vats of nutrient solution and antibiotics. Part of the experiment worked fine. With proper recombinant encouragement, their newly ambitious cells recreated perfectly operating genitalia. But from that point on, things went awry. The leg bones fused, articulated like a spine. Where new legs were supposed to grow, large and powerful fish-tails sprouted.

The military was not apologetic. The experimental subjects were reminded that they had known they were taking a huge risk. The men (men?) were relocated to a larger, common pool, where they began to forge a joint identity as mermen. The Pentagon's liaison to the research staff hinted at the possibility of them re-enlisting, being formed into some kind of special services unit. The idea of being kept together, belonging somewhere (and the accompanying training in underwater communications, demolition, navigation, flora and fauna) kept many of them from going into shock. But there were some men who could not live in such a drastically altered form. Gary woke up before one desperate man in his dream figured out how to commit suicide in a tank with smooth aluminum walls.

The house suddenly seemed threatening, and claustrophobia propelled Gary outside, back down the trail to the lake. Where the hell was his friendly swimming companion? The hot afternoon sun was soothing, and made the goosebumps fade from his bare skin. Once more he scanned the lake and saw no one, until he went to the end of the dock. "Ready for another round?" leered the handsome face.

"I'm not sure. I had some pretty weird dreams."

"Come into the water and tell me about it."

He slipped nude into Martin's element. But instead of talking they wound up sexing, even more frantically than before. Gary barely made it back to the camp by curfew.

The next off-day found him back at the house. And the next. The sex was good, but Martin would not allow Gary to touch him, nor would he engage in any kind of penetration. Gary accepted it after awhile, assuming that since Martin was calling the shots, he could change things if he wasn't satisfied. The brief heat of Martin's semen, jetting between the cheeks of his ass, before lake water washed it away, became an erotic trigger that always made him come. Then he would get out of the water, go inside and eat, take a nap (always marred by more weird dreams), and eventually come back outside for more sex. When he left, Martin would still be in the water.

One day, the strangeness of the repetitive dreams made it impossible for him to respond to Martin's light and authoritative touch. As the lusty grin on his friend's face was replaced with genuine concern, Gary knew he was falling in love with this man, and instead of making a joke about not being able to get it up underwater, he haltingly described the dark visions that troubled him. Eventually even his muscles tired of treading water, and he relaxed into Martin's tattooed arms, wondering how he could keep both of them afloat so effortlessly. Then he happened to look down, but off to one side, the way his father had taught him to look for fish in a brook. And he saw the lower half of Martin's body for the first time. The two-fluked tail was muscular, dappled brown like a rainbow trout and undeniably masculine.

"It's true, then," he said thoughtfully, and wondered why he was relieved. Probably because he had known the truth for a long time, but had not let himself acknowledge it. Martin was a mer.

"Yes. Do you want to hear the rest of the story?"

He did. His body signaled urgently that he wanted something else, too, but he made himself wait.

"One of their own scientists betrayed them. She had spent years developing a way to communicate with dolphins, killer whales, and other intelligent ocean mammals. The military had gotten wind of it, taken over her project, and taught the pinnipeds to carry explosives and conduct underwater sabotage. A lot of the animals were injured or killed during carelessly conducted exercises. She was supposed to teach each of us how to work with a dolphin partner. A weird variation on the K-9 corps. Somehow, she found out that they intended to use us to staff underwater nuclear missile silos. She also found out how they intended to replace us. The mer-virus is in our semen. We can make any man into a mer. The military counted on our isolation from "normal" humans to encourage homosexual activity if anybody was reluctant—and like the hypocritical bastards they are, they knew we wouldn't find out prematurely because we wouldn't dare fuck around as long as we were under their supervision. One night she sneaked out to our tank, told us what the score was, and gave us the location of the underwater base they had already built, for us. Then she let us loose. We found it, and it wasn't well-enough guarded to keep us from making it our home."

Gary postponed dealing with the full import of this by quibbling about details. "How do you live underwater? You still breathe air, don't you?"

"For the first six months we have to use our lungs and can only live in fresh water. Then we get our gills and have to go salt-water, full-time. I'm getting my gills soon." Martin took Gary's hand and ran his palm over his chest. He could barely feel the edges of raised half-circles—the gills that were about to break the surface and become operational. "I've never seen the ocean base. I'm one of the new ones—a recruit. We could see it for the first time together, Gary. I won't tell you it's easy. They want us back, and we'll have to convince them it's less expensive to just leave us alone. But if we win the war, we could build a whole new world. We're far from helpless. We have the missiles that were left in the base. We can threaten to expose their medical experiments to the media. It's your chance to get away from—"

"Stop. You don't need to tell me." Away from Old Mother Bassett and his satchel of vitamin pills. Away from Aaron (who would probably be consoled by the fact that his ad would be cheaper to run without the phrase "no strings"). Away from the stifling closet of the racing circuit. Away from the boredom of staying in peak physical condition for no good reason. He would never have to come out of the water, and he could be surrounded by gorgeous, available men all the time—and it would mean something besides a trophy or a scholarship.

"Give me that seafood," Gary snarled, laughing, and dove for Martin's rigid cock. He ran his tongue up and down the fat vein on the underside only a few times before Martin's hands found his head underwater and urged him to take the heart-shaped head into his mouth. He licked around, inside the piss-slit, his lips rolling back and forth across the coronal ridge. Martin's grasp on his head grew tighter, and Gary's teasing was soon rewarded with a thick, slick dick opening his throat. The first dose of semen spurted into his mouth almost immediately, and he swallowed every drop of the salty, sticky cream. "All I can say is, I hope we have to do this a lot to change me," he sputtered, surfacing.

Martin laughed. "We can make it last a little longer when we don't need to come up for air. When you have a real swimmer's body."

"Soon, my man, soon. Hold me. The way you usually do. But this time—go all the way."

REVOLT OF THE NAKED
D. V. *Sadero*

Dr. Jason left the Dome, hurrying down to the main street of Talanta. His mind continued to focus on young Oslo, who was playing a dangerous game. As part of the deception, Jason was worried a little about his own safety and a great deal about Oslo's, a man for whom he had developed tender feelings.

He found the tent of the official dealer in Nakeds. Dr. Jason appraised the stock as the dealer stood by respectfully. Only one of the Nakeds impressed him, a pale-haired young man squatting on his haunches on the pale pink grass. Behind his long reddish-brown cock, a large pair of balls sagged nearly to the ground in the afternoon heat.

"Let me see that one," Jason said.

The dealer called the Naked over and ordered him to stand in front of the doctor. He said, "He is a used Naked. Those two over there are new."

The doctor thought the new Nakeds were not very good specimens, but he said nothing, just looked closely at the used Naked, noting with approval the head of rich and thick blond hair, the frank, handsome face and its blue eyes, the well-muscled arms, and the small but work-hardened hands, developed chest, and flat, labor-firmed torso.

No doubt brought in from the outlands by some farmer, Dr. Jason thought. He closely examined the Naked's large, smooth, heavily foreskinned cock, then had the dealer order him to turn around.

The neck looked strong but not too thick, and the back was well muscled, wide at the shoulders and deeply tanned. It tapered to a small waist that ended at the curves of two small, rounded buttocks. The legs consisted of well-developed thighs on finely sculpted, rockhard calves.

Dr. Jason put his finger in the crack between the Naked's buns and found the asshole firm, without scar tissue, and tight. "What is his name?" Dr. Jason asked.

"Vek," the dealer said.

Vek, Dr. Jason thought. Like all Nakeds, given a name of three letters and one syllable. Not even allowed a decent human name. Perhaps Mario can get along without—no, he cannot. I know what would happen to him, sooner or later. I can't bear the thought of his being harmed. Of ending up among the Fucked.

In a short time, the Naked was purchased, and the dealer ordered Vek to obey his new master.

"Follow me," Dr. Jason said, starting down the main street of the town of Ultima.

Vek had hoped that a new voice would not command his will so completely as Dayton's had, but he found it as impossible to resist.

In a short while they had walked the winding path up the hill and reached the doctor's prefab house with its view of the town and the Dome. Made in the airy, many-windowed style suitable for hot climates, the building's roof overhung its walls, creating a veranda on all four sides.

Dr. Jason ordered Vek to wait just outside the door. He went inside. "Mario, Mario!"

A young man with large green eyes and light brown hair and a wiry, neatly muscled body came into the living room. He looked a good deal like his father and, like him, wore only the briefest of loincloths. "Yes, Dad?"

"Happy nineteenth birthday, son." Jason embraced Mario in a big hug. "Vek, come here."

The slave stepped into the room.

"This is for you, Mario," his father said.

Mario gazed at the well-muscled Vek. "For me? A Naked? All my own? Wow, that's great!" He threw his arms around his father and hugged him tightly.

"You must take care of him," Dr. Jason said. "Re-member, he is completely subject to your will. But still he is a human being, so you mustn't abuse your power over him."

"I'll take good care of him, Dad."

"Vek! From now on, Mario is your master. You will obey him."

Vek bowed his head.

"Lie flat on that couch" was Mario's first order, "Spread your legs wide" his second. When Vek obeyed, Mario loosened his waist cord and pulled the restraining pocket of cloth off his hardening cock and tightening balls. He straddled Vek, framing the slave's butt between his powerful young thighs. "Oh, Dad, he's beautiful! He feels so good, he smells so fine." Mario spread the slave's buns. "Oh, Dad, he's pale white down in there, just beautiful."

Dr. Jason smiled and handed his son a crudely made little pottery vessel containing a lightly scented grease. "He's also tight, Son, so you may want to use some of this."

Smiling to himself, Dr. Jason stepped outside onto a little patio back of the house, carved out of the hillside. Through the open window he could hear Mario taking his pleasure.

Sounds gentle enough, Jason thought. He had not wanted Mario to have a Naked. He hated the idea of men in slavery. But he knew he was one of the few men on the plateau who felt this way. Every man, when he came of age, had to have a Naked for protection. Some had their Naked from the time they were twelve or thirteen, but it sickened Dr. Jason to see boys ordering men about and often mistreating them. And he was sure the boys' fathers were just showing off their wealth.

It was a compromise with his principles, but he could see no alternative. The society of men here in the Uplands was sick. There was no way around that.

For some weeks, since Mario's sudden maturing, Dr. Jason had worried about his son's safety. Though men rarely bothered boys, and were punished if they did, among adults outright rape was far from rare, considered not a crime but a sport. Seduction was a pastime, and men boasted of how many Freemen they had fucked. No man could really trust another. No man wanted to be among the Fucked, but most wanted to put other men into that unfortunate category. Oh, there were couples who got beyond the hang-ups of the society, the hypocrisy and pretense and brutality among Freemen, but they were few.

The powerful prejudice against being fucked that almost all men had was ridiculous. It dated from the time after the women died, when men turned to men for sexual satisfaction. Those who fucked were admired. Those who got fucked were the weak.

In the past, Mario had been deferred to as the son of one of the doctors who kept the race of man going. But now Mario was in his bright youth, with light brown hair flowing around his handsome face, deep green eyes, well-set shoulders, smooth skin, and good proportions, his beautiful little curve of ass, that long pink cock, its head covered smoothly with a thin, pale foreskin and his hard, smooth thighs. Jason knew that his standing in the community would no longer protect Mario, so now his son had a young and powerfully built Naked to accompany him everywhere.

Jason sighed. He knew Mario's other father wouldn't like him having a Naked, but there was no choice. Mario being one of the Fucked was unbearable to think about. He went to the window and leaned on the sill and gazed fondly at his son. Mario was running his long pink penetrator of a cock in and out of Vek's ass, slowly and with an almost rapturous concentration. Jason could see his son was completely lost in the world of physical pleasure.

Mario's father felt a strong urge in his groin, and was glad that Valor would arrive early tomorrow. Valor who was a Jungle Man who was Mario's other father and the love of Dr. Jason's life.

Evening. Where Ultima's two main roads cross, in the heart of the community, many men had gathered at the huge plaza at the beginning of the annual Birth Festival. Some were farmers who had come into Ultima for the annual holiday. Others were men of the town. All were looking over unfamiliar faces and untried bodies.

At one side of the plaza stood the Earthist tower, a high, thick turret of stone, built over many years by believers in the Earthist faith. Several of them now stood guard in front of the tower. A lot of men in the plaza found this amusing, since nobody had any reason to attack the Earthists, the last few believers in a religion whose great days were many years past. Middle-aged men thought of it as the desperate faith of their fathers, born in the terrible days of the plague. Most young men thought of Earthism as ancient history.

Crude stands and booths had been set up on the other three sides of the plaza. They offered a wide variety of goods: sweets, red wheat gruel and other foods, small clay pots of love-grease, clothing in the form of cords and strips of cloth, blankets and such for babies.

Dayton, now comfortable among all the buildings and men, strode with his son through the crowds, aware that he was attracting many admiring glances. His cock curved forth in his loincloth, which he wore low-slung and loosely binding, since he was half-hard with excitement at seeing so many beautiful men with such fine asses on them.

"Come on!" He tugged Reno around the corner. They went along a street lined with doorways, full of men in the skimpiest of loincloths, lounging and standing about near torches in cocked-hip, consciously sexy poses.

Every time Dayton showed interest in a man, the man would turn around slowly, hoping to fire him up by showing his butt. And Dayton, like many other men strolling up and down this block, was obviously turned on, his loincloth barely restraining his great slab of cock.

Dayton's son Reno looked here and there, showing nothing but curiosity, as Dayton noticed. "Who are these men, Father?" he asked

"Whores," Dayton said contemptuously. "The Fucked. You pay them and go in those little rooms and fuck them, or anything you want. Like with Nakeds. Except they don't *have* to do what you tell them. They're Freemen. It's kind of a kick to shove it up a man who's so depraved he's takin' it just for the money…. But I'm not payin' for it tonight—you can bet on that—not with all this free stuff walking around. Whew. You, uh, didn't get hard?"

"No, Dad."

"Yeah, well, I just wanted you to see this street…. And even better is what's at the end of it. Come on."

The lane of whores ended suddenly at an informal garden. Its numerous trails led into thickets of enormous ferns and bamboos surrounding a large central plaza bare of anything but thick white moss, its borders illuminated by wheat torches. This area was called the Field of Love.

Most of the men who wandered about here were cleaned and combed, their bodies fresh and new with recent applications of jungle water. The men, children of a race engineered geneti-cally for space travel and the tough existence of pioneers in strange and difficult environments, were all so much alike that any difference was a matter of pride, treasured, exploited. It was not enough to be bright, tall, handsome, muscular, horny, and hung. A man was happy if he was paler than others, or had an especially light or dark skin, was short and slight (a true rarity), or had great height, a curving cock, or was somewhat thinner or heavier than others—anything that would set him off from the rest of the men.

Men stopped to chat, sized up one another, and frequently they coupled up and walked off together into the deeply shadowy labyrinth of greenery.

Dayton sent Reno to walk around the town, cautioning him to stay where there was good lighting. Then Dayton set out to try his luck. He hit on men who were the type he liked: finely muscled, light boned. Some of them disliked the crude way he came on, reaching down to handle their balls and cocks with hardly a hello, as if they were no more than Nakeds. Others kept their distance, seeing Dayton as a beefily muscular, heavy-calved, massively hung farmer and fearing he might try to overpower them and shove his cock up their ass. It was exactly what Dayton had in mind.

After he struck out a few times, Dayton noticed his cock was aching with horniness. Obsessed with the velvety scrotums he had fondled, he sniffed his fingers. He thought of going back up the street and paying for a whore, but he had his pride. And it was still early.

Dayton found a number of other farmers in a corner of the plaza playing at dice under one of the torchlights. Two of them were old friends from nearby farms, and they brought him into their game. For the moment, the pleasure of gambling submerged sensual thoughts.

Deeply engaged in winning and losing, his red and green coins, Dayton still found it hard to keep his eyes off one of the other players, a townsman who was tall, beautiful and blond, his body pale from being hidden from the sun. This was a vanity some of the townsmen indulged in, to differentiate themselves from other men, especially the well-tanned farmers.

Dayton was excited not only by the pale skin but also by the man's flanks: thighs not thickly muscled like his own and those of most farmers, but long and flowing in line. And he admired the man's well-built but slender chest, his flat torso, defined and lithe, and his beautiful face and blond hair. Much to Dayton's pleasure the man's thick pink prick and deeply red balls were often visible, swinging this way and that as he spun the pebbles on the hard dirt. But what he admired secretly at every opportunity was the man's small white buns. So firm, Dayton thought, and probably an unfucked hole.

The man was named Zagreb. When he had wiped out the two farmers and his leatherlike purse bulged with red and green coins, he took a challenging stance and raised his voice. "Hey, doesn't anybody want to play anymore? Come on, you country boys, loosen up with your stones."

"Well, *I'll* bet with you," Dayton said, facing Zagreb.

Reno, who had come back from wandering the few streets of the town, ran up to him. "Father, isn't that all the coins you have?"

"Quiet!" Dayton roared. He turned back to Zagreb. From every side, farmers' voices whispered to him that Zagreb was a professional gambler. But Dayton merely drew himself up to his full height. In his most arrogant manner, he said, "Listen, city-boy, if I lose, you get my stones, all these"—he held up his heavy purse—"and my ass. And if I win, I want the same from you."

"You wouldn't know what to do with an ass!" Zagreb sneered. "Come on, bet stones against stones."

"What's the matter, city-boy?" Dayton barked, attracting the attention of many men nearby. "Too scared to take my bet?" He reached down, jerked his loincloth aside, and waved his meaty cock at Zagreb. Clear fluid lurking in the large slit began to drip and fall to the ground.

Zagreb laughed. "Scared? Shit! Listen, farmer, I haven't drilled a country guy's hairy, dusty, Naked-fucked asshole in a while. Make it your coins and your ass against mine, farmer." Zagreb ripped aside his loincloth, spilling into everyone's sight a very long and pale cock, its pink head peeking forth through thick puckers of white foreskin. The cock dangled down over a huge pair of red balls. "Think you can bear to lose it in five throws?"

"Done!" Dayton cried.

"Done!" Zagreb was sure of the dice-tossing skill he possessed in his long white hands. No ham-fisted farmer had a chance of beating him. Besides, he had been having bad luck lately, and had been barely able to get enough coins together for the annual festival. But Zagreb felt his luck had returned. His purse was filling up again. He needed to win a few more times, just a few more times.

As dozens of farmers, townsmen, and whores watched and made side bets, Dayton and Zagreb each knelt under the flickering illumination and began to play.

Zagreb won the first throw, but Dayton did not seem to care. In fact, as Zagreb was beginning the second round, Dayton calmly, almost absentmindedly, stroked his big, dark slab of half-hard prick. He appeared more a man amusing himself at his leisure, or flirting with another man, than someone risking social and financial ruin.

Zagreb won the second throw.

Dayton did not look upset. He still fondled his meat, which stood out hard now, its fatness greater than the width of some men's wrists, its thickly foreskinned head larger than a boy's fist.

Zagreb figured that Dayton was waving his cock around on purpose to get him upset, so he looked indifferent. Still, occasionally his eyes stole a quick glimpse of the farmer's enormous ugly meat. Zagreb made his third throw. He came up with a very high number.

Many of the men watching had their hands on their crotches,

kneading their meat. A few had pulled their cocks out and were jacking them as they watched.

Dayton took the dice in hand, threw them, and beat Zagreb's throw by one point, evening the score.

Now the crowd was pressing in. Townsmen wanted to see the loudmouth farmer get it, and farmers ached to watch Dayton fuck the smartass pretty-boy gambler.

A smiling Dayton let his prick jut forth stiff and big for all the world to see as he stroked his big brown compacted balls.

Nervous despite himself, Zagreb tossed the dice onto the ground. He scored higher than before. Smiling, he picked up the dice and dropped them into Dayton's brawny hand.

Dayton threw the dice. His count was the same as Zagreb's. Zagreb threw again, then Dayton.

"I won! I won!" Dayton cried. He snatched the bag of coins from the cord around Zagreb's waist, snapping the cord. The brief loincloth slid down Zagreb's leg, leaving him naked.

Suddenly paler than ever, Zagreb began to back away from the burly Dayton. He backed into the grip of several large farmers with erect cocks.

Smiling and moving his big hand up and down his big dick, Dayton approached Zagreb.

"Please!" Zagreb gasped out. "No! Townsmen, friends of mine, help me! You saw this game. This sweaty farmer didn't win fairly, and his friends are holding me prisoner. Townsmen, help me!"

The townsmen knew that Dayton had won fair and square. Many of them suspected that Zagreb was a crooked gambler, and he was generally thought of as overly impressed with himself. Nobody was inclined to battle for Zagreb.

After a silence that told Zagreb much, he addressed Dayton, who was standing in front of him, looking Zagreb's pale body up and down and smiling and stroking his own cock, making sure its great length pointed straight at the gambler. "Anything!" Zagreb said. "I'll give you all the stones I have, and I've won good money tonight."

As he talked, he struggled, but the farmers held him firm. Then, at a signal from Dayton, they forced Zagreb to his knees on the moss at the edge of the plaza, between two brightly burning wheat torches.

Dayton lubricated his dark cock, then crouched down over Zagreb. He pulled back his stretched and glistening foreskin, revealing a blunt red cockhead of considerable size. Gripping Zagreb's shoulders as he knelt, Dayton slowly and steadily shoved his ironhard cock into Zagreb's ass.

Zagreb screamed and fought to get free of the hands that held him down and the cock that was entering him.

Dayton slowly moved his meat in and out of the small, hard white butt, dog-fucking and smiling with pleasure all the while.

Hands moving on exposed, engorged cocks, the crowd gazed in silence at the two men, the farmer crouched over the gambler, clearly and plainly fucking him for all the world to see. Dayton lowered his big, muscular body down onto Zagreb, forcing him flat to the moss. He wrapped his powerful arms around Zagreb's arms and chest and at the same time signaled his farmer friends to let go of the gambler's body.

Set free, Zagreb strove to escape, twisting and turning in Dayton's grip. Each writhing movement only excited Dayton more. As his victim squirmed and screamed, the farmer pumped his prick in and out of him, faster and harsher.

Zagreb's excited muscles throbbed and twisted around the ever-more-deeply-invading cock, and Dayton felt his juice rise suddenly beyond control. It blasted free of his balls and blazed up his huge and vibrantly stiff cock to shoot forth deep into Zagreb. Dayton loosened his grip, rose up on his arms, and thrust his prick harder than ever into the man beneath him, pounding repeatedly against him, making it clear to the men gathered all around that Zagreb was not even struggling anymore.

Dayton's cries of acute pleasure combined with Zagreb's groans and screams to make a weird animal sound. Finally Dayton rolled off Zagreb and lay on his back beside him on the moss, at the feet of the watching men. Breathing as if he had just run a marathon, Dayton lay laughing and gulping in great breaths of air. Half-swollen now, its head still partly engorged, flaming red, and cupped in thick dark foreskin, his cock relaxed obscenely onto his abdomen. Drops of come drooled from the large slit onto the hairs and muscles of his belly.

Shakily, Zagreb rose to his feet in the crowd. He saw for the first time that the men all had hard cocks. One farmer's rough hand reached out for his pale body, then another. Zagreb twisted away, fled the torchlight for the darkness. A group of the men, most of them farmers, chased after him. Lounging on the moss among his admirers and friends, Dayton watched, laughing all the while.

FANTASY BOARD
Kyle Stone

WELCOME TO THE LAMBDA GATE
the Electronic Friendship Board linking the
Gay, Lesbian and Bisexual Communities
from around the world
=operating 24 hours a day=

over 8 Gigabytes of on-line files

*Chatting	*Bios	*E-mail
*Gifs	*Fantasies	*Games
*Messaging		*AIDS info

Come play with us!

Enter your HANDLE.............
Enter your PASSWORD..........

>>Hit any key to continue...............................>>

*THE LAMBDA GATE**MAIN MENU*

1* Message Area *public   2* E-mail *
                                 * private messages *

3* Bios…Just the stats, man.   4* The Hitchin' Post

5* Fantasy Board   6* Gifs * Grasps *
—a place for stories   * Shareware *

7* Games   8* Internet *
                                   * Newsgroups * E-mail *

9* Gateway: access to GayNet, and the Overseas Connection

10* Need help? Press <?> at any screen or <Y>ell for sysop!

========
>>What next?…> 1
========

```
========
```
*MESSAGE*AREA*
FROM: TIGGER...TONY
TO: ALL
SUBJ: HELLO
```
========
```

Hello. Anybody out there? My name's Tony and I'm new at
BBSing. My uncle bought me this computer for college and it had
a modem with it. I saw the ad for the Lambda Gate in a computer
paper, so here I am. I'm just looking for friends. I don't know if
I'm really gay or what, but I think so. Anyway...

I had this buddy in high school—we were both into gymnastics and some track events. One day he let me suck him off in
the equipment cupboard. It was dark and hot and smelled like old
gym socks and sweat and mildew from the uniforms. I was so
excited, I thought I was going to have a heart attack. We had put
the equipment away after team practice a hundred times before,
but this time there was a charge in the air that had nothing to do
with neatness! Neither one of us said a word. He pulled the door
shut, and I went down on my knees in front of him in the dark as
I heard his zipper slide down. I reached out and there was his
cock, hardening in my hand. Growing, reaching toward me. The
sour-sweet smell of him rose up around me, and I almost fainted
as my lips opened around him. Then his balls were in my hands,
warm soft furred sacks, swinging low, filling as I sucked at him
greedily, as if my life depended on it. He came, fast and hard,
and I drank him dry. It was a shock when he pulled away, tucked
himself in and left me in the dark. I stayed there a long time. I
jacked off till I came on an old T-shirt. Soon after that, he got a
girlfriend, and he didn't have so much time for me. I really miss
him.

I'm 19 years old, with black hair and brown eyes and a medium
build. I'm 5'10" tall. I guess I'm okay-looking. I love watching guys

work out, especially if they have a lot of hair all over and the sweat gets it all matted against their skin. That gets me hot! Sometimes when I see that, I throw a real boner, and it's embarrassing. Anyone else ever do that? In the steam room I try to see if maybe some other guy has an erection, too, but it's too hard to tell. What I really want to do is reach out and touch someone! Then I'd know. I think it'd be really great to roll around in all that steam and get it on with some hunk and then go and shower off together. But that hasn't happened yet. It never will, I know that. I guess I'm really too shy. So is anyone out there? I'd like to meet some guys around my age. I don't go to bars or other gay places. I know there are organizations, but I can't join anything now. I live at home. I don't have any gay friends. It's hard. And I'm horny all the time! Is there anybody there?

TIGGER

========
+tag+ Don't pick up the pho-@#$%!&...NO CARRIER
========

<Quit> <Save> <Reply> <Next> ?

```
========
```
*MESSAGE*AREA*
FROM: HONCHO
TO: TIGGER
SUBJ: HOWDY, GUY!
```
========
```

A great big howdy from the old head HONcho man here over on
Board # 4, The Hitchin' Post. Jes you git those cute little buns
down here to the front porch, you hear? These tired old eyes sure
feel good restin on yer bodacious bod, stud! Sounds like you
gonna fit right in with this rowdy crew! Hairy pelt steamin in the
shower? Yahoo! You wanna throw a boner, boy, go right ahead!
Throw off any clothes that might git in the way, while yer at it,
stud! Jes watch them pervs go down on their knees!

HONCHO....the head butt-wrangler down on the ranch


```
========
```
+ tag + A hard man is good to find. Oh, yeah!
```
========
```

<Quit> <Save> <Reply> <Next> ?

```
========
*MESSAGE*AREA*
FROM: REEDR
TO: ALL
SUBJ: STORIES
========
```

Hi, all—

My handle's REEDR and I write erotica—well, okay porn. :) If you're interested in finding out just how hot, twisted and weird I can really get, check out a few of the stories I uploaded to the Fantasy sub-board (that's screen 5, for the BBS impaired). Let me know how you like them, guys. If you drool enough, I just might let you see some more! <VEG>

```
========
+ tag + "Don't torture yourself, Gomez—that's my job!"
========
```

<Quit> <Save> <Reply> <Next> ?

========
*MESSAGE*AREA*
FROM: FRANK FOUNTAIN
TO: ALL
SUBJ: YO, SPORTS
========

What I want is real simple. I want to have a bunch of hot sweaty guys down in the basement, and I take off all my clothes and climb buck naked into the big tub we got down there, see? So then all these guys gather around in a circle and take out their dicks and start pissing on me. And their hot hard wetness hits my skin and sends jolts of pleasure through me. First I just lie there and let my skin soak up all that wet heat, feeling each golden stream dance over my chest and belly, coat my cock, wet my balls. Then the guys start to run out of water one by one, like a tap turning off, so they start to jerk off, ramming their fists up and down those shafts.

Pump...pump...slap...slewp...I don't even see their faces anymore, you know, cuz all I see is those dicks, dark red and luscious, being pumped for me. And then I feel the first spurt of cum, SPLAT, right on my face. So I snake out my tongue and start to lick it up, still hot from the man's body.

And then it really starts to happen. One after another these guys start moaning and shaking and shouting and that thick creamy spunk starts hitting me all over. My own shaft shoots all by itself, turned on by all that man juice...like being plugged into something, know what I mean? And I know I'm moaning, too, just smelling all that sex and rolling around in it. My whole naked body's covered in cream, my hairy legs and chest and arms caked with the stuff! So then I crawl up and hang into the edge of the tub and start to clean them off, every one, all those dicks, some cut, some not, most of them still semihard. So I suck and lick and drink down all of them, drawing them inside me as much as

I can, drawing in their taste and feel and smell and sound, so it's all inside me. And I cum again. I'm hangin' onto the side of that big tub so's I don't slide down, crouching in all that hot hot jism and piss, and my cock's shooting off like a fuckin' hose, man! It's so wild! Know what I mean?

Wanna cum with me?

Frank Fountain==: ;

                    .
              .
        .
           . .

          pissin' in the wind

========
+tag+ This face is leaving in 5 minutes. Be on it!
========

<Quit> <Save> <Reply> <Next> ?

```
========
*MESSAGE*AREA*
FROM: ULYSSES
TO: ALL
SUBJ: NEW USER
========
```

I have been lurking in the shadows, as it were, and decided it was time to introduce myself. My lover has been on the board for over a year, so I feel as if I know some of you already. I am a professor of modern languages at U of MR. I'm 47, keep fit by swimming and enjoy giving formal dinner parties, going to the opera and ballet, and the occasional evening of dancing. I read mysteries by the bucket and write very bad poetry. Don't worry. I do that last only in secret. I am rather technically challenged, but working to overcome it. The sysops have been very generous with their time and assistance, for which I am truly thankful. I enjoy chatting, once I figure out how to get into chat mode. Please bear with me.

ULYSSES

```
========
+ tag + A loaf of bread, a jug of wine, and <occupant>.
========
```

>>log off: Y/N ? Y
THANK YOU FOR USING THE LAMBDA GATE!
Tell your friends about us!
GOOD-BYE
@#$>!+...NO CARRIER
****

<<<

It had been another rotten night. Damon looked through the glass wall into the garden room where Kenny was sleeping, one arm thrown back, hand open, trusting, childlike. The early sun was caught in his golden hair and played over that delicate face, bringing for an instant the illusion of a healthy flush. Damon looked away. It was still too early in the day to work in the garden.

He went to the kitchen and brewed fresh coffee. It was decaf, but the wonderful aroma did almost as much for him as the caffeine used to do. How Proustian, he thought. The smell bringing back the whole experience so strongly he could taste the rich dark flavor on his tongue. Evenings at the Orient Café when he was a grad student, talking, using words and ideas to touch and explore the young men around him. He had never felt secure enough to brave a more physical exploration. It had taken a long stay abroad to loosen his reserve. And now he was once more using words and ideas, although on a much more fundamental level, to cruise men again, this time electronically. He took the hand-turned mug of coffee back to his office, switched on the computer and logged on to the Lambda Gate.

>*Welcome to the Lambda Gate, Ulysses! Your logon is being announced now.*

Immediately after these words scrolled by, a private message flashed on the screen:

/P: TIGGER to ULYSSES: Hi! Wanna chat? I'm new around here, so bare with me.

/P: ULYSSES to TIGGER: Hello. I'm fairly new at this myself but I had a good tutor. You're doing just fine. Hold on. I'll join you in chat mode. /C *** >Are you there, Tigger?

>*Okay, I see ya. Ulysses is some handle. You a history buff or wat...oops, what?*

>*In a way. Ulysses was an ancient Greek who fought in the Trojan War. On the way home, he had some wonderful adventures.*

>*Adventures, eh? {grin} Those Greeks were really into it with guys,*

weren't they? How about you? Wot r u into? Wot kind of adventures are you looking for?

... ... >Sorry for the delay. I had to close the door. Now, where were we? Adventures? Yes, I suppose you could say I am looking for adventures. But I'm not sure yet just what kind. I feel cut off from life lately.

>You want to reach out and touch? {grin}

>Exactly. OTOH, perhaps I am too old for such fantasies.

>What's OTOH mean?

>On the other hand.

>Oh. How old are you?

>I'm...47.

>I'm 19 and I like older guys. You don't have anything to prove, right? From what I hear, I couldn't stand those s&m types in the bars. U know...stand and model.

>You have a lot of experience? <G>

>O sure. Laugh! At least you've had a chance to have experience! Like I read about all these stories about gay life in the old days—

>The old days???

>Sorry. I mean the 70s and 80s and that...like in Randy Shilts's book...something the band—You know it?

>And The Band Played On.

>Yeah. I read it in the library. It sounds like I missed a lot. And now...I live at home. Ack! Gawd, I'm horny! I wish you were here right now.

>I am here, Tigger.

>Grrr...What do you look like? I haven't read your bio.

>I'm just under 6 feet, gray eyes, reddish brown wavy hair, slim build. No spectacular baseball bat between my legs, but everything's in working order.

>I bet! I'm getting a hard-on just thinking about it! I'm sitting here in nothing but my Jockey's, man. My dick wants to play with u'r dick! I'm getting wet, man! There's precome oozing out my slit. OOoooyow!!!!!!!! Let's get together, ok? Where do you live?

>*Actually, I'm in the downtown area, near the university.*

>*I'm in the north end. Wanna get together? We can't meet here, 'cause I live at home, like I said before.*

>*I would like to meet you, but I'm afraid that's out of the question. I have a lover. He's the one who got me interested in the BBS, so I joined to find out what was so interesting.*

>*And what do u think?*

>*I'm beginning to understand the, ah, attraction. I spend a great deal of time here, now, myself. I hope I haven't wasted your time, Tigger.*

>*My name's Tony.*

>*I'm never sure about the etiquette of chatting. My bio makes it clear I'm not looking for sex. I hope I wasn't leading you on.*

>*That's okay, man. It's been great talking to you.*

>*I enjoyed it. BTW, are you really sitting there in your Jockey's?*

>*Wadda you think? {very evil grin}*

>*Good-bye, Tony. <smile>*

>*Chow, Ulysses.*

*//*** [TIGGER has exited chat]*

*//****

"'Chow'," Damon muttered in disgust, but he was smiling. He keyed on his 'busy' signal so as not to be accosted again, and went back to reading files.

But his mind wouldn't let him concentrate, and his groin was disturbingly aware of the sexual energy of the messages, even at this early hour. "Why aren't they going to work?" Damon grumbled. But what was really worrying him was his own reason for being on the board. What was the quest he was setting out on? Most of the men seemed quite clear about what they were after, if not sure how to get it. But him?

In the beginning, he was jealous of all the time Kenny spent at the computer. He didn't understand what his lover could be getting from it, and it angered him to be shut out because of his lack of knowledge. The Lambda Gate was one more thing coming between them at a time they needed to be closer than ever. It was one more thing they couldn't share, one more thing that seemed to belong to the young. He knew this wasn't true. Unlike some of the older professors in his department, he used a computer all the time. He even used a modem to access the library and send the articles he wrote to a few colleagues for comments. But that was his job. Serious. Work. On the other hand, the Lambda Gate was fun. For a while it became a rival. Until he decided to get to know the enemy.

His reasons for logging on for the first time were simple; he wanted to understand what Kenny found so fascinating, wanted to share this important part of his lover's life. He wanted to be able to talk to Kenny about these electronic friends. But the world he discovered intoxicated him. It was frightening in its possibilities. The attitudes he found also disconcerted him, and he realized—perhaps for the first time— that he had never known real temptation.

How many invitations to sex had Kenny accepted? How often had he gone to have coffee with a friend and ended up in the bed of some BBS member? It was so easy. So very tempting. And the idea hurt like hell. To Damon it made a travesty of their five years together when he had barely even looked at another man.

"I'm insecure," he told himself. "That's all it is. The usual lot of the older man in a relationship like this."

But now he felt himself being pulled gradually into the beguiling flow of the boards. He found himself looking forward to it, being energized by it. Sometimes he wished he could take some of that energy and channel it to Kenny, but in a way, Kenny was using that energy, using it to fuel his interest in life, and Damon was determined to remain a part of that life, no matter how much effort it took.

He was absorbed in reading a message about the possibility of Hawaii's accepting gay marriages, when a fresh cup of coffee was slid in front of him.

"Having fun?"

"This is an interesting proposal, don't you think?" Damon took a sip of coffee and wished he could bury his face in Kenny's crotch and munch his way through the gray track pants to the loose, living flesh beneath. The image was so strong his hand began to shake and he set the mug down hastily. He was shocked at himself.

"Do you think a piece of paper makes that much difference?" Kenny asked him.

"Perhaps not to us, but—"

"Hah! All we'll be getting is a death certificate!"

Damon winced. "What I was going to say was that it would make a difference to the men starting out. It's an established rite we have been denied too long."

"Yeah, yeah. I'm going back to bed."

Damon felt his eyes prickle with the hot traitorous tears of anger that caught him so often unawares lately. Sometimes he felt he was being punished for trying to grab a little happiness while there was still time. And they had been happy...until three months ago....

Damon turned off his 'unavailable' symbol. He needed distraction. Almost at once he was paged.

/P: TED E. BARE to ULYSSES: Hi! How's it hangin', stud?

/P: Ulysses to TED E. BARE: Hello. I don't think I've talked to you before, have I? Automatically he keyed in the chat sequence. *>There. That's better.*

>So, read any good books lately? {grin}

>I doubt that what I read would cause many 'grins' to anybody!

>Boring, eh? I know what you mean. Just looking at the paper's enough to bring you down these days. 'Course with me, takes a lot to bring me down. {snicker}

>How 'up' are you? Having typed the words, Damon was startled by his sudden temerity. A tiny thrill ran through him.

>About half mast, so far. Looong way to go yet, sport! Keep talkin'

at me! That way both yer hands will be busy and mine will be free to roam...

>*Why should I do all the work? What happened to a fair division of labor?*

>*Never heard of it! You must be one of the legal eagles, huh? All words, no action?*

>*I precipitate a fair amount of action from time to time, TED E. Don't tempt me!*

>*Temptation is my middle name, baby.*

>*That doesn't start with E!*

>*Right here in River City! Wowie! I'm at three-quarter mast now, dude! Jockey's are getting damp. Mmmm. That hum is starting, you know the one?*

>*Hum a little louder so I can sing along.*

>*You getting hard, too?*

>*There is a definite...reaction.*

>*Zowie! I just pulled my Jockey's down, and my cock is standing at attention, just licking the cool air trying to get...closer...closer to you, man!*

Damon shifted his position on the swivel chair. He felt as if he and Ted E. Bare were connected by threads of electrons as surely as if they were in the same room, only on opposite sides of a screen. And yet he didn't have any desire to pull down the screen; because, without it, he would retreat into his decorous shell where sexual needs and fantasy were doomed to remain silent. He had a clear picture of the young man...he knew he was young.... In his mind, Ted was a more robust version of Kenny. Damon unbuckled his belt.

>*I'm here in front of you, Teddy. Tell me what you want me to do.*

>*You know what I want, dude! I want you on your knees in front of me with your mouth open...wide open...so I can ease my way inside...slide over your teeth...glide down your throat...ooooooooooooo that's sooooooooo great! And you look so good on your knees...your eyes bugging out like that...your face turning red...*

>*Just be careful, Ted. I do have teeth, you know. I'm not that ancient.*

>*Don't I know it! I can feel those teeth now, nibbling on my cock-head, your tongue...*

>*Ted, sorry, I have to go. Talk later, okay? //****

Damon wiped the sweat off his forehead and stared at the screen. He had never left chat so suddenly or without warning! He logged off before anyone else could accost him.

His heart was beating fast. His hand trembled slightly as he touched his cock through his trousers. "Kenny," he moaned softly. He went downstairs and into the sunroom, to find Kenny just sitting down on the cot.

Without saying a word, he went over and knelt beside the bed. He slid his arms around the slim waist, reaching under the elastic to run his hands over the soft peach fuzz low on Kenny's back. He hid his burning face in his lover's lap. Kenny laid a hand on the back of his head for just a moment.

"Getting warm with all that 'hot chat'?" he said.

THE MAN IN A UNIFORM
Kitty Tsui writing as "Eric Norton"

I was once a boy. A boy who loved to fanta- size. A boy who grew up with an intense love of books. I devoured everything I could get my hands on. My library card was my ticket to adventure.

I read about the exploits of the Hardy boys, Robin Hood and William Tell. But I also read the stories of Charles Dickens, Alexandre Dumas, Jules Verne, Somerset Maughm and Ian Fleming.

I was an only child, and a bastard child at that. I read avidly because I was an alien in an alien land, and the only thing that connected me to reality was stories in books. I was born in Singapore to a Chinese mother. The man who sired me was an American serviceman. An older man, an officer I think.

I've felt different all my life. At school I was bigger and taller than all the other kids, and though my hair was black it was tinged with red. And I have blue eyes. I never cared much for school or sports, but the library drew me like a magnet.

I remember that day as clearly as if it had been yesterday.

A tropical storm hit the city suddenly, rattling windows and corrugated tin roofs. Rain fell in sheets. It was summer and I wore thongs on my bare feet.

The storm passed as quickly as it hit and I bicycled to the library so I would have new books to read that weekend.

It didn't take me long to replace the pile I returned. I wrapped them carefully in plastic and placed them in the basket of my bicycle. It was then I noticed the man. He wore a starched white uniform with gold buttons. The creases in his pants were as sharp as the cutting edge of a cleaver. He smiled at me, his teeth blazing white as the uniform he wore.

Shyly I returned his smile.

The sun broke through the clouds. For some reason I didn't jump on my bicycle but pushed it beside me as I walked, fully aware that the man had fallen in step behind me. Down the street a vendor hawked ices. As I drew close I heard a voice.

"Hey, kid, want a popsicle?"

I turned my head. The man held out some paper money.

I nodded. Coconut popsies were my favorite.

He bought two popsicles and we walked down the street side by side in silence. My mother and I live on the outskirts of the city so we walked for some time. Presently he engaged me in small talk. What was my name. How old was I. What did I like to study in school. Did I have hobbies. Did I have a girlfriend.

"You speak good English, kid, for a native."

I didn't tell him that my mother tutored me for the day I would go to America. That was her hope for me. To go to America and find her man.

As we got closer to where I lived he slowed as if sensing my growing unease. A public bathroom loomed ahead. It was really a series of holes with a wooden floor elevated above a pit. Grass screens formed the walls and the roof was fashioned from a sheet of corrugated tin.

The man jerked his head in the direction of the latrine.

"I gotta take a piss," he said. "You too. C'mon."

I leaned my bike against a tree and followed him as if in a dream.

The place was empty. The man stepped up to one of the holes, feet apart. He unbuttoned his fly, slipped his whole hand inside and drew out the most enormous cock I had ever seen. He took a long piss, then shook it.

"C'mon over here," he commanded. "Touch me."

I couldn't move, my feet were rooted to the ground. But I could not take my eyes off his organ. He walked towards me holding it out like a gift. As I watched I saw it swelling, thickening, the purple head breaking out of its covering of skin.

"Don't be frightened, I won't hurt you," he said. "It's like sucking on a popsie. Hey, get over here. I'll teach you."

He came so close I could smell cigarettes on his breath above the stench of shit and urine. He took my hand and placed it on his cock. I flinched when my hand contacted his flesh. It felt like a hot coal, pulsing with heat.

"There, that's right," he coaxed, "wrap your fingers around it."

He took my hand in his, like my calligraphy teacher introducing a new written character, and guided me. He moved my hand up and down his shaft. I could feel it throbbing as if it had a life of its own, independent of the man. Then he bent towards me and kissed me, thrusting his tongue inside my mouth. I started to recoil but he held me tight and there was nothing I could do but work my hand as he willed it and surrender to his mouth. Suddenly he gripped me hard and increased the speed of his hand on mine. He released my mouth then and grunted as he climaxed, his semen shooting out into the dirt and splattering my bare feet.

He left me there in a daze. I noticed the heat for the first time, and the humidity thick around me like a wet blanket. Heart hammering in my chest I lifted my hand and tasted the sperm he had spilled on me. It was my first taste of a man.

It's been so long since I've had a man's semen in my mouth I can no longer remember its taste.

THE MAN WITH A GOATEE
Kitty Tsui writing as "Eric Norton"

I took my best friend Rog out to dinner at the Neon Chicken, one of my favorite restaurants in the Castro. It's unfortunate for the neighborhood that it's no longer there. They served great salads, amazing pasta dishes, and of course an array of chicken specialties. It was a small intimate place with subdued lighting, attentive waiters and a good wine list, the kind of place where one can comfortably eat alone.

Though we had reservations for eight-thirty, it was a popular eatery so we went upstairs to wait at the bar.

Rog had just started a job as arts editor of a gay newsweekly and he was chattering excitedly about his co-workers, and the new entertainment pages that he was to inaugurate. It was interesting at first but when he went on and on about the alcoholic publisher, the klepto reporter, the dyke-drama-queen photographer and the nellie secretary, my attention drifted.

I looked around me. Someone caught my eye immediately. A man sat at the other end of the bar smoking a cigarette. He had dark brown wavy hair and a goatee that looked so black I wondered if he dyed it. Except for his goatee he was clean-shaven but a shadow stained his cheeks and jaws and spread down his throat. The bartender called out a name and the man I was studying put out his cigarette. As he walked by I noticed a full basket in the crotch of his 501s.

When at last we were seated it happened to be one table away from the man with a goatee. He looked at me and I felt myself drawn in by his eyes green as emeralds. I swallowed hard, my mouth suddenly dry. He gave me a barely perceptible nod and I began grinning like a fool.

"Uh huh, and what was that all about?" Rog inquired. He looked at the man in question and screeched: "Eric, you whore!"

I don't remember what I ordered for dinner but I know I had crème brûlée for dessert. It's my favorite and I always have it with my cappuccino when I'm there.

The man ate slowly, his attention focused on the food in front of him though the restaurant was packed with men eating, drinking, laughing and cruising. When he finished he leaned back in his chair waiting for a refill of coffee. He looked at me, a smile on his face. I returned it.

"Oh, great," Rog said, rolling his eyes. "I guess I'll be going to the bars alone tonight."

Right Rog, I wanted to reply. Instead I sighed, remembering with a pang of guilt that it was his birthday.

"Course not. Come on, ready to go?"

I signed the credit card slip and stood, flashing the man a smile as I walked by him.

After having drank wine at the restaurant we switched to beer. Rog was single again and cruising like it was going out of style. The bar was packed, the music loud, and I was getting a headache.

"Rog!" I shouted, "I've got to get some air."

He nodded impatiently and waved dismissal, entwined as he was with a man.

The cold air in the alley felt good. I stretched, yawned, thought perhaps I should just go home, I'd had a lot of alcohol. From the darkness behind the dumpster came the unmistakable sound of men fucking.

Suddenly I heard the snap of a lighter and glimpsed a face in the darkness as the flame flared momentarily. Just as quickly darkness returned and all that remained was the glowing end of a cigarette. I started. Had my eyes deceived me or was it the man with the goatee?

Someone stepped out of the darkness as if he had heard my question.

"So, we meet again, pretty boy."

I gave him a look that said plenty.

"And this time don't disappear."

I went inside and kissed Rog.

"Happy birthday, darling. I gotta go."

"Whore!" he laughed, wriggling his ass at me as he danced with yet another man.

On the way to his place we stopped at Orphan Andy's.

"We're having coffee," he announced. "I plan to keep you up all night."

My half-hard cock responded immediately. It throbbed and began to swell as my excitement rose.

When we got to his apartment he took me to his bedroom and pulled me onto the bed with him. It was a huge bed covered with a down comforter so soft it felt like a cloud. He leaned over me on his hands and knees, green eyes boring into mine. His full, sensuous lips framed by the dark goatee brushed my cheeks. Then he kissed me hard, his lips warm, his whiskers grating on my skin. He pushed his thick tongue inside and I sucked.

Even while thus engaged he managed to undress me. When he lay on top of me I felt his hard cock against my thigh and my heart pounded in my chest. I started to undo his 501s but he pushed my hands away.

He continued kissing me fiercely, probing with his tongue, teeth knocking against mine. I groaned as his hand closed around my cock. He lowered his head and rubbed his goatee hard on my nipples till they felt raw. When he finally took them in his mouth and sucked I gasped out loud; they were so sensitive. My balls ached. I thought I would come with just his mouth on my tender nipples. I shuddered with pleasure, waves of joy spasming through me.

He licked up the crease between my thigh and my groin and took me balls-deep into his mouth. I yelled as he engulfed me. He was incredible, his mouth about drove me crazy. My nuts tightened and it was all I could do to keep from spurting right then.

When he released me he growled:

"On your hands and knees."

I complied quickly, spreading my legs wide. I could feel his hot breaths on my asshole. He knelt behind me and spat into my crack. He opened his fly and drew out his cock. I heard him working spit and precum onto it. He took a fistful of my hair and pulled me to him as he entered, a pole of fire penetrating me to my core. He fucked me slow and deep, each time pulling me so hard against him that the buttons of his fly dug into my flesh.

He started grunting and thrusting faster and I thought he was about to come but he pulled out suddenly. He leaned back, then pushed in from a different angle and his cock-head began hitting against my prostate. I let out a long cry as I climaxed, white streamers of semen shooting onto his black comforter.

He continued his assault, driving his stiff rod into me. Finally I lay my head and chest on the bed while he battered my ass. I lost all track of time, aware only of the man's cock assaulting me. Slow, hard, deep.

He pulled out, turned me over and kissed me, his mouth as

rough as his cock had been. He moved his whiskers over my cheeks, my throat, grating against my skin. I knew he wasn't finished with me and my asshole was begging to be filled again so I wrapped my legs around him as I drew him in for a kiss.

His tongue parted my lips as his cock penetrated me. We moved like this all night long, his tongue in my mouth, his cock in my ass. It felt exquisite. We moved like this all night long.

IOWA
Patrick Moore

Descending gouged, pitted stairs, the music pounded aggressively into Patrick's ears. There is only a partial recognition of the music in a sex club, and it often seems to be coming from a far distance. The muffled quality allows it to be truly a backdrop; but, even so, snatches of clarity occasionally break through. "You cannot touch reality...you're living in a fantasy..." This club had been open for more than a year, but Patrick had never visited it before. It had been on the edge of his mind several times, but somehow he had never gotten to giving the West Side address to a cabdriver. The space was enormously impersonal and must have been a truck garage. That coldness was now important to the carefully cultivated ambience of brutality. If masculinity means playing at being hetero, few of the men here worked toward that. Rather, they were gay men playing a game, exploring roles which they created in this concrete bunker that could serve as sound stage and set. The renovation from garage to nightclub consisted mainly of throwing up a few black walls to separate the coat check from the bar from the stage from the sex room. You could almost feel the lumbering movements of the truckers who had once parked their rigs here, near the river, always near sex. How many of them had parked and then walked across the highway to the piers? In those days, the piers would have been alive with sex. Everything was alive then. The men would have slid out of the trucks, unsticking their dicks from sweaty underwear, wanting to toss off a few loads before going home to wives and girlfriends—a few stinking loads thrown into mouths and asses that waited patiently by the river. Then they would attack. The mouth that had, moments before, been an object of desire would appear accusatory in their panicked minds. Then fists would strike out, trying to erase what was true, what was undeniable, what would always win out. Maybe their rage at hidden desires was not sated even then. Maybe, after emptying their dicks, they would rampage down the streets with blood-spattered bats. Finally exhausted, they would take their bloody hands and stinking cocks back to women who chose to believe, who bought into a debilitating lie.

The crowd tonight was altogether more healthy in its sexual persuasions, and the club had a welcoming feel for all of its industrial environment. The men tended to be talkative. This subset of the gay world knew itself well, and friends were made easily after seeing one another week after week. Coming to these spots was still an act disavowed by many gay men. Sleazy, they would have called it, as they made their way to summer houses featured in decorating magazines. Repulsive, they would have spat, while all the while they yearned for it. Every gay man yearns for the release of anonymity and pure physical pleasure unencumbered by the constraints of love. And while they sit smugly over foie gras at La Grenouille, the images hover above ruby-red banquettes. Images of degradation and exaltation. The gay men order stuffed zucchini blossoms, but they wonder whether a fist would really go up their ass, whether handcuffs would ache after hours of wear. The gay men who sculpt perfect hairless bodies for themselves open their throats to chardonnay and wish it were piss, wish they could give themselves fully and utterly to another man in the way unique to their breed. Tonight the men in this industrial wilderness in Chelsea enjoy themselves heartily because they know that there is relief in acting on impulse and stepping over the line. No going back. No return.

Patrick walked, glided, leaned against a wall and moved on again. He wound deliberately through the maze of rooms, not ready, not quite ready, to do anything but move along. "Aaah!" he moaned as he leaned against the stage and felt the drug boost incredibly throughout his entire body, lengthening and pulling at him. His torso felt miles long, unwieldy and dangerous. His legs were sharp spikes dug into the ground for stability. He trailed his quivering fingers along the edge of the stage, studying the soft emanation of light from the strip of glow tape that marked the border and guided the performers safely in the dark. Onstage, a man in a black leather hood had been hooked to a giant torturous wheel that waited, still now, for its orders. The wheel also had a slightly ridiculous game-show quality to it, as if one could spin the naked man to win a refrigerator or a mobile home. The man on the wheel had an overly muscled body, Patrick thought. His true body was hidden by layers of muscle that served as a defense from anyone seeking to touch the vulnerability that he sought. He lacked the normality, the everyday quality in his body that drove Patrick wild. The man on the wheel hung slack against the restraints lifting him from the ground and securing him for use. The wheel was tended by two men who conferred about the next course of action. Patrick wandered in a circuit around the stage, trying to hear what the two wheel men were discussing. The music drowned them out. "Gonna set you free…Rock your body…The music gonna set you free…." One of the men stepped away from the wheel as the other started to turn it slowly, steadily. One picked up a whip as Patrick lost interest, getting ready to move toward the bar with the slaps and screams building predictably.

Nearby, a less-predictable scene presented itself. On a lower platform, adorned only with a rough sawhorse, teetered an unlikely creature whose birth was possible only in a club such as this. This woman—and Patrick assumed it was a woman—was sheathed wholly in white vinyl. After taking in the entire form of her, Patrick decided to begin once again at the feet to try and fully comprehend this creation. The feet, in and of themselves, were a study in perversion. The white heels were cripplingly high, causing her constantly to sway to and fro, in danger of imminent collapse. The shoes were met immediately above by the legs of the bodysuit, which encased the thick body underneath. The only real clue, and it was hardly conclusive, as to this person-age's sex was the swelling in the suit's chest area. As to the head, this was the area that crossed some boundary, moving the look far beyond the possibility of simple fashion. Large, frightened eyes stared out from the cutouts in the white hood. The eyes were garishly made up with false eyelashes and powder-blue shadow. The stare of those eyes made Patrick feel as if he were going to hyperventilate. This was an animal. Humanity had left the eyes that stared out so intensely that one could almost ignore the huge ponytail of straw-blond hair exploding like a volcano from a hole at the crown of the head. The creature's eyes were suddenly obscured as an unnoticed attendant grabbed hold of a milky vinyl arm and threw the form over the sawhorse. In its own way, the look of the dominatrix was even more radical. She was extremely short and wore a tweedy suit with a tailored skirt. There was an English aura to the mistress, a short Vita Sackville-West just in from the garden to adjust her pearls before picking up a riding crop and getting to work. The first strike of the crop on white vinyl was the most shocking for its lack of sound, only a muffled thud and a far-removed groan from inside the sack. As the blows increased, the high heels became more and more precarious, with only the sawhorse preventing total collapse. After some time, the maitresse simply walked away, lit a cigarette, and began to chat with a group of unimpressed women to the side. The slave, beyond standing, slumped farther forward and shook its ass in appreciation.

"Is your name Patrick?" The voice startled him and he turned to a nondescript, skinny young blond with wire-rim glasses. He wondered why anyone would wear wire rim glasses to a place like this. The face made him slightly nervous because he was sure he had never seen this person before.

"Yeah, that's my name."

The guy had a strangely nervous way of hopping slowly on one foot. His voice was smarmy. "Did you go to Carnegie-Mellon?"

"I'm sorry, but I don't think I know you," Patrick said, and started to turn away.

"Oh, yeah, you remember me," the guy said, and introduced himself. Patrick had a bad habit of not listening when people told him their names. If fact, his memory was very poor in general, and he still had no recollection of this wispy blond at college. However, his interest was reignited when the guy lit a joint and offered it to him.

"Thanks. I could use some. I think I might be a little too high."

"Me, too," said the blond. "I just did some crack. Usually I like to snort heroin, but tonight I bought some crack over by my house. I live on East Fourth."

"I've heard a lot of people died last weekend from heroin. You should be careful of this new batch on the streets; it's supposed to be very pure." Patrick had never taken heroin, but he saw it as the most extreme of drugs. His estimation of the blond grew slightly now that he knew him to be a junkie. "Thanks for the smoke. I'd give you some coke, but I just did the last of it," he said, lying.

"That's okay," he said, somewhat cooler. Patrick noted that the guy's hopping dance had increased. "Well, uhm, I have to go to the bathroom. Just wanted to say hello. See you around." Then he was off.

"Coke whore!" Patrick spat, walking away from the stage where the man revolving steadily on the wheel was developing an irregular pattern of red whip marks on his body.

Too, tttttttoooooooo, high. Peeeeeeeeak. "Jesus Christ!" Patrick muttered as he flung himself onto a bar stool in the nick of time, just before falling over. He pushed his back hard against the bar, harder than he realized, and had the distant sensation of the vertebrae of his spine grating against the counter edge. At this apex of the high, he had no sense of and no regard for his body. A constant grinding of the jaw whittled down his molars imperceptibly, and his tongue followed an undeviating path along the back of his teeth. Patrick's body may as well have been the heel of a shoe that scuds and sticks in whatever lies in its path, milling the objects in the street. With his legs sprawled before him, Patrick attained a precarious balance on the stool while making it appear an indifferent pose. Each point of contact, though, was absolutely necessary to prevent an undignified pitch to the floor. Feeling structurally sound for the moment, Patrick examined his reflection in a mirror facing the bar. His skin was very white and his hair very black, an important contrast demonstrated by everyone from Diana Vreeland to John Kennedy. His eyes were inscrutable, too much, and he tried not even to look at them. These were no longer the shocking two-color eyes he had in high school, created by colored lenses. No, these were real eyes and all the more terrifying because of it. His eyes were blue, but at this instant they reflected no light, swallowed all light, until they appeared an unequivocal black. A rational person would have noted that after taking drugs, the pupils dilate. But in this setting, they appeared malevolent, prone to violence, ready to accept another's violence. He shook his head once or twice. Closed his eyes and breathed. For an unmeasured interval, there was no sound. The mute button had been hit; the soundproof door had closed; the leather hood had been zipped shut. No sound, no light. Another breath and it all came charging back into focus. As his eyes opened, Patrick's hand floated up to his bare chest, framed by the black leather jacket that hung open to reveal his tits and stomach but camouflaged the problem "love handle" area. His chest was lightly haired. From a distance, it looked almost bare. He was pleased with his chest most of all, he decided. In this one area, he was satisfied. Lower, his hips could stand to be thinner but didn't look bad in the long black denim shorts which ended just past the knee, revealing strong calves disappearing into black high-top Converse sneakers. He let his hand run over his chest and stomach while letting the coke take him past a half-understood point. His body was a thing now and he was satisfied. Two entities—him and his body. "You can't hurt me now," he thought.

And then Patrick lost himself. "Yes, yes, what I want. Don't think. Nothing. Don't think. Do." He threw away his body, an object that could be used or not. He wanted the control. "Why don't you do it to me…" the music lulled. "Tell me why…Why don't you do it to me…" He wanted to be controlled by one man. That man stood directly in front of him. "Use me," Patrick thought, as his blue-black eyes bored into the eyes of the man in front of him, and the man in front of him walked between Patrick's legs, walked forward and took control. One person can appear miraculously as salvation, as death, as punisher, as redemption, and this one person positioned his leather chaps right between Patrick's legs. There is no reason to look for the right person, Patrick knew, because when the factors are right, he simply appears. You can walk all night and never find him. But when the time has come, just throw yourself back and let him appear, more complete and perfect than could be planned. "There is magic," he thought. He believed that his want, unleashed by the drug, had conjured up this man, summoned forth a physical incarnation of the emotional flood.

He thought of a book he had read that was a string of commands, imperative sentences for hundreds of pages. "Check this out…" the music said. Give yourself over. At the exact moment of breaking, surrender yourself utterly. Dress yourself for sacrifice and expect humiliation to reveal a path. Move a bit lower than you thought possible. Destroy your physical self as an experiment. Find out how far down you can go. Pray and think religious thoughts at inappropriate times. Think of your parents during sex. Think of your penis during Holy Communion. Pretend to have Tourette's syndrome at an office party. Break down in front of a homeless person. Tense your asshole until it itches while eating at "21." Listen to old disco on a Walkman while crying at a funeral. Close your eyes and disregard the hand exploring you. Find beauty in the ugliest moments. Talk about AIDS while fucking a man hard. Make hatred a way of life. Hate yourself most of all. Sit in church and list every tragedy created by God. Show pictures of your dead lover to potential tricks. Wear expensive suits with no underwear and a buttplug. Go to galleries and tell artists their work is unimportant. Make a mark on your body and see how long it stays. Cut off your long hair. Keep the hair in a glass jar. Cut your fingernails to the quick. Keep the clippings with the hair. Regard everything as a record. See yourself in history. Estimate how much time is left. Be wearing a long skirt and motorcycle boots when you finally break. Curse every writer you have ever known. Have one last drink at Trader Vic's. Don't invite Madonna. In the flash when you are about to disappear, turn to the photographers and scream, "At least I was famous!"

"Stupid, thank God," Patrick thought as soon as he heard the man's voice. This was not an affected stupidity, but the real item. That's what he wanted. Tonight he craved the erotic mundane.

After asking Patrick's name twice, the guy just looked at him. He seemed not to have heard or to be able to understand. His hair was cut in an ugly, slightly-too-long style framing his Italian New Jersey face and mustache perfectly. Patrick let his hands wander slowly around the ample, hairy chest and rub the firm beer belly, asking the guy his name.

"Joe," came the answer. Patrick almost lost control. Could it be more perfect? He hardly dared ask the next question. "What do you do for a living?"

"Construction," came the answer in an almost-retarded, mean-spirited voice. "My body gets real tense from work. 'Specially my shoulders. What I need is a good rubdown. You ever do that? You into that?"

"Oh, man!" Patrick moaned. "Let me take care of your body."

"You like this body?"

"If I were to put together a picture in my mind of the perfect body, it would be yours. Your proportions are magnificent because you're not too tall. The rest of you? It'd be hard to say which part turns me on most. The chest, maybe. The arms, maybe."

"What?"

"I said I love your body and I want to take care of it," Patrick said, kneading the man's shoulders.

"Mmmm, that's what I need. Wanna come give me a rubdown for a couple of hours? That's what I need. I'm kind of sexed out, but I need somebody to relax me."

"Let's go, man. I don't want to waste one minute I can have my hands on your incredible body."

"What?" Joe asked as they walked out.

Patrick was talking, talking fast, but he had absolutely no idea what he was saying. "So fucking high," he thought, and heard Joe say something. "What'd you say," Patrick asked.

"I live in Brooklyn. You mind?"

"No, I don't mind."

"Good, I'm gonna pick up some ribs in Chinatown on the way. Hungry?"

"Hungry? Are you kidding? Do you want some coke? I'm gonna have a little more." Patrick opened the vial as they were driving down the street, but Joe seemed uninterested. Patrick was talking again, about massage techniques, mapping out exactly how Joe wanted his body handled.

"You know, this is great, Joe. Because when I do coke, I feel really horny, but I can't get a hard-on; so I really appreciate the chance to just make your body feel great. It would really turn me on to start massaging you right away when we get to your place, even while you're eating. I mean, I could even start on your feet while you're sitting there eating. Would you like that?"

"Yeah, I guess." Joe was driving down the Bowery toward Chinatown. Patrick was sort of praying that they weren't actually going to a Chinese restaurant with him in this condition, but he had given way. He had given in to whatever happened. He just wanted to give.

The streets of Chinatown were mostly deserted at this hour, the neon lights flooding color over the empty pavement and random groups of young men. Always atmospheric, it was threatening when empty and quiet. The rules changed. Patrick was rubbing the length of Joe's hairy arm when they pulled up in front of Wo Hop. "Get me an order of spare ribs," Joe ordered, casually handing him a ten-dollar bill.

"Oh, you want me to go in?" Patrick was in no condition to go in to a strange restaurant at the moment, but was also completely at the service of this man.

"Yeah, man, you think I'm gonna leave my car on this street? These Chinks would swipe it in a minute."

Walking down the steps, teetering slightly, Patrick pushed open the door to Wo Hop. As he had feared, it was mobbed with people. Having given his order, he stuck near the cash register and tried not to sniffle. When he heard the door open behind him, his entire body tensed tighter. "Two cops, two greasy fuckin' cops, wanting fried pork, just like Big Daddy up in the car. Man, hurry it up," he thought, looking intently at the menu. The cops couldn't have cared less about the wired-up little fag next to them, though. They were thinking about grease. They were thinking about pork. They were thinking about fried wontons. They just wanted their food and didn't give a fuck.

There was a shrill building of voices in the back of the restaurant. At one of the tightly spaced tables sat a towering black drag queen, hair teased to the ceiling and piss drunk. She looked disgustedly at her food and pointed an imperious finger to it. She flicked at the pieces of pork with her long red claw. The waiter was having none of it, "That what you order."

"I didn't order no dog-meat salad, baby," said the drag queen, putting her hand on her ample hip.

"That pork. That good."

"Get me some chicken foo and take this back to the soup kitchen." The drag queen must have been well over six feet before the heels, and her legs seemed to take over the entire restaurant. Her calves were the size of small children. Most of all, her face was one of those expanding faces; the more you looked at it, the bigger it got. Now she took another slug of beer and seemed to resign herself to the food.

"That good. That what you ordered."

"Oh, run along, Ling-Ling, and get me some duck sauce," she shrieked, and started eating.

Patrick could smell the pork in the bag as they crossed the Manhattan Bridge and traveled past Williamsburg and Park Slope. He could tell they were going a long way, farther than he had been in Brooklyn, but he could also tell it was too late. There was nothing to do. Nothing that could stop this. He had no interest in Joe's descriptions of the Italian, black, Jewish, Puerto Rican, and Irish neighborhoods. "Creeps," he thought. "Sexy, stupid pigs." He ran his hand over the jeans that kept him away from Joe's hairy flesh. "Man, I can't wait to get my hands on you. You're the best."

Pulling up later, he didn't know how much later, Joe turned off the engine in front of a depressing-looking two-story suburban house. The sun was beginning to come up, and neighbors were coming out of the house next door. "Get down," Joe growled, pushing Patrick toward the floorboards. When the neighbors had gotten into their car and left, Joe said, "Okay, hurry up and get inside."

Joe followed Patrick up the flight of stairs with his ribs. As the door opened, the house revealed itself to be extraordinarily ugly, neat, and mundane. "Perfect!" Patrick thought. "Better and better."

Joe told Patrick to take off his clothes in the kitchen and put them over the chair. Joe paid no attention to this disrobing, made no comment, but pulled off his own jacket and proceeded to dump the ribs onto a plate. Patrick continued to stand naked in the middle of the kitchen as Joe sat down heavily at the Formica kitchen table. "So get to work on those feet," Joe mumbled through a mouthful of ribs.

Patrick had imagined this but never done it, never known how to get to this point and make it real, not an act. It was real, he knew. It was really happening. The erotic tension of it, the perfection of this guy's attitude, made him short of breath. Squeezing beneath the table, he began to unlace Joe's shoes and carefully pulled them off. He also carefully removed the gym socks. The feet didn't stink. Running his hands over them, Patrick was unsure whether or not he wished them to stink. From above came a disembodied voice: "So how you like those feet?"

"Beautiful," Patrick whispered as he rubbed each toe separately, thoroughly. He examined them carefully. The toenails were cut short, and each toe had a short tuft of hair. The arch of the feet had longer, silky hair that merged at the ankle into a darker forest hidden by the jeans. There were hard calluses on the heels, and he made a mental note to work particularly hard on softening them with lotion or oil or his tongue.

"What's your name?"

"Patrick," he said, without wonder at being asked now for the third time.

"Let's go in the bedroom," came the voice. "I want you to get to work."

Joe's bedroom was as ugly and as neat as the rest of the house. Macho guys were often rather babyish about their surroundings and neurotically clean. The house had obviously been furnished at thrift shops and garage sales. Joe lay a towel on the bed, saying sternly, "If you use any of that cream on me, don't get it on the sheets. And stay away from my asshole—I don't like to get fucked or nothin'."

"Of course," Patrick said, unable even to imagine fucking this guy. He watched from the corner as Joe got undressed. Joe's body was the most beautiful thing he had ever seen. It was perfect in its mixture of muscle and fat. He had a rather hairy chest and a firm, bulging stomach. His dick was unremarkable and soft. The arms were defined naturally, by work rather than a gym, just as Patrick liked. But it was particularly his legs and ass that drew Patrick forward as Joe lay facedown on the bed. This man looked as if he were wearing a pair of hair pants. His totally smooth back sloped down to meet a clear line of hair beginning at the top of his buttocks. Soft, thick black hair that covered both asscheeks and became impenetrable toward the crack. The strong legs were similarly covered.

Patrick gasped as he straddled Joe to begin to work on the shoulders. "What'd you say?" Joe muttered.

"Your body is perfect. It's the sexiest body I've ever seen."

"Oh, yeah," Joe said, sleepy and bored. "Not too hard and take your time. I want a real thorough rubdown."

Patrick had finished the remainder of his coke in the bathroom, and the drug exploded once again against the back of his head, focusing all of his perceptions closely on the flesh that he touched.

While thoughts raced through his mind, his physical attention was focused completely. Do a good job, do a good job. He wanted only to please this man, and he tried his hardest as his fingers firmly but gently worked the smooth layers of muscle encasing the back. In its way, this was a totally nonsexual act. Patrick tried to think of it in that way. He tried to think of it as a job. "I have a job to do. Do it well." This job was to make a man's body relax as deeply as possible. He would work as long and as hard as was required of him. Doing a good job was the reward. Being allowed to touch this flesh was the reward.

His hands moved silently along the back as Joe started to snore. Asleep, no attention paid to the efforts. It was assumed that he would do a good job. Time has no meaning when there is no sound. And there was only silence and a softly sweating man beneath Patrick's hands. This man in his silence commanded a respect that had nothing to do with stupidity and taste. Patrick wanted to lose himself in this service. And he had lost himself. He heard his thoughts tumbling along: "I'm gone. There is nothing left of me and if I concentrate, if I focus myself completely on his masculine pleasure, I can disappear. So beautiful…absolute normal perfection."

Patrick didn't understand the dual thoughts that raced through his mind as he worked down along the side of the hairy asscheeks. Stroking the sleek coat of hair with his hands, he continued down the legs and began working the feet with cream. There were two separate minds within him. Two minds that sat beside one another, pouring out thought. The one thought of nothing but loss. In that mind there was only pain and memory. In the other mind, there was only attention and a growing void. This was the mind that he strove toward as he lowered his tongue onto Joe's foot, distantly hearing him moan. With the smell and taste of the foot, pain retreated a bit. Sucking on a toe, Patrick could no longer see fevered, pleading eyes looking at him. Chewing lightly on a callus, he no longer felt the empty bed waiting at home.

The coke was surging through him. His throat and face and teeth and nose were completely frozen numb. Yet, in his brain of loss, there were shots of bright light ricocheting back and forth, reflecting off one another and building brighter. The lights were thoughts. The lights were feelings. The lights were sensations. The lights were words: "Leave me now. Please, my darling, leave me now. We will never again find one another, so leave me now to end in some way, to finish in my fashion. Love is not sex and sex is never love. So I humble myself. I offer myself as a tribute to your memory, which I beg to leave me now. Each night I will lower myself toward a waiting man who is not you. These men are not you, and I do not want them to be. I want only an infinite succession. I want only a row reaching toward oblivion when I can no longer think but only perform these services. I can no longer see your pain. I can no longer see your wasted face and body and the intricate swirl of lesions. You are gone, my darling. You have left me now. I no longer feel you. I no longer see you with me. There is only absence. Now is the time for my pain. I paid tribute to your pain, and now my time has come. The glory of my pain blossoms within me, limitless in its blinding power. I walk alone in a dim room, pacing. There are no tears here. There are no tears for me. I am alone. My tears for you are dry, and I have none left for myself. I am alone. Each day I will scoop out a bit more, until only the fragile pristine shell of walking death remains, and they will pass me and say, 'Where is he? Where has he gone? What is that pale shadow that moves like stale breath against the wall?' I am gone now, darling, and so are you. That is our bond. That is our marriage. That is our pact. We are, each of us, gone. Gone, darling. Gone."

Joe's front side now appeared to Patrick. It was less erotic than the back, but his job was not to judge, only to service; so his hands and lips lowered themselves to arms and pits and nipples and stomach and legs and balls, and he wrapped his hand softly around a throbbing cock. "Is this what you want?" he asked Joe, begging. "I want to do what you want me to do." There was no answer from Joe's snoring lips as Patrick worked his hand slowly up and down the cock. Only one mind now, only the empty mind, only the mind that holds nothing and is hard, hard. With hardly a groan, the cum boiled out of the cock.

Patrick sat there on the edge of the bed, looking at the sunlight piercing the drawn blinds with increasing strength. In the weak light, the body beneath his hands was even more mundane. It was even more glorious to him in its imperfections revealed by day. He knew there was no need to say or do more. There was no task left but to leave silently. That was an important task. Simply to leave.

So he did, after roughly pulling on his clothes. Patrick walked out into the blinding summer morning with the drugs still racing, demanding attention. This was New York. This experience was New York, and it was cold, mean, and he was tired of coming back for more. He was cold even in the sun as he walked down streets that became larger and became highways, and he looked now at the ocean. He found himself at the ocean—or rather, across from it—separated by innumerable lanes of traffic and a sign that said, Welcome to Sheepshead Bay. It took some time to find a path across the lanes of traffic and then to pull himself over the low wall to the sand. The sound of the water was more imagined than real with the roar of cars speeding past, but the thought of it calmed him. The sun had warmed his numb body, and sweat was pouring down his back, soaking into the porous leather of his jacket. He let the jacket fall to the ground, and then stepped out of his shorts as well. He didn't bother with the sneakers but walked quickly up to his waist into the water. It was neither cold nor warm, filthy nor clean. It simply surrounded him and erased the lower part of his body. He looked down and his lower half had disappeared into the slow-moving waves. "Good," he thought. "Gone." And he moved forward slowly, away from New York. He moved so that he could feel each inch disappearing. Now only his head remained above water. He turned to look at the city, but it wasn't there. There were no skyscrapers or neon signs. There was only the concrete wall dividing the thin strip of sand from the road and the brownish-gray houses on the far side. He did not fall, he let go. He released himself into the water carefully. For an important moment, Patrick was not sure whether he was above or below the water. Then, closing his eyes, he knew he was below and moved his lips steadily, saying, "I'm gone, I'm gone, I'm gone, I'm gone," until finally he was.

THE BIKER AND THE SLUT-BOY

Hoddy Allen

If, one hot summer night, in the back room of a crowded bar, in a steam bath, or in a downtown city park known to be cruisy in those days, if there was a big-shouldered biker with long black hair and another longhair collared and licking his boots, chances are that it was Simon holding the leash. And chances are that it was Al on his hands and knees, licking the road dust from his bossman's boots while they waited for the action to come their way, which, in those days, always did. For a while there the two were quite notorious as word about them spread from coast to coast.

I'm surprised. "You're the Slut-Boy!" I exclaim, right in the middle of Al telling me this story. Al nods and blushes deep red, and I sit back in my chair and shut up.

Everyone's heard the stories about the Biker from the East and the Slut-Boy he took cross-country one summer on the back of his bike. They're stories that still make the rounds of the club scene today, when the bar talk turns to nostalgia for the good old days and the "time before." I myself had heard the stories many times, but I had no idea they were talking about my Al. That's my name for him, short for Alley cat. Back then he had his own name, but not the one he used when he hustled.

I'm surprised, not shocked, to find out that Al hustled in his younger days. It was his way out of the suburbs, he says, his way to live downtown. For most young people to survive downtown, he says, there's either the low-paying jobtraps, if they can get one, or there's government checks if they can score one, or there's the relative freedom of places like the Canal.

The Canal ran through the middle of Al's hometown, a winding, twisting, man-made waterway with tree-lined, scenic parkways for traffic on either side. By day, it was a tourist trap, with tour buses and recreational vehicles rolling past monuments and markers, picnic spots and parkettes. But by night the eastern side of the parkway was a hang out for the downtown kids who would stand under the trees along the road to watch the nighttime traffic roll by.

Al had his spot under a maple in the stretch of the parkway they called "Track Three." He had no idea what the other two tracks were for, but for nearly a year he was out there, in his spot, three nights a week, blowing cigarette smoke at the traffic rolling past him, and waiting for one to stop and roll down a window.

I'm trying to imagine Al in those days; a "skinny, long-haired, jaydee." That's Al's description of himself with about a year's worth of smarts and about the same amount of attitude. He was a little guy back then, with a boy-muscled body, concave belly, and tight little pecs that must have been just handfuls on his smooth-skinned chest. Dressed in an old denim jacket, the cuffs dirty and stringy and worn, with a tight T-shirt or a loose tank top underneath it. Al says he never thought of himself as the type that most wet dreams were made of, back then, but I can see how the look must have done all right by him.

Especially in those too-tight jeans of his, his only pair at the time, he says, stuffed into a pair of brown Frye boots, the leather on them old and cracked and stretched out by his feet. I can see him, the long, yellow and brown hair falling down around his face that he'd flip back, flashing that green-eyed stare of his at the traffic rolling by, just to catch their attention. Then they'd notice the basket he had in those too-tight jeans of his, and that cute, fuckable bubble-butt of his as he got into the passenger side of a car.

But that's just my fantasy of how Al must have looked in those days. Simon liked his looks, enough to take him cross-country on the back of his bike that summer. That's part of the story about the night the Biker and the Slut-Boy met, but the truth from Al was that he didn't like Simon very much at first.

He was busy scanning the traffic. It was a hot, crowded, noisy, mid-summer night on the Track, and the Trade in the traffic along the parkway was almost nil. It was also the middle of the month and the government checks weren't due out for another week. That left a number of kids on the dole cash-starved enough to try their luck on the Canal.

Al hated it when he was just another pretty face in the mid-month crowd along the parkway; his chances of scoring even his usual one that night almost down to zero, due to the major assortment of boys that were available to the pick-and-choose Trade in the traffic rolling past.

Almost down to zero. A long red car pulled up to his spot. Al stepped off the curb, but the car squealed its tires and sped off.

It was a slow night for the traffic. Nothing but tourists from the suburbs and gawkers taking in the roadside show. Them and the hecklers, and the hagglers trying to give kids twenty for it, and the sad scene that night almost made Al want to quit the business for good.

Almost. He could still pull one in. He was, after all, a regular face on the Track, a landmark along the Canal after nearly a year of hanging out under the trees. And if there was one thing Al knew about the Trade in the traffic of his hometown, it was that they knew enough to rely on the landmarks along the parkway instead of on the fresh new faces just passing through.

He stepped off the curb again, this time for a small green sports car, it's paint job black and shiny in the streetlights filtering through the leaves overhead. It pulled up to his spot and rolled down a window. The driver of the car looked past Al when he tried to stick his head in to see if the guy was looking for company; but before he knew it the guy shook his head and grabbed the stickshift. The car roared off down the parkway and Al turned to go back to his spot under the tree to see someone standing there, leaning against the tree trunk and looking Al over like he was merchandise, which he was that night.

"How much do you charge?" the man asked.

A nice-looking guy, not that much older than Al, and not that much taller either. He was a big-shouldered, big-chested kind of guy, with long black hair that he kept tied back tight into a tail that rested on the left shoulder of his black leather bike jacket.

Smooth faced, with black eyes shining in the streetlights overhead, he had a smug look on his face as Al checked out the tan, square-toed boots on the guy's feet and read the motorcycle logo stretched across the white T-shirt he wore under his jacket. Al shrugged. Why the hell not, he thought, even though the guy didn't strike him as the type who would want to pay for it. Hell, the man could have charged.

"How much you got?" Al asked him—his standard opening before he laid down his price for services. He stepped toward the biker, casually, cautiously, as the guy looked him over once more.

"For you?" the man considered. "Dinner."

Al turned his head to scan the traffic again. The hair down around his face covered his expression as he shook his head and rolled his eyes at the offer.

See, "Dinner," to Al, would have been considered a "gratuity."

Not that any of the Trade in the traffic of his hometown ever took him out to dinner afterwards. It was usually back to his spot on the Track with fifty dollars more in his pocket, his usual fee for services. Al decided that the man standing in his spot did not look like the type to have fifty dollars to spend on such services, so he decided to call it a night, his first scoreless night in a long, long time.

"I'm resting," the Slut-Boy said to the Biker the first night they met. It was a bath house reply at the time, which meant either, "I am not interested," or "Fuck off," depending on how it was said. Al lit a smoke and turned to leave the Track, but the long-haired biker followed him down the parkway.

"So you're off-duty now?" he said. "The meter's off?"

"Look man," Al spun on him, flashing a hard-assed, green-eyed look. He flipped his hair back and glared.

"I'm resting. Okay?" he said. And he muttered something else, as he picked up his pace along the parkway to put some distance between them.

"So when do you stop shaking it like a money-maker?" he was asked the next night. Al nearly jumped out of his skin, then he turned to see who it was standing next to him in his spot under the maple. He shook his head at the biker's persistence, flipped his hair back, and shot the guy his look.

"You don't get it, do you," Al told him. "You want it for free? Check the bushes in the park. You got to pay for it, this side."

"You mean you never, ever, do it for free," the biker wanted to know. His long black hair was untied and falling down around his face and the shoulders of his jacket, and he had a calm, curious expression on his dark-eyed face to match the hard-as-nails stare he was getting from Al.

"And let the word get out to the Trade I'm giving it away?" Al told him. "Shit."

"Well, actually I'm new in town," the biker told him. "So I don't know much of the Trade to tell that to."

"Then what are you? A sidewalk social worker? You want to be a pimp or something?" As far as he was concerned, after nearly a year on the Track, Al had seen and heard it all before. From the con jobs to the rip-off artists, he was no longer impressed with anything anymore except a straight, upfront, cash deal with the Trade in his hometown.

"No," Simon patiently said to him that night. "Actually, I'm a photographer," he began, but Al cut him off.

A car slowed to a stop at his spot, a big gray- white sedan-type car, and Al stepped off the curb for it; anything to get away from the man who'd been messing up his time for the past couple of nights. He stepped around the front of the car to the passenger side door and grabbed the handle.

"Then go take a fucking picture," he yelled back at Simon, and he got into the car without even checking out the driver first. It was a bad move on Al's part. He slammed the door closed and the car squealed its tires and sped off down the parkway with him, leaving the biker at his spot.

"What do ya mean, take my fuckin' picture," the driver shouted at him over the music blasting from the dashboard. The driver was a big guy, kind of fierce-looking, with a panicked look in his eye and a white-knuckled grip on the wheel as he floored the pedal and raced away from Al's spot on the parkway. The guy kept checking his rearview, and he kept glaring over at Al as Al shook his head and waved his hand at him.

"Aw, nothing to do with you, man," he told him. "There's nothing to worry about."

"C'mon, it's cool," he said, just as the car screeched a left off the parkway. Al fell against the guy's shoulder in the turn, and was pushed back to the passenger side, hard. He thumped his head against the window, and as stars flickered out around him, he rubbed the bump on the side of his head and caught the driver glaring at him, lip-curled, as he drove.

He could smell the booze on the man's breath, see the sweat

beading on his forehead. And Al could feel his own fear rising cold as ice inside him, as the car lurched a right off the street to an unlit service road that took them deeper into the heart of the downtown park.

One of the stories I heard about those two was that the Biker once rolled one of the Slut-Boy's tricks. Far from the truth, but the story Al tells me is wild enough. Imagine being a kid trapped in a speeding car as a bad trick takes you further along a dark, bumpy service road into a deserted park at night. Al had always been able to spot the psychos, the Bad Trade in the traffic of his hometown, but he also knew that every kid on the Track eventually turns up a number. His was up that night, he thought, as he was grabbed and pulled, kicking and shouting out of the driver's side of the car, and was dragged across a clearing toward the trees by his hair.

He swung his arms behind him, dug his bootheels into the ground as best as he could, cursing and swearing and yelling for help; but the trick had his fist twisted up in Al's hair so tight it brought tears as he was yanked along, stumbling on his bootheels.

A shout stopped the guy. He turned, taking Al around with him to see who it was. Al managed to tear his hair loose from the guy's grip with a yell, and he tumbled out of the way just in time to see someone leap from the dark left by the trick's car headlights, and wrestle the big guy to the ground with a thud.

Simon wasn't a big guy, neither was Al. But between the two of them they probably could have taken the larger guy down with no problem. But Al kept his distance from the two men scrambling in the dirt, kicking up dust in the headlight beams as they struggled, and he was wide-eyed with panic and shouting at them.

"What are you doing? Just what the fuck are you doing?"

It took some effort, but Simon did get the upper hand. He scrambled onto the larger man's back and managed to twist the guy's arm up to his shoulder blade. The trick bucked and kicked and tried to shake Simon off of him, but Simon shoved the guy's face into the dirt; then he looked up at Al, surprised.

"What do you mean, what am I doing?" he shouted back. "I thought I was rescuing you."

"And fuck my face on the Track for good?" Al shouted back. "Shit."

The man on the ground pushed his head up and spat dirt.

"Listen to the kid," he said. "His ass is grass on the Track from now on."

Simon shoved the trick's face back into the dirt again, having had enough of this. The "Code of the Canal," or whatever they call the rules the Trade in that town went by, made no difference to him at all. He dropped a knee into the guy's back to hold him down, and he used his free hand to go through the man's pockets.

He found a wallet, tossed it to Al's boots. Al stepped back from it; then watched as Simon fished out a pair of handcuffs from the trick's jacket pocket and a rather nasty looking hunting knife from a sheath on his belt. Simon tossed the knife at Al's boots as well, and Al stared down at it, white-faced and swallowing hard.

"So how much do you charge?" Simon asked him.

"Twenty? Thirty?"

Al looked up from the knife.

"Fifty," he replied, somewhat indignantly.

"Then if he's got it, take fifty."

Al picked up the wallet and flipped through its contents.

"Why don't we just take the whole wad," he said. Why the hell not, he thought, in for a penny— "There must be a couple of hundred in here." But the look he got from Simon shut him up.

"Take fifty," Simon told him in a tone of voice that surprised Al. No one on the Track ever spoke to him that way before.

"Do as I say."

"All right, I'll just take fifty," he said, and he was surprised by his reaction. He took two twenties and a ten from the wallet, and tossed it at the trick's head.

"Good," said Simon. "Now you owe me a dinner."

He clicked the cuffs around the trick's wrists as he held them behind his back. Then he stood up and planted his boot in the middle of the guy's back; and they left him there, handcuffed, face down in the dirt with his headlights on and the car radio turned up full blast to wear down the battery. On their way back to where Simon had left his bike Simon tossed the keys to the trick's car into the Canal. He kept his hand on the back of Al's neck as they walked. Al's knees were shaking from the close call.

"Now all you got to remember is that what I say goes," Simon told him when they got back to his bike.

He was sitting on the seat, one boot up on the fender, and he grabbed the front of Al's T-shirt and twisted the material up in his fist so he could pull Al in close for a warm, wet, open-mouthed kiss that Al could feel all the way down to his toes. None of the Trade in that town ever kissed him like that before. Knees still trembling, his arms limp by his sides, he got lost in the kiss, eyes closed, until he was jerked back.

"You're cute," Simon told him looking Al over, a smug grin on his face, his dark eyes scanning. "But I'll bet you're a lot of trouble."

"I won't be," Al told him in a small voice that sure surprised him to hear it come out of himself. He shook his head, near to tears as he tried to assure the Biker, but Simon grinned even more and shoved Al backwards.

He landed on his butt on the dirt with a thud. He looked up, stunned, at the Biker leaning back on his bike and stroking the length of his cock in his jeans.

"You'd better not be, Slut-Boy," the Biker warned him as he crooked a finger at Al.

"You better not be," he said, as Al came crawling on his hands and knees in the dirt to the toe of Simon's boot on the fender; only to be stopped in mid-crawl, when the Biker swung his leg up and planted his boot sole against Al's face.

††††

That was the real story, says Al, about the night the Biker and the Slut-Boy met. A far cry from the rumors that flew around town for the next couple of nights as cop cars "trolled the tracks" and "frisked the faces," and "leaned on the landmark along the parkway a little," to see what they knew about one of their own kind and his "pimp" who rolled one of the Trade who complained. But the Biker and the Slut-Boy were long gone out of the city by then, heading west on Simon's bike.

"We'll have some fun," Simon said. "Get laid, and go take a look at the ocean."

He wasn't Al's "pimp." Boys don't have "pimps," says Al. And "pimp" is such a TV-word for it anyways, he says. But that didn't stop the rumors and the stories about those two as they made their way south from Al's hometown to the cities around the Great Lakes and the Midwest; like the one about a bar in one town that nearly got raided the night the Slut-Boy was selling blowjobs under the table at happy hour; or the one about a certain, well-known business man, a pillar in the gay community of his hometown, who was kept tied up and tortured in his own basement dungeon/playroom for days on end while the Biker and the Slut-Boy ate him out of house and home upstairs.

Or the one about the time the Biker tied the Slut-Boy to a tree near a rest stop somewhere along the interstate one afternoon, and charged truck drivers ten dollars each to fuck his face.

The truck drivers were actually members of a local city fuck club, dressed up to look even more like truck drivers than they already did, as was the cruising fashion in those days. And they were paid ten dollars each, but they did it for the glory and for the fun of it more than anything else. The Biker took pictures, and they were hot shots of the Slut-Boy...

...On his knees, stripped to the waist. His wrists and ankles bound with greasy rope to the tree trunk behind him. He had a vague, spaced-out look in his eye, his hair sticky with come, stuck to his cheeks and his forehead. Come dribbling off his chin, each man was pictured taking a turn with him, fucking his mouth, shooting their loads on his face.

There was one shot of him surrounded by truckers' cocks, spent and limp, held up tight in rough trucker fists before his face. Two of them were tangled up in his hair while another one slapped him, left and right, in the next shot.

There was another one of him, his face stretched in an agonized howl as a work-booted toe pressed the head of his dick into the ground between his knees; the next one showed his face as his dick stood up straight and hard between his legs after it had been ground into the dirt that way.

There was another shot of him, his face a mix of agony and pleasure as a rough trucker hand milked his hard cock until it exploded in an arc of come expertly captured on black and white film. And the last shot in the series showed his head slumped forward, exhausted in his restraints, while the men who had used him stood by an old panel truck parked behind the tree to complete the fantasy setting, and drank beer while they decided what to do next with him.

That was the story that accompanied the photos, a black and white spread called "Truck Stop," which followed "Saloon Slut," and "Executive Stress (or the Biker's Revenge)." They were photo-stories that began to appear in the gay skin mags that summer and fall; photo-plays by the Biker, featuring the Slut-Boy himself in all kinds of sexual adventures, wherever they went on their trip out to the west coast that summer, and for a while there Simon's features were considered the best the mags had to offer in one-handed reading entertainment at the time.

—And I'm surprised, not shocked, to suddenly associate that face in those pictures to the one resting his head against my thigh now, as he tells me what really happened that summer—

They had fun, that summer, on Simon's bike roaring into town after city on their way out to the coast; cruising through steambaths and back rooms, warehouses and parks and the clubs that made up the scene in those days. Wherever the action was, back then, the Biker and the Slut-Boy were sure to have been there, at least once.

Even down through the farmlands to towns that didn't seem big enough to have a scene; out along the interstates through the flatlands and down into desert country, they still found the scene. Often the Biker and the Slut-Boy made history in those places. Or at least they gave the locals something to talk about for a while.

Sometimes, it was just for the kind of entrance they'd make on a given scene, like the times the Biker would lead the Slut-Boy into a club or a bar on a collar and leash. At a disco in the southwest, Simon cuffed Al's hands behind his back and had him follow through the crowd on the dance floor to the club's then notorious back room, just to leave a wave of puzzled frowns and eyebrow-raised expressions in their wake.

And, notoriously by local standards, the back room in that club took on national proportions that night with Al on his knees in the dark, licking on every boot Simon pushed his face on to.

"Just do as I say, Slut-Boy," the Biker told him as he pushed his face on to the toe of yet another fancy cowboy boot, using a bootheel to the back of the Slut-Boy's head.

It was like the night they spent in a bath in one town when they finally got out to the coast. Their first night in town, and Al spent it blindfolded, hands cuffed behind his back, kneeling before a hole in the wall of a cubicle while they waited for the action to come their way.

It did. A dick slid through the hole and found the Slut-Boy's mouth. It fucked his face a couple of times, then it pulled out when the guy on the other side of the wall heard the click of the Biker's camera as he snapped off a few shots of the scene.

Another one slid through the hole a few moments later, one of the one's Simon had arranged earlier to show up at that particular hole for the shoot, and it worked Al's mouth like a pro for the camera.

Then a long, thick, monster of a cock slid through the hole, a hard and veiny thing with a more-than-a-mouthful head, all red and swollen. It advanced slowly through the hole, and it found Al's mouth; Al who couldn't see it, but could certainly feel it stretching his mouth wide open as he struggled to accommodate its width.

He gagged on it a few times as he swallowed it, but he managed to suck it in, inch by inch; and as he tried to get it down his throat, the owner of that now-legendary dick, soon to be immortalized in the mag that would publish those pictures later on that fall, grunted and sighed his pleasure from the other side of the wall.

"Oh yeah," the Biker kept saying, snapping off a few more pictures of the scene. He couldn't have been more pleased.

"That's right, Slut-Boy," he told Al. "Make it happen," and the guy on the other side of the wall exclaimed.

"Hey, is that really the Slut-Boy in there?"

"The one and only," Simon called back.

"Sheeit. They told me at the desk. I didn't believe it. Is my meat gonna be in a magazine?"

And in the name of the talent alone, working on his dick through the hole, the guy blew his load down the Slut-Boy's throat that night, probably the biggest load Al ate all that summer. The guy then let the Biker pose the Slut-Boy with his dick for a few more shots of Slut-Boy staring up at what he had been sucking on while blindfolded, and letting it rest on his upturned face so he could feel its weight as he watched it soften and drool out the last of its load on his cheek.

The photo spread featuring the monster dick made the mags by late that fall, but by the time they got out to the west coast, the Biker and the Slut-Boy had already caught up with the reputation they'd been making for themselves through the pictures Simon took and the action they found along the way. After a summer of steambaths and back rooms, parks and warehouses;

after a summer of photos of bikers and farmhands, cowboys, soldiers and sailors, the Biker and the Slut-Boy had arrived.

"That's right, 'Slut-Boy,'" the Biker would tell him during a shoot. "Make it happen," he'd tell him, and it would.

"Yeah, but the Slut-Boy?" Al complained one afternoon.

They were sitting on a bed in a motel room, outside of a town on the southern coast. Simon was flipping through magazines that had his pictures—Al's face—in them, and he was laying them out on the bedspread. None of the story lines Simon wrote to accompany the film he sent to his partner back east ever referred to Al as "the Slut-Boy." Yet all a publisher had to do in those days was put the words, "Slut-Boy Inside" on the cover, and loyal readers, like myself, would buy them up, just to see what he was into now.

For a while there, the Biker's photo-features were like the gay man's "Perils of Pauline," a serial of sexual adventures featuring the Slut-Boy himself in a number of predicaments, like getting bound and gagged by horny marines on leave in one photo spread ("Shore Leave"); gang-fucked by cowboys in the trailer park in the back end of a rodeo ("Sweetheart of the Rodeo"), trapped by a gang of gay bikers in their roadhouse on a Saturday party night ("The Biker's Buddies"); chained to a steel girder by construction workers taking an extra long break in ("Hardhats' Lunch").

Al blew cigarette smoke at the magazines Simon laid out on the bedspread, pages open to his work, and he sighed again about the name he went by in those mags.

"Would you rather 'The Cocksucker Kid?'" Simon teased him.

"Or how about 'EZ Virtue,'" Al tried.

"Or the "'Mouth that Whored,'" Simon jumped in with, but Al made a face.

"Not funny, Boss," he warned.

"What can I tell you," Simon said with a shrug as he laid out the mags. "The crowd calls them as they sees them. There's enough guys who've heard me call you that. They see your face later in the fuckmags and put it together."

"Yeah, but," Al said, "how do they know to call me that, out here?"

"Please," said Simon with a sigh. "You've never heard of telephone, telegraph, tell-a-gay?"

Which would have been true enough of the scene back then.

Everyone had friends someplace else. Everyone went out, in whatever town or city they found themselves in, to look for the action, to find the scene. Everyone met in back rooms and steambaths, and phonelists and phonebooks were often long with numbers and time zone reminders.

Because it was a time when a slut could be a slut, and a slut back then was simply someone getting more action that you were. Like the photo-fantasies strewn across the bedspread that afternoon—some of which I still have in a stack of old issues of mags I used to buy in those days.

I keep them on the top shelf in my bedroom closet, take them down once in a while when I have nothing better to do. To think that all this time I'd been beating off to the Biker's pictures, I'd been looking at pictures of Al, my Al—

The bed covered with shots of Al sucking off truckers, licking biker boots, rimming sailors and getting fucked by cowboys, men in cop uniforms, army fatigues—Al sat on the edge of that bed, bitching about the name he went by in those shots, until Simon swung a leg up and pushed his wool-socked foot against Al's face. He shoved him to the floor with a thump.

"But you are a slut, Boy," he said.

It was like the way the Biker set the scene for the men he got to pose for "Bath House Butthole," a full-color spread this time, to show off the new tattoo on Al's butt: the red-eyed snake curving an S around his right buttcheek, its green scale tail looped around his asshole, shaved and spread for the occasion. The artist who did the work was also one of the models for the piece, and he was more than pleased with the display of his work; the Slut-Boy himself displaying it, on his elbows and knees, wrists and ankles tied to the frame of the cot in the tiny room.

The Biker had swatted the A-shaped brand up by Al's hip, a mark that had been there long before the faked branding scene they had staged for the conclusion of "Sweetheart," and he spoke to the men crowded in around him, towels wrapped around their waists.

"What can I tell you, grade-A fuckmeat right here. Just give me a lot of good come shots for the boys back home."

The "boys back home," were those of us who were sure that our wildest fantasies were really happening somewhere else, to someone else. The Biker's pictures confirmed it, and the rumors and stories about them flew before them as they made their way up north along the west coast interstate.

After all, it must have been quite a sight to see them make their entrance into a given scene the way they usually did that summer, into a bar or a club, a back room or a bath. The big-chested biker with long black hair, hardball shining black eyes with the smaller longhair following behind him, green-eyed and shy as he followed his Boss, either collared and leashed or hand-cuffed. But what must have really been a sight was to see how the Slut-Boy looked up to his Boss, always fetching him his beers, lighting his joints for him when they stepped outside with a group.

Al always called Simon "Boss," and it took him quite a while to get used to the attention, his face now recognizable everywhere they went on their way up the coast. Some nights in a bar he would just sit in a corner and keep his eyes on Simon, who would be playing a game of pool or two, and he'd try to ignore the looks he'd get; some from fans, some from those who were just jealous as they took one look at the little longhair in their midst, and put the face they'd seen in the magazines to the one in the barlights.

But it was in the back rooms and the steambaths where the Biker and the Slut-Boy really made their reputations, and the stories live on these days when the bar talk turns to the good old days. Like the one about the cocksucking contest they held in one back room one night, just to see how many the Slut-Boy could take.

"That's right, Slut-Boy," the Biker would say as he tugged on Al's leash. "That's right, make it happen."

And it did.

Like in "Frat Fuck," a full-color leg and crotch fantasy—a four page spread that came out late that year. It was the Slut-Boy himself playing a fraternity pledge, and the Biker following him on his knees with his camera as he snapped off shots of Al...

...On all fours, scrambling between Frat-boy legs, some in jeans and sneakers, others in shorts and bare feet, whitesocks and sweatpants, as he took a paddle-whack on his scarred and tattooed behind while he crawled between them. The frat paddles were borrowed, each had a different insignia on them, and Simon had to use one of them to give Al's butt a few more whacks, just to bring up a blush on his cheeks for the close-up shot afterward.

And it took quite a while for Simon to get one shot that he wanted, a tableaux of the Slut-Boy on all fours, a crushed beer can balanced on his butt, while three streams of frat piss hosed him down, soaking the hair falling down around his face, dripping off the arch of his back and shoulders. It took quite a while because one of the men Simon got to pose for the piece was pee-shy, and he had trouble aiming what little stream he could muster so that it would hit the side of a yellow dogfood bowl placed at the Slut-Boy's face, just so the Biker could expertly capture its splash against the rim on color film.

There were shots of the Slut-Boy sucking frat cock, licking frat feet; getting kicked while crawling from room to room in the frat house where more frat boys waited. Once, the same four models changed leg-and-footwear to create the illusion of there being a house full of frat boys to fuck him and step on him, beat his butt and piss on him some more.

The last few shots of the spread, laid out comic-strip style complete with dialogue balloons and sound effects, showed the Slut-Boy's ass sunk in a garbage can, arms and legs sprawled out over the sides, while a frat arm pulled a screen door to the house closed. Two of the models, guys who would agree to show their faces in Simon's last piece with the Slut-Boy as his star, played passersby in the last shot, and the caption over one of their heads read:

"Will you look at that. Somebody threw out a perfectly good cocksucker."

The rumor was that the Biker dumped the Slut-Boy, because the Slut-Boy tried to rip him off. But the truth, according to Al, was that he was out the night they were robbed.

He was busy, scanning for the Trade in the traffic of a city three thousand miles away from the town where he grew up, on the northern west coast. It was a late summer night in the city, a quiet night in the Zone—that town's name for their track, their strip, their stroll—and a cool ocean breeze was sweeping over the downtown blocks from the harbor, making the air smooth and salty sweet. He was standing on the corner of a business district—the office block crowds long gone for the night—leaving the dark streets below the brightly lit high-rises to the Trade and the traffic in that town. And the scene in that town that night, with its car-to-boy ratio about even, almost made Al want to stay in there for good.

Almost. He couldn't help but feel something was wrong.

Not with where he was, or with what he was doing. Though he wasn't Al's pimp, Simon did send Al out to work on occasion that summer. It gave the Slut-Boy something to do while the Biker made contact sheets, wrote story lines and prepared the film he sent to his partner back east. All it took was a few questions asked at a local bar about when and where, and about the kindness of the local police in any town large enough to have a track for boys. There weren't many towns where Al could make more than his usual fifty, but at least there weren't many towns where he had to drop his price.

As a matter of fact, the Slut-Boy himself once earned three hundred on an agency call. But out on the stroll he was just another pretty face. Maybe a little familiar to some of the Trade in the traffic of that town passing by his spot, but Al kind of liked it when he could take a break from being the Slut-Boy once in a while.

But he couldn't help but feel there was something wrong, that night. Not with the guy who stopped his car at his spot and rolled down a window—a nice guy, a little timid, a little bit smaller than Al but older, balding. He drove Al to a nearby alley, where he proceeded to make a meal out of Al's more-than-a-mouthful in the front seat of his car. The Slut-Boy himself rarely got sucked in the magazines, so he sat back, pushed the guy's face down into his crotch, and he stared out at the Dumpsters in the alley, trying to enjoy the suck, but he was distracted by whatever it was that was bothering him that night.

There was nothing wrong back in the Zone, either, when the guy drove Al back to his spot with fifty dollars more in his pocket. It was back at the hotel where they were staying, a gay hotel, just not a great hotel; and when he got there he found that the door to their room had been kicked in.

"We've been robbed," Simon said from inside. Al stepped in carefully to find the room strewn with their packs and clothing, the drawers from the dresser/table/mirror pulled out and dumped over. Simon sat on the bed and stared at the closet, its contents pulled out and dumped, and he sighed.

"They got our leathers, our cash, our grass and my camera," he said.

The bathroom where Simon had been making contact sheets had been ransacked. The counter and the sink were a mess of chemicals and broken equipment. Al sat on the bed next to Simon and shook his head.

"I called my partner back east," Simon began. "He'll be sending us some cash, but it'll take a few days to get here, and I've only got a ten in my pocket for food."

"I've got bucks, Boss," Al said with a shrug. It wasn't the money he was worried about. He was more upset about the loss of his Boss's camera.

"Ten. Birdyfood." Simon muttered.

"Boss, I've got bucks."

"Sorry pal, but it's going to be tight for a couple of days.

"But Boss."

"No."

And Simon shot Al a nasty look that surprised him.

"I've got fifty in my pocket, a couple of hundred in my boot." Al persisted, but Simon wasn't listening to him. He grabbed his Boss's shoulder and tried to tell him it was all right, but the next thing he knew he was shoved off the bed. Al landed with a thud in the debris on the floor, and he looked up, stunned, as Simon got to his feet and approached him, shouting at him:

"Just what the fuck do you take me for, Slut-Boy? Just what the fuck do you think I am?"

Al scrambled backwards in the mess and backed himself up against the wall. Simon grabbed him and pushed him against the wall so hard he made the pictures bounce. He'd never seen the Boss that mad before, and it scared him. And it made him mad.

"What do I take you for, Boss?" he shouted back, seething. "For one big fucking jerk," Al said, and he stomped out of the hotel room leaving Simon to the mess. He did not come back to the room that night.

No, he wasn't Al's pimp, but that didn't stop Simon from sending him out for the night when he had other things to do.

It got Al out of his hair while he worked on his photo-stories, but, in a way, it was also free publicity: the Slut-Boy himself out on the stroll, keeping up his image as a hustler plying his trade. But not once that entire summer did Simon ever touch a penny of Al's money, even though he could have made a lot on him, especially through the escort services.

Al checked into a steam bath and locked himself into the little room he got for his bucks. He spent the night fuming on the cot in the room while the club's speaker-music thumped overhead, and men in the rooms around him humped and grunted.

Simon was upset, not so much over Al's offer, but over the robbery, the loss of his camera. Al knew that. But what stung him the most was the way his Boss reacted to the idea of living on what Al earned on the stroll, like his bucks weren't good enough.

Still he went back to the hotel room the next day. Simon woke to see Al standing at the door to the room, glaring at him from a safe distance. On the foot of the bed, Al had left a box in a brown paper bag. Simon pulled it out and looked at the lid.

In the box there was a plastic camera, the kind sold in kits that are used to take pictures of birthday parties and Christmases. Two rolls of color film were included in the set. Simon looked up at Al.

"And I still owe you a fucking dinner," Al told him. "So get over it."

"Get over it," was a relatively new gay phrase at the time.

Because it was a time when anything was possible, when fantasies did come true. Like the Biker's pictures in the magazines; like the time the Biker had the Slut-Boy strung up to the branch of a tree in the middle of a cruisy, downtown park in a city in the Midwest one afternoon, hanging by his wrists with his jeans pulled down to his boots.

This story about those two still gets passed around in the clubs these days. A true story, according to Al; and the park, notorious by local standards, took on national proportions that afternoon, as Simon ran his hands up and down Al's chest under his vest, pinching tit, grabbing skin, and slapping his butt left and right until the Slut-Boy's cries and hollers rang through the trees. It must have been quite a sight to have been cruising that park and come across the scene going down between the long-haired biker and the hustler waiting for the action to come their way.

A few curious faces peered out from the bushes at first, some with frowns, others with familiar puzzled, eyebrow-raised expressions. A few stepped into the clearing with big grins on their faces and bulges in their jeans, and soon in the clearing was a circle of men, some standing, some kneeling before them. An impromptu orgy was beginning in the woods that afternoon as joints were passed around, little brown bottles of poppers twisted open until the air around the trees filled with smells.

"That's right, Slut-Boy," the Biker said into Al's ear as he played with his ass. "That's right, make it happen."

And it did.

Because it was a time when parties could erupt at any moment, like the one in the woods that afternoon. Men leaned against tree trunks playing with themselves as they watched. Other men got on their knees before them. And Al, in the middle of it all, hollered and grunted and groaned as he was touched, pinched, spanked, played with, fucked, sucked by the men who came up to play with him at the Biker's invitation.

They took turns fucking him, they grabbed his tits and pulled on his balls. The Slut-Boy was helpless to do anything but pull down on the rope keeping his wrists over his head; and to feel fucked-out, so much his eyes rolled back into his head time and time again as he was entered repeatedly and used.

At one point there was a guy, a big burly type with callused fingertips and hot, smoky cigar breath, breathing down his neck and pulling on his tits while he fucked the Slut-Boy. Another guy on his knees before him was driving him crazy with sensations as he chewed on the head of his dick, actually biting the skin, while Simon stood before him and fed him his tongue.

The party in the woods lasted long after the Biker cut the Slut-Boy down from the tree branch and took him, fucked-out and exhausted and staggering on his bootheels, back to the hotel where they were staying. He had to use the rope around Al's wrists to keep Al's arms tied around his waist as they rode the bike back, and Simon really didn't care how it looked when he led the Slut-Boy through the hotel lobby, his wrists bound in front. In the room, he pushed Al face down on the bed.

"So tired, Boss," Al said into the pillows.

Simon reached under him, and pulled Al's jeans down to his boots. Al moaned.

"Please, Boss," he begged. "Fucked-out. No more."

"So?" said Simon as he kicked out of his boots and squirmed out of his jeans. He got on the bed, lay beside Al, and ran his hands all over the Slut-Boy's buttcheeks, over the burnscar and the snake tattoo; making Al squirm at the slightest fingertip touch to his hole, fucked-out and swollen, the pucker pink and distended, glistening with lube and sweat and come.

"Who's Boss," Simon wanted to know.

"You are," Al sighed. "You're the Boss."

Al groaned and whimpered and squirmed, his hands bound under him, as Simon's finger pushed easily past the squeeze of his ass muscles, fucked-out and helpless to resist, and began to finger-fuck him until he was sobbing in the pillows.

He wasn't Al's pimp, but Simon sure loved sending Al out to work; as much as he loved setting the Slut-Boy up in the gang-bang scenarios he created for his pictures, and testing his mettle in the back rooms and steambaths. It might have been something of a voyeuristic thrill for the Biker to see the Slut-Boy in action, taking on a number of cocks. But it was when he could take his turn with him afterwards, that seemed to really turn the Biker on.

"Oh, please, Boss," Al would beg him, throat sore and jaw-tired if he'd been sucking a lot of cock, tongue-dry if he'd been licking a lot of boot leather. Fucked-out, Al was helpless to resist Simon's advance as he rolled over onto Al's back, pushing his dickhead past the tired, futile squeeze of the smaller man's fuck-hole; making him take just one more dick up there. His.

Maybe it was like the main event, like coming home. It would have been sloppy seconds for sure, but Simon seemed to like Al's hole soft and slick and loose enough to move around in. He sure liked the way the Slut-Boy's hole just gave itself up to him that way.

Especially if Al hadn't come yet. His pent up agony only added to Simon's pleasure as he took advantage of him, fucking him until Al's insides were numb with overload. If Al had come, it was because Simon made him come, several times, until Al was shooting blanks but still horny.

That was when Al's hole was at its easiest. He fucked him on the bed in that room until Al couldn't feel it any more; Simon taking his pleasure, bringing himself close to adding his load to that of the other men who used Al's ass that afternoon. Al could barely feel the hot gush of Simon's load bathing his insides as Simon groaned and jerked and shot on top of him. He could barely feel the hot flush of piss Simon always gave him afterwards, to douche him out; but he fought to get up from under his Bossman's weight, and race to the can. Simon laid back on the bed and laughed.

And that was what really happened that summer, says Al, stories and rumors aside. The Biker and the Slut-Boy may not have been the last of their kind, but things were changing, and by the late fall of that year, Al and Simon parted company.

Nothing too dramatic. No fights. They were walking along a beach one day in a town up on the northern west coast.

It was a pretty city, mountains on one side of the skyline, the ocean on the other, and the scene in there almost made the both of them want to stay in that town for good.

Almost. Simon had been very quiet all day, saying nothing; a little too preoccupied with something as they looked out at the ships in the harbor.

He had his shirt slung over his shoulder. Al was barefoot, his boots and socks in one hand, and a can of pop in the other. He was having trouble keeping up with his Boss, who seemed to be walking the shoreline a little too fast, and he dearly wished the Biker would get over what was bothering him.

Simon scanned the horizon line for a bit, letting the waves lap at the toes of his boots.

"Well, I've seen the ocean," he finally said, and without another word he turned, crossed the beach, and headed up the hill that would take him up to the street. Al tossed the pop can and hurried up the hill after him.

"And? That's it?" I ask.

Al shrugs: "That's it," he says. "Simon sold his bike and flew back east.

"And left you stranded."

"I wanted to stay. He offered me plane fare back home, but I liked it up there. So I found a room, got a job."

"On the stroll?" I try, using what I guess must have been too TV a word for it, for the way Al looked at me when I said it.

"A real job," Al tells me. "And I got a big, fat check from Simon, too. Modeling fees." Al grins at me.

I shake my head, not shocked, just impressed I guess. I feel like asking for an autograph, it is the Slut-Boy himself kneeling by my chair, but I feel a hard-on coming on instead.

I squeeze the base of my cock and it stands up straight between my outstretched legs. I'd been playing with it all through Al telling me this story, and now my dickhead's throbbing and swollen.

A little drop of precome oozes from the slit. Al sees it, and licks his lips.